I0580815

THE LICH'S BLADE

BOOK 3 OF

THE WINGBREAKER SAGA

BY

STEPHEN HAGELIN

*This book is dedicated to Effie and Calder, my wife
and my son, who have weathered so much and overcome.
You will forever inspire me with your endurance.
Because of you a faerie gets their wings.
~Stephen Hagelin~*

Fhoraena

THE SHADELANDS
STANAEDRE
ESTENNA
MIDSYRON
SORANIL
NORENAN
THE ICE WASTES
WELLSEY
PYRINCEL
FASSEN
GAERSHEIM
ROSENKRAUN
THE CHERIM FOREST
FROREHOLT
GAERLIN
EIRENAU
FRORIN
ARTELL
HARYN
ORENTON
FIRLIN
SILVI
SENDRA
ASKELUND
JANUE
AELA
MUERLUND
CAPHOLT
AELAÉTE DESERT
CHISLETON
WEIR SEA

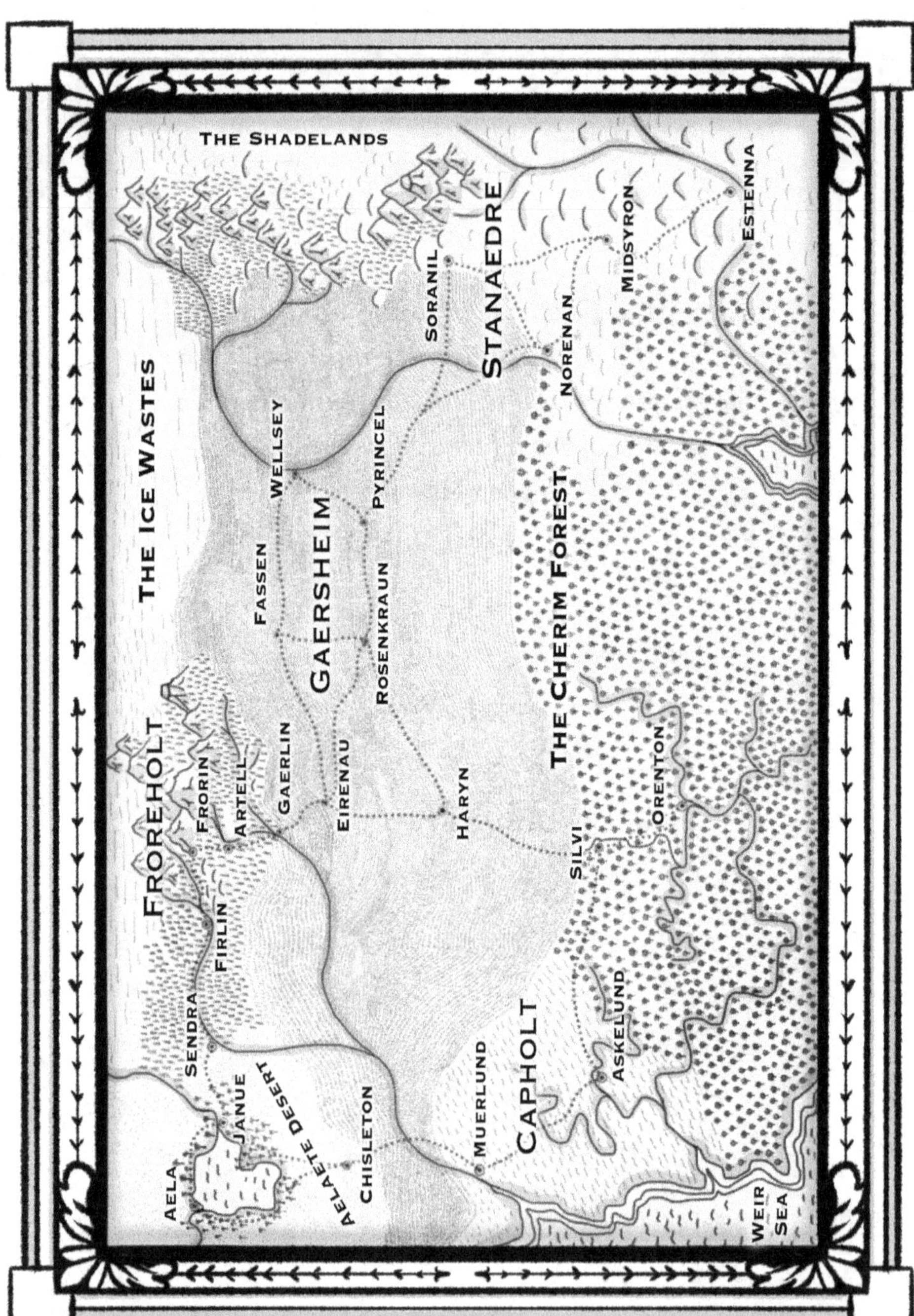

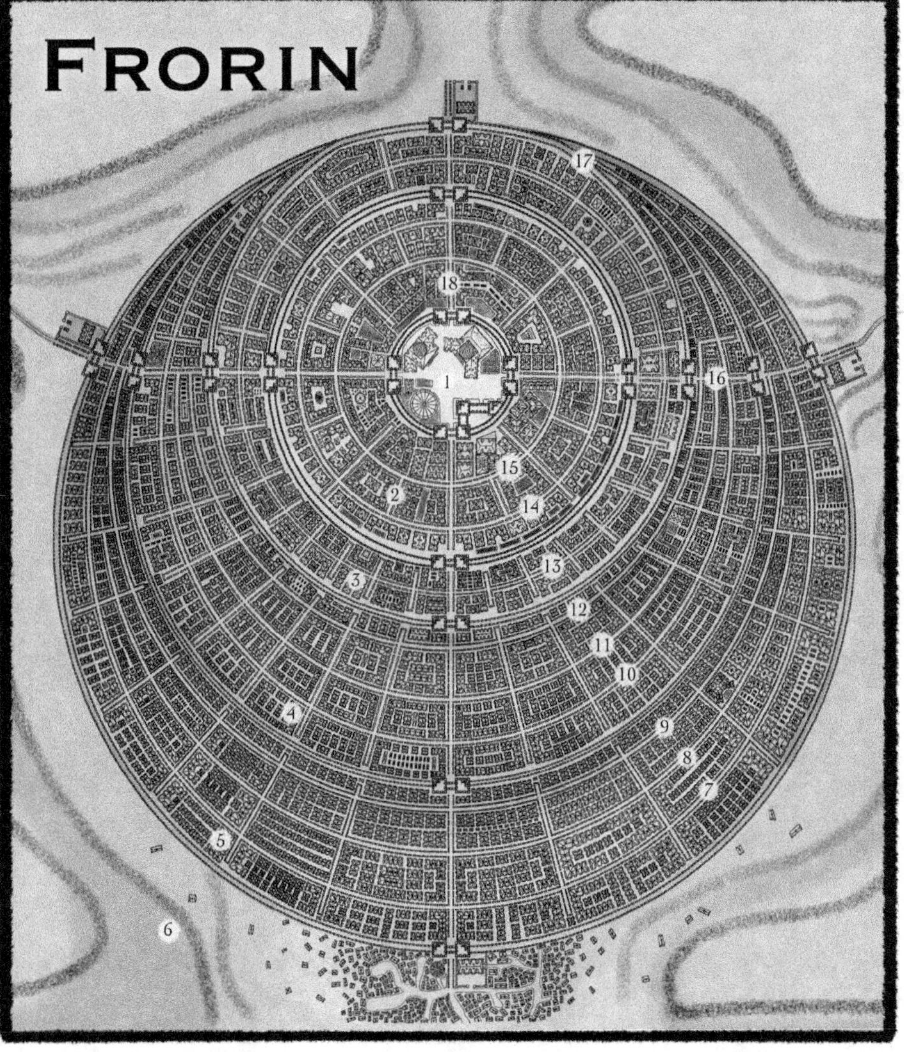

FRORIN
1
2
3
4
5
6
7
8
9
10
11
12
13
14
15
16
17
18

TABLE OF CONTENTS

The journey will continue

Prologue

Fassen

Faerie Hunter Bounty Office

Grifton Francis

Grifton stared up at the heavens as if inspecting the underside of a cracked cistern, the water leaked, pouring over the city, flooding the streets. Beaten by the rain drops, he was not crushed, as he stood tall under the meteoric droplets which were dashed to pieces on his stone-armored skin; or riven in two as they passed by the granite-coated serrations on his misshapen wings. His red-lined, serrated bone-steel sword traced a shallow fissure in the pavement as he dragged it behind him, leaving a trail that led all the way out through the East Gate, into the Forest of Grass, to where he had almost slain his foes, and where he should have died.

He flexed his drooping wings, which were only partially repaired with bone-grafts where Leif had maimed him, and he read the letters on the signboard—traced in gold and green metallic paints—which glinted in the baleful amber light of the street-lamps. He'd arrived at the doors of the Faerie Hunter Bounty Office and attached bank.

He stepped up onto the veranda of the doorway and pushed on it with his orphaned shoulder, but it didn't move. He strained against the door and felt the shivering of a bar through the glue-bark wood. It was quiet as he listened at the crack, but all around him the deluge filled the city with a death-song for his brothers. It was wordless, naturally, but so was he.

Grifton slid his sword between the doors and leveraged it against the door bar, in a few quick tug-and-pull movements, he sawed through it with his toothed blade, and kicked the doors inward, dragging the blade behind him.

The clerk, Norran, froze and stared at him with a stack of papers clutched to his chest, and a clean pen held in his mouth—which he dropped immediately. The papers followed soon after, as the clerk rushed toward him, then turned on his heel, and ran behind the counter, where he rummaged through his drawers until he found a tin that sounded with a dull clatter from its loose contents.

Grifton watched his progress disinterestedly and fell back on the bench beneath the bounty board with a sigh. "I have an urgent bounty request."

Norran returned with gauze in one hand, and a needle and thread in the other, and then dropped both when he saw the hard chitinous bone that had sealed up the wounds. "...w-what is it-t?" he stammered, face white as a Lich, as he continued scanning Grifton's wings, shoulder, and the bony lines that had closed the smaller gashes and cuts he'd earned facing the two currently most famous, and soon-to-be infamous, new Hunters.

"The immediate authorization to pursue and kill the renegades, Leif Aellin, and Fryn Martin—for their sympathizing with the plot to embarrass the king of Gaersheim, and for killing my brothers, as well as members of the House of Vassidel, and the Grass Guard, and for crippling injuries to myself."

"You can't mean..." Norran's eyes widened and his hands shook. He seemed torn between disbelief and shock. "...to go after them?" he asked. Running back to the desk and not finding the papers he needed, he started going through the ones on the floor.

Grifton ground his teeth. "Do you think I won't?" That earned him an audible and satisfying "gulp" and a meek nod from the clerk. Running his hand through his hair, he chuckled. "Also, submit a request for the investigation of the veteran Hunters Chanterelle the Blackbow and Yarrow the Silverblade. They helped Leif and Fryn escape, and may yet be with the fugitive who has the Harvest Crown."

Norran swallowed and wiped a drop of sweat from the corner of his eye so it wouldn't fall on the pages of his pocket notebook, in which he wrote furiously. "I will send an urgent notice to the President, at once, since his approval is necessary for any such investigations, but for now I need you to provide a full statement of the events, and sign and date… if you can… if it was your dominant hand that you lost, then I can notarize it for you."

He grunted and closed his eyes. "We suspected their involvement as soon as the Earl invited them to a celebration… what with his Waverly heritage... I shouldn't be surprised if he wants to cause trouble."

Norran floundered, setting a blank sheet on his writing board, and dipping his clean pen into his nearly-empty bottle of ink—which almost tipped over in his haste. He started taking down Grifton's account in shorthand, wings shivering, cold, the doors still blown open and forgotten, blots of ink spattering on the pages as he wrote, and the rain threw itself on the street and the mist filled the entrance of the Bounty Office.

Interlude 1

MOONLESS

Forest of Grass

Great Road to Rosenkraun

Lia

The rain fell in a smattering drizzle on the roof of their carriage, which rocked over the ruts in the muddy, pebbled soil as they made their long slow march to Rosenkraun—the capitol of Gaersheim. With the constant rain, Lia was relieved their driver could sit on a covered bench, since it hadn't let up since they'd departed two days ago. As they approached the heartland of their enemies, protected by the diplomatic status of their host, Lia swallowed, worried for her daughter sleeping in her lap, mourning for Leif and Fryn who had surely died so they could escape.

She couldn't bear to recall how she'd just left them behind. Guilt gnawed at her stomach, and she couldn't speak of it. Yarrow kept watch on their surroundings from the driver's bench, but with the mist and rain obscuring everything outside, Lia doubted very strongly he'd be able to detect any dangers in time. She suspected he rode up there to escape the desperate silence that had filled the carriage ever since they'd left Fassen.

Nora lay under her cloak with her head held gently, protectively, in her mother's arms, breathing deeply in her sleep, her little wings shifting as if she were dreaming that she flew. Lia brushed a few stray curls out of her face and glanced over to the opposite side of the carriage's lounge seating. Trel and the Princess played cards distractedly, silently, making mistakes and not calling them out. Princess Savis would not hear of Lia's report of the events, of Fryn and Leif falling, or of the gruesome way they ended. She insisted, in a quiet, stammering voice, that it was impossible, that Lia had imagined what she saw, and that they would soon be reunited in Rosenkraun.

It was a joyless harvest, she decided. The shortest season, the longest month, and they weren't even halfway through it. Whispering a threadbare prayer, she closed her own eyes, trying to remember what little of the teachings they had been able to preserve and pass down. Here a little, there a little, mostly damning and despairing. Her people wallowed in disgrace and covered it with pride.

"You cry, you weep, and wash with tears, and rise again to play. But I will scrub and polish, and I will wash away; and those who wait and linger, and those who stay to pray, will they see and listen? When they see my day?"

It was likely that no one heard her quotation or would have any idea of who had said it first. In fact, she didn't remember clearly if it was Forry, Darsin, or someone else, but she looked out the window, wishing for the day. Rainwater streamed down the glass, and the clouds were full and dark, converting what should have been the morning, to mourning, and the mourning to night.

Lia closed her eyes, and leaned back in her chair, drifting off into a fitful and tiresome sleep.

~90 Years Ago~

Frorin

Sky District

Aldyr

Sometimes the wind blew like a whistle through the shabbily-bunched-up buildings, roofs sagging under the weight of their own shingles; sometimes it assailed against the walls, tossing the towering invisible tips of the pines like so many blades of grass, carrying away anyone foolish, or unfortunate, or poor enough not to be indoors; sometimes dying like the last breath of a singer as she waved and departed the stage without even an acknowledgement from the crowd of her having sung in the first place. Sometimes, it didn't blow at all, and the air only moved with the idle shifting of those who pushed through the streets.

Dangling his feet over the eaves of the one-bird aviary, scanning the carts that wandered up the foothills road under the last light of the scarlet-tinged sunset, his wings twitched, coated in a delicate layer of frost, as he searched for the one thing he wouldn't leave without: a single leaf of mint. In his ragged pockets, he had a few things of value, such as the shard of strange, currant-colored quartz he'd found while wandering the foothills of the mountain. No one told him not to anymore, every find valued, relied upon, subsequently counted on, expected.

One of the carts wobbled under the weight of the greenery heaped over its bed, barely contained by the tarp tied down too-tightly to its hitches. The driver held onto the reins of his fat hare lazily, as if his hands were drained completely of their strength, but beside him, a young fee with bright, dancing eyes looked up longingly at the walls of the city—the only region Aldyr had yet to explore. They were obviously not wealthy, but they had rights of trade. Even a one-day payment was impossible for him or the other residents of the unincorporated district.

Heart-beat pounding, ear-tips flushed, he flitted down toward them, hovering beside the driver, trying not to look too closely at the pretty fee, as he coughed once and attempted to raise his voice to catch the attention of the driver.

The driver ignored him, possibly not hearing him, perhaps so focused on his path that he was oblivious to everything else, probably shunning him outright. The fee only gave a cursory glance in his direction, blushing and looking away from his tattered clothes and the vest he'd buttoned over his chest in lieu of a shirt.

"I say, mister!" Aldyr yelled, blue light trailing away from his drained wings as he fluttered to the ground and jogged on his scrawny legs to keep up. "I say!"

The old merchant grumbled something to the young fee, who was probably only a year or two older than Aldyr, maybe less, considering how his younger sister was as tall as she was... they kept on driving their cart as if he had no presence or existence at all.

Aldyr stumbled over a pebble in the street, scraping his knees as he continued to reach out to them, until they turned the corner of the ascending street and passed out of sight. His stomach rumbled, so he formed a pearl of ice and swallowed it to give it something to work on, and rose to his feet, rubbing the frozen scabs on his knees, determined not to fall behind. He ran heedlessly, avoiding or brushing against the other drably-dressed pedestrians who looked on in confusion as he passed, his jaw set grimly, and his weakened wings fluttering to enhance his sprint. As he wound around the curve of the road, he saw the cart pulled up at the checkpoint gate, the driver consulting with the guard, waving a blue ribboned scroll around with one hand. Another guard in the light-blue tunic and decorative silvery plated armor poked through the greens on the cart, checking for urchins, stowaways, or contraband.

Aldyr slowed to an exhausted stop beside the gate guard surveying the trader's license, hands on his bloodied knees as he gasped for breath. The guard handed back the scroll, and turned his sour gaze toward him, as he sneered, "What do you want, sky-dweller?"

Not having regained his breath, Aldyr held up a hand for a moment, and straightened purposefully. "I need to buy some mint."

The guard's eyebrows rose, and he tapped the hilt of his sword in thought. "You sell things for mint, you don't 'buy' it."

"No, you don't understand," Aldyr corrected, "I…"

"Do you have one of these?" The guard interrupted, jabbing a finger toward the scroll that the driver of the cart had just accepted. "No. You don't. Without one you cannot buy or sell goods in the city, unless you are a resident of the city, or have a business permit for the day."

"We are not *in* the city," Aldyr insisted, leaning forward, rising on his toes for effect. "I just need…"

"No!" The guard declared, slicing the air with his hand in a quick chop as he frowned, and his flat gray eyes shifted from their earlier businesslike, pleasant light, to a tint that was colored and highlighted with disgust. "They are at the city gates and will not be accosted by any vagrants or vagabonds. The gates of the city are a part of the city, you cannot trade here."

"Fly off," grunted the old man, spitting over the edge of the cart, "leave me be."

"I'm not a vagrant!" Aldyr complained, losing what strength he'd had left to stand. "I *live* here."

The guard waved the cart through, and the gates parted, pulled open by the massive chains and pulleys built into the towers separating the wild land and the wild city from the civilization contained within the walls. The driver flicked the reins, and drove the tired hare through the opening, and as the doors began to close, the guard crossed his arms and stared smugly at the boy looking with desperate longing after it, hopelessness closing in around him.

"But… I just needed one leaf!" he yelled, and finding one last burst of strength in his wings, he darted through just as the gates were about to close, and flew over the cart landing beside the fee. "Please sir, I need one mint-leaf! I can pay!"

Shouts from the guards on the other side announced the opening of the gates again, as Aldyr held out the shard of crimson quartz in his palm. "This is valuable—please, for my sister."

The fee had been cringing away from him, but she relaxed and looked up at him as he held the red gem before the driver, her blue-yellow eyes shining with curiosity and compassion.

"It is an expensive herb to transport without wilting," the driver huffed, eyeing the stone dubiously, "how do I know this stone is worth my trouble and expense?"

"Stop that boy!" came a shout from the wall, as two guards lounging by a nearby guard post scrambled to attention, and the officer from outside appeared at the mouth of the opening gates.

"It's just one leaf…" the fee said, her voice low, as if she were afraid of the guard hearing their transaction.

"Hmph." The driver replied, "fine, but be quick and fly off." He pocketed the stone and jerked his thumb over his shoulder.

Aldyr smiled, nodding repeatedly as he reached out to grab a leaf from the piled-up greens in the cart sticking out from under the tarp. As he plucked one of the huge leaves, a gauntleted hand gripped his wrist, and he was yanked off the cart into the air and slammed back down into the ground. A tremor ran through his feet to the tips of his wings, as the hard stones bruised his bare heels, and he felt a terrible crack form in one of the small bones of his foot. He failed to bite back the yelp of pain, succeeding only in biting his cheek, as he flailed and tried to escape the guard's powerful grasp. He was released, tears running down his cheeks as blood filled his mouth, his foot swelled, and his wrist bruised; and his heart broke as he watched the driver ignore him, guiding his cart down a side street and out of sight.

"You *dare* to fly in here? Scum!" The guard hissed, eyes burning with rage, as a cool frost collected on his wings and arms. "I'll teach you to come inside our city," he smiled cruelly, closing his fingers into fists. He dragged Aldyr by the collar of his vest through the door of the gate tower, and up the stairs onto the battlements, sputtering threats and curses with each jostle and bump. Shock settled over the boy, and he stopped crying, even as he was knocked around—he was frozen, in time, in every sensation and emotion—numb.

Other guards scurried out of the officer's path, faces white, wings pulsing and twitching to an anxious beat, as he finally reached the top of the tower and swung him bodily over the battlements so that his weak legs dangled and his wings shivered limply over the eighty or so wingspan fall. Ignoring the tower lookout, the officer stared into the depths of Aldyr's eyes, judging, mocking, waiting perhaps for his conscience to kick in. His free hand went to his coat pocket, and he withdrew a cigarette, lighting it with a tiny, magical strike-lighter. He took a drag and let the blue smoke trail out of the sides of his mouth as he pondered his prey.

Aldyr never let his eyes waver or blink, fearing what would happen if he lost the contest; thankful that he hadn't blown the smoke toward him, though already it caused a terrible itch and his tired tear ducts began to work again. He held onto the officer's wrist, resisting the instinct to look down, to fail at his test.

The cigarette's ash grew too long, and it broke apart, scattering grayish smears all over the officer's uniform, dispelling the silence they had created. The lookout stepped forward, reaching toward his arm, concerned wrinkles forming around his eyes. "What are you doing, Captain?" he asked, his fingers just about to close around his sleeve.

"Hands off," he said, spitting his cigarette at the other guard, who batted it away so it wouldn't singe his uniform. "I'm just going to teach this pigeon a lesson."

Aldyr spared a glance down, since he hadn't been the one to look away first, and swallowed. He wouldn't be able fly further than a wingspan for an hour at least, and he was staring down eighty, likely more.

"Let the boy go," the other guard pleaded, voice shaking as he shrank back from the captain, "don't do this…"

The captain tightened his grip, arm shivering exhaustedly, as he answered with a sour gleam in his eyes, piercing through the other guard's resolve, "he does not exist."

Aldyr saw it reflected in the flat gray mirrors of the captain's resigned eyes, the cold glaze, the limp lids—a long fall and a quick death. He struggled then, twisting and writhing to free himself from his grip, weak wings fluttering, legs kicking about as he tried to wrestle his way back over the battlements. The captain snarled and grabbed him by the throat with his other hand, squeezing, fingertips digging into his tendons, pressing on his nerves so that a paralyzing pain lanced down his spine, and he almost stopped his struggle… almost… As the captain's fingernails drew blood and his heart threatened to beat itself out of his chest, he reached up, gathering what ice he could into a hardened sliver, and stabbed the captain's arm.

The lookout reacted first, yelping in shock, before the captain looked down, eyes widening at the sluggish dripping of blood as it trailed down his arm to dribble along his chest plate and uniform. Then, he ground his teeth and redoubled the pressure on Aldyr's neck, so that a black haze surrounded the edges of his vision, and he felt his arms going limp. Over the guard's shoulder he could still see the mint leaf where it had fallen in the street, somehow unharmed, as everyone stopped in their tracks to watch, horrified at the boy held bodily over the edge of the wall. No one intervened, merely stood by gawking at him, helpless as he was.

He dug out his sliver of ice, half-frozen blood thickening the shard, and held it up loosely, pointing it toward the captain's face, extending its length with all the elemental strength he had left. The sliver grew thinner, longer, and redder as it assimilated the blood, and Aldyr watched in that slow moment as the captain's pupil dilated, focusing on the needle point just before it pierced through his eye, and out the back of his head.

Aldyr's vision faded to black, even as the captain's grip failed, and he began to fall. He floundered, scrambling to grab *something* on the way down, and thumping against the ledge of a stair window, too small for an adult to do more than stick out their head, he clung to it, and slowly, so slowly, he pulled himself inside.

Shouts echoed from the courtyard, but the lookout above was dumbstruck for almost a minute, before he started yelling incoherently, first to see if the captain was alright, and then for someone to find a doctor to remove the ice. The boy, blood on his fingers, bloody fingerprints leaking from his neck, stumbled down the stairs, and collapsed at the doorway.

"He's alive!" one of the guards declared, pointing at him deliriously. But no one moved, stricken either by fear or indecision, as he crawled to the center of the square, where he bundled up the leaf, and hobbled back through the gate.

Whispers followed him, all the way back home, down every alley and through every passing window—the rumors of his story spread faster than he could walk. Finally, he fell at the door to his family's hovel, a daub and wattle shack, with a pine-bark door, and a chimney that looked like it'd been made by ants, and he passed out, just as the door swung inward, and he saw the hazy outline of his mother's worried—no *fearful*, face. He felt the leaf being taken from his hands, and relaxed.

Selina would be able to breathe.

The Next Day

Aldyr woke, not to the sound of Selina wheezing, or choking on her own saliva, not to his parents arguing in the back room about who would forgo their food, nor to the hacking and retching of a drifting wood-alcohol swilling drunk, but to a knock at the door. He sat up, tossed aside the towel that had been thrown over him as a blanket, and nearly bumped heads with his sister, his only sibling, as she leaned over him protectively.

"Aldyr," she said, hugging him too-tightly around his chest, stifling, almost like the fingers that had pressed around his neck, "you're awake!" He pushed her back slightly, at a sudden click at the latch, and stared nervously at the door.

The door creaked as it was opened by whomever it was that had come, and a head peeked in through the shadow, announcing in a gentle, but somehow dangerous voice, "That is good," as he smoothly closed the door behind him. He was dressed in a gray cloak, with a nondescript but well-made tunic of a silvery gray with pale blue lining. At his side was a plain black scabbard, with a silver handled sword. "I am relieved to find you well."

Aldyr frowned, feeling his sore neck with one hand. Who was this fae, coming in here; did he intend to finish him off? His eyes darted to the sword at his side, but he didn't answer.

Selina though, rushed about, trying to make their squalor somehow more welcoming to the stranger in the cloak, though he ignored her, watching Aldyr closely—gauging him. As she finished what cleaning and straightening she could, his little sister sat down on the cot beside him and folded her hands in her lap over her dirty beige dress and waited for the stranger to speak.

He coughed, but said nothing, letting the silence draw out, until finally, the boy couldn't take it any longer.

"Why are you here?" he demanded softly, not breaking eye-contact.

The stranger's mouth twitched into a momentary smile, as he noticed the mint leaf hanging from the rafters by the fireplace, only a small piece cut out for Selina's medicine. "Rendal," he said simply, discarding the word like he had no more use for it.

Selina raised an eyebrow but didn't voice the question she obviously wanted to ask.

"What do you want, Rendal?" Aldyr asked, noticing for the first time that his parents weren't at home.

"That was the guard's name. I thought you should know."

His sister frowned, fidgeting nervously with the hem of her plain, threadbare dress.

Aldyr looked down, bunching his tiny fingers into fists in his lap. "And?"

The stranger brushed his cloak back and crossed his arms, as if preparing to give a lecture, tilting his head and shifting his wings with amusement playing across his lips. "You have a choice, child. Those in the Assembly would have your head, or your wings, in an earlier age, for your crime."

"I…" he started to say but was cut off with that same sharp chop that the other guard had done, slicing his hand through the air.

"I was not finished." He looked at the leaf by the cold, bare fireplace and sighed deeply. "I cannot agree to this. You do not exist. You fell from the tower, and Rendal died with you." He turned and took hold of the handle of the door, swinging it open with a flush of red pulsating through his frost-covered wings, shame, or anger burning through his unexpressed words.

"What choice?" Selina blurted, standing, rushing forward to grab the end of his cloak.

The stranger paused, and placed a kind hand on her head, still looking away. "Live, unknown, as if you were dead, or come right now with me."

Selina let go of the cloak and took a couple steps back, shaking her head. "N-n-no… but then…."

"Why should I?" Aldyr asked petulantly, massaging the bruises on his neck again; it was still sore and the scabs were shallow, threatening to bleed again at any moment.

Turning to look him in the eyes, resignation and sadness surrounding him like the gray cloak he wore, he held the door open with one hand and beckoned with the other, saying, "You will enter and serve the city. As my student, you will still not exist, but you will live," he nodded toward Selina, and the leaf, "and she will be taken care of… if you follow me."

A chill settled over him, as a sense of danger and hope hung in the air like the static charge during a storm. He stood and walked forward, oblivious to the pain in his ice-encrusted foot, and the skinned portions of his knees. "What will I do?"

"Serve the king more rightly in Rendal's stead. I am the Third Hand, the sword prepared even as open palms are presented in peace. If you follow me, I will train you to serve in secret whatever the king demands."

"I will." He hobbled by his sister, wrapped an arm around her shoulders, and kissed her on the cheek. "It'll be alright, Selina, I'll see you soon. Wait for mama, she'll be home any minute now. Tell her I'm safe."

He closed the door on his way out and bit his cheek as he heard his little sister whimpering in the house. He looked up at this stranger, setting his teeth determinedly. Even if it meant serving the city that refused to acknowledge him, he would do it for Selina.

They walked, but he didn't notice his surroundings as they passed all the slums, back to the gate laying open and silent like the grave; where he was stared at and whispered about, as he strode awkwardly with his ice-formed cast. They meandered along the main roads, through the Pine District, past its giant manor for the governor there, the Hill District, through the crowds of well-fed commoners, the Rain District, with its Bounty Office and Hunters rushing about importantly, the Snow District with the nobles and their empty streets, until at last, they stopped before the checkpoint for the Crown District—with the palace and the Grand Assembly, buildings he'd only heard of and imagined, towering over the walls, filling the gigantic courtyard, with liveried Royal Guards tracking his movements with their eyes, as motionless as statues, and just as pristine.

They ascended the steps of the Grand Assembly, and Aldyr feared that he'd been deceived, and he was truly going to die after all, or be made wingless, and cast out into the wilds. But, instead of following the magnificent hallway to what could only be the main chamber, they went down a marbled flight of stairs, and through a series of winding halls and tunnels, until they stopped before a steel door cast with an image of a sword piercing a coin.

His guide shoved the door into its sliding pocket easily, as if it weighed nothing at all, and entered the succeeding chamber with perfect posture, shoulders back, spine erect, wings folded neatly.

"Master Bersi!" called someone from inside, as rushing footsteps brought a young fae in a matching uniform, with a sword that seemed less-used at his side. "Who is this?" He asked, stopping short of his associate in shock.

"My new student. Assign him to a room and equip him. Oh, and enroll him in the same class as Lyenel." His guide directed, waving Aldyr away as he left down a side passage deeper into the building.

"Hmm… with Lyenel, eh? He's not very nice putting you with him. What's with your leg, kid? Never mind, follow me." Unconcerned, the new stranger led him down the opposite hall, babbling about who-knew-what until he stopped before a plain pine door, and fell silent. "Well, it seems you've joined the school. Can't imagine why you'd be interested so young, but not my business to question the Master. What is your name?"

"Aldyr," he replied tiredly, scratching his neck.

"Aldyr. Aldyr what?"

"Havrshyk."

"Hmph, okay then, Havrshyk. I'll have you go in there and take a bath and get dressed. I can't introduce you to your classmates looking like you just clawed out a weasel's eyes." The guide smirked and thrust open the door, revealing a large single bedroom, with another chamber off to the side, presumably the room with the bath—just for him—a luxury that he'd never needed, or desired.

And in that moment, as he stumbled through the door, he regretted looking for that leaf; hated himself for it.

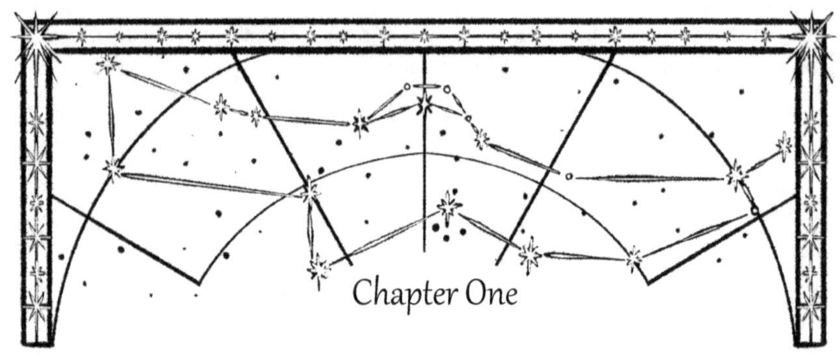

Chapter One

SPARROW

Without even the moonlight to see beneath a blanketed sky, Fryn resigned herself to observing the outline of the city from the limb of a pine tree by the stray lamplight that glowed in the dim night. Her jacket collar flapped against her neck in the brisk wind, so she extended the armor-coating of her ice to it, freezing it in place. She frowned and forced herself not to bite her cheek, or her tongue, or her teeth, or anything else, and therefore have to use her precious reserves of blood to heal herself needlessly… again.

Leif, or Havrshyk, perched a little further down the branch, dangling his legs over the edge, thick black frost coating his clothes, his wings, his face, even changing the color of his normally sandy-blond hair to a reddish black. He was in a full Lich state, and he sneered contemptuously at the sleeping town. Fryn was glad she'd frozen her stomach, as it tried to twist at the sight, but couldn't.

"Fryn," Havrshyk said, glancing over at her from *his* eyes, ominous green reflecting the few pinpricks of lamplight from the ground, "we should slip in and check the Office."

She ran a hand through her frost-cleaned silver hair and suppressed a sigh. "Not sure what good it'll do." Fryn flicked angry eyes in his direction, her hand still partially covering her face.

Leif's smile was as cold as she felt, but then, it wasn't really *his*, and that was why she felt cold. "If they haven't caught on to us there yet, we could send a letter to one of your associates and obtain information about my body—after all, that's all I want. Once I have that, you can both go your way."

She considered arguing that point, pinching her chin as she looked away. "That's well and good… but…"

Havrshyk laughed, a short, cruel bark, and then a sigh, as he rose to his feet and stretched his arms over his head. His once red-lined wings, tinged purple from the odd combination of elemental flows and mixed blood, scattered a few loose fragments of ice as he splayed them out to the sides. Leif did not laugh like that, he was more lighthearted, more relaxed, more awkward yet endearing. He did not laugh as if he observed fae from above.

"You found yourselves getting involved in this problem long before I intervened," he cautioned, lowering his arms and meeting her eyes. "Besides, I don't owe you any help, best hide in the marshes or something when we're done, because… ha, ha, whoever was behind that plot to embarrass the Rosenkrauns is still out there and they won't settle with 'shaving half a chin.'"

She gave a small smile and shook her head. "You're trying to sound like Leif?"

"What, you're from Frorin and you haven't heard that one? May have fallen out of use then…" He crouched on the edge of the pine branch, preparing to jump, as he added under his breath, "perhaps it was just another Sky District phrase," and leapt out into the air, diving with arms and wings pulled in to descend more quickly.

Fryn followed, just slightly behind, as they flew across the city toward the northwestern borough of Gaerlin: a vaguely triangular section of the city on the lowest slopes of the riverbanks, where the road to the water could be seen winding up three switchbacks to the hilltop by the evenly-spaced lamps.

The air smelled like dew, cattails, and mud which had gathered where the river slowed in its lazy curve around the city. It was one of the few sections of the river that were tranquil enough for boating or transporting cargo. She also noticed that the streetlamps only lit the main roads, and only the occasional oil-lamp lit certain areas of the riverbank, probably just the major trade warehouses or offices, she supposed.

They pulled out of their dive one after the other, snapping to a hover, and landing on the muddy pebble-stone courtyard of one of the walled warehouse complexes. Overhead the clouds promised rain, and wind, funneled by the riverbend and the walls, pressing against them as if to cast them out.

"We don't belong here," she said, flicking her eyes around each of the shadowed corners, half expecting to see a drifting patch of ice-dust, like the northern wastes. She shivered. Her frozen skin crawled with the sense they were being watched.

"Oh? I thought it was less a psychological condition and more an established fact," Havrshyk replied.

She kept herself from biting her lip, barely, as he insulted her with another fae's voice. Her wings flushed almost red in anger, but she wrestled it aside, and sneaking over to the streetside exit, she peeked out.

"But I'm right," Havrshyk added, "once you are supposed to have died, then everyone pretends that you did... and who you are now, is an apparition, an impostor—just as I am an impostor for *him,* we are for ourselves."

Despite her sense of being observed, the streets were empty, quiet except for the slight whistling of the wind through an almost-shut gate. Fryn glanced back at him with a false smile. "You've thought about this quite a bit, huh?"

A raindrop splashed on the cobblestones, sending bits of mud and dirt scattering under the impact, but it was much lighter than the rain in Fassen, with drops the size of her hand. She wondered if it was usually a thick mist, rather than a sprinkle.

Havrshyk took a long time in answering, pondering as they silently walked along the dark river. Perhaps nearly as long as he'd thought about it.

"When did you become a Lich?" he asked softly, almost in the same self-conscious way that Leif would usually talk. "How did the people around you react?"

For a moment she saw again the snow-dust blown in the wind across the Ice Wastes flats, she smelled the warm, almost-cloying perfume of the glacial flower, and heard her childhood friend laughing capriciously as she shook the stem of the flower to make one of its tulip-shaped petals fall. The rest, she refused to see again.

"Fryn?"

She closed her eyes, and the image faded. "I was a child, and when I returned, I didn't know what I had become, and I instinctively hid it… after a few years, well, there was no hiding what I'd become."

Havrshyk laughed. "You were lucky." He looked up at the clouds, and another raindrop splashed over his head. He sighed, and brushed ice shards out of his hair.

Fryn watched Havrshyk staring up at the sky, wondering if perhaps he were not the monster described so often in the stories she'd been told of the Viper, Lancer, and Lich.

"You know, I only helped Mythrim, because he let me out… and to make things right."

What could be righted by poisoning people? she wondered. "We need to find the Bounty Office if they have one. It's only been a few days… there is a chance they will not know." Fryn scratched her neck and looked away, trying to shed the crawling sense of discomfort that had begun clawing away at her disgust for him, revealing something in her she didn't expect, something uncomfortably similar to sympathy.

Her temporary partner nodded, more to himself than to her, and walked out into the street. She followed him, barely hearing his response. "It's better if they don't find out we've been here."

"I doubt they'll be able to predict what we're after," she replied.

"But they'd know that you'd go home?" he suggested.

"Ah, yes, perhaps they might."

The oil streetlamps were unevenly lit and unequally spaced, and for some reason that bothered her. It made the town feel more like a haphazard conglomeration of individual houses or businesses, than a livable, unified city.

"After all," Havrshyk added offhandedly, "it is only natural to go to one's friends—and you, well… we, have a reputation. Your actions in Frorin spread quickly, unfortunately, so it will be much more difficult to move in secret."

Fryn paused in following him to do a quick circle of pacing, and then, realizing that he'd gotten further ahead, she rushed after him. The Bounty Office, such as it was, sat in a cramped space between two large buildings. Gaerlin did not have a much of a Commission presence, and often they only had two or three local Hunters, who never did much business, or make a name for themselves. Havrshyk stopped before the single door eying the peeling paint of the sign with a mixture of disgust and distaste. Two things Fryn had always considered synonymous… until that moment.

He checked her with a sharp, questioning look, and then shrugged. "Keep your hood up, and your cloak clasped. Hide your Bloodknife, and pretend you are merely a fee seeking help with a small problem. I will be examining the bounty board, and when you come in explaining your problem, I will offer to help you out."

She nodded. "That could work."

Havrshyk grinned and pulled on the door. He frowned and pulled on it again. Then, grinding borrowed teeth, he pushed—and accomplished nothing.

"I suppose they are such a small office they do not need to operate through the night."

"Your powers of deduction are astounding," Havrshyk answered in a low monotone. "Well, that could make things easier. We are going to break in."

"I don't think that is…"

"No time to think, break the lock, and cover your face." He wrapped the tan scarf that Leif had worn at the Harvest Festival around his face, and then donned his hood, tapping his fingers on the hilt of his Bloodsword subconsciously. "I'll keep an eye out for guards…"

She sighed but drew her Bloodknife and applied the tip to the keyhole, then, pressing herself in the shadowed stoop, she pressed and twisted while reshaping her blade into a frozen key; her unpleasant companion watched both directions of the street. The lock clicked softly, and the bolt slid free, so Fryn pushed softly on the door, and peeked in; it was dark and still, like the catacombs where she and Leif had waited for the Guardhouse Ball.

Stepping inside, she brushed off the peeling flakes of gray paint that had attached themselves to her fingertips as she'd worked at the lock and scanned the single clerk's desk to the right. It was shielded by the same kind of glass that separated the clients from the clerks, that they had at the Bounty Office in Frorin, but with the messy, paper-cluttered desk, and the half-drained teacup, it reminded her more of the drunk wine-thief she'd first caught, than of Caelyn who had helped them so much before.

Havrshyk ignored her and examined the bounty wall. In the span of only a few days, news of their 'crimes' had already spread this far—the Finch Post was fast, but the Commission's Messengers were much quicker. Established routes and single destinations made that easier, Fryn supposed. There was one poster with a poorly drawn image of the two of them, that listed incredible, but mostly accurate charges against them: killing officers of the Grass Guard, killing other Hunters, nobles in Fassen, conspiring to embarrass the King of Gaersheim, and of being accomplices to the theft of the Harvest Crown. Beside this, there was another poster for Lia, but it appeared for the moment that Trel and Yarrow had escaped being marked. Fryn nodded to herself, relieved, that at least they had *that*.

The Gaerlin office was much smaller than the ones in Frorin or Fassen, and if the arranged items on the stained surface of the clerk's desk were any indication, the fae was likely older, and spent the majority of his time smoking a pipe. As Havrshyk took a turn staring at the posters, she stepped around to the desk and smelled the ashtray, a mixture of pine needles and tea leaves—hinting that the clerk was not well enough off to purchase Cherim tobacco, or anything else for that matter.

This information was useless however, so she sighed, and opened the three drawers built into the pinewood desk. One was stuffed with crumpled notes, shopping lists, and ironic doodles of various fee and fae with exaggerated facial features. One had a bottle of ink, a blotting cloth, and paper, and the third a bottle of a whiskey she'd never heard of before. *Agedwood,* it said, in sloppily arranged letters, and as she took out the bottle and uncorked it, she decided that it probably tasted like it sounded.

She still had her nose nearly stuck in the bottle when Havrshyk startled her from her thoughts. "A bit early for that," he said lightly.

Fryn corked it and put it back in the drawer. "His life can't be much better than mine," she replied.

He didn't comment, but instead went down the hall, and followed the stairs to the narrow second story where she could hear him rummaging around the various cabinets, and drawers, looking for who-knew-what. The idea had been to see if they were already being chased, not to leave a trail… Glancing back toward the desk, she contemplated tasting the whiskey, but simply shrugged and went over to the door, looking through the crack around its edge down both directions of the street. Two figures ambled along the quay, fortunately moving away from the Bounty Office.

Gaerlin was not much of a city, as it sat on the banks of a stagnant river and had no valuable natural resources. Whatever reason there had been for founding it there was long forgotten or used up, and now it simply *was*. If anything, it deserved the name Fassen more than Fassen did.

They didn't even have a starlamp to light the way to the Bounty Office here. One lamp was lit, and the other guttered out as she looked at it. It was like going back three hundred years, to the time before artificers and their craft became somewhat affordable. That was just one more thing the Commission had funded and made a fortune in trading, at least until they kicked Stanaedre out of the Commission.

A dull clatter sounded from the next story up, as Havrshyk searched, and Fryn decided to examine the back rooms on the ground floor. Their objective was simple, and already accomplished, so she wondered what Havrshyk thought he needed.

"Mint," he muttered irritably, "a backwards town like this without even a proper bank has to have some lying around in the open!"

A loud crash shook Fryn out of her reverie and she flew up the stairs, brushing through the doorway to the offices and the clerks' lounge. Paintings hung crookedly from the walls, a sofa's cushions had been thrown about, and a low table upended, and the china cabinet had been knocked over, spilling its shattered ceramic shards all over the dusty black rug. Havrshyk stood, shoulders rising and falling with his excited breaths, and his wings shivered with a wave of electric frost.

"Why are we here?" Fryn asked softly, her voice nearly catching, as she wondered if he'd turn his frustration on her.

Running a hand through his hair, fixing it with a layer of frost, he turned on his heel and regarded her with a blank frown. "We have nothing, only power, and even that is limited. We have no money, no food, and our blood is a limited resource. Have you not considered the precariousness of our situation? We are on the run, not because I killed those hunters, but because you sided with the wrong fae. We have no one to rely on, and if we continue on in this way, not only will we be unable to reclaim my body, but you will not have Leif, and we will slowly wear away."

"But we can remain frozen," she argued, "in full Lichform and we could simply fly straight there!"

Havrshyk laughed hollowly and was silent for a moment as he stared at the floor. "When you are in a full Lichform, your body cannot replenish its reserves, neither do your elemental capacities refill without limit. In an active state, you slowly consume yourself and your stored energies, unless you are able to constantly consume the lives of others. And if you are unwilling or unable to do that, you need to eat, and rest, and allow your body to heal. *I* was frozen in my own ice, trapped, till Mythrim got me out."

Fryn swallowed.

"It merely allows you to push past your needs for a time, but if you use it too long, and wither too much, then you will not be able to recover without a full transfusion. Do you think I was fine after Mythrim let me go? I was barely functioning, and *that,* after he donated some of his own blood!"

"I didn't know…" and she hadn't because she'd never been forced to freeze herself for very long… for some reason she'd never wanted to. She wanted to be alive. "But then… Leif!?"

"His time is short, because he only has so much blood on which to live, and if we do not reclaim my body in time, he will simply fade and only I'll be here. And… if I must use my blood, then both of us will die."

Fryn frowned and lowered her gaze.

A glint of light shone off of a bit of metal from among the ceramic shards, so Fryn bent down and recovered a dirty 5-mint coin, and then another, the remains of a petty-cash bowl among the china. Havrshyk watched silently as she searched, and in the end, she held about 50-mint in her hands triumphantly.

"That'll do. Now, let's find something to take from one of the nearby shops. We'll need food."

Closing her hands on the coins, and shoving them in the pocket of her waistcoat, Fryn shook her head. "I will not rob an honest fae; to take from our enemies is one thing, Havrshyk, but to take from our friends is not Arta's way."

"Arta?" he sneered, "A foolish, tragic king, and all his line. What use is it to follow him or his ways?" He bit his lip, no longer frozen, and a drop of blood ran down his chin, and fell onto the ground.

Setting her jaw, she met his eyes. "You don't mean that, you can't believe that… anymore."

"Why shouldn't I? After what they did?"

"You were wrong, Havrshyk, to kill those fee at the party."

He didn't respond right away, but instead sighed and went back down the stairs. Outside, Fryn could feel a cold and humid wind blowing in from the river with a cloud of fog through the partially open door. Finally, as she followed him to the door, his wings drooped and he answered, "Once you lose your trust, it's not an easy thing to take it up again. Even if I wronged his children, my king betrayed me first."

"He'll not betray again, I think," Fryn said hopefully. "I wonder now if Prince Ieffin knew that you were in there…in the sword…and thought to give you an opportunity to see the world a little better. Maybe he knew that if they simply let you out, you'd turn on them; maybe that's why he gave your sword to Leif."

Having fully drained himself, Havrshyk released an invisible, frozen sigh. "I think you give him too much credit... But f we're not going to rob a bystander, what would you suggest we do?" he asked, pulling the door open and stepping out into the street.

As his foot hit the cobbled ground, he rocked back with an arrow lodged in his shoulder, and his eyes hardened as he whirled back around—and not losing his balance he flew in a jagged arc toward the Main Street where two Hunters stood with longbows drawn. The jaundiced light from the streetlamp flashed along his black sword, as he cut two arrows, one after the other, out of the air, and lunged forward, to impale one of the Hunters on the end of his sword.

Fryn beat him to it, flying between Havrshyk and his prey, deflecting the sword with her blade and slamming an ice-encrusted fist under the Hunter's chin. Her wingburst-backed attack threw him back into the wall of the nearby warehouse, and he collapsed unconscious—but thankfully alive—to the ground.

"We are *not* killing innocents..." She hissed over her shoulder.

The other Hunter took a step backwards as he dropped his bow and went for the sword at his waist, eyes flicking between them, and the blood-weapons they bore.

"We'll need blood to keep going," Havrshyk countered, pursing his lips, "and we shouldn't let them know where we are."

She held up a hand, forestalling any more excuses for the inexcusable, as she spun on her heel, and kicked the sword out of the Hunter's hands, and followed through with a chop at his neck. He too fell to the ground. "No one dies unless they deserve it, Havrshyk."

"We are all dead anyway, Fryn, just pretending to be alive," Havrshyk mused.

Froreholt had at one time been a more religious or superstitious place, Fryn remembered, during the first few generations of their kingdom. Her people had venerated their founder and his heroism... not that they'd ever thought of him as more than that officially... but Arta had said many depressing things—such as the statement regarding his defense of the first Lich, saying that blooded or bloodless, none truly lived.

"Or we're all alive," she countered ironically, checking the pockets of the Hunters for spare mint, "we should be able to prove our innocence of the charges... but only as long as we remain so." The hunters had precious little mint, so she only took five from each. "The Francis brothers violated the Commission's code, so we can still argue our innocence there."

He 'hmm'ed. "With what we saw there, who can say that those with bounties on their heads deserve them? Is even the word of kings and presidents to be trusted?" Leif's tan scarf fluttered in the breeze, so he froze it back into place around his neck and looked at her with a smug, condescending smile. "By what absolute authority do they hunt us? Justice?" His smile faded and he shook his head. "The Commission is as corrupt as ever."

Fryn stood and looked back toward the Bounty Office once more, and then toward the water. Then, she began to run. Tired of all of this, wishing to end it all quickly, to put this whole nightmare behind her, to hold Leif in her arms... To not look into his face and see another fae sneering back; she ran all the way down the street, and around the sharp bend, following the path to the riverside. Havrshyk ran after her, not even bothering to ask what she was doing, perhaps reading the atmosphere correctly for the first time.

The foggy air cast a gentle layer of frost and then ice over her clothes, her skin, her hair, but she didn't stop until they ducked out of the last streetlamp and stood on the very edge of the largest pier, staring out at the marshy reeds peeking up above the surface of the water, barely visible in the gloomy dark.

She halted at the end of the pier with the toes of her boots just sticking over, but Havrshyk kept going, out over the water, flying off toward the other side.

Fryn waited for that feeling of distance, hoping and longing for a severing of that connection of her heart to Leif's... in the same moment mourning him and wishing she could be free. Havrshyk vanished from her sight, but in her heart, she could still sense him as the distance between them began to shrink, and Havrshyk returned, landing on the water, with a patch of ice forming beneath his feet. He floated before her with a blank expression, waiting.

Looking once more over her shoulder in the direction of the Bounty Office, knowing that she and Leif didn't deserve any of this, Fryn froze her stomach solid, and flew in an ice-scattering wingburst out over the water, with a chilling wind so severe that the surface of the river froze momentarily as she passed.

They had sixty mint to spend, but if word of their bounty had already gone before them, they might not be able to even use the money without risking another attack. Even with the opportunity to purchase food, they might have to starve. Fryn intended then, to avoid fighting as much as possible, and to run and fly as far as they could every day.

Despite the season, they had reaped a harvest they hadn't sown, and so they fled in the same eager and frantic way the springtime sparrow flew. Casting out over the river, Fryn looked down at her starlit reflection, but her mournful face was only visible for a few seconds before she had to look up and check her heading, narrowly avoiding one of the gnarled roots of an oncoming tree. She cursed Havrshyk and wondered how similar misfortune had brought them to such different perspectives.

~16 Years Ago~

Frorin

Rain District

Fryn

Fryn pulled on her yarn, undoing the pearls she'd attempted to put in place for the fourth time, and despite her frustration, she almost enjoyed unraveling the end of her scarf more than knitting it together. The bright blue yarn fell in a growing spiral on the table, as she waited for her mother to finish her story.

Her mother was knitting her own scarf, not from yarn, but from white thistle-down that she complemented with a vibrant purple pattern. "It was because of her jealousy over Arta's attention that she killed Yndril, tamed the ermine, and made it bite her head clean off!"

Fryn groaned.

"Yes, quite terrible, but see Yndril didn't die. Her head fell one way, and her body, the ermine ate; but Arta was close behind them. Fora thought she'd tricked him, but he was far too wise you see. In only a few days he flew over the ice fields, and he landed in the flower-fields, with his spear of light the only means to see. Snow fell far thicker in those days, covering the land in snow so deep you could bury our city twice, but not a flake touched *him*."

Resetting her needles, Fryn diligently began again. "But the stars show Arta fighting the serpent?"

Her mother 'tutted' and shook her head. "That's another story altogether child, now hush, your father will be home soon, and I'd like to finish this part of the story."

"Yes, Ma," Fryn supplied, continued her work, biting her lip in thought.

In contrast, as Fryn focused, her mother was able to extend the length of her scarf without any thought given to it at all—and she wove her tale just as quickly and skillfully. "Centuries before he faced Fora and the viper in the valleys lost to time, he tracked the ermine in the winter through the tunnels in the snow. Finally, he found her head, frozen and preserved, and he wrapped it in his wings. The light in her eyes remained, and no one had ever died before, so he kept searching for the rest of her. He found the ermine sleeping, and seeing the red on its jaws, realized the truth, Fora's greatest crime, and using his light-bound spear he pierced its eye and cut open its stomach, and fished her body out."

"Gross, Ma, why are you telling me this?" Fryn complained, setting aside her knitting, and shifting in her chair so she could reach over and drink her chilled tea.

"Because it's important, dear. A spear was not a weapon at the beginning of time. It was a lamp, or a lantern, a way to find and guide and see. The world is very different now, much has changed, since jealousy made death appear.

"Arta laid out the pieces of her body, and placed her head above her shoulders, but nothing happened. Then seeing the light in her eyes, he brought the light of his spear above her, and he called out to her to return. He cried over her, marveling that she could be before him, and not there. He wondered if this was what the Wing-Giver had meant when he warned of that thing we now call death... but the Wing-Giver gave again, and as Arta wept over his fallen bride, her frozen body fused together piece by piece, until her frost-covered eyes flickered open, and she took her second first breath.

"And unlike all who came after her, she never died again. But at that moment, she did not remember who or what she was—nor did she remember her husband, though she was grateful to have someone with her when she woke..."

"She forgot him?"

"Perhaps it was a mercy to forget. She was the first Lich, reborn from a traumatic death... but all she'd had before had been stolen and lost." Her mother finished one last loop, and then tied it off, and set her completed scarf aside. "Now, I believe I hear your father downstairs, are you hungry? I imagine he might be dying to eat."

Fryn nodded and hopped off her chair, flitting down the stairs after her mother. Sure enough, he was busy brushing crumbs off the front of his shirt as he moved to hug them both. He picked Fryn up and swung her around with a laugh and set her down beside the kitchen table. "I saw Harissa today, Fryn," he said cheekily, not really even noticing his wife's outstretched hand, scratching his head, and mussing up his silvery-gray hair.

"I didn't think you'd be going to the outer districts today..." her mother complained.

He waved her off. "I thought it would be good to invite her up to play sometime, show her around the Rain District parks."

"Just as long as Fryn isn't going down there, we agreed, remember that moving up means making changes."

He nodded, suppressing a frown as he moved to the table and noticed the array of cold meat and hare-cheese. "We'll talk it over and arrange for her to visit. In the meantime, however, I think we need to eat."

A lazy snowflake drifted through the open window, neatly brushing past the frozen curtains, as it settled on her desk; a dark-stained, pinewood, child-sized desk. Fryn wasn't worried that it would damage the finish. She pulled her feet up under her frosted blankets, bunching the turned over covers in her hands as she stared at the strangely welcome visitor, but she *was* worried the flake would wobble and fall off to shatter on the slate tiled floor. It was covered in delicate, perfect spines of ice-crystals so purposefully constructed, she wondered if the story about Yndril in the snow might be true.

She had lived forever, despite the fact she had died; the firstborn of the Wing-Giver, the eldest, fairest, the one who'd shed more tears and blood than anyone ever to be born upon the surface of the world. Arta's bride, and Arta's bane, the reason why there were three moons in the star-filled sky. Harissa always complained—or had, before they'd moved last year—that mothers told their sons to be like Arta, but none wanted their daughters to be like *her*. She wasn't a role model, even if it wasn't her fault, she was the haunting story, not even a cautionary tale, just a tragedy. But then why did her mother keep telling her the tale of Yndril? Because even a tragedy is important?

Fryn threw off her blankets, or well, she tried, but they crumpled back with a soft crunching sound—she had suffused them with a brittle frost layer for comfort and cleanliness—and she flitted out of her bed and landed before her desk, leaning over the snowflake to inspect it without touching. It glittered with the reflected and refracted light of the blue-tinted starlamp at the street corner, and the Commission Bank's clock tower discreetly chimed a quarter past eleven.

Her father's snore sounded softly down the hall; they often left their doors cracked open. Fryn smiled as she heard a soft creaking of springs, and a quiet "oof" as her mother woke him with a nudge so he'd turn over. It had been her idea to move inward, allowing the rest of the clan to make use of her business connections, maybe even improve the position of the Martin Clan. Touching one of the spokes of the snowflake with her fingertip, Fryn rolled it back and forth with a smile widening, cheeks pinching a little as her dimples fully formed; what need did they have to change?

She picked up the snowflake and tossed it up in the air a couple times, catching and throwing, higher each time, wings flicking idly as she played. After about the fifth time, she fumbled to catch it as a slight rumble went through the floor, and it fell, breaking into slivers and shards that spread out across her feet and the tiles in a wide arc, with a shockingly loud tinkling sound. Looking around, her heart racing, Fryn waited for the sound of her parents' door hinges, ready to bolt back into bed at a moment's notice. A breath of wind blew in from the hall, tossing her short bangs out of her face, and rustling her half-frozen curtains, with a moist heavy warmth like the breath of a giant beast.

A faded orange light flickered and reflected off the wall outside the door, so Fryn crept forward to see if perhaps, her father had lit a lantern and was coming to put her to bed again. In her mind it was not her father, but Arta, and not a lantern, but a glowing spear. As she rounded the bed, she looked first at the playful reflections that danced in the mirror of her nightstand, and then at the source, a wave of orange, red, and yellow flames that had somehow silently extended from under the door in the middle of the hall, creating an impenetrable wall of fire and smoke, separating her from her parents. Her mother had frozen the stove's coals herself, and Fryn had held them in her hands, playing with the lines of charcoal she scraped across a sheet of paper to draw with, delaying every minute she could before being sent to bed.

But there, just beyond the door, intense heat, worse than the glaring summer sun, assaulted her and the thin second skin of ice that she had decided to coat herself with constantly—now melting and dissipating like the morning fog. But still, she didn't move. Her eyes were fixed on the door on the other side of the fire, waiting for some sign of movement through the smoke, for her mother's voice to command her, reassure her, compel her. She couldn't tell if time itself had frozen, or if her heart had stopped its beat, but she felt a jolt travel up her spine tingling all the way to her wingtips as she expelled the burst of energy and her time began to crawl, shouting down the hallway, "Fire! Wake up!" She faltered backwards, stumbling and landing on her rear, adding under her breath, "help me…"

Dully, she was aware of the clock-tower ringing its bells frantically, and the yelling of the guards outside the window over her shoulder. Water splashed against the kitchen walls, and Fryn cringed at the gasping of the steam, not looking away, waiting for her parents to come, only shrinking back when the rush of air from the broken kitchen windows shifted the direction of the fires, and they rushed into her room—catching on the desk chair, her curtains, her bed, chasing her all the way to the open window. Her wings felt limp and all her strength seemed to fade, as a rising panic brought her climbing on the desk on which the snowflake had settled, and she stuck her hands out the small opening on the bottom half of the window.

They lived on the second story of the duplex house, and she saw that the bottom floor was completely engulfed in the conflagration, flames licking up the side of the building just below her, from the neighbors' child's room. Hands pressed against the window, she pulled back inside, frantically searching her burning room—her parents would find their own way out, but she would have to save herself. Standing on her tiny desk, she held her breath, hoping that her heat-weakened wings would have the strength to fly, then, steeling herself, unable to shield her hands with even the thinnest layer of ice from the heat, she jumped. The window exploded outwards around her in as many shards as had the snowflake, gleaming incandescently in orange and blue, and red from the slashes on her arms as she fell.

Fryn fluttered her wings with all she had, and spun, spiraling downwards like a broken kite, as the pavement met her face first, and a blanket of darkness fell coolly, and blessedly, over her from above.

~Two Days Later~

Frorin

Snow District

Fryn

Her life had shattered like that snowflake, Fryn decided, beautiful, but fragile, transient. She sat up straighter so that her ice-molded cast wasn't pressed against the window of the carriage, so that the Guard Captain sitting across from her wouldn't be able to meet her eyes, so that she'd find a position, perhaps, more comfortable when they hit a bump. Even now, he crossed his arms, putting creases in his otherwise crisp ceremonial uniform, glacial blue, and white, like the Crown-Guard, official, inspiring, ultimately disappointing.

"Ms. Martin," he admonished, as if she were merely being childish, "you ought to listen more attentively when an adult is speaking to you."

He'd blathered on long enough, she thought, but merely flicked her eyes back to stare daggers into his. He stiffened momentarily, a small mercy, but resumed his lecture, radiating importance and elemental warmth as if that would put her more at ease. She countered his heat-element as she could, intensifying the frost on her side of the carriage.

"Instructions were left in your parents' will that you be raised in the Snow District, educated, and trained as an upstanding young woman of worth—not to be returned to your *crim... uncouth clan*."

Fryn sighed, and doubled up on her melting layer of ice, smiling slyly as her frost coated and stiffened her pale-blue dress, and the silly white gloves that climbed well past her elbows, or rather one elbow, since she'd broken her right arm. Still, she wasn't in the mood to talk.

"Come now, Ms. Martin, you are already eight years old, this petulance does not become you." He shook his head and looked out the other window, finally reading her mood.

Less than a year after leaving their clan, she was supposed to be someone entirely different? *Stupid*, that's what it was. Fryn took a deep breath, and held it, as they passed through the gateway of a long drive leading into a courtyard of fine gray stones. The building they parked before was *three stories* tall, had steps leading up to a covered patio, and a set of gigantic double-doors. A fae in a clean black suit stood beside the door, regarding her through the window with an emotionless twitch of his long, gray mustaches. Was *he* the one who would be raising her?

He descended the steps to the drive and opened the carriage door, deftly lowering the footstep and holding out his spare hand for her to exit, but he didn't speak or meet her eyes. The captain huffed, uncrossing his legs as he waited impatiently for her to move. Indeed, even this butler seemed intent on her being quick, as his wings shifted and pulsed with a flush of blue.

She took his hand and stepped out onto the flagstoned courtyard, spinning around awkwardly because of the cast on her arm, and the bruises on her legs, and the binding keeping her from using her wings. There were two outbuildings, one, a domed aviary wherein she heard the chirping of a finch and the cooing of a pigeon, and the other, looked to be a carriage-shed. Everywhere she looked around the miniature estate, she marveled, for they were near the northernmost corner of the Snow District, and she could see the walls of the rings connecting just beyond. The long arms of the estate itself stretched out like wings, from a central tower, and as she began to ascend the steps to the porch, she heard the pattering and clattering of many small feet running around the building, chasing one another down its halls.

The doors parted before they even reached the top, and she saw him, tall and thin, but balanced like a sword. He didn't notice her at first, instead focusing on his butler, and the captain, a wan smile on his pale face. Inside, Fryn could hear children, not so much playing, but practicing, training, with the occasional 'ha!' or 'oof!' or victorious laugh, as five children all close to her age were sparring with padded sticks instead of knives. One was alone, a girl with bright and cheerful eyes, and straight black hair like the fae who stood now in the doorway, long and styled in the same kind of braid, with matching blue ribbons.

Fryn started, falling back as the fae addressed her; her fall thankfully caught by the butler who helpfully pushed her back upright. "Welcome, Fryn Martin, to Bersari House, I am Baesil, Baesil Bersari, Grandmaster of the Swordhand-Pa…Soft-Point Fist. Please, come inside." He bowed slightly, sweeping his hands to the side, ushering and welcoming her through the doors. Fryn found herself moving before she even realized what she was doing, walking in, scanning her surroundings in a mixture of awe and disbelief. *This* was where she was supposed to live? High vaulted ceilings, a pure white plaster dome, blue-stained glass windows, with hand-carved moldings, curtains and drapes free from even a speck of dust—cleanliness and poshness oozed from the very walls of a school that trained its children how to kill.

The five children in the center of the circular foyer paused in their practice to stare at her. Three boys, with messy but somewhat styled hair, raised eyebrows or sniffed as she entered, and returned to their practice. One of the girls was drawn back into the fight because of her partner, so that the lone girl with black hair was the only one who continued to examine her. She had a playful smile, and her wings pulsed excitedly as she ran forward, bowing with a clumsy flourish just like the Master.

"Welcome! I'm Pyran Bersari, but you can call me Pyra." She leaned in and added softly, eyes flicking up toward the Master, "That's my dad…"

Fryn smiled, then let out a small laugh, some of the weight of her life falling from her shoulders like a shed layer of frost. "I'm Fryn, nice to meet you."

"I'm bored, daddy," the girl declared in response, throwing her arms straight up in the air. "Let's play!"

The Master sighed resignedly and waved her off. "Be back by dinner and show Fryn her room!"

"Yay!" she replied, hearing, probably, nothing of what he said, "Bet you can't find me, Fryn!" flew off down a hallway and took a sharp turn, flying out of sight.

Fryn was stunned, only for a second, and then electrified, as she started walking, slowly from the soreness in her legs, determined to find the little girl.

She wouldn't lose.

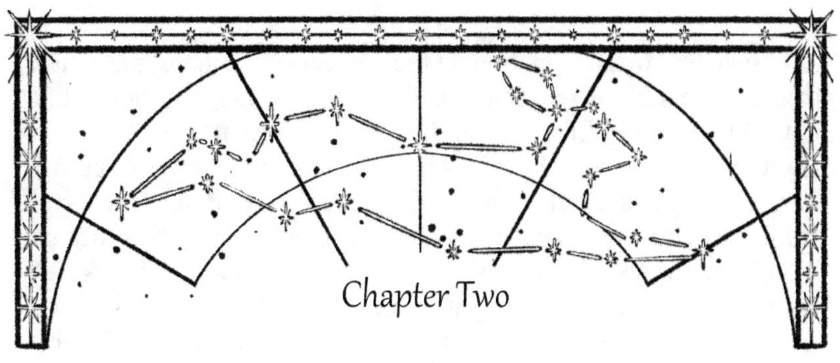

Chapter Two

Hare

Artell

Fryn

Aside from Frorin, Artell was the only *real* city of note in Froreholt. Though it was comprised of only one ring, Artell was protected by an impressive stone wall, which surrounded a city that clung for its life to the bluff of rock overlooking the river like the lichen that had followed them all the way up its course from the stagnant docks of Gaerlin. From their vantage point on the eastern wall, they kept their hoods up, and concealed their weapons as best they could as they surveyed the Artell River's churning rapids hundreds of wingspans below. The locals called them "The Bones of the River," or if they were feeling really inspired, "The Serpent's Grave," and Fryn would have swallowed at the vertigo-inducing sight, if she had any saliva left. She blinked and continued to stare down into the ravine. She half imagined it was instead, a river of bones, and shuddered as she thought of the wingshards and gravel that filled the alleys of the Weasel Cairn.

Not even a fluid-elemental would dream of swimming through that river, and it was said, (hearsay again), that its depth was greater than the height of a pine tree. Fryn did not believe them, but she had no incentive to prove them wrong. Whatever its depth, the narrow river had cut a sharp channel through the rocky cliffs, and provided a natural barrier that protected them from the dangers of the Forest of Grass.

Havrshyk was lost in thought too, pondering, perhaps, the chunk of ice he kept in his mouth to distract from his hunger. They could not afford to be in Lichform in the city, or to use their elements to any great degree, so… Fryn grit her teeth, and tightened her belt… they could feel the toll of going without food these last five days. While in Lichform, it was just a numbness, but with the full rush of blood in her veins, it was consuming. More than once, Havrshyk had argued with her that they ought to have killed those hunters, since the nutrients in their blood would have sustained them longer and they wouldn't have had to risk being seen in the city. She'd ignored him.

A gust of wind tugged at her hood, but she held onto it, and a fresh awareness of the city and its inhabitants took hold of her. It was a little like dreaming, with a wobbliness to her knees, a fragility to her wings, that made her feel like she was drifting even when she gripped the battlements of the wall with all her strength.

"How do we move, in Lichform, when there's no blood to give us strength?" she asked softly, eyes flicking toward the corner of her vision to see if any of the passing guardsfae had heard her.

He didn't move at first, just took a deep breath. Then, slowly turning toward her, he leaned his back against the battlements and closed his eyes. "You don't know? Hm… that's… what was it again?" He considered the question carefully, and, she could tell, he drained partially to alleviate his hunger. "In the absence of physical energy, we control our bodies by drawing on our elemental reserves… but if we are in Lichform, and then empty our reserves, we must either draw from our blood again, or remain paralyzed and frozen—or get a transfusion of fresh blood full of elemental energy."

It made sense.

"We need food, Havrshyk, my reserves are spent, and my blood is weak." She drew her knife slightly from its sheath and frowned at its anemic pink color. It was still a Bloodknife, but it was as empty of motive power as her elemental energies. Her wings hung limply behind her back.

"Then let's find something. I have an idea." He pushed off the wall and wavered down the steps to the street. The eastern quarter of the city, or sector as they called them in Artell, was a modest residential area. They had no slums on the level of Eastwall in Fassen, or as Fryn considered the entirety of Gaerlin, but the shops and houses all bore the same ugly lichen stains that she would expect a poor district to have. The 'park' was really just a bed of moss in an empty lot where a pine seedling had risen just to the height of the wall, and children chased each other around its spindly trunk.

The city was composed of four sectors, with the Ridgelord's Estate in the center. It was awfully similar to Frorin, just different. The north was the richest sector, with large houses and a few merchants of the greatest standing, and the west was predominantly a trading district, and the south… well, she didn't know what they had there. Fortunately, Havrshyk was heading south, through a curved alley that brought them conveniently and unnoticed to a large square.

She glanced out into the market curiously, staring at the mass of faeries that stood about, or sat, or hawked wares from unsheltered booths, or handed out leaflets at the entrances to the square… or a myriad of other things. The volume of their speech threatened to drown out her own thoughts, and she forgot, just for the moment, the gnawing urgency of her hunger.

Everyone looked excited, or agitated, or something… as they bustled, and shuffled, and rushed around the congested square—but there were no ribbons, or speeches, or bottles of wine, or snacks— nothing to justify such a gathering. Fryn subconsciously refused to enter the crowd and waited in the alley with her hand pressed weakly against the wall.

Havrshyk wasn't nearly as concerned, stalking out with an almost Leif-like swagger, and Fryn spotted the glint of a five-mint coin in his hand as he threaded through the idle faeries and vanished in the crowd. The only hint she caught of him moving around back there was the occasional glimpse of his overlong tan scarf, looped around his neck and frozen in place so that the two tails of the scarf dangled down his back under his wings. Yet another marker of his time, Fryn thought; in Frorin that style of wearing scarves had since become old-fashioned and was usually done ironically for parties. Leif would wear it that way, possibly since it was originally an Aelaete fashion, but that just increased the irony. Havrshyk continued to do so; whether it was to imitate his host, or because it was the fashion in Frorin 70 years ago, she couldn't say.

The wait dragged on. He moved from one corner of the square to the other and back, on who knew what strength, until he finally slipped out of the crowd and returned to the alley with a small cottonwood-canvas satchel in hand. He crouched in the alleyway behind her, and rifled around in the bag, and stood up with two small skewers each of dry-roasted hare, and blackberry pips. Wordlessly, he passed her the blackberry one first, and his face flushed with full blood as he slowly took one bite and sat with his back to the wall.

Even though she wanted to devour it immediately, she had learned well enough that hunger took time to build, and time to tear down… as Master Bersari had phrased it. She could almost hear him now, explaining how shocking it would be if one were "suddenly" starving, and how similarly, the body went into shock if it were suddenly full. She took a nibble of the blackberry pip, and nearly cried from relief. It was sweet, filling her blood with much needed sugar, and it was juicy, refreshing her dried-out throat. After that first bite, she dreaded the dried out bits of hare, but hoped by the time she finished the berry her concerns would be unwarranted.

It took them nearly fifteen minutes to eat that one skewer of fruit, and once they had finished the meat, Fryn was feeling nearly as revived as if she'd had a transfusion.

"So," Fryn said, using a sliver of ice to pick her teeth, "what is all that?" She pointed at the crowd with her toothpick. It was still as busy as ever in the square, and its occupants showed no signs of leaving anytime soon.

Havrshyk sat on the ground, gnawing on the end of his skewer, as if the sliver of wood still had something to nourish him. His eyes flicked up to hers, and then back to the stick. "You aren't going to like it."

She narrowed her eyes and listened with one ear, trying to pick out something, anything… nothing.

He sighed. "Leaflets are being handed out by Commission messengers and many end up in the gutters, but," he pulled out a crumpled piece of paper from his bag, "the majority of the townsfae are reacting predictably."

She snatched it and scanned it with a scowl. Sure enough, it mentioned their bounties, but worse, it advertised a petition by the Commission to deny the ascension of the Pine-Martin to the rank of low-nobility, on the grounds of her supposed involvement in the conspiracy against the Gaersyn Crown. A proposal submitted by President Hans, the King of Gaersheim, and apparently, the Lord of Wellsey—the same one who had canceled his engagement to Princess Savis.

"This all just smacks of a conspiracy alright, but theirs!" she hissed quietly.

"They're trying to gain popular support, and potentially catch us by advertising the bounties even to the common fae, not just the Hunters or Guards. I don't like this at all… they're after something else, something big—this is just like the Stanaedre Coup…" Havrshyk insisted, peeking around her to scan the crowd, and smiling as a passing fee crumpled one such paper and threw it menacingly into the gutter. "I guess your cousin is popular even in Artell… I can see why though, hah… More than a few just tossed the fliers away in front of the messengers."

Fryn smirked despite herself; despite the fact that her current partner had imprisoned Leif inside his sword. "You know you stood her up?"

Havrshyk frowned, which looked odd on Leif's face, since he didn't like to frown. "That was part of the plan, but if not for that, I might have enjoyed the evening. She's more…" he waved his hand vaguely, "vibrant, more social than you."

Fryn shook her head. "She's certainly that."

He was about to continue but was interrupted by a young fee who appeared suddenly in the mouth of the alley and addressed them in a slightly lilting, quiet voice. Her accent was odd, with harsher 'ch's and 't's as if she were from Renholt or had spent a great deal of time there. "Are you two, by any chance… any relation to…" she began, her face obscured by her charcoal-gray hood, and the darkness of the alley. She presented them with one of those fliers that had been handed out.

"Of course not," Fryn interjected, with a tight-lipped smile, "you have no idea how often we are confused…"

The fee lowered her hood and revealed a thin, pretty, but severe face. Her eyes gleamed mysteriously as she pursed her lips. "Are you hungry?" she asked, bringing up in her other hand, a small cloth satchel bulging with savory-smelling goods.

Havrshyk oddly said nothing, his eyes darting between the bag, the stranger's well-meaning face, and the space behind her in the square.

She looked down shyly, and stammered, "I saw you buying food, such small portions, and I could just see it in your eyes…"

Fryn swallowed, still tasting blackberry, and glanced at the flier in her other hand. "Why?"

The strange fee looked around quickly, swishing her long black curls out of her face, and checked for eavesdroppers, before advancing into the alley. Then she added in a whisper, "I'm sympathetic." Her almost clear, cloudy-white wings twitched nervously on her back, smaller than normal, but likely suitable for short-distance flight.

Sympathetic to what? Fryn wondered dryly. Our true plight, or whatever we're accused of?

"We are grateful for your sympathy," Havrshyk commented, rising from the ground. "But I'm not certain I understand."

Leif would have laughed at that statement and said something about how it is fairly certain he doesn't.

She stepped deeper into the shadowed alleyway and whispered. "I know who you are, and I can help you… but we can't talk here. There are too many people."

"And who do you say we are? We are merely simple travelers low on supplies and funds," Fryn answered, checking that she had enough blood to form a blade if needed. Her elemental reserves were basically shot, and her blood was too thin to form anything more practical than a pink icicle.

"The Serpent and the Lich, the two most feared of the constellations," she replied with an ironic twist to her smirk, as if she thought there were other more fearsome signs for the superstitious to revere. "I would help you if I can, but you must follow me."

Havrshyk shrugged, and Fryn sighed. Meeting the stranger's eyes, she felt a slight shiver and a confidence that she meant them no harm. Giving her a quick nod, Fryn asked, "What is your name?"

Their guide whisked by them with her dark gray cloak swishing in the manufactured breeze, so that they could barely make out the thin leaf-shaped wings that sprouted from her back. They were small, and gold-lined—and, as Fryn had thought before, it was apparent that flying was difficult for her.

"Alyra," she shot back over her shoulder, struggling to rise to a hover, "this way, quickly. Hans sent out these fliers where he thought it most likely to find you."

"I don't see how they caught on to us so quickly," Havrshyk complained, flying after her. "But I wonder if we could walk, I'd rather conserve my energy."

Alyra gave him a wry laugh but kept flying, leading them in a race down the dark alley and taking a sharp right turn. "Not an option, I'm afraid. The Hunters here are already searching for you. Several guards were rumoring about a suspicious couple of drifters who were seen lingering by the Serpent's Grave. Even now, three teams of Hunters are scouring the four sectors of the city," she explained, darting nimbly, without even a hint of difficulty, around corners, and into tighter spaces than they would normally dare to fly.

Fryn found herself admiring her jagged grace, as if she had memorized the path and flown it a hundred, or likely more, times. Under the flapping cloak, she saw Alyra was outfitted in a rugged gray vest and blouse, with pants covered in loops and pockets, jingling with small tools, trinkets, and mysteries and on her belt, at the small of her back, were two crossed crystal handled daggers.

Their journey through the city was winding, circling, tracking, and back-tracking, even revisiting that same market they'd been to before, as if she were narrowly dodging and sweeping around the Hunters on their search, and it was getting dark by the time they stopped on the wall at the north-eastern edge of the city. Panting, Alyra took a minute to catch her breath and without explanation, she dove over the wall, following the cliff-face toward a tiny glimmer of light, the barest hint of it visible against the rock. She swept down to land on the concealed terrace and walked under the lip, passing out of sight.

Fryn shivered, not from the chill air, and spared an unconvinced look toward her companion before she noticed the approaching glimmer of a Guard patrol's lantern below the wall. She flew, erratically, weakly, after their long journey, and half fell toward the terrace with Havrshyk close behind. She spun, no longer using any strength or flight to avoid the notice of any guards above, and barely slowed to a halt before she would have crashed into the lip of rock. Alyra stood with her back toward them, facing an immense hardbound door that was the only other object in the three-wingspan-wide space.

Admiring his surroundings with a low whistle, Havrshyk grinned. "I'd heard the rumors…but I didn't know for certain."

"Know what?" Fryn asked, watching Alyra as she knocked unceremoniously on the iron-banded door.

"The city of Artell was originally a bastion against the east… some even suggested that it was built to guard against Jakaren and his like." He scratched his chin and closed his eyes. "Hm… yes, full of stockpiles of arms, and equipped for imprisonment, interrogation, espionage. My master told me he used to get his reports and logistics through here."

Alyra's hand froze, as she was about to knock again, and shot a quizzical look at him, reevaluating him with her steel-colored eyes. "I wasn't aware that Master Yarl was a member of the Swordhand-Palm."

Fryn avoided looking at her partner, as she covered a yawn.

Before she could continue her line of questioning, the door swung inward of its own accord, and their guide ushered them into a natural cavern hallway that was lit with only one glaring white starlamp every twenty or so wingspans. She tossed them a raised eyebrow over her shoulder as she walked ahead lightly.

"Indeed, this safe-house was in disrepair for at least fifty years since its previous occupants were in office here." As off-handed as her remark sounded, Fryn could feel the tensing of her partner's muscles and the quickening of his heartbeat through the bloodcrafted link—the link she had accidentally created with Leif, not Havrshyk, when she'd saved him after their encounter with the Venomsword.

Havrshyk tightened his jaw, choosing not to comment, wisely— Fryn thought. Alyra continued nonetheless, "unless I am mistaken, the order lost favor with the king, and was disbanded."

"I had not heard of this Swordhand-Palm until this year," Fryn interjected, "it appears that my school was founded on its principles, but for more publicly appealing uses."

Their guide nodded as if she were already aware of that fact and stopped abruptly before another door just like the first. She spun around, hands swishing back her cloak, as she bent toward them and said in a soft voice, almost conspiratorially, "I have friends here, who may be able to help you escape the notice of the Commission for a time, but follow my lead, and do not trust them *too* much. We all have our wants, and needs, but some might charge a trying price to sort you out."

Before either of them could answer, she turned on her heel, took a deep breath as she gazed up at the door and grasped its latch determinedly. She pulled it open, and strode in confidently, whistling from the middle of a tune.

"Back already, Aly?" A squeaky-voiced fae wondered from inside the room.

"Back already," she affirmed, and beckoned them to enter, "with company."

Fryn stepped in first and picked out the owner of the childish voice instantly. He was lounging in the most uncomfortable posture on a stool beside a makeshift bar on the far side of the room. His mussed brown hair was barely parted in front of his face so that only one of his eyes gave any hint of the dense freckles he was so obviously trying to hide. He sloshed his mug of hop-scented ale, oblivious to the flecks that splashed onto the unmanned bar, and his already dubiously stained shirt-sleeve, as he examined them out of the corner of his eye and down his nose simultaneously.

"Drifters," he scoffed, "we aren't recruiting, we're not a hostel, and we don't take in strays," he informed, looking away from them and taking a deep draught of his ale. Fryn repressed a frown at his attitude, and found she was more surprised by his youth—he had to be only seventeen, or eighteen, and yet he had the arrogant attitude, and the over-sized mug, of a much older brigand.

They hadn't discussed a story, or identity, and they both watched him, and then glanced at each other, for several moments before Alyra intervened. Their guide settled on a excessively discolored bench before a matching table and waved them over to the opposite side. "Have a seat, and don't mind the weasel, he has a way of popping up where he's not wanted."

The freckled youth nursed his ale as he thought of a suitable retort, and finally, bangs floating back to reveal the victorious glow in his eyes, he snapped, "And this quail has an uncanny knack for accepting other bird's' unwelcome chicks!"

A passing grade. Fryn smiled; Leif would have enjoyed this. Her stomach twisted as she looked over at her companion, at the darkened hair, the scowl, the shadowed eyes, and the black sword at his waist. *Havrshyk... As soon as you have your body back, I'll break you once again.*

Alyra burst out into a high-pitched, but melodic, and somewhat husky laugh, and went quiet. "Geran, these are no chicks. Why don't you run along and fetch someone useful?"

"Hmph," he snorted, nearly choking on an overlarge gulp, as he slipped off his stool and slammed his mug down on the bar, and obediently, unwillingly, slunk off down the hall muttering curses under his breath.

"Well… for the time being we have some peace and privacy," Alyra said, folding her hands on the table and closing her eyes for a moment. They snapped open again urgently and she leaned over the table to whisper, "my associates here *can* help you, but I would beg a favor in return." Her delicate, gold-lined wings shifted under her cloak, and one of them actually batted it aside to poke out oddly, while the others were hidden.

Havrshyk mulled on that and caught Fryn's eye, holding it for a second before nodding to himself and answering her. "Before we can attempt to restore our names or investigate the forces behind the conspiracy we've stumbled upon, we need to slip out of the public eye, and escape the notice of the Commission."

Fryn opened her mouth, and was about to contribute to the conversation, when Alyra cut in. "So, you imagined that coming north, back towards Frorin, where your only allies might be found, would be a good idea?" she asked incredulously, lifting one of her carefully sculpted eyebrows at them. Her use of 'l's and 'r's were soft and lilting, but the 'th's and 't's were over-enunciated. A southern dialect perhaps? The Francis brothers had a rougher accent, and they were from at least as far south as Haryn.

Before she could answer, Havrshyk spoke first. He dismissed her eyebrow-raising with a nonchalant wave and examined the unlabeled bottles and mini casks at the ramshackle bar with an unimpressed eye. "We have business in Frorin that cannot wait."

Fryn's neck itched, and she spared a glance down the hall, but for now it seemed no one was listening in. She focused on Alyra with a friendly smile, and added, "Indeed, it is a pressing matter, as urgent perhaps as avoiding notice. So, if you can help us get to Frorin quickly and avoiding detection, you would have your favor."

Footsteps down the chiseled-out hallway announced the return of the weasel-like youth as well as one other, as Alyra leaned in closer and whispered, "More on that later then." She swiveled around to face the tunnel with her arms and legs crossed, and coattails swishing as she put on a snide smile. "I thought I asked you to 'get someone useful," she commented dryly, wrinkling her nose. "That smells like Werys' perfume… if you can call it that."

'Werys' presented herself in the opening of the hallway with matching crossed arms, wearing an asymmetrical coat belted tightly at her high waist, and buttoned over a full chest, which blossomed with a large, possibly stuffed and tucked-in crimson scarf. She frowned at Alyra, ignoring them, as her full lips pouted and her large blue eyes stared daggers. Her straight brown hair was braided and pulled back into a bun, in a style Fryn had used frequently, but with her shallow cheeks, and large face, Werys looked like a washed-out, amateur copy of herself. The 'perfume' as Alyra had graciously called it, was a sickeningly sweet and sour scent not unlike smoke and old meat, with hints of marjoram, and rosemary. Fryn discreetly blocked her nostrils with a thin layer of ice and breathed shallowly through her mouth.

Alyra however, ignored the smell, and locked eyes with the young fee. "We need a bird."

"A bird?" she asked, noticing them for the first time, eyes narrowing as she recognized them. "Ah… yes… I see. That can be arranged." She shifted her attention back to them and smiled, falsely, Fryn felt. "We are no friends of the Commission, but there must be more to our benefit than simply inconveniencing our enemies."

Fryn opened her mouth at the same time as Havrshyk, but before either of them could answer, Alyra interjected, "I will arrange payment, but first, kindly find us a bird. And, Geran, you help her too, we are in a hurry."

Werys bit her lip and turned on her heel, and was halfway to the hall when she paused, and stomped back to grab her companion by his shoulder to drag him out behind her. "…fetch a handsome price too… least she's worth something…"

The whispers faded, and Fryn checked her reserves. The small amount of food they'd eaten was now fully digested, and she was hungry, even more than before, and gauging the amount and quality of blood in her veins, she could still only fashion a letter opener of a blade. It was belted around her leg under her skirt, but it was so much reduced that it kept threatening to fall out of its sheath. Fryn hoped she wouldn't need to use it anytime soon. Havrshyk's sword hadn't shrunk as much as she'd expected, possibly because he couldn't draw on Leif's blood which was, for the most part, trapped there.

When it was quiet again, Alyra sighed, let her shoulders slump, and turned back to face them. "Back to the matter at hand, my favor…"

Finally, Fryn was able to get a word in, and she seized her chance quickly, replying, "as it is within our power we will repay you for your assistance."

Havrshyk coughed into his fist. "Provided we arrive in Frorin in safety of course."

Alyra smiled mysteriously and looked over at the bar, her finger tracing a pattern on the table. "My favor will require your presence, therefore, your safety in the meantime is my primary concern."

Fryn raised an eyebrow and shared a glance with her companion. "Could you be more specific with your request?"

"I require an introduction to an associate of yours, who would most likely only accept an audience with me if I were in your company," she answered cryptically, shifting her wings as if loosening the tension in her back and shoulders.

Ieffin? Probably not, Fryn thought, Harissa perhaps… but she warned us against meeting with old friends.

"Before you ask, I cannot at present be more specific. Suffice to say, I will accompany you until we meet them," she added pointedly, facing them with a sense of urgency as a footstep sounded down the hall.

Havrshyk ground his teeth and whispered in her ear, "that's a large inconvenience for one favor."

Fryn almost agreed. "But as she helps us, it becomes less and less so."

Werys reappeared at the mouth of the hallway, alone, wearing a pouty frown—which did nothing to improve her sour face. "We only have the one bird," she said, uncrossing her arms and waving one distractedly, "old Mulberry."

Alyra frowned. "The Magpie? It will do." She dragged out the last syllable and curled her lip. Standing in a swift motion, she fluttered her wings and waved for them to follow her. "As spirited as the beast is," she said, "it is faster than many of the other options."

Following her erratic flight through the twisting turns and odd intersections in the rock, Fryn wondered if there were a good reason why all the slower birds were already in use. *"Oh Leif, you'd have something clever, or foolish to say about that, something to brighten up this horrible day,"* she thought, biting her lip as her frustration began to escape her control over her blood flow, and she felt her cheeks flush pink with anemic blood.

Leif flew beside her, but he was so far away. The link she'd created when she poured her life into his heart to heal him felt congested, hazy, as if they were separated by a membranous film. His heart was there, but his blood was not; he was with her, and yet he wasn't—a contradiction not just in terms but in fact. *Soon enough, he'll return.*

Alyra distracted her from her musing, as she fluttered to a stop before a gigantic set of double doors. A humid breeze breathed on them, and moisture collected on the walls, and a droplet fell from a single stalactite that had been overlooked when the original excavators carved out the tunnels. Their guide strode forward proudly, and pushed the doors open easily, even though they towered in the wide space that rose to a dark dome overhead.

"Behold," she proclaimed, arms wide and eyes flashing, "our humble rookery."

"What's humble about it?" Havrshyk asked, chuckling, almost in a Leif-like way. The cave opened up around them like the stomach of the mountain from their esophageal path. Yet it wasn't dark. Dimmed starlamps radiated warm light off and around the nests and birdhouses built into the various nooks and ledges so that dried golden grass glowed as if alive, and the floating dust motes and the single drifting bit of down seemed to be frozen in the air. In the hushed silence, a pigeon cooed sleepily.

Alyra shrugged and spun around to face the far wall of the cave and mimicked the odd warbling call of a magpie. Fryn and Havrshyk waited with bated breath for something to happen, for a massive black-and-white bird to come swooping down… but nothing happened. Their guide sighed deeply, and whistled again, but still, they couldn't detect any stirring.

Finally, when she couldn't bear it any longer, she simply yelled and stamped her foot. "Mulberry!? Get down here, right now!" The force of her shout seemed to fill the space, nearly compelling Fryn to rush forward to obey, and she was not surprised when a sheepish, and enormous, magpie descended from the uppermost nook and landed with a huff, its feathers all puffed out.

"I know you weren't sleeping, you little chirp!" She added, wagging a finger under its beak. Its head bobbed, and it shrank back as far as allowable under the circumstances. It was already saddled, with a large multi-rider set that looked like it had taken several rabbits' worth of leather to make.

Werys arrived behind them, unhurried, if a bit annoyed as Alyra continued to berate the bird with increasingly colorful language. "We saddled it, of course, but you know how he likes to slink off looking for shiny things. Stupid bird."

Havrshyk looked about to respond, but before he could, Werys cut in again with a sharp motion of her hand. "We wouldn't even have him if the previous owners hadn't left his egg behind—why they or anyone would keep magpies is beyond *me*."

Fryn adjusted her Waverly-green cloak and swallowed purposefully. "Thank you for preparing the bird, but we had better be on our way."

Werys' eyes flicked up to meet hers, and hardened, as the irritating youth joined her at the mouth of the hallway. "How much are we getting paid for this, Alyra?"

"Enough," she replied, dragging Mulberry's head down by the reins, to stop him from cleaning his feathers so they could board.

Geran sneered and crossed his arms, trying to lean against the wall in an intimidating way. "10,000 mint-worth?"

Eyes widening, hairs on end, Fryn felt a shiver of frost settling over her, freezing her clothes to her skin, and she hardened what she could of her knife in its sheath, solidifying what remained in her stomach. "Even Mythrim was only worth 5,000 mint, and we had to share that. And *that* was for an infamous, veteran assassin."

"Follies, and fools," Havrshyk cursed, "it's already that high?" His hand tightened on the hilt of his Bloodsword, but he didn't draw it. "This is just like before..." Fryn could feel the quickening of his heart, and she took a deep breath, waiting. "They always betray a lich... and that is always a costly mistake," he added softly, more to himself than anyone else. But she heard it.

Geran pushed off the wall with his back and stuck his hands in the pockets of his ratty brown coat, showing his crooked teeth in an unpleasant smile. "Of course, Mythrim had never shown himself enough to warrant such a high bounty, but you have surpassed him in notoriety so easily. Perhaps if you were more cautious you would have followed his example."

"And perhaps, Geran, you shouldn't irritate our guests who have surpassed the assassin?" Alyra chided with a tense laugh. "We wouldn't want you to embarrass yourself."

"I'm embarrassed just standing next to him," Werys said pointedly, jabbing a finger toward her companion.

He scowled but continued to face them. "Alyra's right about your perfume, Werys, it smells like something you'd use to gas out a wasp nest."

"Fryn, Leif," Alyra interrupted from the bird's back, "climb on up, if we continue arguing with these idiots, we'll never get going at all."

The light shifted slightly, not growing any dimmer—but changing its quality as if the color in the room was being washed out. Alyra frowned, and Fryn agreed, as a cold tingle intensified at the base of her neck. The air was charged, not figuratively, but electrically, and she could smell the metallic tang of ozone. Leif's hair stood on end, and a tendril of sparks arced up from the ground to Havrshyk's fingers.

Geran took his hands out of his pockets, revealing a dual set of steel daggers, and Werys snapped a whip that snaked up from the bird bath behind them. "I'm not satisfied with any less than 10,000," Geran hissed, "and I know they aren't worth a quarter of it. The Commission must want you desperately."

Alarm radiating from their guide, Alyra dropped from the magpie's back in a flutter of her cloak, hands reaching behind her back to settle on the crystal hilts of her knives. "You don't want to cross me, Geran," she warned, "I'm not good at showing restraint."

Funneling all her blood into her knife, Fryn checked her reserves. Her Bloodknife was still thin, and it looked more like frozen wine than blood, and her elemental energies were barely sufficient to maintain her Lichform.

Alyra yelled, and flew forward in a surprising wingburst, just a grayish blur as her small wings fluttered faster than any normal fae could or would fly, to compensate for their size. Her blades danced out, cutting through the water whip that Werys had drawn, with their crystalline polished edges catching and retaining the light.

Geran leaned forward, under Alyra's following slash, and the shadows of more attackers shifted on the floor before them. Fryn spun horizontally in the air, almost as she had when she had danced the Acorn, and kicked blindly with an ice-encased boot. She struck something, and a satisfying grunt made her smile, as she opened her eyes and caught sight of her assailant recoiling with his sword lodged in her icy armor, and his hands holding his diaphragm, as he wheezed for breath.

Fryn ripped the blade free and scanned for more enemies. Two fae were harassing a spitting and cursing Havrshyk, and Alyra was facing off both Geran and Werys. But she didn't have time to be casually watching, as her attacker found his feet again, and came at her with a stone-skinned fist. She side-stepped his obvious charge, and even before she knew what she was doing, she'd moved passed him, sunk her Bloodknife in his back, and ripped it free after a few seconds of draining him dry. Unlike the hunters she'd spared in Gaerlin, this criminal group needed none of her sympathy; she also needed the blood.

Her knife swelled, though she couldn't fully assimilate the blood yet or absorb it either, to avoid shocking her veins with fresh, strange life; she focused on keeping her head as another fighter appeared behind her. She grasped the blood in the knife with the forefront of her mind and drew it out into more of a lance-like shape as she instinctively froze and formed it into an unbonded weapon. As the new attacker flew at her with a long sword aimed at her neck, she ducked under the swing and lunged upward, spearing him through the thin leather armor covering his chest, and in a flash of inspiration, she released the spear in a cloud of ice-shards, blasting him off to the far side of the cave.

It was a net-zero gain for blood, but she'd killed two of the attackers.

Havrshyk skidded around a kick from one fae, and a sword-thrust from another, as he pointed with one hand toward the one and lunged through the other with the tip of his black sword. The sparks he'd gathered sprang from his outstretched palm and burned a hole in the chest of his other attacker.

Ten seconds, thereabouts, Fryn imagined, they had been fighting. Alyra stood by the entrance, Werys' cold lifeless eyes staring up from her prone corpse, one long gash in her throat, and Geran huddled as if crushed, against the tunnel wall, one of Alyra's crystal daggers in his chest. His hands were gripped at the handle, as if he'd tried to pull it out, but couldn't. Alyra wiped one dagger on Werys' jacket, and then retrieved the other, cleaning it in like fashion on Geran's vest with a relieved head shake. "I hadn't intended to cut ties completely, but they would have been fickle friends in the end."

Looking over at Fryn, who lowered herself to a seat on the edge of the bird bath, she smiled sadly. "It appears that my colleagues are not in agreement with me. A pity. Why they would side with the Commission in this is beyond me, but we would be better served leaving now before any of the others return." She sheathed her knives, and once more hopped up onto Mulberry's back, and gave the startled bird a comforting pat on the neck. "Don't worry little chirp, it'll be much better out there. Less blood in the air."

It seemed to take her word for it, as its ruffled feathers lay flat again, and it shuffled from foot to foot as if eager to be going. Not really wanting their blood in her veins, Fryn drew on some of Leif's blood, hoping to keep it out of Havrshyk's control, as she redrained and put away her Bloodknife. She climbed up behind Havrshyk, heart racing from the short combat, but her unease was still as fierce as the day two weeks ago, when Havrshyk had been restored. Hoping to restore her own blood reserves, without relying on the deaths of others, Fryn found a biscuit in one of the saddle's bags and munched.

The bird chortled and hopped up into the air. Apparently, there had been a screening wall, for as they flew up and around a winding turn, they flew out of the cliff side and up into the cloudless night sky. A humid wind buffeted them, and they angled north towards the far-off glimmers of the nightly dancing lights. Small swirls of orange and purple, and green, and yellow, shimmered just beyond their sight.

She curled her hands into fists, bunching up her cloak, and shivering. Not from the wind, or cold, or frost, but anxious, excited, afraid. *"Leif,"* she thought with a smile, *"soon, so soon, it will be* your *face I see… not his…"* The long tan tails of his scarf blew past her cheeks, and she almost buried her face in it, but it was not the same.

Frorin

Fryn

Two weeks could hardly be called an eternity, but Fryn had heard Leif equate much shorter periods of time with drastically longer eons; that said however, the lingering hunger that had haunted her since their flight from Artell remained in the background—stretching, attenuating every second of her perception.

Observing Frorin from a safe distance, Fryn perched in the last pine tree on the road just south of the city. Had it always been this isolated and bereft of company, so small?

No trees grew north of the city, so this pine was as close as they could come unnoticed. Only one challenge remained. How could they enter the city without being revealed?

"What reason did we even have to found this city?" Fryn marveled to herself, scratching her chin.

Their strange new companion, Alyra, snorted in hearty agreement. "How can you bear this cold?"

Fryn didn't bother answering the obvious. Every Fee and Fae was born to a certain element. In some countries, the various elements were more evenly distributed, but in a place like Froreholt, Ice and Wind were the most common, and like any civilized society, the faeries of the city were good at making themselves comfortable despite their climate.

Aldyr couldn't abide the silence though; he shaded his eyes and gritted his teeth. "This city subsists on the coals of its outcasts... and was founded to appeal to its undead queen."

Only Mulberry, their Magpie, chortled in response. Fryn was too put-off by his statement to compose a rebuttal, and Alyra just looked confused.

Havrshyk leapt off the branch much as he had when they approached Gaerlin, but this time he didn't bother to soar, he drifted down slowly like a snowflake until he landed unimportantly on the road, where he shifted his wings under his coat, and hid his sword amongst his coattails.

Oddly enough, Alyra soon followed him, likewise hiding her wings, and weapons, so that soon she looked harmless, and uninteresting as well.

Fryn gave Mulberry a raised eyebrow and shook her head. "Am I the only one who doesn't know what we're doing?" she asked him, ruffling the feathers in his fluffed-up neck when he replied with a smug croak. "You too, huh? Well, here we go then, stay here I guess." She sighed lightly and then dove toward the ground, leaving a bored Magpie behind.

Chasing a snowflake on the way down, Fryn caught it, and spun it away with a twirl, as she landed smiling. For a moment, the fun and the whimsy of it, mingled with the closeness of home, distracted her. That faded quickly when she met Aldyr's eyes—-how could she be happy when Leif was locked away?

Fryn bit her lip in thought, following the others idly, as she realized that despite her circumstances, she was certainly happier than before. She was glad to be home, and she knew that soon she and her partner would be reunited.

Though she had never been to the city before, perhaps *because* she hadn't, Alyra led them up the winding slope of the south road. It followed the curve of the foothills toward the high plateau on which the city was founded with a gentleness that belied the altitude, and the distance, such that hours passed with walking before the walls of the Pine district appeared like an aurora on the horizon.

The city was massive. Layered on the crags of the last hillock before the Ice Wastes to the north, so that its districts were separated not only by their walls, but by their height. Dimly, Fryn could see a glint of light on the far-off domes of the Grand Assembly and the Palace of the King in the very center of the city.

Thin trails of smoke rose from a few of the chimneys in the city, but for the most part, fires were only used in the poorer neighborhoods, and there, only when cooking was necessary. Most of the inhabitants of the city had enough elemental affinity that warmth was not the greatest issue, and so the air smelled lightly of the northern flowers, and the sweet sap of the pines. Fryn closed her eyes as she remembered happier times, and allowed herself to hope that the end of their troubles was near... and then she opened them and looked at the nearer districts. The Pine Crescent was almost shabby looking from the outside, its wall clearly made of a different level of craftsmanship, and before that, Fryn saw, and *really* saw, the shambling mess of the so-called Sky District. There was no room on that elevation for a planned district, the screes and the rocks were too uneven, broken, and rough to allow for a manicured road or organized residences. Instead, the ragged region outside the last wall was a scattering of wrecks, crooked houses and shacks that huddled on whatever level patch of ground they could find, regardless of how close together, or how distant they were from each other.

Stranger still, no smoke rose from the chimneys. The closer they got, the more Fryn narrowed her eyes, and stared in awe. They were all partially frozen, constructed of mud, and pebbles, holding their shape more because of the intense cold, than because of any intention put into their construction. Bits of hay and lichen stuck out of the mud walls, but not one of their occupants peeked out of their pine-bark doors.

Aldyr glanced back at Fryn as they passed the first scrap of an abandoned building on the outskirts, with an expression that bordered on gloating. "I guess you've never seen the city from without..."

She swallowed a pebble of ice she'd been mulling over and looked away. Just down an alley, two children watched them pass by with dark, suspicious eyes, and lightless, limp wings. Across the way, she noticed another brooding fae watch them with guarded, yet distant eyes.

Forgetting herself, Fryn looked back to Aldyr and asked him, "What do they do here?"

He shrugged. "It's been almost a century Fryn, but they look just the same." He was silent for a moment, and then shook his head as he explained, "They exist." The last word was almost spat as if he were trying to convince himself of that fact.

Alyra's teeth chattered as she seemed about to ask a question, but then, looking at the quiet strangers watching them from the shadows, she frowned. "They ignore us," she said, "almost as if *we* were the ones who don't exist."

"We don't, remember?" Aldyr replied, smirking. "Now if my memory serves, the gate should be up ahead. When we get close, try to copy what these Sky Dwellers are doing. Look as if the traders that will come up behind us are not even there at all, and we will be able to slip into their carts after they are inspected."

Finding herself surprised at not knowing, Fryn wondered, "Why do they inspect the carts?"

"Sky Dwellers, Fryn," he answered, spitting on the ground. "The city doesn't even recognize them as citizens of Froreholt, let alone Frorin. They do not exist and cannot be allowed to bring their squalor into the presence of the respectable folk in the higher districts."

She furrowed her brow but had to stifle any more comments as they rounded a bend in the road and looked up past the living ruins surrounding them toward the monolithic gates of Frorin. All things considered, the barracks beside the gate, and the tall square towers on either side, created an impressive image. As Fryn felt her hope welling within her at the sight of the gate, and the guards standing so carefree on either side, she wanted to encourage her onetime enemy that his freedom was almost within grasp... but... he was shaking. Havrshyk glared at the gates as if he were barely able to restrain himself from ripping them apart with his hands.

They were saved from that imminent disaster by the rattling sound of a wagon's wheels approaching from behind. Absently, they stepped off the road and into one of the alleys out of the view of the guards to where two little girls were drawing pictures in the dirt with twigs.

Fryn gave them a smile, as she noticed the crudely drawn shapes of fee in dresses with swords in their stick hands. Though one of the two returned her smile, the other one paled and led her away into a side passage and out of sight.

"Don't frighten the children Fryn," Havrshyk chided, leaning around the corner after the wagon had passed. "They'll never let you close enough to hurt them."

Why would she want to? Shaking her head, and ignoring his comment, Fryn looked out as well. The wagon was being searched by one of the lazy guards while the other one chatted with the driver and pretended to examine his trading license. Only licensed traders or travelers were allowed into or out of the city. Even before becoming a Hunter, Fryn's citizen's license had granted her access to the all the districts except for the Crown District, because she had been a ward of the Soft-Point Fist School under Master Bersari. Her Hunter's License granted her slightly more clout—or it had for the short time she'd had it.

Fitting a hand into her coat's hidden pocket, Fryn retrieved both licenses, her Hunter's License being marked with the scales of dagger and coin, and the citizen's license printed with a silver embossing of a snowflake. That snowflake would be important enough to grant entry without question... but would the guards know her name?

Aldyr nodded at her with a grunt. "Even if they don't know to stop you, they keep a record of everyone who enters and leaves the city. No one can know that we are here. Not even your friends." He narrowed his eyes as he saw the Snow District insignia on her citizen's license and closed them as if remembering a bitter experience.

"I think they're done inspecting the cart!" Alyra warned, and then darted out on a quick wing, fluttering under the tarps and into the bed of the wagon.

It was already moving, and was being waved through the opening gate, Fryn and Havrshyk had missed their window of opportunity. Alyra peeked out of the tarps at them with a worried expression, so Fryn just gave a subtle wave and pointed at the wall, mouthing "later" hoping she understood, but also secretly relieved to be separated from their tagalong.

Havrshyk sighed, some of the tension in his shoulders loosening as he straightened. "Why must she follow us?"

"She did give us a ride, saving us days getting here," Fryn offered, "but my guess is that she also has a secret she doesn't want to tell us."

"I can only imagine what that is. Did you see her blades? And why was she hiding in one of our old way-stations?" He asked and waited as another wagon approached. This one lumbered up the only paved road in the so-called Sky District, the one that led traders and the significant up to the capitol. All of the other paths were little more than dirt game trails made by passing faeries on the lichen covered rocks. This large wagon was covered by a gray tarp like the one before, but its contents bulged out underneath, large green leaves that sent forth the sweet cool scent of peppermint on the wind.

Aldyr stiffened.

Fryn was about to run forward to climb inside, but he reflexively grabbed her hand and held her back, eyes wide as he watched an old fae argue with the guard.

"Not this one," he whispered, transfixed.

"We don't know if there will even *be* a next one, come on!" She hissed, dragging him out of the alley and then flitting behind the wagon. Havrshyk froze as she climbed into the back of the wagon, and wiggled under the leaves, so she reached out, and pulled him in.

"Some mighty assassin you are… What, are you allergic to peppermint?" She shook her head and shoved him down as the guard who'd done the cursory inspecting jabbed the end of a lance into the leaves.

The tip of the lance pierced her shoulder, but Fryn froze, draining herself so that no blood would coat it.

The lance retreated, and the mumbling of the confused guard was barely audible. "...swear I hit something in there... must be dirt..."

She bit her cheek at the pain of her shoulder, slowly healing, spending some of the precious little blood she had left to repair the damage.

Havrshyk looked out between the leaves at the slowly closing gates, focusing on a far-off shack up the hill to the west. "I wonder what happened to them."

"To whom?" Fryn asked properly, following his gaze.

"My sister."

She bit back any response. It wouldn't comfort him to know they were probably long dead. Even a long-lived faerie might reach eighty, but Aldyr had been imprisoned in his twenties for ninety years. Even if his sister was younger than him, she could not still be alive.

As if he'd detected her line of thought, he muttered sadly, "Maybe she lived long enough to have children, maybe they did too. But no one lives very long in the Sky District Fryn. Even I didn't."

"How did you get into the city?" She asked.

"I killed someone. What did you expect?"

Fryn sighed as she reflected on the gates that closed with a trembling thud. "I did, too."

Havrshyk shook himself from his depressive thoughts and looked up at her in surprise. "Who did you kill?"

"I killed my friend."

He smiled. "I killed an enemy, perhaps I was lucky?"

Fryn didn't comment; she just watched through the mint leaves as their wagon rolled straight up the South Cardinal toward the next check point. The guards this time didn't even bother checking the cart, as if no one could possibly make a mistake at the entrance to the city, but instead merely asked to see the driver's papers. In seconds, they were in the Hill District, and a short time later they reached the Rain District.

"Where is this trader going?" Aldyr muttered to himself. "We can hardly slip out while it is moving on the main roads."

The wagon finally pulled to a lurching stop, and Fryn had to brace herself against the side to stop from knocking her head against it and causing a loud noise. Aldyr was out in a flash, flying around the corner of a building, with Fryn not far behind.

"Need to avoid running into anyone we know," she reminded herself, as she knelt in the shadow of a cultivated mushroom cap and examined her surroundings. The cart full of mint waited in a wide courtyard, ringed by a low wall of cut gray stones. To her left, a manor house loomed, with bright gold trim, and green copper shingles, and to her right, there was a large warehouse with what looked like an attached restaurant. The windows were shuttered, and steam rose from the small chimney on its roof.

"This is oddly familiar," Fryn said examining the signboard outside the smaller building, "Frosthall Estate Wines, tastings 2-6 pm."

The last time anyone had gone there was about a month ago, when Leif had been poisoned by Mythrim during the Guardhouse Ball. Cheerful voices argued inside, and furniture scuffed and thudded as the workers set up the tasting hall for the day's work.

It was late morning now; Havrshyk nodded to her with a sly smile. "It is only poetic that the first place in this city we visit on our way to reclaim my body is so close to where Leif cut off my head."

She flicked her wings and looked over at him with a frown. "Did you feel it?" she asked, resisting the urge to touch her neck.

His answer—merely looking over his shoulder with glazed eyes—was enough. She knew the pain was insufferable, yet he had not had the option to die.

Hoping to stir him from his mood, and excited at the thought of being so close to restoring Leif to his own body, Fryn gave a small smile and pointed out toward the street. "Are you ready to go get your body back?"

He blinked. "The sooner the better, Fryn," he said.

Before they could move however, they were interrupted by Alyra appearing around the corner with flushed cheeks, as she darted into the cover of the low wall, rubbing her cold hands together.

"I didn't know if that wagon was ever going to stop," she complained, "it was difficult to keep up."

Fryn wished she hadn't been able to.

Ignoring her, Havrshyk gripped the hilt of his Bloodsword and stared out the gate toward the Vineroad. "Just a little farther now."

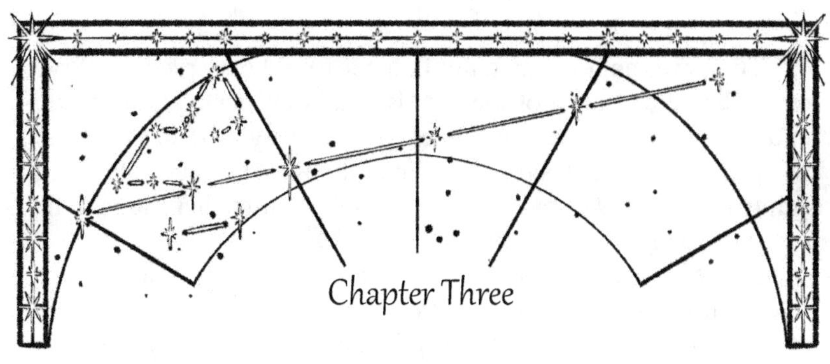

Chapter Three

LANCER

Frorin

Fryn

The stonework of the Guardhouse was covered in a marbling of old ice. Frost clung to the windows, and the unpaved part of back alley and loading dock was blanketed in a thin layer of powdery snow. Fryn scanned the yard, listening, hearing nothing but silence broken only by the soft tapping of a ladle against a metal pot from the basement door.

She went down, one slow step at a time, crouched and ready to leap into the air. The door was left open a crack, and as she peered through the opening, her frost-rimmed eye was obscured by a layer of fog which took a moment to clear.

Warm golden wood covered the floor, polished meticulously, gleaming under the flickering light of a single oil lamp. *"Starlamps are too expensive for the serving class sections, I see…"* she thought with a small smile forming at the edges of her mouth, though no dimples appeared on her cheeks.

She pulled it open just wide enough to fit through, and crept inside, cheeks hot from the wash of kitchen air down the hall, and waited for the others to trail in after. And again, the only sounds came from the kitchen, three doors down on the left, where only a glimmer from inside gave any sign of movements in the Guardhouse.

There was an hour or so until dinner would be served, but Fryn remembered that most of the guards would either be out on patrol until a few minutes before dinner, or they would be in the office wing, on the opposite side of the Guardhouse. She snuck along the empty hallway and carefully put a hand on the hilt of her Bloodknife, peering around the doorway into the kitchen.

Sure enough, Lillen stood with her back to the door, humming a sweet, cheerful tune as she bent over the oven door to slide in a tray of what looked like dark brown rolls. She wore the regular serving suit, a black and white themed blouse, jacket, and skirt, with white leggings and ribboned shoes polished to reflective perfection—but against all that lack of color, she wore a pale blue, pink-ribboned cooking apron, with its tassels looped symmetrically at the small of her back between her blue-lined wings.

The counters, the stove, and her hands were covered in a catastrophe of white flour, but it had somehow been prevented from dirtying her clothes; so that the smudge of flour on her apron seemed gratuitous. Her heart leapt to see a familiar face, but Fryn set her jaw and moved on. Havrshyk was right. They could not contact anyone they knew. The wine cellar and the crypt that lay below were just a turn or so further down. Aldyr's body, and Leif's freedom, were just a few wingspans away.

Footsteps thudded overhead in the direction of the stairs leading to the kitchens, so Fryn hurried, taking a right at the end of the hall, and then a left into the wine cellar, flitting past the stairs to the main level. Pushing through the heavy door, they entered the same cellar where she and Leif had once stolen a bottle of wine to hide out and wait for a party; the party where they had finally been able to kill Mythrim. The dust on the racks was gone and there were fewer wine bottles now. More affordable, drinkable vintages seemed to be the norm as well, as if they had decided to stop accepting payment in goods.

The back wall of the wine cellar was now lined with shelves, and racks, where an expanded armory now hung, cleaned and ready for a moment's use. Longswords, halberds, crossbows, and axes rested under protective layers of cloth; but at the center of the wall, standing proudly uncovered, were shining silver lances. Fryn caught her breath as she saw her face in the bell of the handle of the first one and scanned its two-and-a-half wingspan length, from leather grip to needle point.

Havrshyk reached out one hand to touch it, and Alyra watched them curiously, 'hm'ing to herself. "First at Artell, and now we find it here—Arta's name, his spear..." he intoned softly.

"You mean his preferred weapon, yes? I doubt that his actual lance really exists, or if it does that it'd be here," Alyra commented disinterestedly. "Is this what you came here in secret to steal? I don't see how we can take a lance out of here unnoticed."

They both gave her a disappointed look and then resumed their inspection of the silver lances. "Ieffin's reforms are going forward then," Fryn said at last, "I knew he meant to rearm the Guard and rely less on the Commission, but I didn't realize he'd restore the Lancers."

"No Swordhand-Palm, however," Havrshyk said with a long sigh. "That time is passed. Now, for what we came for." He narrowed his gaze, as if searching for some forgotten memory, or following some obscure clues. He paced before the weapon stands, his boots shuffling a bit as he barely dragged his toes across the boards, until he caught on something, and nearly fell over.

The dim light seemed to illuminate the space far better when it was clean, and Fryn recognized the inset ring in the hidden trap door to the catacombs. Havrshyk hesitated, kneeling before the door, hands shaking as he gripped the ring and pulled open the hatch. It was as silent, cold, and black as it had been a month ago, and there were no flying arrows or loosed poisons—no traps of any kind. They filed into the dark after him, and Alyra closed the door with a whisper as they waited for their eyes to adjust.

Fryn bit her lip. Havrshyk wouldn't be able to make the same kind of electric light sphere that Leif had, and it was only by the gentle glimmer that radiated from their wings that they could advance without falling over or getting lost. She led the way, being the only one who had been where they were trying to go, or at least the only one with any memory of the place. From their infrequent talks on the subject, Fryn gleaned that Havrshyk had been completely insensate, or comatose when Mythrim had broken him out.

She sent out a thin layer of frost over the ground which climbed up the walls to the low-hanging rocky ceiling, which caught and enhanced the light from their wings a little more, so that she could see the turn on the left to the section of the catacombs where they'd waited with wine and sandwiches, unknowingly eating over

Havrshyk's grave… where Leif had first kissed her. Her wings shivered, and she pushed forward against the torrent of unease that washed over her.

Even with her frost outlines, she didn't stop in time, the toes of her boot slammed against a stone, and she fell face first over a large slab of granite, scraping her cheek against a sharp piece of glass. Blood flowed to the area immediately, and she froze it shut to heal. Sitting up, Fryn held her face in surprise; she'd cut herself on the bottle that Leif had opened and disliked, and when she placed a hand up on the nearby ledge of rock, she bumped into the empty lamp that had glowed cheerfully on their picnic in the dark.

Then she gasped.

Havrshyk watched her with concern lining Leif's eyes, and Alyra sat on the slab with her chin resting in her hands, elbows perched on her knees. "What's wrong?" she asked softly.

Fryn pointed into the yawning maw of the alcove in which Havrshyk had once lain for seventy years, with the empty weapon mount above it matching the empty grave. "It's not here…" she whispered, barely able to form the words with her throat constricting and her chest pounding. Her control over her ice faltered, and a healthy trail of blood slipped past the ice in her cheek down to her chin, falling to the ground in slow droplets, unnoticed.

"There's something here," Alyra replied, picking up the bottle of sour wine, uncorking its cut neck and sniffing the contents. "Never mind, there's nothing of *value* in here."

Sparks danced around the edges of Havrshyk's wings as his shoulders stiffened and his jaw clenched, frost encompassing his whole form. "Then *where* is it?"

Fryn opened her mouth to answer, but far off down the tunnel, a soft 'thud' sounded from the entrance, and Fryn glanced around for a place to hide. Seeing nothing better, she squeezed into the grave-prison Havrshyk had once occupied and wedged herself as far into it as possible. "Come on, hide!" she hissed.

Alyra nodded and followed, as best she could, finding just enough room beside Fryn so that they were packed in like preserves.

Havrshyk froze. "I wouldn't go in there with your body," he said, nearly choking on his attempt at humor. He swung his head around, several times at least, before his face fell, his strength crumbled, and despair creased his hollow eyes. He stumbled closer to the hole and flattened himself on the ground behind the headstone—the closest he could allow himself to return to his tomb. His scarf nearly covered the whole of his face, and he shook his wings so that they were hidden under the folds of his grass-forest green cloak.

Reminiscent of when they had first hidden there, Fryn's heart pounded until she drained it so that it had nothing on which to beat, and she strained to listen. One… no two… three approaching? She clenched her jaw and focused. There were two, clearly defined by the tap-tip-tap-tap of two walking almost completely in sync. Leif would have found some other better idea for hiding there… he had… but she could not do *that* if it weren't actually him. And what would they do with Alyra? Well, *she* could hide in the grave.

The steps weighed heavily in the air, pressing down against her back, making it harder and harder to breath. She drained completely, not needing the oxygen to see, think, or be. Havrshyk let out a subdued moan, but he didn't move, and Alyra's eyes fluttered shut. The weight continued to worsen but at least she could bear it.

The footfalls fell silent at the start of the turn, and a whisper of a voice wafted down the hall.

"…ure you heard some…ing…?"

The gruff tone was familiar, and for a moment it brought a rush of hope as she recognized the grudgingly friendly voice of Captain Gunter, recalling with a smile how the tip of his newspaper had fallen in his tea and attached itself to his mustache. But in an instant, this was replaced with dread, as the footsteps turned and wandered with a growing glowing orange glimmer that chased away her memories and left her mind a blank.

Gunter's companion's voice came through clear as the light filled the hallway. "I was certain," Lillen said tremulously, as if she were scanning the walls and the plaques of the dead with a mixture of distaste and reverence. "The door wasn't shut like I'd left it, and there was a bit of water trailing in from the door."

"A thief, in the Guardhouse, most unlikely, most unusual." Gunter grunted and coughed. "Has the boy returned from his apprenticeship? Perhaps one of his former companions thought to pinch his salt…"

"Why is there a gravestone there?" Lillen asked, and a shadow shifted across the far wall, as if she had raised a hand to point before the lamp.

The gravelly response he gave was not enough, so she pressed with a polite, "Hmm?"

He came closer to the hole, and for a moment, Fryn felt a heartbeat not her own, as Havrshyk's panic nearly peaked and his hold on his Lichform waned. "There was a criminal that Mythrim released from here, a relic long thought dead. Fortunately, for all their presumed faults, Leif and Fryn killed him."

Lillen gasped, and Havrshyk's heartbeat intensified, Fryn could feel the heat of the blood that was now rushing fully through his veins. "But… imprisoned… in a grave?"

"There is nothing here," Gunter stated, sounding almost unconvinced, "Let us return."

"B-but why, why would they do that?"

"I do not presume to understand or question the decisions of our previous lords, now come, we must have the tea ready for our guests."

Seconds passed, footsteps receded, and after more minutes than Fryn could care to count, she climbed out of the hole wondering how and why they hadn't walked all the way down the hall or noticed the obvious tracks in the dust.

She crouched beside Havrshyk's prone form, placed a hand on his shoulder and whispered, "Come, it is passed," surprised at her own welling compassion for the one who'd robbed her of her friend, her companion… her love.

The walls of the grave had pressed in on her, and she had been close to panicking in those few minutes of being inside—what would that have been like for years without end? His callous disregard for loyalty or love, or his lack of mercy, his bitterness, all seemed so much more *right* and *just* than she could have swallowed before.

Alyra crawled out of the alcove, arms shaking as she pressed a hand on her temples, whether from the lack of oxygen, or from the lack of space, or the previous night's exhaustion, she couldn't tell. But she fell to a seat on the headstone and held her face in her hands.

"…the silver city on a hill… they said… the pinnacle of light, magic, and beauty… they said… but this," she waved a hand around the subterranean grave, "belies all the innocent splendor I was promised. There is an old darkness here, I can feel it, claws of the dead gasping at the choking roots of the living." She shivered and fell silent.

Fryn set her jaw, recalling her conversation with Havrshyk in Gaerlin, how they had been shamed, and despised for having lived. Ever since Arta, who'd fought for ages, and crossed the continent from one end to the other looking for his bride, only to find that she had died, his children had resented those like her, who'd managed to survive.

Master Bersari's face had changed in that moment he'd realized what she was, his fatherly concern for her welfare, his adoptive love, soured in a second, reflecting in his eyes his wish that it was not her who had lived, but his own daughter instead. Ever since that day, he'd treated her only as a student who boarded at his school, training her stricter, harder, longer, than any of his Guard candidates.

Alyra looked up and met her eyes, as if sensing her mood, her own eyes wet with the tears that both Fryn and Havrshyk had frozen to keep back.

"This land is harsher and less forgiving than it seems," she said cryptically. "A mess of contradictions and pleasant lies."

"Thanks," Fryn asked with a forced smirk, "if I knew where you came from, I could return your comments more appropriately."

"It doesn't matter where I'm from, but where I'm going," she replied, standing, and dusting off her clothes. "And no, I'm not telling you that yet either."

Havrshyk calmed slowly, only now climbing up from the ground. "What do we do now?"

"We need a place to lay low and gather information. If we don't know where it is, we can't go get it," Fryn began.

Alyra glanced into the grave. "There is no need to be so secretive now," she said, pointing into it, "I have gathered what you seek."

"Oh, have you?" Havrshyk wondered sarcastically.

She stared into his face, eyes darting pointedly toward the black sword at his waist before shifting to the empty weapon mount above the grave. "I may not know a great deal about Bloodcrafting, but you need the sword bearer's body, don't you?" And she shifted her gaze to Fryn. "Your husband cannot use his full range of abilities to heal himself, can he?"

She blushed despite herself. "We were never married…"

"Ah, it appears I was mistaken, partially."

They stood awkwardly, in a circle around the headstone, fingers tapping on elbows, slow breaths and sighs, until Fryn decided to break the silence even if she didn't know what to say. "I suggest we try to speak with Ieffin, see what he did with the body."

Havrshyk laughed hollowly, as if noticing how close Alyra had come to the truth. "Sneaking into the Crown District didn't work out so well last time."

"It was midday," Fryn countered, "and Leif hardly looks like he's from Froreholt," she explained, wandering down the hallway a bit, slowly, so the others could follow, and she wouldn't trip. "If we go in at night, we might have a better chance of meeting him. He likes to work late; he might even be at the Grand Assembly."

"Half-drunk perhaps, but working nonetheless," Havrshyk agreed with a small head shake.

Frorin

Pine District

Harissa

"You are a fool," Harissa said, resting her hands on the crook of her cane. She sat in the same chair her father used to occupy with a brilliant red and green scarf stuffed into the collar of her coat.

The hapless messenger's wings drooped under her pronouncement, bowing his head as if he felt her words were unjustifiably harsh. "It is all true my lady, the King of Gaersheim will not relent. Either we allow the Commission's Hunters access to all Districts equally, or they will withdraw from the city."

She pinched the bridge of her nose with her fingers and sighed deeply. "Then *he* is a fool. The Pine District has never been welcoming to the Commission, and we don't plan to be now, when they are trying to frame my cousin for high crimes!"

"The prince insists that we must make some concessions, to allow their agents to work within the city. He said to remind you that without their assistance, your father might not have been avenged.

She uncrossed her legs and let the tip of the cane slide through her hand to hit the floor with a sharp rap. "Do not say such disingenuous lies in my presence. Fryn avenged my father, the Commission gets no credit for what she did. She would have done so whether there was a prize to be paid or not." Inhaling sharply, she narrowed her eyes at the cringing fae. "I will allow only one. Tell

Ieffin I suggest he do the same if he ever wants his bid for independence to succeed."

The messenger, wearing the sky blue and frost white tunic of the Crown Guard, bristled. "My lady... say what you will to me, but my prince, your future king, deserves far greater respect than you give."

Harissa almost snorted, but she found that would have been false. As she considered it, she did respect him, as long as he kept his white gloved fingers far from her crescent. Instead, she said:

"Did you know? The Pine District used to be considered outside of the city? For hundreds of years, these slums were managed, and overseen, and protected, by my ancestors—completely separate from the kings and queens of Frorin. They didn't want to consider the poor, and the honest, and the industrial as part of their prosperous and artistic society, and so we were not considered citizens.

This last wall between us and the Sky District was built by my family, and we *made* the Crown acknowledge our right to live here. When the guards tried to chase off our builders, we speared them on their own lances, and when that conflict grew so great that the guard was depleted, and the crown's power emaciated... that is when the Commission was allowed to intervene."

The messenger looked up at her with his mouth hanging open dumbly. "So, it's your fault?"

Harissa groaned. "No. It is not. And I will do what we did to them, to the Commission, if they try to take our home. Before I was ever acknowledged in the nobility, I was a pauper's princess, so tell Ieffin that I am tired of looking at the slums beyond our wall, as much as he is, and that I plan to demolish all the buildings, and that I will carve out a new crescent road and erect another wall."

Shrinking back before her rising voice, the messenger scrambled to his feet and flew back through the door. In his haste he left three unopened letters.

Jaeson leaned in through the burgundy curtains with one of Harissa's signature cocktails in his hand. "That was well said, sister, but you might have included in your warning that the inhabitants will not be harmed."

She took the offered drink and drained it dry—marveling at how she could handle the alcohol since being bonded to the bone-sword, how strong, and invincible she felt. Looking down at the bone cane in her hands, and the trailing, glowing lines of red imbedded in it, she felt the resonance of her ancestors, pushing her toward a new age.

"Jaeson," she replied, waiving a hand dismissively, "he should know me better than that by now... I just wanted to correct the impudence of that fae."

"Mhm," he allowed dubiously, "but why are you pushing for the new wall so soon?"

She held out a hand toward him for a new glass and was not disappointed. This time she sipped it delicately, as if the grimmest topics she could ever discuss involved poor luck at cards. "I read the history… of the city, of the crown, and of us. A storm is coming, and if we do not build a wall, then all of the lives in the Sky District will weigh on us forever."

He shivered and made a drink for himself.

Together they brooded, ignoring the somber music being played on the stage below, and the fee and fae who had taken to coming nightly for the dances, open to all, that separated her from the exclusive society of the rich in the Snow District.

As applause sounded, and a song ended, Jaeson whispered into his glass, looking out of the balcony toward the assembly below. "Word is that Fryn was seen in Artell."

Harissa smiled.

"You don't think...?"

"No Jaeson, I don't. You trained them better than that. I can only imagine what incredible need or threat drove them to return. Let it be known, quietly, that it is common for faeries that look suspicious, but are in fact harmless, to wander our streets, and to leave them be and unharrassed."

He smiled. "Agreed."

With that, Harissa leaned down and swept up the letters. Only one was directed to her, the others were addressed to Captain Gunter of the City Guard, and to Master Bersari... Fryn's old instructor, and foster parent.

In the end, they'd escaped the catacombs easily. No one ever seemed to look in their direction, and they slipped around one corner after another without incident, as if enveloped in a cloud that muffled their steps and averted prying eyes. When they finally arrived at the shrub where Mulberry had decided to take a nap, one foot tucked neatly in his feathers, they all took a deep breath of relief.

Alyra spun on them, wagging her finger, her thin lips pressed into a line. "I didn't know what you were looking for, but if we were going after a *body,* I would have liked to have known about that... seems somewhat important, no?"

Havrshyk crossed his arms. "It didn't concern you. You were the one who insisted on tagging along with us... a little over a day ago."

"Perhaps you could be more open about who it is you are trying to meet?" Fryn asked off-handedly, sparing a northward glance at the Crown District's unnecessarily tall walls.

Alyra's rigid expression twisted into a frown as she shivered from the cold, which was turning her lips blue and her skin white, not unlike Fryn's face in Lichform. "Not quite yet. Once we've left this city, perhaps."

They fell silent, stationary eyes unfocused, frozen, and glazed, set in a grim and ambiguous determination. The wind whistled through the nearby alleyway, losing breath like a flutist's overextended note for an unsympathetic conductor, lazily shifting a stray delicate snowflake into the center of their circle. Mulberry chirped, shifting from one foot to the other, but they all were lost in their thoughts. The snowflake settled, and broke apart, vanishing in a silent shattering of tiny shards.

Breathing a long slow sigh, Fryn brushed her coattails back and sat down on the stones, resting her chin in one hand, wings shifting beneath her cloak pensively. "Fortunately, the Commission has not caught up with us yet. Doubtlessly, they would go after our friends first, and have exhausted their primary leads. All that remains then, is to know their secondary plans. Where are they lying in wait for us, and further, what do they have to do with the crown in the first place?"

Havrshyk 'hmm'ed but didn't comment.

"Why not go to Aelaete then?" Alyra asked, crossing her arms in the folds of one of her thin coats. "I doubt they could track you there, or even elicit the support of the locals… but if they search here, I am certain they will find someone who has a grudge against you," she suggested, presenting her point with the tip of her finger raised in the air, her fingerless gloves doing little to protect her slender digits from the cold, which had already descended upon her clothing in the form of an insistent, brittle frost.

Havrshyk adjusted Leif's supposedly warm scarf, a tan, knitted garment so infused with his ice that it acted as little more than a cold compress, and his eyes lit up with a mischievous smile, as if imagining something awful and compelling, and alluring at the same time. "You insisted that we meet the Prince; and obvious strategy or not, he is the only one who knows where the body is. I feel we have no choice but to proceed." As if resignedly, the wind picked up again, tossing his hair back out of his face.

It was still early, perhaps only 8 o'clock or so, but the deathly stillness of the post-morning rush impressed on Fryn the sensation that the city was somehow empty and desolate, like the Weasel Cairn. She rose to her feet, swaying briefly, second-guessing her decision not to steal the blood of those lowlifes in Artell only for a moment as she caught her balance with a grim, firm, set in her jaw. "I just hope you know how to put it back."

Havrshyk blinked, and his wings stiffened, as a tendril of sparks raced from one wingtip to another, before bouncing to the hilt of the sword and then dissipating into the ground. "Hmm… I hadn't even thought about that."

Her small wings almost chattering from the cold, Alyra crouched and pressed her knees together, crossing her arms around her chest. "Wouldn't that be one of the first questions, Leif? Why even put it back at all?"

Havrshyk rolled his eyes, and walked closer to Mulberry's fluffed form, where he'd tucked his head under a wing, and puffed up to hold onto his heat. "Stick closer to him," he suggested, pointing wearily, looking as if he really wanted to correct her, but was afraid to tell her the truth, "The sword needs its body, I can't maintain what isn't mine."

She nodded idly, mumbling under her breath. "First I'd heard of such a thing."

Fryn stretched her arms high over her head, wings splaying out under the morning sun, and bent over to touch her toes, her silver hair mostly pulled back into a bun, though her now slightly-too-long fringe fluttered in the breeze. Straightening up again, she crossed her arms, and cleared her throat. "I suggest a round-about route. We are going to the Crown District, but a path from this side of the crescent counter-clockwise to approach from the northwest would probably take us there unnoticed. We'll need to skirt the intersection of the walls, but if I remember correctly, they are fairly lax around the changing of the Guard at the North Gate."

Havrshyk shook his head and coughed discretely into his fist. "That would lead us by the Soft-Point-Fist school. You really think that's wise? If I were a Hunter, I would definitely look there."

"We should visit the Stone Market then," Alyra suggested, "Even I have heard that it's the place to buy anything and everything you might need in Frorin. Perhaps we could find some kind of disguises there?"

Fryn let an mischievous smile creep onto her face, though she banished it quickly, and Havrshyk gave her a raised eyebrow. "I think I might know someone who'd be willing to help us down there."

Alyra nodded, probably just eager to get out of the cold, and Havrshyk sighed. "I think I know where this is going."

"Just don't ruin the surprise," she said, walking over to Mulberry and patting him on the side. "But where do we hide the bird?"

Mulberry dug his beak out from under his wing and blinked a beady eye the size of her head, snorting as if he were about to be left out of something interesting—he was though. Alyra regretfully ducked out from his fluffy chest feathers and shivered as she caught the bird's eyes and pointed off toward the pines. "Fly off, Mulberry. Return when I whistle."

The magpie bobbed his head, and just as a cloud drifted over the sun, he took wing and vanished toward the south. Fryn wondered how they'd be received at The Pheasant, the entrance they had used to access the Stone Market last time, but shrugged, and donned her hood. "It's not too far, Alyra, you'll be fine." She started back down the alley to access the Ringroad, not looking back to see if they followed.

Frorin

Stone Market

Fryn

Fryn marveled that Camilla had not recognized them, or at least she gave no visible sign, or subtle tell; no strange strain in her voice. She let them 'eat' at the round table, but this time Leif didn't complain about the mushroom soup, since Havrshyk had no qualms with eating nutritious food. Their funds were limited with only forty mint left over from their small-time theft in Gaerlin. In their haste, they hadn't thought to take anything from Alyra's hideout in Artell, and now, they spent their last mint on a meal that left Camilla more than a little dissatisfied.

After slurping down their soup, Fryn rotated the table-top just like Harissa had done before, and the hidden doorway opened in the paneling of the wall. They retreated inside where a pull on the wall-sconce in the stone-brick tunnel closed the way behind them. They padded softly down the low grade for a long way before reaching the door.

Condensation clung to the walls and dribbled down to a small drain by the entrance to the Market, and Fryn felt a tugging at her stomach, whether dread, or a premonition or a memory, she couldn't say, but she reluctantly pulled on the latch and stepped out into the cylindrical defunct storm-drain that the city's underground had converted into a clandestine marketplace generations ago. It was getting later in the evening but even so, the street that led down to the Hub was busy with merchants chatting at their stalls or stepping out of their wall-side doors to run errands. It was as bright and warm in the market under the city as if it were a warm summer day—Alyra was visibly relieved.

The chatter of faeries filled the hallway, and the trio of renegades paused at the open door, stirring with a start when it closed fast on its own behind them with a loud 'thud.' Pushed forward by the sound, Fryn led them down the lane, behind the central aisle of small booths, where she recognized the Yardall merchant selling the sub-rated Sceppe at a special offer. If he noticed them, he didn't give an indication, since he was busy pushing a small tasting cup into the hands of a fae in a black cloak, who stood almost a head taller than everyone around him. She wasn't surprised; shady characters would likely be as common as aphids on a rose.

They ducked in through the door to the tailor's and Fryn stopped short in the entry and pasted on a smile as the overbearing and overweight, little tailor gave a cursory welcoming glance in their direction. He was busy wrapping a measuring tape around the bust of a buxom fee in a faux silk gown, with puffy sleeves, and a frilly, lace-covered neck, that somehow accented the low neckline. The fee was probably in her thirties, since she was wearing enough make up to look like her mid-twenties, and she had a permanent pout. Her irritation was obvious, her eyes bulging out at the tailor who had squeezed a little too tight—for he had seen *her* and *his* eyes threatened to pop out of their sockets. His mouth worked for a few moments, to no effect, and it was the fee who finally 'harumph'ed and sat up from her chair, taking the tape along with her.

"Such lasciviousness, the insolence!" she declared, spinning on the tailor to wag a condescending finger. "I've never been treated so terribly, you pompous, bulbous, debased little fae!"

She huffed, crossed her arms, and pushed rudely past them and out the door, leaving the tailor's shop not empty, but as silent as if it were. The tailor pointed at them in horror, but Fryn's patience had run out, and she decided that it would be far more expedient to break the silence herself. "I see you remember us, very good," she began, peeking past his shoulder to be sure that there was no one else inside the store, "We have a favor to beg of you." She jerked a thumb toward the door and glanced pointedly at Havrshyk, he nodded and opened the door long enough to flip the open sign to closed, and then locked and barred the door.

"F-favor, you say? What do you want with me...?" The tailor stammered dropping his measuring tape to the ground, as he rounded the chair and stood as straight as he could on his short, little legs, as if he could stare them down successfully.

Havrshyk crossed his arms and glared ominously. "We need a disguise."

The tailor paled a bit, taking a half-hearted step backwards as he unwillingly averted his gaze. "That's right, you're wanted. Ironic, but... it's almost as if you are in the exact same position you were in last month." He studied Alyra behind them, but seemed relieved that it wasn't Harissa with them, since she had sewn his shirt-sleeves together the last time.

"Funny," Havrshyk agreed, not smiling, as he walked over to the far closet and scanned the various uniforms and high-fashion knock-offs. He paused, hand hovering over a cream and blue colored coat, with silver buttons, and finely embroidered piping; it was as if he had touched a static charge and was still standing there electrified. He pulled it off the rack, and examined it more closely, narrowing his eyes as he allowed a tiny, genuine smile to play on his face.

"You have a good eye," the tailor commented warmly, in direct contrast with the way his hands were shaking, clasped behind his back, "that is my study of historical Crown Guard uniforms—for reenactments of course."

Alyra flitted over and admired the coat, eyes bright as she asked, "Is this what I think it is?"

"Indeed, taken from the paintings in the Martell Palace. There are many lovers of art and history, even in the Stone Market," he explained, his stiff wings and shoulders relaxing as he spoke, "I am part of a small group of such tasteful individuals, and we recently planned a reenactment of the pinnacle moment of the Stanaedre Coup."

Fryn however, was not one of those 'tasteful' individuals. She coughed politely, but forcefully, and regained his attention. "We require current uniforms, for Crown Messengers, *not attorneys.*"

"Attorneys?" Alyra asked, momentarily distracted from where she stood, arms stuck through a slightly-too-large historical Crown-Guard jacket. "I don't think that would be a good choice, especially since Leif is so tan; why he almost looks Moraskyn..."

"That's a little unbelievable," Havrshyk replied, "I'd be hard-pressed to hide two extra wings."

She blinked but resumed trying on the jacket. "This is very comfortable, but appealing," she commented, more to herself than anyone else.

They ignored her, and the tailor bustled about, trying to locate something appropriate. The Crown Messengers were fast and few, passing largely unnoticed through checkpoints, or on occasion over the walls unhindered. It was the best choice, since they could avoid direct contact with any of the guards and receive only a passing inspection, however, they usually traveled alone.

As Alyra tried on the correct uniform in one of the curtained-off alcoves, Fryn leaned in close to Havrshyk's ear, and whispered, "We'll need to separate and infiltrate the district. I recommend that we meet up in the waiting room of the Grand Assembly. One of the servants could notify the prince that there's a messenger waiting for him there."

He shook his head, though he distractedly followed the tailor with his eyes. "The Palace does not operate so conveniently, Fryn. One of us will have to speak to the prince himself; ask for his location, and march there purposefully."

She frowned, calculating what she knew of the layout. "I don't think I could do that."

"I could find him," he answered, absently accepting a folded-up uniform of charcoal gray and glacial blue. "I've walked my share of that estate."

"Who were you Havrshyk?" she asked gently, her distrust softening as she remembered, just for a moment, his horror-stricken face when he'd frozen before the empty tomb, incapable of drawing any nearer to his grave.

He released a long slow breath and ran a hand over his face, wings and shoulders slumping. "I did not exist."

As she contemplated the deeper meanings of his statement, the tailor handed her a set of trousers, which he had deftly trimmed to her size; a size which he had been too eager to take. Fryn snatched them from his hand and stalked into the other changing stall just as Alyra poked her head out and then waved at her to come into her chamber.

Practiced as she was at the Soft-Point-Fist, a deceptively direct style of combat, Fryn was able to change her forward direction with a simple pivot around her forward foot and slipped inside. Their one-time guide, now simply a tag-along, was fidgeting with her jacket, and trying to force her wings through the slits in the back. Outside the curtain, Fryn heard Havrshyk give an impatient 'huff' and trod into the now-unused changing stall.

"No matter what I do, Fryn, I can only shift one or two wings into the holes," Alyra was complaining, but Fryn wasn't listening. Her eyes had drifted idly toward the coats and skirts, shirts, belts, and so forth that hung on the wall. A dreadful chill pervaded the air, and Fryn felt her eyes frozen stiff so that try as she might, she couldn't look away from the daggers that hung from their belts on the plain brass hooks. They were crystalline, luminescent white, with tiny golden veins—it was almost as if, but no, Fryn couldn't believe that. Still staring at them, Fryn absently held onto the jacket so that Alyra could turn her back and slip her hands and the very tips of her wings into the uniform to more easily shrug it on. The light had a delicate violet hue that barely shimmered over and against the golden-white veins of the crystal knives, as if they contained a very different sort of life of their own.

Alyra successfully donned the jacket, spun in a flourish, and began buttoning the front, but as she looked up at Fryn, her face fell, and she carefully took her knives down from the wall. "You'd better get dressed, Fryn. I can help you with the coat."

No… Fryn shook her head, her eyes growing distant. "Something isn't right.…"

Outside, the tailor coughed, probably worried that he'd be "cheated" once more (despite the fact that he'd been paid last time).

"What?" Havrshyk demanded, his hand spearing in at the side of the burgundy curtains as he thrust them aside. "You mean after all the trouble I went to putting this on…?" He was indeed wearing the messenger uniform, but it was somehow too wrinkly, and hung a little too baggy on him, as if he had lost weight since his measurements had been taken.

"We must go," Alyra agreed, and began throwing off her uniform, uncaring that Havrshyk was standing *right there*, as the tailor *and* Havrshyk both turned their backs, faces flushed, and wings shaded red.

"You mean now?" Havrshyk asked, surprisingly not contradicting her, but stepping into the other changing room, and if the sounds were any indication, he was also changing back.

"Right now…" Fryn whispered. The cold inside her heart was growing, and it felt as if a frost, not comfortable or beautiful, but defiled and deadly, was starting to surround them.

Within moments, they were in their own clothes again, except Alyra, who for some reason, had enhanced her clothing with a set of leggings and the classical jacket, resized, of course. The tailor waved them off, not even bothering to make them pay, as if he had something far more important on his mind.

"You should be going," he advised, his voice slightly slurred, and his eyes glazed, as if he were barely aware of what he said.

As they awkwardly said farewell and stepped back outside—though "outside" was a loose term in the Stone Market—Fryn felt an immediate sense of relief. They had, somehow, forestalled what would have been a disaster. Who cared what they wore or where or when they went? Ieffin was their friend, and Savis had said that he was someone she would always trust. Let the Hunters come and cause an incident. It was time to expose the shadows behind the dark.

The trio stood on the step of the tailor's shop listening to the idle banter of the faeries in the street as they joked, hawked wares, and shared rumors. Clair's employee was still serving Sceppe, and Fryn wished that she could go see him, ask advice, get a drink... but it was not a sound idea. No. Shattered snowflakes, and burned-out fires flickered in the back of her mind, it was not a time for cheer; she would regain, redeem what *he* had stolen.

"There must be another exit," Havrshyk said, walking ahead a span or so, "which will take us much closer to a suitable place."

"Mm." The shadow of a threat had not moved on; the tightness in her chest remained. As they moved to follow him, on his subconsciously-chosen path, Fryn felt a tugging at her mind, a resistance as it were, not against her movements but a slowing of the impulses that would cause her limbs to move. Not an electrifying motive power, but a waning, draining, haze that seemed to hold her back in place. It was there, behind them, talking to him, tasting his Sceppe, pretending that he cared. She could feel the burning of his eyes, the bloodlust that she had only sensed but once before, and even that memory had faded, half-forgotten, seldom remembered, and never sought again.

So now we are the hunted, she thought to herself, stiffening, and loosening, as she began to turn around. *I will not be a victim. I will not be the prey.*

Alyra had been walking beside her, and even as Havrshyk went quickly on ahead, she had stopped with Fryn and was searching her face concernedly. The twitching of her small gold-lined wings betrayed her anxiety.

Why is it always in these moments, she wondered, her eyes widening in shock as she beheld the cloaked form of the fae who stood beyond, *always in these moments, I recall that fear?*

He held a tiny tasting glass, filled only with the last drip of Sceppe, but he didn't finish his drink; he watched them with a dark glow to his shaded eyes. He was a stranger, but somehow the hostility that radiated from him felt so familiar.

The marketplace stood still. Time crawled. Stale light from brassy, first-generation starlamps streaming in corrugated lines, and Fryn found her fingers closing around the hilt of her Bloodknife even as the stranger drew a wicked luminescent blade. Striations of red and black marbled through his crystalline sword with an aura of stagnation.

Fryn found that she could not recall the Yardall fae's name, but she leapt forward, streaking through the air, her black knife flashing out in an invisible arc as she intercepted the sword, and crouched atop the tasting table, arm straining against the attacker's unnatural strength. She ground her teeth, stared into his statuesque eyes, but said nothing, as the Sceppe fae fell backwards, and out of the way.

Her attacker flew, or fell, or leaped, spiraling over her guard, end over end as he brought his sword in a heavy sweep horizontally at the level of her neck. She had extended a small field of frost around her body, a mist through which she felt the oncoming path, so that she barely dodged under the cutting blade and stabbed forward and upward in a rising charge.

The tip of her Bloodknife scraped against a hidden chest plate, just beneath his black robes, and she felt her arms go with the diverted strike, as he brought up his knee and pinched the blade.

She released it—flying back with a wing burst, just a little late; he raked her arm with his clawed gauntlets.

Havrshyk's voice yelled urgently as his sword passed through empty air, and Fryn saw his face mirror the concern and affection that Leif had shown before… there was something in there, a part of him still—perhaps in some way Leif had taken control when Havrshyk had frozen in surprise? She smiled, not caring that her Bloodknife had been taken, and thrown off behind the market stall. Leif had moved in answer, not Aldyr, and that was enough to give her hope.

The pale color of his skin had faded, and it was Leif! He crouched there, hair blonde, skin dark, returned to power for the moment. His green eyes stared daggers up to guard against the vengeful glare that the strange attacker gave, and his black sword rippled with a wave of ice and sparks, exploding, outward, upward, in a wave. Through the arc he swung it, throwing the enemy back, with sharpened crystals of ice and blood shattering despite the electric blaze.

The stranger shuffled his wings out of his cloak, and fluttered back expertly in a tight curve, settling to one knee a few wingspans behind them, separating them from Alyra with a sly smile curling on his tight-lipped face. His hood fell back, and his long dark hair rustled in the slight breeze, revealing his angular, dark-skinned face, his burgundy eyes, and his six wings splayed out of his back.

"I've found you, *Lassesh*," he said, in a clipped and slurring accept. "You did not think we would let you go? Nowhere is too far for us to find you..." He directed this to Alyra, and both Fryn and Leif stood there stunned.

Weren't *they* the targets here?

Alyra had stood back during the first part of this encounter, but now she glared at the six-winged stranger, with one of her daggers held behind her back. "*Geletoth drassash, pelitoné*," she hissed.

He made a 'tut' sound at that and changed stances. "It is not nice to call me a monster, when I still have my wings..."

What? Fryn wondered again, picking up her Bloodknife and trying to figure out whether a fight was going to continue, and if she would be involved.

Alyra appeared as a blur in the air, streaking by with her crystal daggers flashing in the amber light of the nearby lamp, her blades danced forward, one narrowly missing the attacker's face, and the other merely scratching the shrouded armor on his chest.

He stepped back, parrying the following attacks and battering her aside in his inexorable approach… to the alarmed fae behind the market stall.

The Yardall employee had drawn a knife and was holding onto it with white-knuckled hands, as he was attempting to crawl under the table. The crystalline sword swept down at an angle, shattering the table, and scattering broken Sceppe bottles in a shower of golden, malted rain all over the Sceppe seller. He covered his head, cowering as it fell apart around him.

Fryn watched in horror as she realized that this stranger was not going to spare him, not seeming to care that he was harmless, only caring that the merchant had decided to side against him.

Leif flew before the falling blade and caught it on the edge of his jet-black Bloodsword, hair standing defiantly on end. Tendrils of sparks arced up from the stones to his wing-tips, the tails of his scarf, and to his fingers on the sword. They pressed against each other, straining, as one and then the other appeared to gain the upper hand—the Moraskyn pressing down on Leif, and Leif sinking into a better stance.

"You will not harm him," Leif promised, eyes glowing with the amount of sparks flooding through his veins… Fryn could feel them, such a current of power, so alive that she thought it would surely damage him too, it boiled in his blood; his heart raced at more than twice his normal rate, and she found her heart matching it with ease, as she drew instinctively on some of his blood to enhance her own.

The stranger sneered. "His life was doomed the moment he drew a knife," he said, throwing back his wings, and pressing Leif down lower. His wings continued to glow, and radiate a sense of power, darkening the light and bending it, as he pushed Leif with increasing power and weight. Even the motes of dust in the air seemed to fall to the ground under the pressure.

Still blocking with one hand, Leif twisted from his hips, and opened with a charged fist into the soft, unarmored section of his stomach. He was blasted back, twitching, into the market stand opposite the Yardalls' scattering the horrified vendors and shoppers who had gathered around them to watch. One of them stepped forward to help him up, but he merely grabbed the offered hand, and tossed the fae aside. He flew up to his feet with a shout, "I will crush you for that, you snake!"

Those crowding around shrank away from him, but he gave them a glare. "Fly off! You'll suffer the same fate as *them*!"

Alyra knelt beside the seller, carefully helping him up and away from the fight. "Come this way, uh…"

"Terrin," he supplied, "thank you."

As Leif rushed forward to face him, Fryn watched their surroundings, and checked to see if he needed any support. So far, she didn't see any Guards or Hunters coming after them, but after an event like this, even the Stone Market would be policed. "Leif," she said, hoping her voice carried over the clanging of their swords, "we need to… *fasset*."

He grunted, slashing slowly across his armored chest, unable to draw blood. "Further in, he says!" His movements slowed, as if he were moving through water, but Fryn could feel Leif pouring more and more sparks through his muscles to combat the thickness or weight in the air.

She frowned. Leif really *was* in control, for the moment anyway. But if so, then they might not need Havrshyk's body after all. She didn't care if *he* were trapped in a sword for all time, no matter how he had tried to manipulate her feelings. She retreated, scanning the hallway in the direction of the entrance they'd used to enter the Stone Market.

The heaviness of the air followed after her, and the light dimmed under the deepening shade. The ground shivered, and the stones vibrated with an unsettling power.

Looking back, she saw Leif slicing through the thickening air, Bloodsword glowing with a reddish light as he charged it full of his sparks. The attacking fae's sword flowed easily through the murky air, unaffected by the increased gravity, and he was able to deflect Leif's sword and slam it home into his shoulder with a grimace.

Leif pulled back, letting the sword slide out of the wound, as he twisted from his hips, and launched forward with a charged palm strike with his free hand, directly into the fae' stomach. This time, the armor was no protection as he sizzled, and streaks of lightning ran around his wings and the various plates under his robes. Leif stepped back, holding his shoulder, and narrowing his eyes as the blood from his face drained and the injury began to seal.

Through their bond Fryn could feel Havrshyk tugging and drawing Leif's blood to heal the wound, as if he didn't feel like sharing his own.

The Moraskyn fae was only stunned for a moment, he glared at Leif with renewed focus, and sheathed his sword at his waist, as he reached out with one hand, jabbing the air ominously with his finger. As he did, he tore a black hole in the air, and grabbed it, seeming to compress and intensify it into a tight sphere in his fingers, as he spun, and lobbed it toward him.

The light twisted around it, and the air was pulled into it, as the ball arced past him, eating away any of the material it flew through until it stopped in midair, and then exploded in a wave of cold darkness, leaving a spherical hole in the wall of the stone market. The edge of its effect had even carved out some of the stones, and the supports of an awning over the Tailor's shop so that its one remaining support snapped under its weight, and it crashed to the ground in a cloud of dust and fine ash. The fee and fae who'd watched in silent curiosity panicked, turning from the scene in horror as they realized that it might soon involve them in the destruction as well.

Fryn gulped.

The stranger was already stabbing the air again, and grabbing two spheres this time in either hand, he twirled, leaning into a lunge, tossing one toward the fleeing crowd, and another toward Alyra and the Sceppe seller.

Fryn could only choose one. She flew in the direction of the first one, hoping Alyra could dodge the other. As she got ahead of it, she slashed with her Bloodknife across the ground, flooding the air and the stones with her frost and raising a crystalline barrier... if that would even be enough.

It was completely sublimated. She could feel the wave of nothingness as it got closer to her face, and watched in slow motion as it trimmed the edges of her fringe, and then retreated back into the empty circle it had carved. It left an even wider circle than the one thrown at Leif.

Alyra shoved the seller down between a pile of crates, as if that would protect him, and flew towards the second one, gliding under its path, and slashed upwards with her crystal knives. It ricocheted! Whatever material her blades were shaped from, it contacted with the ball as if it were solid like anything else, and she snapped it up into the ceiling.

The roof shivered under the weightless impact, and a yawning hole formed in the center.

Gravel and stone, loosened by the crater, tumbled in from the street above, and a few faces peered in—some even wearing the uniform of the Guard.

Neither Fryn nor Alyra had time to spare for the confused faeries above, as they darted back toward their foe. The Moraskyn agent raised a hand toward Fryn, blasting her backward with a pulse of invisible power, as he brought his blade up into a guard posture facing Alyra.

Her first blade encountered his with a clear ring, and a flash of light, and her second followed soon after, deftly cutting the ties of his cloak where his neck had been a moment before.

They danced back, her slashing and advancing, pressing him back toward an alley. Alyra didn't spare a look in their direction, but Fryn knew, if she didn't grab Terrin and Leif now, they might be noticed by the guards who were shouting questions down into the hole.

"Are there any injured?" One of them asked, landing on top of the rubble, and scanning the darkened market.

A few relieved sounds came from further back in the market, as faeries made their way cautiously around the rubble, and up out of the hole. Most would not like their names on record, Fryn supposed, seeing as how they ran a market known for its dubious reputation.

Two other guards followed the first, ushering the spectators out, so Fryn flew back to Terrin, who was still covering his head and cowering behind a box, and she grabbed him by the shoulder and shoved him toward the guards. "Get out of here!" She pressed, turning back toward Leif.

Terrin hobbled on a twisted ankle toward the first guard, his wings glowing with relief, as the last of the spectators escaped.

Fryn was almost to Leif, where he leaned back against the remains of a merchant stand, his shoulder almost healed, when she heard Alyra give a sharp, pained cry, and watched her get thrown out of the alley, across the street, and collide into the opposite wall.

She fell in a heap, her wings twitching, and her crystal knives clattering to the ground beside her.

The other two guards stood atop the pile of rubble, waving Terrin up, who tripped over a rock at the foot of the slope. The first guard was stepping down toward him to help, when the Moraskyn fae stalked out of the alley; he held a black orb pulsing in each hand, alight with misty tendrils of cold.

His burgundy eyes flicked toward the guards.

Fryn recognized the one on the ground; she'd kicked him through a window at the Guardhouse Ball.

One ball flew through the air at a dizzying speed toward the two guards at the top of the pile, and Fryn was already moving before the stranger had finished his spin and thrown the second aimed at the lower guard. She could only save one.

The first ball impacted the face of one of the guards, disintegrating it in a puff of black smoke, so that his companion had only a moment to stare in horror, before the circle expanded and he was gone. Not even a boot remained... just a twirl of wind and ash.

Appropriately, Fryn snatched up one of Alyra's daggers, kicked the last guard in the stomach, and deflected the second ball into the sky.

The poor guardsfae was knocked unconscious, his head cracking on the loose stones with a resounding 'smack', and Terrin wailed, as Fryn zipped back toward the Moraskyn fae.

She decided not to approach in the same low stance Alyra had, because he would expect that, as she wingbursted overhead with a downward slash, one of Alyra's daggers in her left hand, and her Bloodknife in the other. His eyes gleamed, darkening as the light writhed away from him, and the lamps were drained of their power, winking out one by one in a rush. He blocked her strike with his one hand holding his sword, grinning, as he held his free hand out, palm down, and pushed against the earth; and the power blasted Fryn up and over, deeper into the Stone Market.

She skidded across the paved stones into the center of the circular drain that had been converted to the central hub of the market. Its high domed ceiling had been carved and built directly into the wall separating the Rain and Hill Districts, and Fryn caught her breathe as a few more of the starlamps were snuffed out.

She heard Leif even before she saw him, as the Viper zipped into sight, sparks trailing along his wings and blade, cutting through the enhanced gravity; his power spinning with him, he lashed out with a kick that sent their attacker sailing through the air directly towards Fryn!

She ground her teeth in frustration as Leif stalked into the dim light of the last remaining starlamp, the one placed at the very center of the dome—apparently too far for the Moraskyn's effect to reach. He rubbed his sore shoulder, and leaned on his sword, sparks dissipating, and his blood fading from his face.

How could this fae be drawing power from the lights? Fryn wondered, changing her grip on the knives that she held.

Leif nodded to her tiredly and raised his sword in the same Swordhand Palm stance that Aldyr had just recently taught him—held out, like a foil, as he prepared for one last charge.

Shouts came from the hole in the tunnel behind them; more guards rushed in.

Leif and Fryn charged at the same moment, one above, one below, as the stranger grabbed another sphere of the void and it changed into a long shadowy blade, and he blocked Fryn's strike with the dark blade, and Leif's with the crystal one, and he held his ground. The stones in the ground began to rattle, the air grew heavy, and he parried Leif's strike, and stabbed him in the side, before turning on Fryn, slashing at her feet so that she had to jump, as he kicked her back, spun again, and kicked Leif in the head, so that he crumpled.

He rolled across the stones to the center of the space, barely dodging a crushing heel kick from the stranger who landed right where he'd been a second before. He stood between them and the direction of the shouts, and Alyra and Terrin.

Fryn readied her Bloodknife, standing guard over Leif's dazed form. He had a savage bruise on his forehead, where he'd fallen headfirst on the stones.

"Give up the exile, Hunters, or I will be forced to destroy you too," he offered, eyes darting around the abandoned market as he searched for his prey.

"I am not in the habit of turning over faeries to be killed," Fryn replied with a smile, "and I am quite skilled at killing those who try to stop me."

Fryn drained Leif completely, he had Havrshyk's sword after all, so he'd be preserved; he was in no position to support her at the moment anyway. As she hardened, and enhanced her Bloodknife, it folded many times over, congealing into a long black blade with crimson waves. She'd never used this much blood before, but it might just be enough to create a weapon sharp enough to cut through his mysterious power. Whether he was increasing the weight, or gravity, or whether he was thickening the air, she couldn't say. The only power that had been able to land on him so far, was elemental.

"The wings are the sails, the land is the sea…" she muttered, "Behind is the gale, I break upon thee." Master Bersari's voice echoed in the back of her mind, recalling one of her very first lessons, when she was ten years old, and she discovered what it meant to soar. Fryn sped toward him, using her wings to rush forward, and downward, so that her legs burned, straining against the increased gravity, and she rose with her Bloodknife outstretched like the point of a lance—using the crystal knife in her free hand to deflect his guard—as she burst into him. Her knife caught on the edge of his chest plate, and there was a ringing, echoing 'crack' in the air as it splintered around the tip of her blade, and she pressed on, through the armor, so that it bit into his flesh.

He gave a hollow groan, what would have been a scream if she had not just collapsed his lung; his wings went limp, and the sword fell to a clatter on the ground.

He wavered on his feet, but Fryn noticed a flicker of movement, as the stones shivered beneath him, and sunk a hairsbreadth into the ground, in a growing circle as a wave of gravity pulsed outward and threw her back.

She flipped over backwards, returning all the blood that she'd borrowed from Leif, so that he shook himself awake… with black hair, and icy eyes… Havrshyk had returned to power.

He rolled to his feet even before the blood had started flowing in his veins again and followed the direction Fryn had given with her eyes, over the crowd, toward Alyra who now stood behind them with Terrin at her side, apparently unnoticed by the onlookers.

Her foe struggled to breathe, sheathing his sword, as he stabbed the air with both hands, so that tiny spheres formed at the tips of all his fingers and he lazily shot them everywhere, into the hallway, toward the guards, into the dome, and at Fryn.

Fryn dodged and blocked one with Alyra's crystal blade before it could hit Leif and looked back at the stranger anxiously.

The Moraskyn glared at her, mouthing an unknown language, and the darkness intensified around him. He stood hunched over, with a hand on his chest, and his six blade-like wings went limp.

Surprised shouts, and alarm echoed from the tunnel, the dome began to crumble around them, and Fryn saw Alyra dragging Terrin from the mouth of the tunnel.

The sphere of blackness enveloped the stranger, and he vanished, with only a word of warning as he went.

"I am not finished…" His sour, rasping voice spat, "the exile… must die…"

There was no drifting cloud of ash at his departure. Instead, a blinding flash of violet light, and the scent that lingered after a lightning strike.

Alyra supported Terrin's limp body, waving Fryn over for help, as Leif shook himself, and led them through the last undamaged hallway out of the central dome. His hair was black again, and his face cold.

They had defeated their foe, for now at least, but Havrshyk was still in control.

Shouldering through one doorway, then shoving through another, they took turns through a long series of connecting hallways, passing between shops through the interlinking doors. First, they moved one way, then they looped back through the other doors deeper in, cycling three times to confuse any guards who might be chasing them.

Fryn only felt relief when they exited the last door out of the Stone Market, this one having led them through a long meandering path along the walls, so that they came out into the Rain District from a door built directly into the wall that was made to look like the inside of a storage shed.

Terrin had recovered somewhat, though he limped, and mouthed something quietly under his breath. Alyra nodded and donned her hood. "It will be a rushed flight," she replied, "but if we hurry, we'll be able to hide at the Yardall's warehouse where he works."

He guided them around the bend of the Rain Ringroad, and past the oddly abandoned eastern gate of the Snow District. The guards had likely rushed toward the emergency further out.

Terrin did not lead them through it however, but instead toward the outer ring north of the Bounty Office. His lodgings were in a small, combined office and warehouse with no descriptive signs or logos, just a street address number tucked under a small stooped roof: 125HY.

His hands shook so badly that he could not get them into his pockets to fetch his key, so Alyra quickly, but gently, found the right key in his coat pocket, and turned it in the lock, pushing it open with her boot. It was blessedly dark and quiet inside. He was the manager of the little venture, and didn't even have an assistant, so they all filed in in a flash, and bolted the door behind them.

Havrshyk deposited Terrin on a low bench beside the entry, likely intended for putting on and removing his shoes, and leaned over him to inspect the wounds on his head and ankle, poking carefully at him with his finger. To his credit, Terrin only winced, sucking in his breath only when Havrshyk spread a cut open slightly to check its depth… and then, he dragged his fingertip down the length of the cut, sealing it with a blueish-red layer of ice.

Frost spread outwards around his shirt and waistcoat, both now horribly ruined, and a fog-like mist rose off him, filling the entry to the office. Alyra scrutinized Havrshyk, eyes flicking between his blood-drained face, and Fryn, narrowing as her wings shifted in thought, pulsing with a slight shade of yellow.

"Thank you, Terrin," Fryn said at last, resting her back against the opposite wall, and sliding down to the ground. "We didn't have a safe place to go."

"…she told us…" he managed, closing his eyes and pressing his lips together in a pained expression. They waited. "... she said to help you, no matter what."

"Who told you?" Alyra asked.

"Clair..." He said, opening one eye as if to say, who else? "She never believed what they said about you… knew that you'd come here."

Seems everyone did, Fryn thought. "Oh Clair," she said, smiling and shaking her head, "glad to know you're still on our side."

Havrshyk said nothing, but went further in, and collapsed into an armchair that sat in the corner of the room, with a cold pot of tea on the table beside it.

"We need to find another way," Fryn said, "but for now, I need to rest."

Alyra seemed asleep already, perhaps when she woke up, she'd be willing to discuss her motivation to follow them after all?

Interlude 2

Fee

~86 Years Ago~

Frorin

Aldyr

Lyenel held out his practice sword with an easy grace, head tilted back slightly so he could look down his nose as well as the length of his sword. His sword-hand foot was forward, his palm-hand foot was back, and he let his empty hand rest limply at his side as if it would never need to see use. His green eyes sparkled with a brush of amber light as he enhanced his vision, drawing in the various reflections from the candles in the four wall sconces surrounding the circular arena so that Aldyr found it even harder to see. They said that glasses were forbidden during training and combat, so the set of spectacles he'd received the week before would be useless unless he were studying—and they often begrudged his desire to do even that.

Lyenel's foot slid forward slightly in the coarse gray sand and he bobbed the tip of his sword in the air. "Are you going to stand there forever, Heavy, or are you going to draw your sword?"

Havrshyk hated that name, and he fluttered his 'heavy', 'icebound' wings irritatedly as he raised his sword and lowered into the correct stance. Just because he wasn't able to fly as far or as fast, or as long… they mocked him—calling him 'Heavyshyk' or 'Heavy' or 'The Glacier'. They had elegant elemental affinities that enhanced convenient aspects of their martial art, such as light, or air,

89

or water… but his ice only made it so he didn't mind the cold, and so that his tendons took longer to stretch. Aldyr wished at that moment, that he was clever, so he could snap back something cutting to wipe that smirk off Lyenel's face.

He charged forward, sand flying up and glittering from the flare of light released when Lyenel stopped dampening it, nearly blinding him, as the sword snaked forward like the head of a spear, catching him in the center of the chest; his own sword was deftly knocked aside by Lyenel's open palm. The point of the wooden sword pushed through the leather guard he wore, and Aldyr grunted at the sharp pain that lanced up to his temples from one of his ribs as he hardened his chest with a layer of ice, too late.

"Too slow, Glacier," Lyenel teased, following through, and launching him off the end of his sword, so that he flew back, nearly hitting the back wall, luckily fluttering his slow wings in time.

"Again," came the voice from above, where Master Bersi was observing their progress for the first time in months. "Aldyr, you must not rely merely on your eyes, but trust your feet, for…" he began, and he and Lyenel, and Aldyr all continued the mantra,

"…The wings are the sails, the feet are the sea, what good are the sails, if the boat cannot be?"

How thanklessly vague, Aldyr thought to himself, *every crumb of wisdom that they deign to give us, is as foolish and contrived as the last.* He narrowed his eyes and held back his now-slightly-too-long black hair with a layer of frost that he combed through with his fingers.

This time though, he would not rely just on their technique, since that didn't work for him, he hardened his training armor with a layer of ice below the leather so that they wouldn't see the enhancements, and he bowed again in the ring.

He charged first. Not the flashy, artistic flourish that the youngest son of the Yardall Clan had demonstrated, but the sharp and powerful jab of a serpent, as he darted forward, edges enhanced with trailing flakes of frost; he performed the same lunge that his opponent had moments before, but in a shocking blink of an eye— marvelous and startling, the Glacier sublimated. He didn't even need to touch Lyenel's sword, as he twisted from the hips, and in direct conflict with the mantra quoted by their master, he performed a wingburst and blew forward, stamping his foot and rising with the movement so that the tip of his sword clung to the leather chest plate that Lyenel had only bothered to strap on loosely, catching and throwing him up and out of the ring.

"Hold!" Bersi commanded, and Aldyr didn't move, he froze in place, sword extended, the palm of his empty hand facing the ground, a cold wind settling in a flurry of mist as his wings remained rigid, and blue.

At the same time, Aldyr smiled, looking at Lyenel's dumbstruck face as he rubbed the back of his head. He had not been fortunate enough to stop his flight since he had been launched at such a high velocity. He eyed his roommate warily, the arrogant light of his eyes fading ever-so-slightly.

Master Bersi wore his usual colors, though not the traveling uniform and cloak this time, he wore the loose robes of his order, The Swordhand-Palm, the third and sharpened, unknown hand of the Crown. It had a slightly open chest, where the tunic was belted off with a short sash that could support the weight of a training sword, and his was sewn with golden thread, befitting his rank as Grandmaster. He gave Aldyr the smile he gave the ones he was ordered to kill, a smile that was warm, and comforting, even reaching his eyes, though his wings were stiff despite their folded, supposedly relaxed posture, a smile that radiated… disappointment.

"Do you understand your failure, Aldyr," he asked, his face impassive, though the vein in his exposed neck pulsed irritatedly. Havrshyk had grown used to gauging faeries' emotional states less from the betrayal of the light suffusing their wings, and more by the less obvious things, the things they didn't know that they should hide. Bersi's wings shimmered slightly with a tinge of red, or purple, but it was so *controlled* he couldn't tell whether it was a trick of the light or a sign of frustration.

He didn't understand. "Of course, Master," he said, less to convince his master than to practice the art of the lie.

Master Bersi tapped his elbow with the fingers of his cross-armed hand.

Lyenel was not convinced, however, and he stomped forward as if he were trekking through a bog. "*That* was *not* the <u>Swordhand-Palm</u>!" he declared, blowing the lid on the whole thing, surprising, probably, no one.

Aldyr lowered his arm, drawing in his excess elemental energies and secluding them in his core, savoring the shimmering sensation that ran along his wings as the remaining ice he'd created dissipated without leaving a drop of condensation. He slipped his practice sword into his belt and matched his master's pose, crossing his arms, and as best he could, tilted his head back like Lyenel. That was more to keep his hair from falling in his eyes again; he'd have to freeze that *again*. "I used the right weapon, in my right hand, and my left was open for use in blocking and chopping, disarming, and grappling… am I missing something, Lyenel?"

Lyenel rubbed his chest and frowned. Apparently even his advanced intellect could not discern the nature of his suspicions. Bersi was another matter.

He sighed, releasing his pent-up tension, closed his eyes, and pinched the bridge of his nose, shaking his head at the same time. "We are… to put it in thematic terms, the Lancer, Aldyr, <u>not the Serpent</u>.

"And…" he said, drawing out the syllable, and the response. "Brought the Viper into our nest, eh? Listen, Aldyr, you are not of the city, so perhaps you mirror in a fashion the wildness of the Serpent, from the Lay of Arta's Fall. We are the lance in the hand of the king, the weapon he used to pierce the hide of his enemy, but you have not mirrored this. You do not rely on the strength of your feet, but your wings instead…" he lectured, turning his hand, pacing a couple steps as he illustrated.

"That makes no sense," Aldyr interrupted, "wouldn't the lack of wings make *us* the Serpent?"

He ground his teeth, and Lyenel's eyes popped open wide, not unlike a constipated fly. "Whether you agree with our mythology, or ideology, or whatever you have an issue with—it is irrelevant— you are here in service to the Crown. It is *he* that you need concern yourself with. You serve at his pleasure, for his welfare, and in the manner and style he desires. You are higher than a soldier, scarcer than his advisors, more vital to this kingdom than all the branches of our judicial system… and if that means pretending, then that is what you'll do!" The tirade came through softly at first, but as his compounding phrases built in their logic and poetry, his voice rose with a tremulous passion, until his breath was spent, and his wings, which had fanned out expressively, folded neatly behind his back. He breathed deeply, and in the silence that followed, Aldyr frowned, narrowing his eyes at Lyenel who stared in awe at their master.

"But, why must we adopt this rigid style? It will not help us fight in flight, or on the chase," he asked gently, hoping that this time his point might be taken more seriously, that his opinions might have weight.

Master Bersi squatted, elbows resting on his knees as he leaned his chin against his fist, and cocked his head slightly, so he could turn a bemused expression toward his shortest student. "Do you understand, truly, what your position is in the service of the Crown? You are not an average Guard, standing at the gates, fighting in the streets; you are the sword that goes unseen, whose style is meant for fighting one, or two opponents indoors, in tight spaces where everyone else is at a disadvantage. You can slip past fortifications, and guards, and kill only the one you are meant to kill. Surely that is more expedient and just, than simply hiring mercenaries like they do for pickpockets and thugs. Remember, your sword is only the tip of the spear, your legs are the haft, and a spear is most powerful against an opponent's attack when it is rooted to the ground."

Thoroughly chastened and partially convinced, Aldyr lowered his eyes and dug a small depression in the sand with his boot, glancing up every few seconds, until he heard his master give a calm sigh. "There is a reason why we fight the way we do, Aldyr, but at present, it suffices for you to trust me, and obey."

"Yes Master," he conceded, but inside, he remembered, that Lancer's wings had been thrown back, as in a wing-burst, to enhance his attack. But for now, he would obey.

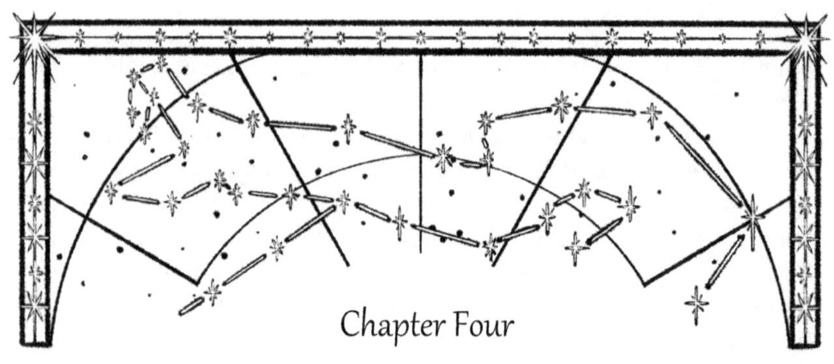

Chapter Four

SERPENT

~Present Day~

Rain District

Fryn

The door flew open as if it had been struck by a storm-tossed stone. With it came the glaring light of the early morning sun, silhouetting the slender form of a fee wearing a burgundy waistcoat, and an amber work dress. Her auburn hair was pulled back and piled high on her head, though a few strands had refused to be restrained, and hung about her face, framing it like a halo with the sunrise behind her head, red-light glowing through her blue-lined wings.

"Terrin!" she shouted, head spinning in a rushed scan of the room, until she found him on the bench and hurried to his side, only slowing to gently wake him up. The forgotten door creaked and shifted under a slow breeze, letting in cold air and harsh light alike. Fryn smiled from where she sat against the far wall, half-buried in the coats that hung from wood pegs just over her head. She'd slept through the night, knees pulled up to her chest, resting her head and arms on her knees.

"Whatever happened to you?" The newcomer asked, fussing with the crust of ice that clung without melting to his wound.

"My lady? Is it you?" he asked, making to stand up to greet her, but she held him down with a firm hand on his shoulder.

She giggled, not like the giggle of a child, but shaken, like one on the verge of breaking down into tears. "Of course it's me, Terrin, you didn't expect someone *else* to have the *key*, did you?"

He stared at her with dull eyes, speechless.

"Good morning, Clair," Fryn volunteered, standing and pulling away from the coats.

Clair froze, wings immediately fanning out and flicking back again as she spun around, pointing an accusing finger toward her, though an impish grin spread out on her face. "Fryn! So, it *was* you? I'm so glad!" And before she even finished her sentence, she'd leapt through the short distance, and had wrapped her arms around Fryn's body in a surprise hug. Clair's arms were on top of both of hers, so Fryn couldn't really return the hug, pinned as she was, and she found that she wasn't sure what she was supposed to do. Hug back? Laugh? Cry?

"Good to see you too, Clair," she said at last, an honest smile pinching at her cheeks, as she tried to pat Clair's back with half of the desired mobility for a hug. After a much longer hug than necessary, Clair pulled back, clasping Fryn's shoulders as she stared into her eyes.

"...Yes... yes, it is," Clair replied, "how are you holding up?"

"I've still got my wings," she allowed, but fell silent as she remembered the strange fae and his mysterious comments about Alyra. "It's not as simple as it should be," Fryn added, looking back up and putting on a smile. "It's true we killed some Hunters... but it's also true we *should* have done so."

Even as she paled a bit, Clair gripped Fryn's shoulder more tightly, and nodded. "I've seen the kinds of things you've had to do before, don't envy it, but... collapsing the Stone Market, was that really necessary?"

Fryn raised an eyebrow at her. "We didn't do that Clair, there was someone else... a Moraskyn, can you believe that?"

She made a "psssh" sound of disbelief. "I didn't think they were real!"

The two of them burst out laughing and kept laughing till they ran out of breath.

Havrshyk came around the corner at last, but his overt color-changes had been softened so that he looked almost as much like Leif as he should. He crossed his arms and leaned back against the wall beside Terrin. "Trouble is, there's someone who wants to pin everything on us, and until we know who that is, there's little to *do* about it."

As if in a moment, she could absorb and analyze everything at once, Clair nodded, her jaw set, and her wings rustling with the eagerness to fly. "There *is* someone who would help you. Me."

"I hope you have room in your heart to help one more," Alyra said, popping in from the back, "I'm Alyra, a..." she glanced between Fryn and Havrshyk hopefully, "...a friend of theirs."

She's awfully quick to call herself that, Fryn thought with a smirk.

Clair didn't object, however, but released Fryn and shook her hand. "Well, it is nice to meet you, Alyra, I'm Clair, Clair Yardall— of the Yardall Sceppe Estate."

"So, I hear," Alyra said, glancing at their hands, where Clair was still vigorously continuing the handshake far longer than was normal. "Even what I tasted in the Stone Market was better than anything I tried in Artell."

She let Alyra go with that, making a loud 'pfft' sound, followed by a laugh. "The only thing worth drinking there is the river." Clair said it as if that made the most logical sense, but even Fryn was confused. "But," she added, "what are you up to, and how can I help?"

Fryn drummed her fingers on her opposite arm, arms crossed as they were, and closed her eyes as she considered her response. "We need to speak with Ieffin, but it's impossible to sneak in, if last time is any indication."

"Tricky, yes, certainly," Clair replied, nodding in thought, "but there *are* ways to meet him. In fact… I might know one such way… but it would take some time, even a few days to arrange."

Havrshyk gave a low 'hm?' And Alyra waited patiently, standing far enough back that Clair couldn't give her a second handshake if the inclination hit her.

Looking over at Terrin, Fryn saw that though his face was still pale, some of his strength and color had returned. Havrshyk had done a good job sealing the cut, not that she expected anything less—he was a far more experienced Lich after all.

"It will be hard for us to wait a few days. Our situation is a bit beyond precarious," she said.

Clair nodded, smiling mischievously. "But you see, it is a brilliant plan. I am going to invite him to do a tasting of our latest batch of Sceppe, but instead of bringing him to the main Estate, I'll lead him here."

Havrshyk coughed. "That's not a good idea. He will have guards, and servants, and they will be put in the awkward position of letting wanted criminals run free, since we cannot allow ourselves to be taken into custody with this conspiracy on our tails."

Alyra's wings flicked in agreement as she added, "The Hunter who is chasing us will be watching for just such a movement by any of their friends."

Despite their arguments, Clair's face set, and she shook her head. "No, I'm afraid we'll have to try. Far better than breaking in, I think the prince will have an easier time breaking out."

"I find *that* hard to believe," Havrshyk replied softly, "the Crown Guard are not so lax as to let their leaders out of sight."

If anyone would know about that, Fryn supposed, he would. "He did move about last time with a great deal of freedom," she offered helpfully.

Clair took their criticism easily but shoved it aside with a wave of her hand. "Don't underestimate our prince. He's a force of nature."

"He's something alright," Fryn said, sharing a look with Havrshyk, "but if you do this, tell us as soon as you find out when he can meet."

She agreed, and with one last pat on Terrin's good shoulder, went to the door, grabbed its handle, and stepped out onto the porch. "I will, but do not leave this building. You're a little too famous now." Before they could respond, she shut the door with a thud, and was gone.

"So, once again we wait?" Fryn wondered.

"I've done enough of that for two lifetimes," Havrshyk sighed, "I'll take first watch at the window upstairs."

Alyra chuckled. "No one knows who *I* am. I will go and get some food." Having said that, she fastened her coat, and was out the door right on Clair's heels. She closed the door gently at least.

"I hope that doesn't cave in on us," Havrshyk commented. He then flew down the hallway, and up the stairs to keep a watch out of Terrin's bedroom window.

"Indeed," Fryn said, giving Terrin a smile as she sat beside him. "Thank you, Terrin, if not for you, we would probably be dead... or nearly."

His smile turned to a grimace as he shifted in his seat. "As I said before, we are in your debt."

"It's paid, I assure you." She rested her chin in her hands and sighed. Alyra had slipped out before they could question her, as if she knew that Fryn was about to demand an explanation for their encounter the day before.

As uncomfortable as it made her, Fryn also knew that if Alyra opened up, she would then deserve to know why they needed Havrshyk's body back; it would only be fair.

Still, she wondered. What business did the faeries of the distant, *very* distant, continent of Moraskyr have here? The Commission's motivations she was beginning to understand... but exiles, and six-winged faeries? It was getting too complicated. All she wanted was Leif back, but the mess involved just kept getting worse.

She huffed and scratched her head.

Alyra had better bring back food enough for everyone.

Frorin

Snow District

Alyra

The early morning wind bit at her cheeks, chilling her through her clothes, so that she had to resist the urge to rub her hands together and shiver and chatter through her teeth. Clair had flown quickly, heedless, obviously, since she hadn't expected to be followed. Now, as Alyra smiled at a guard, exuding, as she was able, the sense that she belonged there, and walked right through the checkpoint unchallenged.

The city was needlessly organized in this circuitous way so that anyone could get lost, but still find their king; she could see the wall turrets and the dome of their Grand Assembly as it marked the center of the city. It symbolized, in a way, how their culture was built and centered on the concept of fairness, justice, and sometimes mercy—all while they entertained mercenary connections, outsourcing the expenditure of justice when the work became inconvenient to them.

She sighed. It wasn't so different in Moraskyr, the names and titles changed, but the same cognitive and moral malaise oppressed them all. Necessity was the easiest way to circumvent the law, or the good. Though she held her hands behind her back, and walked oh so properly, her fingers rested on the hilts of her daggers, as she scanned her surroundings, and felt the weight of the disinterest and ennui of the richest and most important and most successful faeries in the city. None of it really mattered. They drifted by her, through her, obliviously, barely chatting even when they traveled in groups. Only this Clair Yardall had a spark of life, and she trotted with a spring in her step, humming purposefully, cheerfully, as she danced through the crowded street, all the way to the Crown District's gates.

Alyra hadn't sensed or seen anyone following her, and she relaxed slightly now that the assassin that had chased her to Fhoraena had been banished. It was temporary. He would recover, and resupply his satchel of wing shards, and return seeking her head—and vengeance against her new friends. She could sense Leif and Fryn's mistrust, but she also knew that they would not betray her, and in fact would help her on her quest if she asked... but she hated asking for it.

She shook her head, and matched the dreadful march of the Snow District, drifting down the street like the snowflakes it was named after, keeping Clair's colorful coat, scarf, and hair always in her view. She could truly vanish in a place as inattentive as this, so she did. Clair stopped to chat with the Crown Guards, and Alyra merely brushed by them, waiting in the shadow of the gatehouse for her unwitting guide to continue.

"Good morning, Ivan," she said to the guard on the right, smiling brightly as she glanced to the other, "Heinrich."

"Miss Yardall," the one she'd called Ivan replied, "it's awfully early for you to be dropping by."

She *tsked* cheekily. "I'd hoped to speak with Ieffin, he can't have gone to bed yet..."

Alyra's wings twitched worriedly.

"He's probably eating his breakfast by now," Heinrich said, "you might be able to join him."

Clair nodded and walked in. "Alright, I will!" Her path led Alyra across the open courtyard, but again she went unnoticed, and up the steps to the Palace. The steps rose up to the magnificent white-finished birchbark doors, carved with all manner of mill work and trim, without even a single pane of glass. Flanking the doors on either side were tall granite pillars holding up the covered porch, if indeed it could be called a porch. It looked down on the causeway and the courtyard from a high enough point, and with a wide-enough view, that she half imagined that she surveyed a crowd of liveried guards and nobles, attending some rousing speech, or listening to a sobering and unwelcome announcement.

Just as she herself had gone unnoticed, Alyra had not even seen the guards standing beside the doors, silver lances held proudly in one hand, at attention, with white capes pinned around their shoulders, draping carefully along their lance-arms. Suppressing her presence worked both ways, limiting her ability to draw attention, but also suppressing her own awareness.

"Ms. Yardall," one said, bowing slightly with his head, "I wasn't expecting you to visit today."

She smiled. "Neither was I," she returned, "but here I am all the same."

He didn't question her but took hold of the brass door handle and pushed the door inside, so that Alyra had no opportunity to slip by all three of them. Clair vanished within, but she could still sense her urgent, steadfast, mind through the walls. *"There must be some other way inside,"* she thought, tracking Clair's mental signature as she went around the corner of the building, nearly losing her step to the moss-beds, as she flitted across to the next patio. Clair reappeared on the next patio, but Alyra frowned, when she saw that it was lined with windows on all sides and thoroughly closed off. She would need to press an ear against the glass to hear anything. On the other side of the patio, she found a shady spot to duck, and put her head against the wall, emitting the sense that she was just one of the trained shrubs.

Through the wall, she could barely make out the innocuous greetings being exchanged, the abrupt scooting of chairs, and the clatter of fresh dishes being set on a wooden table.

"…what brings you here…?" asked a young fae's voice, surprised, but bright, and cheerful.

"…thought you'd still be in bed," Clair replied, sounding more muffled, as if she were taking off her scarf as she spoke. "I was hungry, obviously."

"Oh, I see how it is," the prince said, "I give you permission to visit the Crown District, and you choose to show yourself here every day?"

Alyra could barely make out the chuckle.

"You do," she answered.

"I have no rebuttal for *that*," he said with a laugh, "but where are my manners?" He clapped his hands twice, and declared loudly and over-distinctly, "Tea!"

There was a commotion further in, and Alyra rolled her eyes as she imagined the clumsy display that must be happening inside—the door being slammed open, a tray of cups and fresh tea shattering over the floor, spilling its hot contents all over Clair's dress... it would be funny if the tea wasn't boiling.

Clair yelped, and the childish voice of the butler spewed out, first obscenities, and then profuse apologies, and then both Clair and the prince broke out into a lasting fit of laughter. This was not the height of the land's elite, was it? It wasn't they, after all, whom she had come to see.

"You'll bring a fresh pot of tea, and see to Ms. Yardall's clothes, get her dressed in something... dry," the prince commanded.

"Yes, m'lord," a fee replied dutifully, "if you'll come this way, Miss."

The door shut, and the young fae who'd broken the tea-pot was muttering under his breath, loudly enough for Alyra to detect, but no so as she could hear what he said. The mood in the room was a mixture of shame, remorse, and a buoyant sense of satisfaction. This prince really *had* been glad to see her, and almost as happy about the accident. Odd.

Alyra waited there, no longer pressed against the wall, just relaxing as the sunlight shifted around the corner and bathed her in a welcome, but sparse warmth. She could still feel the emotions of the two remaining in the room, could almost hear the mumbling thoughts of the miserable butler, and the daydreaming vacancy of the prince.

She'd sensed the urgency and nervousness that Clair had going in, but it had waned with each second of their interaction, and she'd been caught up completely in the prince's mood, his pleasantness, satisfaction, and... something else. It was difficult getting a specific gauge on one faerie when there were four or more around, but, she smiled, Clair went there because she wanted to—not just to help them.

After several minutes, Clair returned, laughing, and chatting with the maid who had escorted her away so dutifully before. "I don't believe it," she was saying.

"It's true Miss, every word," the maid insisted, covering a giggle, "every single day."

"I'll see what I can do then," Clair said, and sat down loudly in her chair.

"Sorry for the wait, Clair," the prince interjected, and Alyra barely heard the sound of pouring water, "I've been trying to train my butler to be more decorous."

"It's the one thing you've failed at, m'lord," the maid added, and then, before she could be scolded, her fading footsteps announced that she'd run off.

"Impertinent little finch," the prince said idly, "still, she's right. He's incorrigible."

"In… encor… what, Sire?" The butler asked hesitantly.

"Never mind that, bring some more toast."

They ate breakfast, laughing, and talking about idle things; Alyra forgot where she was, eyes closed, as she imagined the bright and charming scene that was playing out inside the solarium. It became so easy to not be there, no one would see her, even if they looked—she'd be like another moss hedge, or the stones of the wall.

Finally, when they had finished eating, and the servants had taken away all the food and trays, Clair and the prince sat quietly, sipping tea.

"Ieffin," Clair said gently, pausing hesitantly, "what will you do about Leif and Fryn?"

He inhaled sharply, and Alyra heard his teacup rattle on its saucer, and then clink as he set them on the table. "Clair…" he began in a low, warning tone, "…this mess in the Stone Market... *destroying it*... there isn't much I *can* do. My guard lost a number of fae, and there are more injured. Besides, the Assembly is pushing for the Commission to take over the investigation."

"But surely you can…"

"What, disavow the Commission and cancel our international accords for the sake of two faeries? Even then," his voice dropped to a whisper, which Alyra mostly made out by his emotional state, "we are locked into a long contract, with five years left before renegotiation. It would cause an international incident if we ended the agreement early."

"No, of course, I didn't mean *that*," she answered, "but you could see them, help a little bit?"

"*See them?*" he asked incredulously, rising from his chair, scooting it back abruptly. "I couldn't do that, that would worsen our circumstances even more. It is bad enough that that snake Wellsey reneged on his engagement with Savis, that we've lost half of my generation of the royal family, that the power of the Commission and the other Kingdoms continues to eclipse us even in our own borders—no, I cannot risk making anything worse."

Clair chuckled wryly. "No, I suppose not. But you could make things better."

He went quiet, and another chair moved, followed by the light clinking of the other teacup being set on the table. "Why don't you visit my estate, for a tasting? I'll even give you a tour."

"A tasting, hm… Sceppe is very nice… yours especially… but…"

"But nothing," she replied, "it would be very troublesome for me if you didn't come to visit. You have one purpose, don't you?"

"To safeguard, advance, and serve the interests of the people," he answered, as if from memory.

"Well then, if I am counted among them, serve my interests too."

Alyra smiled. Their banter and the warmth of the exchange was refreshing, for lack of a better word; they spoke without really caring about their difference in station, as comfortable with each other as siblings or old friends. If she read him correctly, his emotions toward her were mixed heavily with nostalgia… old friends or such, indeed. Satisfied that they might actually be of some help, Alyra remembered where she was, who she was, and started back across the courtyard—unnoticed by all.

Leif had Fryn had made good friends. But, her stomach rumbling, Alyra remembered why she had first gone out in the first place.

Frorin

Sky District

Harissa

The Sky District was as lifeless as ever, though the children she saw playing were as cheerful as she remembered when she used to sneak out to play as a girl. The wind tossed her hair in fits, and she rested her hands on the handle of her cane as she surveyed the hillside on which the precarious sections of the Sky District were built.

Jason sat on a stool beside her, raising a compass to his drafting paper and sketching the grade and arc around the walls and their descent. His pine needle tea steamed, forgotten, in a roughly formed mug on the ground—one he had borrowed from one of the locals.

"These crags are a disaster, Jason," she said, gesturing toward the shambling buildings erected against the rocks, crammed together, and scattered above and below each other on the uneven ground. "If we are going to build a wall, we are going to have to level the area, and start down there." She pointed toward the bottom of the slope where the snaking road trailed up a few switchbacks forming a long straight path that gently flowed toward Artell.

He shaded his eyes with his pencil and eyed the point where the once straight road curved to climb the hill. "That will make it a very large district, Harissa," he replied, adding a circle from there, centered directly on the Crown District, so that their plan to add a new wall would create a full circle rather than another crescent. "Are you wanting me to redraft the Pine District as well then?"

Harissa nodded absently, until she realized what he was proposing. "You've got an excellent point, Jason!"

"I do?" he asked uncertainly, "what idea is that?"

"If we begin this construction with an expansion to the Pine District, the Snow District stuffs will complain but leave us alone... Then we can regrade the hillside in the process!"

His wings twitched at her calling the other nobles "stuffs" and he sighed. "We barely have the means to *start* building a wall around the Sky District, let alone expand our own into a full circle. No... I think..." he added, erasing the last circle, and starting with a new line at the northern edge of the city, "that the wastes to the north are not worth including. A new crescent will suffice and keep our project within the realm of the incredible, rather than the impossible."

Harissa frowned, wings flushing purple in annoyance. He was probably right, even if she'd rather that the city were made of circles instead of a mixture of shapes... but correcting districts hundreds of years old was hardly realistic. "I want another gate," she mused, "an easy access from Martin Hall to the Sky District."

He paused in his drawing and shrugged with his wings. "Easy enough to add one on Alder Road, it would open up onto an almost empty plateau. In fact, that area would be a good place to start development." Jason smiled to himself and turned on his stool to look up toward the area above the eastern clump of Sky District hovels, "if we subsidized some of these faeries, they might be able to start a few respectable businesses."

The idea was nice, Harissa agreed, but it would only really work if the Sky Dwellers were granted citizenship, and thereby the *right* to do business. No, the wall would come first.

Glancing back at the winding road leading up to the southern gate, Harissa noticed a trio of faeries in long cloaks, who trekked up to the gate purposefully. They looked worn, and almost ragged from their journey, but the way they stood, facing the guards without care, she grew worried.

The one at the head leaned on a long rust-colored sword, as his tan wings beat angrily, and the guards barred his path.

They seemed to be asking the usual questions, but their hostile posture, and the other guards peeking out over the wall, made her want to get involved. "Jason," she said, tapping the tip of her cane on the bare rock of the outcropping they occupied, "Keep drawing."

He ignored her, already so focused on what he was doing that he hadn't noticed the commotion she was probably going to worsen. She flitted over toward the guards and fairly soon she could hear them arguing. The guard at the head of the group had his arms crossed, and was speaking in an insistent, and steely tone.

"I've seen your Licenses, Hunters, but to gain entrance to the city you still must answer our questions."

The Hunter on the right leaned against his spear, yawning as he answered cheekily. "We're going to the Bounty Office."

The one on the left, a weasel-faced fae with a bow and quiver on his back, laughed. "Don't say thar's no marks in Frorin lordship," he sneezed, but didn't bother to cover his mouth as he did so, "we've all heard what happened to the Markets." His lazy, drawling accent sounded like he was from Capholt, the uninviting bog predominantly settled by mystics and miscreants.

He was probably the latter.

Harissa settled beside the guard, at closer glance, one she recognized. "Good morning, Captain Lydell, are these vagrants causing any trouble?"

She examined the lead Hunter, growing more alarmed and less confident the longer she looked at him. He was missing one arm, and his body and wings were marbled in a hideous chitin like armor of marrow and bone. He glared at her, not saying a word.

Captain Lydell smiled appreciatively to her and inclined his head. "Good morning, Pine-Martin my lady, I am merely attempting to preserve the peace within our walls. Good sirs, the Hunters we generally deal with are more often bankers, and clerks. I do not wish to sound rude, but I would like to inspect your licenses before we allow just anyone holding such a card into the city."

The weasel-faced one spat to the side. "You think I stole this license? It's got me name on it, you crock!"

Lydell frowned but kept his composure. Harissa knew that the guards on the walls had their bows ready in case things got complicated. "It is a simple matter to assume a name, mister..." he leaned in to read the name on the card, "Hadahathalatha?"

He cawed with laughter. "Most jus' call me Hatha. You think I would make a name like this up, you do my parents a disservice."

He flushed. "I would never insult your parents, sir," he replied stiffly.

The gangly fae continued regardless. "I grant you that they deserve it, for all the grief my name has caused me."

Harissa sighed.

"Lydell, after the unfortunate incident in the Stone Market, the Assembly has authorized a total of five Hunters to operate within the city," she supplied helpfully.

"If they are Hunters... did you see him?" The captain asked, gesturing with his head toward the bone-marbled one. "I've never heard of any Hunters as monstrous."

She had.

She gestured toward the three Hunters, inspecting each of their licenses in turn. Hatha indeed was born in Capholt and licensed in Gaersheim five years ago. The spear bearer, Jeldon, was from Rosenkraun, and licensed there, if only a few weeks ago.

The third was Grifton Francis. The Bonecrafter. She felt a shiver as she looked up from his card and met his eyes. They burned with a restrained passion that made her stomach tighten into knots and her wings go limp. Her eyes shifted to the Bonesword, an uneven, serrated blade, deformed with spurs, as if only recently it had been attached to ligaments and tendons. A complex pattern of inlaid spirals of red ran throughout it, and she resisted the urge to vomit.

Grifton's eyes were locked on her cane. He smiled. "I have heard of the Pine-Martin of Frorin, it is true then, that there is power in your bones?"

She refocused on his face and frowned. If Leif and Fryn had entered the city, and caused the collapse of the Stone Market, she could not let this fae inside... but she had no authority to stop him either. Harissa took a step backwards and put on a smile.

"Lydell, I have examined Hunters and their licenses many times, these faeries are who they claim to be."

His eyebrows furrowed, and his wings slumped as if he wished she'd given him permission to turn them away. "Open the gates," he ordered half-heartedly, turning back to the Hunters, "To pursue any marks in Frorin, you need to register at the Office. And, if I hear anything about you causing trouble, or endangering the populace, your right to operate in Frorin with be revoked and we will leave the hunt to other Hunters."

Hatha made a poor attempt at a cackle but it quickly devolved into his coughing on phlegm and spitting a globule of the stuff onto the stones beside the captain's foot. "You'd need other Hunters anyway if they kills us, lordship, unless you think your guards are skilled enough to stop them *this* time."

Jeldon, the Hunter with the spear smiled at that, as he brushed past the captain. "Last I heard these two rookies had defeated the entire guard. Perhaps your focus should be on self-improvement first."

Lydell's wings shivered at the insult, but he stood to the side, crisp and professional. Grifton was the last to enter the city. Before he did however, he leaned in toward Harissa and whispered.

"The lich will pay in blood for my blood, Pine-Martin. I will not let anything get in my way. Stay in your district, or we'll see whose blade can hold its edge."

She ground her teeth, twisting the handle of her cane, itching to draw the blade and find out.

He grinned. "If we find them, bring your sword..." With that, he tromped off after the others, up the South Cardinal, as if they really did intend to go the Bounty Office first.

The gates closed again, and Captain Lydell breathed a really long sigh of relief. "I certainly hope we don't let any more Hunters into the city. Not after Mythrim, and now what your cousin did in the Stone Market."

Harissa's mouth quirked as she fought the impulse to slap him. "She's a Bloodcrafter, Lydell. Her power is simple, preserving herself. I believe there was another Hunter that used some kind of elemental power I've never heard of." She looked off toward Jason, still happily drawing and sipping cold tea.

She had gone there to inspect the ruins. Even after the fight had ended, the weakening of the structure had led to more collapsing tunnels, and broken buildings. Faeries that could not fly well had been advised to walk around the cave-ins, and guards were still swarming the area searching for survivors or clues.

He gave her a shrug, and then, as if wanting to forget the subject, he pointed over at Jason. "Are you really going to incorporate the Sky District?"

She gave him a look.

He withered a little, and added, "There is nothing good in the Sky District... it is a waste... and so might some say are its inhabitants."

"They have been wasted, and the area has gone to waste. There is a difference, Lydell." She smoothed the wrinkles in her coat and then waved him farewell.

There were a lot of things to handle at the moment, and at least for now, Fryn would take care of herself. She rejoined Jason on the hill, throwing one last look toward the city, hoping that Fryn would be alright—knowing that she would. Her brother had made good progress outlining the new Crescent, but he paused, drawing the plan for the new gate allowing quick access from Martin Hall to the new region.

"What is it?" she asked, leaning in to get a better look.

"We should create a new market, just down the road from us. It would be safer, and more reputable, and might bring in more funds if we invite the merchants from the Stone Market. No one is going to be shopping there anytime soon."

She agreed... but... there was a lot to be had if she could rebuild the Stone Market as it had been. "Set up a meeting, out here. We could still use that space, after it is forgotten."

Clair threw open the door with a triumphant laugh, barged in, and collapsed into an armchair in the corner of the office. It had taken a full day to hear back from her, and now, Fryn feared, with the way that Clair's chest rose and fell from her exhausted breathing, it would take even longer. Alyra stood at the corner of the entryway, leaning against the wall, but she didn't seem to be impatient in the least. Havrshyk however, emerged from the back rooms quickly, and when he saw her recovering in the chair, began to pace back and forth. Terrin was asleep in his room on the second floor, and Fryn, well, she sat in the chair beside Clair and laced her fingers, resting them on her lap, determined to wait.

It was a good thing she was determined, they had to wait a long time. In fact, Clair actually dozed off for a minute or two. Fryn's polite cough woke her up.

"Oh!" she shouted, leaping to her feet so quickly, Fryn thought she'd used a wingburst—which would have been impossible sitting in the cushioned chair. "Great news!"

"As out of breath as you came in, I see," Havrshyk commented, sounding just a little bitter.

She whirled on him, pointing a finger dangerously in his face, "None of that now, Leif, or I won't tell you anything."

"You'll tell me…" Fryn ventured, "what's happened?"

"Bad news," she said, to which immediately Havrshyk complained, "I thought you said great news?"

Her wings twitched in response, and she pointed that finger at him again. "Quiet you, we're busy." He sulked, and leaned against the wall, as Clair faced Fryn and Alyra. "Unfortunately, I couldn't convince Ieffin to come *here*, but he was more than willing to visit the main estate and do a tasting there. Everyone knows he likes Sceppe."

"I thought he liked Ceren," Havrshyk supplied, not-so-helpfully.

"He likes Sceppe too," Clair replied over her shoulder, and refocused on her audience. "Which means, that tonight, he will be within arm's reach. You can ask for his help or simply say 'hi' and all in the safety of the Snow District."

"It's not that safe," Fryn found herself saying, despite herself, "there was that one time you got poisoned."

Clair pouted at that but recovered quickly. "Anyway, the Estate is on the northern side of the west arc of the Ringroad, right across from Jenseln's Boutiques. Don't go in there, she's a real gossip, and it will ruin any chance of your meeting the prince in peace."

Fryn knew the place; she'd gone there as a child, with Pyran, to look at all the old-fashioned chandeliers and candelabras that no one needed anymore with the advent of 'affordable' starlamps. Pyran had peered through the shelves, looked through the arms of candlesticks like binoculars, and filled the dusty, but somehow ornate, building with her careless laughter. The memory was, perhaps, another reason not to go.

"…I must return to let my family know. They'll be ecstatic, and furious at the same time… have so much to prepare…" Clair was saying, looking about for her scarf, which hung loosely around her neck. Alyra reached out and lifted up one of the ends with a smirk.

"Looking for this?" she asked.

"Ah… yes…" Clair fastened it tightly around her neck, and swung the other tail over her shoulder, and flitted to the door. "Well then, see you!" She waved and was gone.

Fryn shook her head when the door creaked open and went over to close it properly. "Well, I know where it is, but we need to take a roundabout way to get there. The Ringroad is too obvious, too direct."

Havrshyk sighed. "The quickest way would be to fly toward the eastern gate and then cut across the North Cardinal. There is some risk, but we would only see one checkpoint."

He was revealing too intimate a knowledge of the city, Fryn thought, and she glanced over at Alyra, who nodded sagely in agreement. If she knew Leif better, she'd be surprised… but fortunately, she didn't, and she wasn't.

The city had changed a lot since Havrshyk's time, she knew, but at least the Snow District was as much of a fixture as the snow—it had remained the least affected by time, except for the Palace itself. She remembered what she'd learned when she still lived with her clan in the Pine District, how they had been almost considered non-citizens, how they were not protected, until the Pine-Martin had stepped in.

In their recent history, they'd had a long period of isolation, and decay, but Eljaren, her uncle, had fought for their involvement in city policies, and opening up reputable businesses in the Pine District. Now, it was up to Harissa to hold the crescent together and keep them from being disenfranchised like the Sky District had been.

Alyra buttoned her long-tailed coat closed and tugged tightly on her fur-lined gloves. The hilts of her daggers stuck out at the small of her back, glittering almost like an extra pair of wings, and she hummed a strange melodic tune. "We had better fly on then," she said, straightening up from where she'd finished redoing her laces.

"I am already prepared," Havrshyk stated tiredly, somehow repressing a yawn.

Fryn sniffed. "Then let's go."

They all muttered a quiet bit of thanks to their host on their way out, hoping not to wake him, and for the first time in two days—except Alyra of course—they stood out in the morning sun. The ground was clear of snow, but the air held a crispness to it that Fryn recognized as the exact temperature that water should start to freeze. Only Alyra's breath fogged, since Havrshyk and Fryn were already conserving their blood, and were in a partially-drained state. They stood on a spur of road that had jutted eastward from the lesser ringroad, the Vineroad, and all around the area, chimneys from the offices and warehouses announced that the warehouse and clerical staff were hard at work. No one walked or flew about, probably because the workday had begun just a half an hour before.

Fryn could smell the rich acrid scent of the coal used in the furnaces, different from the peat-fires they'd seen in Fassen. They weren't that far apart, a few weeks distance, but the elevation and the latitude changed a lot. Havrshyk cracked his knuckles, and stretched his fingers like a musician, and looked purposefully toward the west, over the arc of buildings separating them from the gate. "What is he anyway?" he asked softly, of no one in particular.

A few seconds passed with only the stiff breeze blowing in their faces, until Alyra shivered and let out a loud '*brr*.' "At the moment my greatest concern is finding the nearest fire."

Though she had long forgotten what it was like to enjoy or require the warmth of a fire, Fryn still enjoyed the color and the wavering light that it put out; to some degree she still considered it a comfort, even if being around a fire tended to be sweltering, and eventually unwelcome. Just a month ago… well just last season, she'd discovered some of that old warmth again, when she'd inadvertently poured herself into Leif's veins to save his life—his blood had not been taken, but had become acclimated to hers, and she had used his more than once in a pinch. It was vibrant, iron-rich, and prickled in her veins, but was the closest she'd ever been to understanding what it was like to appreciate a fire.

In the face of Havrshyk's glacial blood, and colder mood, she wasn't about to agree to seeking out the nearest hearth, but… she wondered if perhaps Leif might melt him too. After all, it was predominantly Leif's blood that formed the blade now, which once had held his soul.

The roads were empty, most everyone having already arrived at their offices. A few stragglers walked leisurely, not like the lifeless and malaise-infected nobles of the Snow District, but with the measured, purpose-driven pace of the Rain District's middle class. A runner flew by them on the road, paying them no mind, wearing the deep green of the Guldhand Wine Company, and in his black-gloved hand he gripped a leather satchel, likely containing some important news… probably about the Yardall's imminent meeting with the prince.

They started down the arc and took the next intersecting alley to the Rain Ringroad and found that the unendurable silence continued even that far into the city. The clear sky promised a biting chill, and some fresh frost continued to grow in spidery webs across the pebble stones. Alyra breathed slowly, deeply, in and out as they trudged, not wanting to waste any of their energy, saving their wings in case they needed to fight, or flee.

A half-hour walk brought them to the East Cardinal, and the gate, where they encountered the first groups of fee and fae wandering or standing importantly at their posts. The wall separating the Snow District from the rest of the city was cut from much larger stones than the outer rings, carved out of the mountainous hill to create the level district itself. It was nearly fifty wingspans high, so that no one could fly over conveniently, and it was graced with periodic starlamps that illuminated the wall and the road below. Unlike the walls around the Crown District, it did not have towers—those were a recent addition following the Stanaedre Coup.

Fryn adjusted her cloak and pulled her hood down a little lower. She hoped they wouldn't be too noticeable.

The guards, yawning at the start of their shifts, stood too stiffly in their creamy blue uniforms. Their decorative silver armor was polished to perfection, but their inattentiveness, and disinterest in their surroundings tarnished the shining image they were meant to portray. One leaned on his silver lance, eyes tracking a fee in a pretty dress, while the other one sipped a cup of tea—his lance leaning against the wall. Neither took notice of the renegade Hunters. The banded pinewood gates were half-closed, which meant that their entry would be difficult, even if the guards were distracted.

Alyra simply walked up to them, shivering, as she caught the attention of the lecherous young fae with an affected call. "Hello there!" Alyra said, rubbing her arms to stay warm, "I think I have gotten lost. I was just going out for a walk, but I can't find my way back to my hotel."

The fae straightened up a bit, smiling as her foreign accented registered and he examined her attractive dress and coat. He scratched his cheek as he glanced away, not meeting her eyes for more than a second. "Good morning my lady, where are you staying? Would you like an escort?"

The tea-sipping guard ignored them, reaching down to a simple brown teapot he'd left by his boot, and pouring another cup.

Alyra blushed effectively and stifled a laugh. "Oh no, I just need to know whether to go right or left. It was on the Snow Ringroad."

The guards shared a look, and the one with the tea asked, "Was it the one with the needle, or the finch on the signboard?"

She gave him an uncertain look, wings going limp behind her back, shifting so that the hilts of her daggers were hidden.

The first one took her hand, and Fryn frowned at that—such behavior would never be accepted by most fee in Frorin—and he led Alyra through the gate to the road beyond, as he helpfully scanned the view to the north and the south. "Do you see anything you recognize?"

She let out a small groan, as she creatively freed her hand and crossed her arms, pouting. "Nothing..."

The second guard followed them, and he offered her a cup of tea, as he patted her shoulder and suggested she examine the Crown District to see which side of the palace she had been facing and figure out which way to go from there.

She sniffed, looking over her shoulder, through the door, at Fryn and Havrshyk, as she drank her tea. Her wings gave a single beat.

Havrshyk nodded, and slipped across the square, and through the door, and Fryn was right behind him. Together they hid in the guard post, waiting for Alyra to be free of the guards.

The flirting guard looked pointedly at the hand that the other one had left on Alyra's shoulder. She stared at the palace and thought for a minute before she finally nodded, and said, "I think I was more behind it, that way!" She pointed northwards up the ring.

"The Proud Finch then," the guards said in unison. "Are you sure you don't need one of us to accompany you?"

She shook her head, smiling. "I am quite safe behind these walls," she said, "Thank you for your help, and for the tea!" She gave them a proper curtsy and then started down the road to the north.

The guards watched her go for a bit, and finally returned to their posts. The guard who'd been flirting, took the empty teacup that Alyra had used, and purposefully refilled it.

Fryn swallowed.

Havrshyk sighed.

The other guard did too. "Well, now I am out of tea. I'll go brew a fresh pot."

Fryn and Havrshyk, hiding in the inside part of the gate, where the guards waited during night watches while the doors were closed, were right next to the stove. Steam was still rising from the spout of the kettle from its last boil. They flew out, and wingbursted up the road into an alley, turning around and watching as the guard walked slowly in and settled at the table to measure out his tea.

"That wasn't so hard," Alyra announced behind them.

Fryn spun, Bloodknife in her hand as she drained and then relaxed. She'd snuck up on them, as if she'd only been a stray breeze. "Careful Alyra, my reflexes are only quick to start, but slow to stop a strike."

Havrshyk frowned at her and stood. "I did not realize you were so good at acting."

Alyra gave him a smile, and then walked a ways down the alley. "I just knew what they wanted to see. Now, Fryn, I don't know the city too well from here on in, but I am guessing we keep going North."

Sheathing her knife again, Fryn took a breath and walked over to the other end of the alley. "I will lead the way..."

Their trek brought them down an alley behind a carpenter's shop, where the sounds of hammering, chiseling, and cursing echoed from the alley-side workrooms. Fryn almost wished they could see what kind of craftsmanship they sold, but they had other, more pressing concerns. By taking such a roundabout route, they hoped to avoid any prowling Hunters that may be in town. Her blood supply was still extremely low though she had eaten something; it would take days of rest and food to rebuild her full strength without draining fresh blood—that was out of the question. Killing the Hunter in Gaerlin gnawed at her and she didn't want to kill again.

"At least it's clean," Alyra muttered, scanning the sides of the back alley they explored. "Most roads like this are littered with... well... litter, or worse."

"Most," Havrshyk agreed, "in the other districts of Frorin you'd find that too, but here, there is the Street-cleaners' Union."

"You're pretty knowledgeable," Alyra said, sounding impressed, "Fryn, you must be proud of your hometown."

Town? "Of course," Fryn replied coolly, "it *is* the capitol of Froreholt after all."

"Of course," she allowed, "though there are some who are *not* proud of their heritage."

Fryn didn't agree. Even in Fassen, the Waverly both resented and treasured their identity and history, even the bad. "Are you proud of your hometown?" She asked instead.

Alyra hopped over a patch of hardened ice. "Yes," she said, uncertainly, "even though I am not able to return there."

Fryn nodded. Up ahead the alley curved, following the arc of the wall, and they increased their speed as the roads nearby grew quieter and less traveled. Mid-morning, Fryn had suspected would be one of the quietest times of day, when the industrious had already gone by and the indolent hadn't yet gotten out of bed. She'd been right... but still, she found herself draining more than usual, holding her breath, nervously scanning the alleyways that linked up with the Ringroad every block.

After fifteen minutes or so, Alyra, who had taken the lead, stopped suddenly so that Fryn ran right into her, and they nearly stumbled to the ground—only stopped by Havrshyk's quick thinking and a steadying hand.

"What's wrong?" Fryn asked.

She shushed them and stepped behind a few stacked crates. "There are Hunters straight ahead…"

They followed her into the shadows, and peered between the cracks, watching as a duo of Hunters trotted out a side lane and paused at the opening to the Inner Alley. They were young, a fee and a fae, one resting a silver lance over his shoulder, while the other rested her hand on the hilt of her short-sword. They wore matching uniforms of brown and green, and Fryn wondered if perhaps, the Commission had started outfitting its Hunters to be more recognizable for the Guards. They chatted amiably, though she couldn't hear what they said, but she remembered when only a month ago she and Leif had chased after their first mark in what had turned out to be more than just a partnership.

She frowned. The two novice Hunters had turned right and were walking in the direction they needed to go.

"Well, that bites it," Havrshyk snorted under his breath, "unless you want to fight them."

She raised her eyebrows at him. "No, we'll go around." Fryn adjusted her hood and cloak, so that her face was shadowed, and she nodded to Alyra and Havrshyk. "Let's go back on the lane they came from, and circle past them on the main road."

"I didn't expect more Hunters," Havrshyk complained, "Didn't used to be that many here."

She swept around the crates and silently darted down the lane, checking both sides of the street before she rejoined the Ringroad. It wasn't far from the North Cardinal, and it *would* be better to cross it farther from the Crown Guards' checkpoint at the north gate. Maybe they'd been lucky after all? It *was* odd though, that even as Ieffin increased the number of, and improved the training and armaments of the Guard, the Hunters had done the same. It couldn't all be because of *them*, they were footnotes compared to the real villains… unless some of those real villains happened to have their fingers in the Commission's threads… in which case, it wouldn't be absurd for Leif and Fryn to be considered 'extremely dangerous rogue elements'.

They left the rookies behind, and emerged onto the Snow Ringroad, keeping to the inner curve of the curb as they walked the empty street, trying not to look suspicious since they were the only ones around. Anyone could glance out a window and remember them. No one should be out in midmorning, not for another hour at least.

Rounding the road to the North Cardinal, they crossed the street without being accosted, and resumed their course on the southward arc of the wall-side alley that they'd recently had to abandon because of the Hunters and Guards. This side of the city was cleaner even than the east side, as behind all the offices and warehouses they passed, it was immediately evident that the streets were swept, scrubbed, and washed regularly. The air held the stale tang of vinegar, and Fryn recalled that the area was the most highly concentrated stretch of wineries, distilleries, and breweries on the Vineroad. Hops, malt, and the strangely acrid, bland scent of yeast filled the back alleys, and Fryn nodded as she recognized the loading-dock signboard of the Guldhand Company Winery, as well as the iconic Buzzed-Wasp Brewery, a brand whose name she'd heard often, but had never tried. Malt beers, lagers, and honey wine were their specialty, they'd said, but for some reason, Fryn had never cared enough to order anything from them—interesting label aside, which was painted crisply in black and yellow, on their signboard opposite the Guldhand one, depicting a wasp wobbling, perhaps falling, from its perch on a keg of ale.

They only took two steps past the loading dock, when Fryn felt a chill creep up her spine. It was darker than it should have been, and she noticed a few crates that had been stacked farther into the alley than the others. Alyra held back, refusing to follow, as Havrshyk, uncaring, strode forward—ignorant of the sense of danger that the other two had perceived—or maybe, he didn't care.

He continued beyond the crates, exuding a sense of disinterest, as he turned to face them, gesturing for them to follow with a lazy wave of his hands and a flick of his wings. A blurred form darted from behind one of the crates, invisible in the shadowed lane, as Havrshyk drew his sword and caught the black, oiled sword of his attacker with a feigned expression of surprise. Fryn rushed to join him, but no other attackers appeared, and though she wanted to cry out, she bit her lip and looked away as Havrshyk lowered his stance, angled the attacker's sword back, and flicked it out of his wrist.

He leaned in, the tip of his Bloodsword even darker than the oiled steel that clattered to the ground, pressed against the skin of the attacker's throat, waiting, not yet drawing blood. "Who are you?" he asked softly, bending over the stranger in black, who slumped, and fell backwards to the ground… fainting, or a feint, possibly.

Havrshyk knelt beside him, blade across his neck, as he pulled back the hood and looked at his face. He was a young fae, probably only seventeen, or eighteen, and wiry with curly black hair. Fryn noticed a chain around his neck, and tugged on it, revealing a dark green pendant with four white wings spreading outwards from a thorny crown.

Alyra raised her eyebrows at that, and muttered something under her breath, but Fryn knew what it was, and she met Havrshyk's eyes to see if he did too. He didn't seem to care.

"We'll drain him, and leave him over there," he decided, pointing to the crates behind which the stranger had been hiding, "can't very well leave him alive." He changed his grip and pointed his sword at the kid's heart.

Fryn grabbed his wrist and shoved the sword away. "No," she hissed, "it's not right! It's bad enough we have to run like criminals, I don't want it to be true!"

"You saw it, Fryn," he whispered, "He's Cherim. The Immortal Queen never stops her chase, unless you leave no tracks."

"A body leaves tracks that are more obvious. Perhaps he's after someone else, and chose us by mistake…"

Alyra watched them carefully, quiet for a few moments before she blinked and turned on her heel. "He's waking, we should go."

Havrshyk tugged his arm back, preparing to stab their attacker again, but Fryn shook her head, and simply stood, dragging him back by the other arm. "We're in a hurry, let's just go," she said, "still a long way to go, and not much time."

He grudgingly allowed her to pull him away, and they continued at a quick pace, flying past the intersections, to avoid being seen as they went.

Alyra coughed into her hand, shivering as they paused in the alley of a building a couple blocks away from the fae. "What are Cherim?" she asked innocently.

Fryn and Havrshyk shared a look.

Their companion averted her eyes and shoved her hands into the pockets of her coat. "I think some things will not remain hidden for long, such as how little I know of your country… and such things as that fae in the Stone Market."

A door opened across the street, but fortunately, the fee exiting the residence was looking and walking in the opposite direction.

"Yes..." Havrshyk agreed. "What was he?"

"He was a Moraskyn fae," Fryn quipped, "They have six wings, haven't you heard of them?"

He frowned. "I know *where* Moraskyr is," he replied, shifting his wings; the snakelike continents to the southwest of their homeland was one of the remotest lands known to be inhabited. There was no contact, except for the rare stories of the engineers of Stanaedre who had taken an airship out to sea, and who'd been blown far off course in a storm. The stories had been confirmed a few times, but no one had heard of a Moraskyn making the journey until now.

Fryn pursed her lips. "Alyra, what are your daggers made of?"

She went pale at that, glancing over her shoulder as if looking for an escape. "They were cut," she said cryptically, "when I was exiled."

"What were cut?" Aldyr asked.

"My wings." She gave him a surprised look, as if wondering why they weren't recoiling in disgust.

"That does explain why you have trouble flying," Fryn said, "but it doesn't explain how they turned into daggers."

She rolled her eyes momentarily, before thinking better of it. "How did your blood become a dagger, Fryn?"

Fryn closed her mouth. She didn't have a clear answer to that either. It had been an instinctual process, that happened in a moment of extreme danger. She nodded slowly.

Havrshyk looked torn. "So why are they chasing you?"

"It is a long story," she said, "but the main reason they were not content with exile is because I killed the one who cut off my wings before retreating here. They were going to keep them, but I was not going to let that happen." She smiled, shrugging with her wings. "So that is why they are trying to kill me. It was a huge embarrassment when I killed him, but the theft of the wingshards, well, it is the most valuable resource in the world."

"Resource?"

She pulled them further into the alley as another door opened on their side of the street and another fae stepped out. "Do you think a fae with a gravity affinity could have caused such destruction unless his power had been magnified in some way? That *pelitoné* is a wingbreaker, the worst kind. He doesn't use his own wings but steals that power from others."

Something didn't add up about that, but Fryn was beginning to feel a chill, a sense of ominousness that weighed on her, and caused the hairs on her neck to stand up. At the end of the alley they were hiding in, away from the main road, Fryn saw the silhouette of a tall fae entering the alley and turning away from them. Frost climbed up her skin, and she felt her clothing stiffen from the alarm that was growing inside her. Havrshyk and Alyra didn't seem to notice, and as the time slowed to a crawl, she recognized him, his misshapen wings, his marrowy Bonesword in his only hand, and she could feel the edge of his awareness as if he were turning his head in her direction.

Without thinking, she grabbed the other two, and pulled them into the hollow of a side door that faced into the alley, giving them a low 'shh' as she pressed them back into alcove as far as possible.

All three of them held their breath.

The street was silent, except for the heavy footsteps of Grifton, as he trodden down the alley towards the main road.

Havrshyk focused his blood into his sword, Fryn did the same, and Alyra closed her eyes, as if imagining that she wasn't there at all. Oddly, Fryn realized, that seemed to work, as Alyra's body seemed to avoid her direct eyesight, and she instead felt her gaze sliding over her to notice the door, or the wall instead.

Havrshyk ground his teeth, and Fryn just waited, as he got closer, and closer, and so close that he was about to see them—until he stopped. A voice called from behind him.

"Francis!" came the voice, smooth and articulate.

A hush fell over the alley. The only sound was Grifton grinding his teeth. "Jeldon, I've told you before not to call me by that name." His rebuke was biting, and Fryn could almost feel the newcomer shrinking back.

Jeldon's voice wavered a bit as he replied, "Ah, yes, you have... Grifton... I found this strange fae snooping just one street down."

A grunt sounded as another faerie was thrown forward to the ground.

Grifton hummed. "What of him?"

The newcomer laughed awkwardly. "He took a swipe at me with this..."

A moment of silence passed.

"It looks familiar," Grifton allowed.

Jeldon's laugh was even more strained than before. "You should recognize it. This sword is of Cherim make. He's even wearing the winged crown medallion."

"This runt?" Grifton asked, and in a moment there was the sound of the air being pushed out of someone's lungs as he addressed the fae. "Sent out here to hunt Liches?"

A weak reply answered him. "Yes, sir, she will not rest while any walk the land."

He growled.

"I'll not let anyone get in the way of my revenge," he growled, and a slick crunching and squelching sound followed as they heard him stab the boy with his Bonesword.

The strange gurgling and squelching continued for long enough, that Fryn pushed against her fear, so that she could peer around the edge of the doorway.

Grifton had impaled the boy on his sword, lifting him into the air, over his head. His wings twitched, and the sword writhed with marrow-like whips that squirmed and stabbed through each of the boy's flailing limbs, pulsing as if it were drinking his bones. He shrank, only able to emit one strangled scream, as his body was absorbed into Grifton's blade, and a skeletal arm formed from the pit of his orphaned shoulder.

The newcomer, Jeldon, Fryn guessed, stared in horror, transfixed, and he backed away nervously.

With one sweeping motion of his sword hand, Grifton tossed the empty clothes and pendant to the drain and turned.

Fryn ducked back into the doorway, closing her eyes, and hoping he wouldn't look their way.

He tromped closer, and closer, and closer. She held her breath, trusting that whatever Alyra was doing would spread to them, making them less visible than before, as he drew even with them.

And stopped.

"Jeldon," he said tiredly, bones clinking in his newly formed hand. "Don't linger. I will need your spear when we corner them."

He gave an audible gulp, and followed, asking hesitantly, "Are you sure they will be in the Snow District?"

Grifton continued out onto the street, adding over his shoulder, "Mostly sure. Those two always went to the powerful. I am sure they will try to get her king to help them. But... he has no idea what the Commission is about to do to them. What it tried to do before."

Havrshyk twitched beside her.

"What's that?" Jeldon asked.

"The continent only needs one king." With that, they got far enough away that she couldn't really hear them.

All three of them slumped to the ground, breathing hard, trying not to look in the direction where the boy who'd attacked them, had been dissolved into nothing.

A minute or two of slow deep breaths calmed her enough that she snuck out to check the alley's drain. The boy's ruined tunic and trousers were mostly stuffed down the grate, but the pendant had bounced off one of the bars and rested on the stones. The oiled blade was gone. Perhaps the other Hunter, Jeldon, had taken it.

Looking back over her shoulder, she saw Alyra and Aldyr giving her concerned looks, so she pocketed the medallion, and went back to them. "I don't like it, but we can't leave any clues like that lying around."

Alyra smiled, probably realizing that it was less caution that drove her to do it, but a sense of sympathy. "These Cherim, they are from the rain forest, yes? Why do they hate liches?"

Fryn returned her smile, if one without dimples. "I only know the old stories, Alyra. The same myths that say that Fora, as we call Cherim, was jealous of another fee, and was the first one to kill another faerie. She was not pleased when the one she killed came back as a lich and had become impossible to kill. I imagine, if it really is the same fee, and not a descendant, that she cannot abide the embarrassment of such a reminder in the form of other Liches. Or, she doesn't want the competition of another immortal being."

"It's a shame she doesn't include whatever *he* was in her hit list," she said, shaking her head. "Immortality is the subject of many legends, even in my homeland. The path to it varies, I think. The pursuit of it is what first caused the study of wingbreaking in our lands. We call it "soul-burning"."

They fell silent.

Fryn wasn't sure how to respond to that. But it bore some similarities to the legends she'd heard about the Wingless Cult, and their absurd elemental powers.

It was not safe to move right away, what with the Hunters patrolling so nearby, so Fryn settled on the ground near the drain, and waved Alyra over.

"Alyra, they do not know of you, and I believe it will be more difficult to reach our destination during the day. Go to the Yardall Estate, just another block or two westward, and inform the prince and Clair that we will be arriving later."

She was nodding seriously, but before she could leave, Havrshyk scratched his chin, and sighed.

"Don't go Alyra. Fryn, I know of another way, but I think it bears explaining our quest in a little more detail." He pointed with his sword at the drain where the Cherim boy's clothes had been discarded. "You see, I am not Leif Aellin, but am the Lich whose blade he stole." He helpfully presented the sword, pointing with his other hand at its blackened red depths. "Leif Aellin is in here."

Her eyes widened.

"We are after my body, and when I have that again, we will go our separate ways—in the meantime though, I can guide us through the storm drains," he explained, lifting the lid of the drain with the tip of his Bloodsword.

"Havrshyk," Fryn said in a low tone, "didn't you hear what Grifton said?"

He shrugged.

"Fryn, my loyalty to the king died when I was put in that crypt. Perhaps I should have simply let myself fall, and the king die, but I am not going to be bound to this city any longer. Nor am I going to remain bound to you." He dropped into the shallow storm drain, and crouched, waiving them in. "Now come along, these drains are quite confining and I do not like tight spaces."

Fryn shook her head and climbed in, followed soon after by Alyra, who then closed the drain. It was lined with a layer of frost, and cut with sharp square stones, the channel was just wide enough and deep enough that they could crouch or crawl and continue in a straight line along the alley toward the ringroad. It was somehow a comforting thing, crawling on hands and knees, her wings brushing the ceiling, as they avoided the busy road above. It was getting late enough now that the city began to bustle, and wagons rolled overhead less than a wingspan away.

Looking back, Fryn could see the concern in Alyra's eyes whenever one of the wagons rolled over them, but it was not a wide road. In a minute, they were near the center of it, and the channel intersected a wider drain that curved with the road. In the place where the drains met, a pit shot straight down, into unknown depths.

Havrshyk carefully crawled over it and took a turn onto the curve. "Don't fall down there; these drains are designed to funnel rainwater out of the base of the city during a storm, and they lead into a branch of the Artell River. More than a few bodies, or dissidents have been disposed of in that way."

Fryn avoided looking down.

"Frorin seemed like such a lovely town," Alyra muttered, "dissidents..."

Havrshyk frowned but continued crawling. "Times were different then," he replied, "the Crown had a lot more enemies, and far fewer friends."

"They have a lot less power now than before," Fryn said, "a great many responsibilities have been given to the Assembly, and the powers of the Crown have reduced because of such things. When the Swordhand Palm was dissolved, the people were afraid of having a government that was too powerful, and so the pressure to rely on the Commission increased. It's odd how that's become a very different sort of problem for them now."

"It's natural," Havrshyk huffed but didn't add to his statement.

For a long while they followed the Vineroad and were just getting to one of the corners where a radial road led off toward the Yardall estate, when Havrshyk held up a hand, and moved back a hair from the direct view of the grate. He held a finger over his mouth and pointed up.

Heavy footfalls sounded in the stones, followed by muffled voices.

One of them, Fryn recognized as Jeldon, Grifton's new companion. "...have to deal with the city guard one more time, I'll kill myself... need a drink..."

Another fae answered him, but not one she knew. "Can't find a decent ale in this city for Jakaren's sake, that 'bee's ass' beer tasted just like it too."

Jeldon snorted. "Bee's ass? That's too kind, Hatha," he spat into the drain, right onto Havrshyk's hand, and continued, "I'd think it was more like drinking the swamp water in Capholt."

Havrshyk growled beneath his breath, draining into a full Lichform. Fryn put a hand on his shoulder, holding him back, as she shook her head firmly.

"What's got you shattered, Jeldon?" The newcomer asked overhead. It sounded like he was chewing on seeds, or something. "Yer hands're shakin'."

He gave a hmph and moved from foot to foot. "It's Grifton. Everything about him makes my skin crawl, Hatha, he almost dissolved me earlier... I didn't know such monsters could exist, you know?"

Alyra sneezed quietly, and she covered her mouth, as Fryn and Havrshyk shot her angry looks. It was soft enough the two hunters above might not notice... but of course, they were never that lucky.

Jeldon jumped at the sound, as he tapped the ground with the butt of his spear, and muttered, "Did you hear that?"

"Jumping at nothing now?" Hatha asked with a cruel laugh. "It's a street Jeldon, there's faeries walking about everywhere."

"It sounded close..." Jeldon insisted, tapping his boot idly on the grate. Havrshyk scooted further back.

"Yer paranoid, Jeldon." Hatha mumbled something else, but his voice grew quieter as his footsteps led him away. Jeldon moved about anxiously before following him in a rush.

They waited in the cold, cramped tunnel for several minutes before climbing out, just to be sure they would be out of sight.

Alyra whispered an apology, but Fryn and Havrshyk didn't respond to it. They crawled out of the grate one-by-one, ducking into the shadow of a nearby alley; so close to their goal.

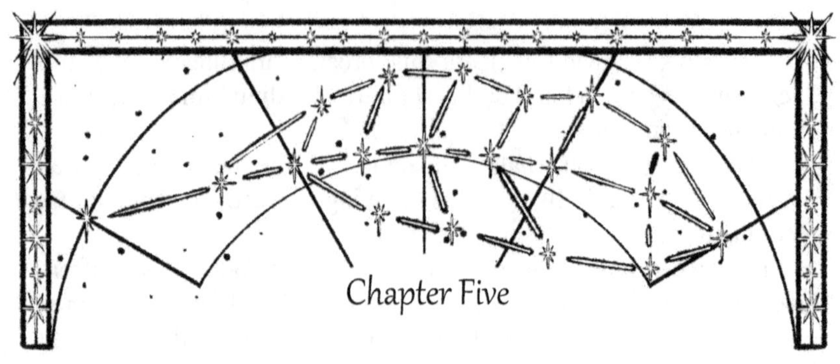

Chapter Five

FEATHER

Frorin

Snow District: Yardall Sceppe Estates

Fryn

An hour of careful dodging around citizens, and one more near miss with Grifton, brought Fryn around a corner, and into the courtyard of Clair's estate. The main entrance was watched by a dutiful doorfae, so she followed the side of the building to the back doors near the kitchens and slipped inside. Havrshyk closed the door after Alyra, scanning the hallway with his eyes narrowed. It was dark.

Clair and Ieffin were either saving on candles and starlamps or had purposefully dimmed them for effect.

"I haven't had to crawl in those tunnels for seventy years," Havrshyk mused, sliding his Bloodsword into its sheath at its side, "Last time I was only depositing a body, not trying to avoid becoming one."

"Lovely," Fryn said, "Everything you tell me about that time period makes me grateful things have changed." She stepped forward, glancing back just in time to see Havrshyk's wings flick and his face darken.

"You kid yourself if you believe the Crown of today is any different," he said, avoiding meeting her eyes.

She pursed her lips and folded her wings. "Perhaps this next meeting will change your mind."

The Estate was quiet, save for the muffled notes of a harp further down to their right, where the long hallways stretched with closed doors, and barely-lit walls decorated in alder paneling, crown molding, and shadowed portraits.

Alyra looked at Fryn with a hesitant frown. "Before we go any further," she said, "I think there is something I should tell you."

Havrshyk looked down the hall toward the music, and the soft laughter.

"And what is that, Alyra?" Fryn asked her, crossing her arms. "We are not troubled going about with an exile. We are somewhat on-the-wing ourselves."

Aldyr nodded and smiled shyly. "I have been exiled from the other side of the world... but there is someone else who was exiled before that I must find at the expense of all else. Where he has gone, I have found, and that through two years of hardship, can only be reached by airship."

Fryn lifted an eyebrow. "And we are supposed to help you with that?"

"In Fassen, you worked with the Earl quite closely, if what I heard was accurate, and his butler Vinellin, right?"

"We did," she admitted.

Alyra laced her fingers together and looked away. "I need his help getting to Elin."

"Elin?" Havrshyk asked incredulously. "That's almost as far away from here as Moraskyr!"

She gave him a sharp look, as if reminding him to speak softly—since they hadn't announced themselves to Clair and Ieffin yet. "It is indeed, Havrshyk," she replied, "and that is one of the reasons I want to go there.

Fryn shook her head, amused. "So, this other exile, why is he important?"

She looked at her feet, as if preparing her words in her head and translating them before she spoke. "My family has always served the... we followed..." She scrunched up her face as she fought to find the right words.

Fryn put a hand on her arm encouragingly, nodding for her to continue.

Alyra muttered under her breath, words unrecognizable in the Fhoran common tongue, *"aleshalyn,"* *"lemorass,"* and finally she looked up and said, "I am the guardian of Hyne, the heir of the Leshal—the ruling clan of Mora."

"And this 'Hyne' was exiled to Elin?" Havrshyk asked, raising an arched eyebrow at her.

"Not exactly. He fled before the Apetin bastard could kill him, so they called it an exile. Those…" Alyra took a deep breath. "Those like him, the one who tried to kill me, cannot go to Elin. It is too far. I am not sure how he found me here. After we get this body back from the prince. I want you to introduce me to the butler. In return, I will help you fight against the…" she shuddered, even her small opalescent wings shivering, "the strange monster who hunts you."

Havrshyk sighed but instead of complaining, he set his jaw and nodded. "I was planning on going my own way after this Fryn, but… I will not ignore her plight. If you and Leif want to escort her to Fassen, or even if you don't, I will help her." He shook his head, turned on his heel, and walked down the hallway into the light.

"But…" Alyra said, "once he is back in his body and Leif is free, why would he help me?"

Fryn wondered the same thing. Was it suspicious or was there something there…deeper than his bitterness, something underneath leftover from an earlier time when he had been more…noble? Deep down, Fryn was beginning to suspect that Havrshyk was still an honorable fae even if he had been driven by the desire for revenge for a long time. "I'd hoped with your ability to read faeries you could help me understand him, Alyra," was all she said, "now come along. I am certain Leif will want to help you and if he hesitates, well, he'll want to help me."

Havrshyk's heartbeat accelerated as he drew up near the entrance to the next room. Fryn could sense the conflict within him by the pressure in his veins. His face twisted, caught between two desires. Freedom, and something else. A lingering sense of loyalty?

Havrshyk drew his Bloodsword and walked out into the room beyond.

The first sound other than a harp was a sharp, bitter laugh, that was punctuated by the gloating giggle of Clair. "…can't forget to play a fifth prime…!" she chided.

As he walked into the reflected light of a fire, Fryn waved Alyra over and they entered the room after him together.

"You needn't be so competitive, Clair," Ieffin admonished in his bright and cheerful tenor voice, so clear, lacking the repressed sorrow she'd remembered. "Shouldn't you be letting me win?"

"My prince," Clair answered with a laugh, "I don't think you'd like that either."

As they entered the parlor area where the game was being played, they were bathed in the warm false-fire of the stylized starlamp in the hearth. It cast shadows and flickering orange and yellow light across the table where the group sat laughing at the pile of cards on the golden oak table.

Clair lounged in a burgundy fall dress, with a modest cut at the neck, black and gold trimming, and a bell that flared out around her hips like maple leaves; her glacial flower perfume was delicate, but noticeable, and Fryn almost revisited a memory best left in the past... she repressed the shiver and memory together, as she focused on not recalling how she'd become a Lich.

Ieffin seemed to be enjoying himself despite the fact that he held the most cards in his hands and was obviously losing. The prince wore an honest and expansive smile, that set his white teeth off against his white suit with his pale blue cravat.

Their momentary joy faded, as they noticed the trio in the entrance to the hallway.

Havrshyk approached, his Bloodsword held in his hands, as if he meant to give it back to the prince. Fryn found a couple of chairs by the wall, and brought one to the table, inclining her head to Ieffin, and Clair with an honest, dimpled smile.

"It is good to see you again, my prince," she said, "and, of course, you too, Clair. This here is Alyra, she is from Moraskyr and has been a welcome addition to our cause."

Ieffin spoke, lowering his hand of cards, face down, in a fan on the table, with a frown. "I am glad, of course, to see the two of you alive... and more or less well... and just as well I am pleased to meet you, Alyra. Welcome to Frorin. Please be seated, we'll have a few more glasses brought in."

Clair's cheerfulness faded, as she nodded seriously. Ieffin's butler, whose name Fryn had forgotten, came rushing around the corner with a tray bearing a decanter of Sceppe and two more glasses: cut crystal with the logo of the Yardall Estate, proudly depicting a variant of the Lancer constellation, where he held a glass held out in toast.

"My prince," Fryn began, bowing her head, as the butler poured her a finger of Sceppe. "I wish the circumstances around our meeting were more ideal, however, we have need of your assistance."

Havrshyk sniffed, Bloodsword resting over his knees. He was polishing it with a cloth in one hand, even while holding his glass up in the other for the toast.

Ieffin smiled distantly. "I have heard of the efforts you expended to protect Savis in Fassen. If it is within my power, I will help you—but I must walk a thin line. The Commission has denounced you, and if my assistance to you is revealed, then I will either have to renounce you or them. You are just two, well three, faeries, and they are an international organization that channels, no, *controls*, the commerce of the entire continent."

"You don't like them," Havrshyk said with a sly smile.

Clair snorted, and then took a sip of her glass. "Everyone knows that, Leif."

"I am not Leif."

The room fell silent.

Havrshyk was still polishing the sword, and then with a smile that looked deep into it slowly shifting red depths, he met the prince's eyes. "I am Aldyr Havrshyk. Leif is in here," he explained, tapping the surface of the blade. "So, the request I am going to make of you is small, and will have minimal impact on your politics. *I want my body back.*"

Clair went white, setting her glass shakily on the table with a loud 'clack,' but Ieffin merely closed his eyes. He didn't seem too surprised, if a little disappointed.

"I should have known that it wasn't an easy thing to steal a Lich's blade." He shook his head and held out his glass for a refill. The stunned butler poured two fingers by accident and retreated behind the couch.

"Where is my body, Ieffin?" Havrshyk asked, "we searched the crypt, and it was gone."

He gave a chagrined smile at that. "Havrshyk, after Leif and Fryn left for the Harvest Festival, I read the accounts of your trial, and I was horrified. I do not consider it just, burying you like they did. I had your body moved because I wanted to give you a better burial. I suppose I should have made certain first that a burial was required."

As Fryn lifted her glass and smelled its contents, she detected a hint of Fassen peat, and took a sip, chewing it, savoring its smoke and rich malt. The alcohol bore no heat, and it didn't flare into her wings or cheeks. Excellence in a bottle. She drank half of what she'd been poured without realizing it, but by then it was too late; she drained the rest and set the glass politely on the table next to the butler.

"We asked to see you," she said, glancing toward Havrshyk, who smiled in response, "not just because we need your help, but to offer you a warning."

Clair gave a concerned 'hmm' and uncrossed her legs, leaning forward to rest her elbows on her knees.

Ieffin scratched his chin, took a long sip of his Sceppe, and then tapped the glass for a refill. "Before you ask, Fryn, Froreholt has relied on the Commission to manage the criminal elements within our borders for a very long time, and many of our citizens have stored their funds within the Commission Bank. I cannot risk injuring the people for the sake of two friends... innocent or not."

"But what of your own safety?" Fryn interjected, "the Commission is not satisfied, and they are moving already to silence anyone who would get in the way of their plans."

"Plans?"

Havrshyk nodded. "If you read my trial, then you know what they once sought."

Ieffin frowned, wings folding as he looked into the false-fire, worry creasing his face.

"When Stanaedre was the guiding force of the Commission," Havrshyk continued, "they sought to control the land by removing our king and running the cities through their clerks. The Coup. They weren't going to crown a new king either. Their mercantile government was so decentralized, they were merely going to remove the laws and lawgivers and let the merchants do business as they pleased."

"One of the hunters who is after us said that the Commission is going to remove the kings... that means you," Alyra added, "it sounds a lot like what happened before."

The prince groaned. "Just what I needed. First Savis' engagement is canceled, now the Commission stages another coup, and I have barely even begun organizing my own forces."

"The Lancers?" Fryn asked, "I saw the armory in the Guardhouse. Are you really going to rebuild our military? After hundreds of years of peace... won't the other kingdoms see that as a threat?"

He shot her a stern 'who-are-you-to-question-me' look but softened. "They aren't ready. Half of those who train in the art of combat are recruited by the Commission, either as the bank's caravan guards, or hunters, or messengers—they have a monopoly on fighters. Those who are not good enough to obtain a license, or employment, usually opt to work for local cities, or teach at martial schools.

"Fryn, we are not ready for a confrontation with the Commission. Hunters are few, but they can subcontract any fighters for their defense."

Havrshyk nodded slowly.

"You want your body back," the prince said to him, "and you want protection from the Commission," he said to Fryn, "and you... what do you want?" he asked Alyra.

She set her glass down gently, bowing her head politely. "I do not need anything from you, your highness, but I do need help from Leif and Fryn to book passage to Elin."

Ieffin's eyes darted around as if he were organizing his thoughts across the surface of the table. "Then I have my price. Havrshyk, you once died to save my crown, and for that, I gave you burial beside Yndril in the hallowed graves of my ancestors, if I give you your body back, it will be for free. Debt repaid."

"Free?" Havrshyk scowled.

"I would make an additional bargain, if you'll listen." The prince gazed at him soberly.

"What is that?" Havrshyk asked, eyes narrowing suspiciously.

"Keep these two alive. As long as the Commission is after them, it buys me time to protect my people."

"What do I get out of this?"

Ieffin met his eyes. "What do you want?"

Clair whistled. Behind her, the butler gasped.

"Fryn is a powerful, and reliable ally, but you were once a Captain of the Guard, and are the last remaining member of the Swordhand-Palm. I know I can trust you." Ieffin's lips pressed closed in an anxious line, and he waited for Havrshyk's answer.

Havrshyk's hard expression softened as he gauged Ieffin's earnest eyes. Finally, he nodded slowly. "I don't know yet. But if I do as you say, I will hold you to your word."

The prince smiled. "That is acceptable. When you have your body back, we may be able to discuss it." He looked to Fryn and Alyra. "This land is going to be facing greater uncertainty and strife, I would ask you to find my sister and take her with you. Whatever happens to me, she is my successor, and she must survive."

"We will do it," they said at once.

Clair sighed as if a great weight had been lifted from her wings. "I actually have one more faerie I invited here tonight. A fee who had a matter of great urgency to speak with you about, Ieffin," she said, dropping the expected honorific.

Ieffin straightened in his seat as a side door opened, and they were joined by a fee in an elegant black dress with a violet scarf around her neck that set off the glossy sheen in her black hair. She rested her bone cane in the crook of her arm, and smiled warmly at them as she gestured for Ieffin to scoot further down the couch so she could sit down.

"Harissa?" Fryn asked, disbelieving, "why... or how... or what are you doing here?"

Harissa scoffed and invited the butler over with a crooked finger. "Get me a Juniper Star, butler," she ordered, and then returned her attention to the group. "Hello cousin," she said, "it was quite obvious when you came back to town. Why did you have to destroy the Stone Market?"

"It wasn't on purpose," Fryn said, "we were fighting for our lives!"

Clair added seriously, "They saved Terrin's life... he has worked for our family for decades and has always been as an uncle to me."

"Did you have to evaporate the city guard?" Harissa demanded, "Ieffin, I am surprised you haven't had them thrown out to the Hunters. Is there something I should know?" Without looking, she held out a hand and accepted a glass with an amber liquid and a frozen chunk of juniper berry instead of a block of ice. She took a sip while watching them with playful eyes.

"There is a lot we should know," Ieffin agreed, "but that topic had not come up yet. If we are ready, I will continue our earlier thread." He gave her a wry smile and fiddled with the chain of his pocket watch.

"How do we get there?" Havrshyk asked, tapping an idle rhythm into the surface of his blade, causing slow, undulating currents within.

"In a way you are fortunate that it is the Vine. Once a year, we commemorate Yndril's Passing, as you know. Traditionally, it has been a holiday celebrated only by my family and a few members of the nobility that we might invite, but something tells me that events are progressing in a dangerous direction, and we will require a powerful action on our part to preserve our kingdom."

Fryn frowned, sipping her drink. He hadn't really explained that thought, so she didn't interrupt.

"Yndril's Passing symbolizes the persistence, sacrifice, and the doubly earned rest of those who have refused to die when in a moment of terrible need. My mother used to say that they were preserved for times of great change. The Lich is not a symbol of the unholy, or of death, but is a symbol of salvation in the midst of most dire circumstances. That is why I moved your body there. I believed that you had lived and died for that rest, Havrshyk... but it appears that we are going to have to revisit that assumption."

Harissa frowned, giving him a confused and alarmed look. "Havrsh...who?" she muttered.

For his part, Havrshyk looked surprised. The king he'd given his life and death to save had imprisoned him as an abomination, but the prince he'd nearly killed had chosen to honor him. His wings shivered in discomfort. "Can't you simply tell us where it is?"

Alyra nodded, but the prince got a distant look in his eyes and let out a slow breath.

"No, I will not have you mucking about like a grave robber," he said cryptically, opening his balled-up hands and then removing his white gloves so he could examine a small tattoo. It was a lance, spearing a coin, and from the redness to his skin, it was recently applied.

It was similar to another symbol Fryn had seen before, when Ieffin had requested that they investigate the death of one of the members of the Grand Assembly... but that had been a dagger and a coin. She'd heard of it. She'd seen it... somewhere.

"No, I will invite those who can attend, commoner, or noble, and will remind our people who they are—and what is at stake—

and openly defy the Commission. If what you say is true, that they mean to take control of our lands, then I am not going to flit about pretending that I can trust them when I can't. I am going to side with you. Publicly."

With that, a hush fell over the group.

Havrshyk shifted restlessly in his seat. "Yndril's Passing is almost two weeks away; what are we supposed to do until then?" he asked.

Ieffin looked at Fryn with an ironic smile. "Do you remember what happened the last time you were on the run?"

She nodded slowly. "You closed us into the Crown District with a murder investigation to distract us."

Harissa snorted with a sharp laugh, and then covered it quickly.

Ieffin gave her a sharp look and then refocused on Fryn. "It was not without cause, Fryn, and the investigation was important. That attorney whose death you avenged, was building a case against the Commission—at my request. That case was going to finally give me the power to deny a renewing of their lease to operate in Froreholt. How interesting it is that he died at the hands of a "renegade" hunter."

Clair's eyes widened but she didn't interrupt.

"So, this time I am going to ask you to tempt them into revealing themselves."

"What?" Fryn blurted. "You want us to bait Grifton?"

The prince narrowed his eyes at her. "Well, yes, him and the other licensed hunters, surely the killers of the Venomsword can handle a few hunters?"

Harissa coughed lightly into her glove. "I might have something to add here, my prince. This does in fact relate a bit to the reason I requested an audience with you. I was surveying the Sky District when these hunters reached the gates. Two seemed capable enough, but the third, this Grifton, was something else entirely. I'd say he was even more terrifying and dangerous than a lich, misshapen, and sewn together from his own marrow. I could hardly call him alive... but his eyes burned with a singular intent."

The prince actually looked troubled at that. He scratched his chin and let out a deep breath. "Even so, I am going to ask. Fryn, Havrshyk, even if you cause just one altercation, and they endanger the city, I can put you in a heroic light, and cast them as untrustworthy invaders. That, immediately after what happened in the Stone Market, should be enough."

Fryn shared a dreading look with Havrshyk, but they both nodded. "I guess we can do that," Fryn said.

The prince smiled and waved his butler over to refill their drinks. "Excellent. Now Harissa, what is this business about, you in the Sky District?"

Harissa accepted a glass from the butler and hid a smile behind a sip. "The Stone Market was destroyed the other day... and I am bringing forward plans to rebuild it on the eastern shelf."

Clair raised an eyebrow at her, but only interrupted to say that she'd get some dinner brought in.

She likely sensed that Harissa had a number of things to discuss—Fryn couldn't complain either—she was quite hungry after their journey through the drains. She just hoped that she could forget the horrible image of Grifton dissolving the boy.

Fryn fiddled with her glass and accepted a refill of some Sceppe over an ice cube. Moraskyr, Elin, the Commission, and Grifton. So many things swirled around her so that she could not tell what direction to fly... except... in two weeks she would see Leif again. Somehow or another.

~Twelve Years Ago~

Frorin

Pine District

Fryn

The streets were as busy, and dirty as she recalled; weary, hard-working laborers and craftsfae marched by, half-pulling their hare-drawn wagons weighed-down by too much wood, or too many mushrooms. The heady smell of sweat, and smoke, mixed with the ringing of the copper-smith's hammer down the way, where he was likely forging something fancy to sell to those who lived within the inner rings.

The Pine Ringroad was a crescent, which only now struck Fryn as odd. She'd spent enough time in the Snow District, where it was impossible to get lost, where she could keep walking till she found her way home, but she had gotten lost within minutes of entering the Pine District.

Pyran took a few rushed steps ahead, wearing a bright-and-dark gray Sanhas, one of the stylized dresses designed by their school to allow formal attendance and martial prowess to blend into one. She wore it right-folded-over-left around her tiny waist with a deep-green sash tied into a tiny bow at the small of her back where her wings sprang out of the slits cut into an almost flower-shaped pattern around the bow. She giggled as the draping sections of her Sanhas swooshed around, revealing her matching trousers and green belt, where she'd clipped a silver pocket watch. (More for show than anything else, Fryn thought, since they didn't have anything scheduled later in the day.)

"It's so quaint down here, Fryn!" she exclaimed excitedly, "Is that *smoke*?"

Though Fryn smiled, Pyran frowned.

"You're not really happy here, are you?"

It wasn't that, but Fryn nodded. She'd realized long before, that she had two smiles, one honest, and one forced, and the only difference was whether her dimples showed. One started to form, but faded. "I'm not really happy anywhere, Pyran, though I'm glad that you came with me. It sounds odd now, impossible, to be unhappy yet glad."

Fryn smoothed the wrinkles that had formed in her Sanhas, a pale blue one, with a silver trim, that she'd been told set off her eyes. The problem, according to Pyran, was that Fryn was as masculine as a fee could be for her age—*she* had started to develop some womanly features, even if she were still a child. It was really just one more asset reinforcing her position as the unopposed ruler of the students at the Academy. Fryn sighed, hand still resting on her flat chest.

"So how far to your family's house?" Pyran asked, winking, as if only she got the joke that Fryn's real family was dead.

Fryn pointed ahead, wings flicking in irritation as she directed her friend, at this point, her only friend, toward the tall building with the wide, covered porch, flanked by a baker on one side, and a tailor on the other, roughly two hundred feet away, on the intersection of the Crescent Road, and the South Cardinal. "Just right there, Pyra, but I'd rather not go through the front door."

"Nonsense!" Her friend argued, and charged ahead on the wing, flitting over to the porch where she waved impatiently for Fryn to join her. There was no reason for her discomfort, really, but Fryn swallowed down her nausea as she walked up the steps and pulled on the brass door handle, not even bowing her head as her friend entered first.

To the left, a small podium, no, a *really* small podium, stood before the youngest waitress Fryn had ever seen. She wore a black dress and a pair of little white gloves, and stared *up* at them, with a few pieces of paper in her hands. "W-w-welcome!" she sputtered, "t-t-to Martin Hall!"

To the right, up on the dais that Fryn remembered dancing on, and jumping off of as a child, the musicians shot them dirty looks, wings drooping at the appearance of *boring* company. Fryn shifted her gaze back to the little girl who peered at her, half out of resentment for being ignored, and half out of partial recognition.

"Hi Harissa," Fryn began, "It's been a couple years."

Harissa, now nine, let her jaw drop, as she stared at her cousin in awe. Her eyes traced the blue and silver interplay of colors in her Sanhas, and then met hers, and froze, as surely as the surface of a lake in winter. "Fryn?"

"Hi," she responded meekly, "this is my friend Pyran, though we just call her Pyra."

"Hi," Harissa said, nodding more to herself than anyone, as she avoided meeting Pyran's intensely friendly gaze.

"Can we sit down?" Fryn asked, for lack of anything better to say.

The main floor was empty, since it was only mid-morning, and above the stairs, the curtains shielding the balcony rooms were all drawn, signifying, Fryn thought, that the entire house was empty— possibly intensifying the frustration that the musicians had had, when they noticed that the first customers were un-paying children.

Harissa led them away, out of habit most likely, and sat them down in a side booth near the kitchen, but out of the sight of where most of the other potential customers might sit. She didn't even drop either of those pieces of paper she carried on the table, but stuffed them, all crinkled, and ruined, halfway into a child-sized clutch bag that she carried under the crook of her arm.

"This is exciting," Pyran whispered over the table, eyes *bulging*. "You have an interesting family, Fryn, almost as strange as my *dad*."

"What is so strange about your dad?" Fryn asked, lifting an eyebrow strategically, "he seems like a proper sort of Snow District Fae to me."

Pyra grinned, showing her perfectly aligned teeth in the almost romantic light of their alcove. "He's got some strange stories, of meeting people in places like this, talking in secret, working for the king… now he's just a teacher, but *I heard* that he used to be a spy!"

"A *spy*?" Harissa breathed, scooting Fryn further into the bench so she could sit down.

Pyra gave her a glance, as if to say, "what did I just say?" And locked eyes with Fryn.

"Ah, yes… that's the rumor," Fryn added, nudging Harissa for embarrassing her, "but it might be nice to have some tea, don't you think?"

"Well, you can help me get the biscuits," Harissa replied sharply, getting up and trotting over towards the kitchens, where the clattering of clean dishes being organized announced that there was nothing going on.

"Oh yes, please," Pyra exclaimed, clasping her hands together, eyes sparkling.

Fryn sighed, "alright… but only because you're too short, Harissa," she allowed, and followed her into the butler's pantry— annoyed that she was still too short herself to really see what was happening on the other side of the passthrough. She found a step stool under the buffet counter and climbed up on the left-hand side by the bread board, to access the cabinet where they had always hidden the treats… sure enough, there were little biscuits in abundance, and a few scones as well.

The pine-nut cookies had been a staple in their family for as long as she could remember, so she set a few on a plate, and added three tiny juniper berry scones, and a ramekin of blackberry jam. Harissa busied herself with the enchanted kettle, filling it from the tap, and charging it with a pained look as she grasped its handle. The light in her wings faded, and they drooped uselessly behind her back, as a trail of steam began to rise from the spout.

"I'm surprised you can use the kettle," Fryn said, scooting the stool back under the counter, and balancing the tray of treats and jam on the tips of her fingers.

Harissa gave her an exhausted look and poured the water into a minty-colored teapot and capped it before even a hint of the herbal aroma could escape. "Well, we're all responsible for something," she answered with an edged tone.

They brought the tea and biscuits back to their table and settled in, Harissa filling matching teacups with pine-needle and juniper tea, as Pyra immediately began cutting open a scone and slathering it up with jam, her nostrils flaring from the excitement. "It's so nice here, Fryn, I never thought your family was this well off so far out of the Snow District."

Technically, Fryn thought, it wasn't *her* family that was doing well. Her family had died in a fire four years ago… all because her father had started his own import business, hoping to prove his worth to his in-laws.

Thankfully, Harissa replied for her. "Our family has governed this district for hundreds of years, it used to be outside of the city, but *we* built the outer wall and claimed it as our own!"

"But what about the Sky District? Who takes care of that?" Pyran asked, suddenly growing serious, except for the jammy crumbs stuck to her cheeks.

"Uh, no one, I guess," Harissa answered. "It's the Sky District, they're poor, and they're not really a part of the city."

"Maybe *you* should take care of them! Your family did that before, right? Build another wall!"

The musicians on the dais, who had been tuning their instruments, shot startled and offended looks in their direction. And Harissa's cousin, Jason, leaned out of the butler's pantry and stared at them, before hiding away in the kitchen. He was ten, just a year older than Harissa, but he'd always been a proud and serious child. The way he sniffed at Pyra's suggestion especially offended her. Fortunately, Pyra seemed oblivious to the Martin Clan's reaction to her idea, and continued blathering on.

"Then, you can govern two districts, reduce crime, bring in more trade and stability, and Frorin will be a better city than ever!"

Fryn set her teacup down with a clatter on its saucer, and was about to rebuke her, but Harissa's eyes brightened and she interjected excitedly, "that's a great idea!"

There was no stopping the flow of this conversation now… Fryn nibbled on a biscuit, and sighed inside, as Pyra caught Harissa in her wake, just as she did with all the other students at the Academy, and Fryn sat there in silence, forgotten. As one hour grew into two, and the teapot was emptied and refilled, more and more of Harissa's brothers, cousins, and aunts and uncles, loomed on the periphery, pretending to work, but secretly listening, caught up in the tale she spun of what and who the Martin Clan could be.

The Hall fell silent though, when the first customer appeared at the door, and everyone made busy, dusting the last of the windowsills, and turning over the last of the chairs, and Harissa rushed back to the door to seat the new arrival.

"Good morning, sir!" she chirped happily, face clouding as she recognized the masculine Sanhas he wore, with its ashy gray, and pale blue detailing, and her eyes fixed on the silver-handled sword at his waist. "Would you like to be seated?"

"I'd like to order the daily special, in a private booth, if you don't mind," he replied warmly, in a voice that sent chills down Fryn's wings.

"Your name?" Harissa asked, leading him toward the stairs that split and circled the musicians' stand.

"Bersari," he answered, eyes forward, not noticing them—thankfully. He ascended the steps, and vanished from sight, but Fryn and Pyra shared worried and thrilled looks.

"You don't think he saw us, do you?" Pyra asked, leaning over the table, nearly knocking her teacup off the table.

"I don't think so…" Fryn said, spying her cousin Jason at the butler's pantry door again, watching them suspiciously, "but I'm a little worried if he finds out we've come here."

Pyran grinned. "But why did *he* come here? It's your family, so I know why you'd come…"

Fryn frowned. "He ordered the special, people only do that if they want to meet my uncle and get some information."

"What kind of information?"

Fryn shrugged. "They never told me, I just think we know a lot about what goes on in this district, so people ask us."

They waited, snacking, and drinking tea, silently. Harissa joined them, and they all shrank into the booth when Master Bersari reappeared at the head of the stairs an hour later, his face grim, and distracted, as he spoke softly with Uncle Eljaren, and descended.

As he took the curve of the stairs, his eyes drifted in their direction, over them, and then back again with an intensity that spoke of a combination of horror, frustration, worry… and amusement. He flew down the rest of the way, stood at the end of their table, and crossed his arms.

"Uh… hi father…" Pyra stuttered, "what brings you here?"

He frowned, though the edges of his mouth quirked as if he were hiding a smile. "Just adult business, what might I ask brings you two here?"

"Fryn wanted," Pyra blurted, then blushed, *damn her*, "uh, *we* wanted to visit Fryn's family." At least Pyra admitted that she was as much to blame for the idea.

He smiled proudly. "I see that, but surely you know what Fryn's grandparents asked when they entrusted her to us. That she not be associated with her, outside influences."

"The Pine District is just as much a part of this city as the inner rings," Pyran decided, wings flushing with a bit of angry purple and red.

"It didn't used to be," he replied, "and that's what matters to them. They are paying the school a great deal, and I can't afford to lose their support, and not just financially. Fryn, Pyra, put on your cloaks, it is time to go."

"But you can't just take her away!" Harissa complained, trying and failing to stand between them.

"I can and will, little finch," he replied, "your father understands as well. Now come." He turned on his heel, and stalked toward the door, expecting them to come, knowing that they would.

"F-Fryn..." Harissa cried, tears brimming as she waved goodbye. "Come back soon!"

Fryn froze her own tears, refusing to show any weakness to her teacher, or Pyra, who openly wailed at the injustice, shaking her head sadly, leaving a scone half-eaten on her plate. As they made the tragic march back to the Academy, Fryn wondered again, why Master Bersari had come, and what kind of information he required, and for what kind of business that he couldn't, and wouldn't discuss.

Only a couple months later, Fryn heard the rumors: Harissa, playing with, looking after, teaching, and enfranchising the children from the Sky District. She'd become something of a symbol for those out-rings, captured by the dream that Pyran had inspired.

~Present Day~

Hill District

Fryn

Havrshyk stood at the corner of the road ahead, looking up at the signboard of a no-name pub, scratching his head. It had been a few days since their meeting with the prince, but they were not much closer to having a clear plan. Nothing except Leif's go-to in all circumstances, 'go looking for trouble".

Alyra was already inside, asking questions and reserving a table. They'd discovered that whatever elemental affinity she had, it had to do with perception, and she could prod their minds to signal them with ease. Fryn had never even heard of such a thing, but she'd never heard of a faerie with an affinity for gravity either. There was something very different about Moraskyr and its inhabitants.

A sharp sensation pulsed through her mind, the signal from Alyra, so Fryn and Havrshyk nodded to each other and then entered the pub, letting the door close on its own behind them. It closed with a loud thud, but few of the pub's patrons even bothered to look in their direction. The dimly lit pub was warmed by a coal fire in the opposite end, down a few steps in an area lined with tables. Immediately to their left ran a narrow bar manned by an oily fae wearing a jute apron and a bored look, listening to a conversation between the two fae seated on one of the stools before him.

One of those speaking with the barkeeper moved a hand to his sword, and the firelight glinted off a hunter's license sewn into a patch on his shoulder. He wore the hood of his dark green cloak low over his face, so low in fact, that it dipped in and out of his ale as he talked.

Havrshyk led the way down the step and into a corner behind the hunter, facing away from him, so that he could eavesdrop. Alyra was up at the bar chatting beside the hunter, her ale sloshing with her animated expressions, and laughter. Fryn took a seat beside Havrshyk, facing away from Alyra and the bar, scanning the common area by the fire.

She watched the other faeries sitting and talking loudly at their tables. A pair of young fee in work boots and aprons drank from their mugs energetically, with tufts of thistledown in their hair and stuck to their sleeves—likely from the textiles shop around the corner. Beyond them, a middle aged fae in a brown duster sat beside the fire, tuning his lute, and picking at a couple strings before settling into a soft melody. He had a tall hat inverted before him, where patrons could toss a mint or two between mugs of ale.

He was plucking the strings in a familiar tune, a surprisingly somber one, for a bustling evening like this—the Bluefire Burglar. He didn't sing, probably sensing that the lyrics would be disheartening for his working-class audience, but plucked away until a passing barfee brought him a stuffed roll and his own frothy mug. It was only after a long draught of the ale, that he plucked a bit louder and began to sing softly.

Fryn half listened to him, also trying to keep an ear locked on Alyra.

You cannot take the fire's tongue,
or steal its blazing heart,
Soiled hands of rabbit dung,
stutter 'fore you start,
She passed you on a finch's wing,
bluefire in her dress,
alight and smiling,
you sought her to impress...

The barfee swept by them, accepting a handful of mint from Havrshyk, as she searched the tables for patrons in need of fresh drink.

"I never liked this song," Havrshyk complained pointing toward the busker, "It's not right for this lot anyway."

You couldn't speak to ask her name,
your wings were red and bright,
she found it such a silly game,
and took off into flight...

The busker was getting the attention of the others, and their talk softened to whispers. Even the Hunter turned around.

Not knowing how to answer her,
you followed in her wake,
she danced upon the rooftop there,
there finally you spake.
Stuttering and stammering,
she took you by the hand,
sputtering and floundering,
she taught you how to stand.
Feet not taught to dance yet,
and fingers made for work,
she fell upon the lancet,
the rooftop formed a dirk...

Alyra stifled a shocked gasp.

This only encouraged the singer, and he continued to strum with one hand, as he took a swig with his other hand before continuing the song.

The fire blue that lit her eyes,
a candle sputtering 'fore it dies,
shouts and calls surrounded you,
but there was naught that you could do.

Fryn hummed, sipping her weak ale. It was slightly malty, without a hint of herbs or hops. A passable ale.

Her stolen fire haunting,
the villagers all taunting,
locked into the stockade,
askin' for your head!

Why'd you have to murder her?
Had no right to talk to her!
Where's the axefae,
Call the axefae,
the burglar has to pay!

He launched into an intense arpeggio of plucked notes alternating with full chord strums, and then slowed into an apologetic rhythm. He paused, drinking down his ale, and then lifting his lute, continued to the end.

Blue the fire you lead astray,
a dance upon a darker day,
but even so you met his eyes,
reflecting bluefire skies...!

He settled back down into his chair and bowed his head to the raucous applause. Bluefire Burglar was always a long and slow song, so the listeners could consider the story each verse told and appreciate the sorrow. But this time, Fryn caught something new.

She met Havrshyk's eyes. He seemed genuinely surprised. "I've never heard it played like this," she said, resting her chin hand.

"I understand now," he said, raising his mug to the busker, "it is not mourning him; but we are meant to see ourselves in him. It is about a class struggle."

"What? No, that's not right. It is just a tragedy, meant to make people melancholy."

"Which part? That the girl accidentally died, or the part where the people kill him because he had no business talking with a high-born fee?" he asked with an edged tone. "Take a look at the Sky District, Fryn, and then tell me truly if everyone in this city is protected equally by the law."

Fryn considered, still keeping an eye on the room and the hunter seated at the bar behind her. She flicked her wings in thought and set another mint on the table. The barfee soon swept it off the table, swapping Fryn's empty mug with a full one, and Fryn was able to sip on the ale as she considered.

Havrshyk said he'd come from the Sky District and spoke as if there were an inherent corruption inborn in the upper classes. Fryn hadn't always lived in the Snow District, that was only after the fire. When she and Pyra had slipped out to visit Martin Hall, Master Bersari discouraged them strongly against going back. Even he, going to visit her uncle for information, had spoken of the outer rings with disgust.

She heaved a sigh and set her mug down on the table. Deep down, all she wanted was to talk to Leif, to learn more about his culture, his family. She wanted to be alone with him, and far from all this chaos surrounding the Commission, and the Crown. Did the Aelaete clans have class discrimination? Or was that simply sibling rivalry?

Alyra spilled her drink on the hunter, who fell off his stool with a yelp and a thud. He landed on his back, sputtering.

"You *stupid*, clumsy wench!" he yelled, and as he was about to sit up, he craned his head back, so that his hood fell and revealed his bloodshot eyes and noticed them. "Wait… do I… I know you…" He stopped trying to get off the floor and fished a folded-up piece of paper out of his coat pocket.

The wrinkled paper had two pictures on it, one of Fryn, and one of Leif, with the scales of justice crest stamped below them—one side weighed with coins, the other stabbed through with a dagger.

"They say justice is rewarding," Havrshyk said dryly, draining his mug. He slammed it down and smiled at the black-haired hunter, "No one said the reward was good."

The room stilled, and in the quiet, Havrshyk drew his Bloodsword and placed the black tip of the blade against the hunter's neck. "But perhaps if you answer our questions, I might let you leave this place alive."

The barkeeper ducked under the bar and rose again with a frown and a crossbow aimed at Havrshyk's chest. "I won't have fightin' in my tavern, traitor!"

Fryn heard the sound of a foot scraping on stone and saw the busker edging around the hearth to grab an iron poker and shoving the barfee behind him.

Fryn drew her knife, scanning the crowd of faeries, looking for the other hunter that had to be here… but there wasn't one. Had this hunter really gone out alone? She nodded at Havrshyk, tossed a 5-mint coin on the table, and strode out through the door.

On the street, the sky had darkened to streaks of purple and orange, as the sun hid behind the mountains, and the moons glowed brilliantly behind a single cloud.

A few moments later, Havrshyk shoved the hunter through the door, a crossbow bolt sticking out of his chest, and tossed the fae to the ground. "Wingless barkeep!" he hissed, ripping out the bolt, and tossing it away. "If you hadn't made me promise…"

"No bystanders," Fryn warned, putting one boot on the hunter's chest to keep him from standing up. He had a mean bruise forming around one eye, and a pathetic expression. "Where's Grifton?"

The hunter stopped struggling as he squeezed one eye shut to glare at her with the other one. "Who?"

"The hunter with the bones…"

"I'm not telling you anything, traitor!" he spat, trying to get her face, but she deflected it with her hand, so that the spittle froze and skidded away down the road. "Just kill me and be done with it."

"You heard him, Fryn," Aldyr said, leaning against the wall of the tavern, color suffusing his face as he redrained and allowed the blood to heal the crossbow wound.

The hunter gritted his teeth and stared her down.

So, she did the only logical thing she could think of. She reached down and cut off the hunter license from his sleeve and pocketed it. "Good luck operating here without a license." She removed her foot, and walked away, waving toward Havrshyk. They reentered the tavern and sat down at the bar.

The barkeeper watched them uneasily, reloading the crossbow. None of the patrons had moved since their altercation, so Fryn sheathed her dagger and put a mint on the bar. "I'd like a bowl of soup, whatever you've got, doesn't need to be hot."

His face darkened. "I won't serve anyone who kills my customers!"

"Then there's no issue," she said, slapping the license down next to the coin, "I merely took this from him so that the outlander wouldn't be meddling in our affairs."

He ran to the door and saw the confused hunter still sitting on the ground, looking around as if trying to decide if it was worth it to try to get his license back.

He gave her a "hmph" and went around to the kitchen, returning with a bowl of soup, hot. "Aren't you supposed to be bloodthirsty renegades?"

"I'm only bloodthirsty if I don't get enough to eat," she said with a smile, "do you know the Pine-Martin?"

He nodded slowly.

"The Commission hired the assassin who killed the last one, barkeep. There's a lot more going on than a couple of renegades."

Aldyr gave her a glare, so she ignored him.

She drank from the steaming hot soup, chewing around the small bits of chestnut and dill. The other patrons started chatting again, and the busker released the barfee to serve the patrons.

She came up to them, conflicting emotions running through the colors in her wings. "What are you doing?"

Fryn set aside the soup and pointed at the busker. "Did you listen to the Bluefire Bandit earlier?"

She nodded, confused wrinkles forming around her eyes.

"There's more than one type of class struggle, and the Commission is not the friend it pretends to be. There are honest hunters, like us, and there are mercenaries, and rogues. I think the prince was right all along. They are a threat to our security, just as we are a threat to them."

She mulled that over and then nodded slowly. She returned to giving ale and food out to the other patrons, so Fryn finished her soup.

They didn't have to wait much longer for the reinforcements to come. The door slammed open, and a chitinous monster of a fae loomed in the doorway. His sword was already drawn and arcing in a swing; it cut through the doorway, cleaving the slab in half, and sunk into the polished pine bar.

Havrshyk was already in motion, he slammed his Bloodsword down on top of Grifton's blade and leapt into him with a powerful wingbursted kick. That... only shoved him back a little.

Fryn felt her wings shivering, and she met his eyes. Tendrils of living bone had woven through his face, threading their way through his skin, and his irises had changed into a sickly beige color.

The transformation he was undergoing continued to deform him. She refrained from touching the Bonesword in the bar and focused on sheathing her forearms and shins in plates of hardened ice. She drained her dagger, filling the plates with her blood, strengthening and hardening them, as she charged through the door, and slid under Grifton's legs.

On the other side of him were two other hunters, the one with the spear, and the weasel-faced fae with the sword.

Fryn darted toward Jeldon whose spear was not quite in a readied position and lunged under its reach. She backhanded him across his face, feeling a satisfying crunch in his nose, and spun around to watch the other fae.

Havrshyk was already hacking at Grifton's back, but even with its infused state, he could not get the blade to sink in. It rang with the dull, hollow sounds of wet wood.

The barkeep stood in the doorway, but ducked back behind the bar as Grifton spun, and launched Havrshyk around in a spinning kick through the broken door and across the hall.

He crashed into a couple of tables, one arm bent at a wrong angle, as he set his jaw and flushed with blood to heal the injuries. The Mountain Fang didn't wait for him to stand, and charged after him, ripping his sword free of the bar as he went.

Fryn didn't have time to watch, as she focused on the fae with the thin sword and the ginger mop of curly hair. He stood in an odd stance, one foot forward, and one back—like the Soft-Point Fist, except that his stance was so low he was nearly crouching.

He sprang forward in a twirl, flaring out into a surprising lunge, so that the tip of his dueling sword scratched off the armored ice plates on her forearms, and she backpedaled enough that Jeldon and this fae were in a line.

This gave her an advantage over him. Her style was designed to fight multiple opponents in a straight line, just like a lancer, but it was more flexible in tight spaces. She settled into her stance, and then burst forward in a sprint. She rushed into a crouch, and leapt toward the swordsfae's face, kicking him back as he blocked, and knocking him into Jeldon's clumsy guard.

"Watch it, Hatha!" he shouted, stepping to the side of Fryn's charge. Hatha grunted but laughed when he saw the blood streaming from Jeldon's broken nose.

"Not so pretty now, boyo!" Hatha crowed, even while springing aside with a flutter of his wings and lunging toward Fryn's back.

She concentrated and ice shards caught the tip of his blade, so she turned, and slammed her fist into Hatha's stomach. He folded under it, grabbing her arm, and rolling backwards, throwing her into the wall of the tavern.

Even fully drained, frozen, Fryn gasped at the impact. Her head hit the stones and bright flashes of light cascaded around her, as she crashed to the floor. The blood worked slowly, sluggishly, to her skull, and she rolled over dazed as Hatha stalked toward her.

Through her spotty vision, she was grateful to notice that Jeldon was still nursing his nose and watching impatiently.

Hatha ran her through with the sword, right in the heart. She set her jaw and froze. The ice climbed up the sword toward Hatha's hand, and as the air chilled around her, she twisted, snapping the brittle blade in half.

She ripped it out, draining completely, unable to complete the healing to her injuries, as she grappled him, fighting to stab him in the neck with it.

He held her back with one hand, as his other aimed the remaining section of his sword at her gut. If she continued, she'd only worsen her condition—and she still had two more enemies.

Fryn flew back out the door, tossing the sliver of Hatha's sword at Jeldon, and landed on the rooftop looking down at them.

Hatha didn't wait. He flew after her in a strange spiral, surrounded in a cloud of mist. Then, as fog filled the street, he vanished.

She kept an eye out of her peripheral vision, listening to the cries and breaking furniture inside the tavern.

It likely took both Havrshyk and Alyra to contain Grifton even in that confined space. She spared a moment of regret for the barkeeper and closed her eyes.

Hatha was a fluid elemental, using the moisture in the air to conceal his movements… but he should know that they were elemental cousins. Frost spread out from her feet, so that she could feel the water forming a rime on every surface nearby.

It did not touch a pair of boots though. Hatha must have been flying. The air shifted around her, and she felt his rush before it arrived. She was too late to move. A knife sank into her back, shattering her crust of ice, and collapsing her lung.

Fryn leapt forward, spinning on the ridge of the roof so that she stole Hatha's weapon again… but he was gone.

She crouched, just in case, and was relieved when a throwing knife spun overhead. The duelist apparently had a bag chock full of tricks. He couldn't fly forever though.

A footfall sounded on the roof beside her, so she slashed with her Bloodknife, and caught another blade on its edge. Behind it, barely visible in the mist, she saw his sneering face. "Ya got better sense than I thought!" He slipped back into the fog, appearing at her back with a quick jab.

She grabbed his wrist with her free hand, and slammed home her knife into his arm, raking it up toward his face.

He followed that first one up with another dagger in her side, causing her to hesitate long enough for him to vanish again.

She groaned in frustration, letting her blood flow freely through her body to heal her wounds. As the cracks in her skull knit themselves together, and the pain of all her stab wounds ate at her, she resisted the urge to scream and ripped out the dagger in her back. *How many does he even have?* she wondered.

As the last wounds sealed, and she crouched low, listening for his return, her Bloodknife faded to an anemic pink. All her recent efforts to restore its edge had been wasted against this hunter, and she hadn't even faced Grifton yet.

A shudder reverberated through the slate roof tiles, and a dark shadow crashed up through the roof and landed just a few feet away. It was Grifton. He shifted wearily on the roof, howling with rage. She couldn't see clearly enough to tell for certain, but he didn't appear injured in the least.

"I'll find you, Viper!" he yelled.

Fryn slipped down the roof on a wing, not daring to make a sound by running on the tiles, and in through a window to the rooms inside the tavern.

The interior was destroyed. Impossible tears and claw marks scratched across the walls and posts, and beams were torn in two; it seemed that every piece of furniture had been broken into pieces. She didn't see any of the tavern's patrons as she descended, but the barkeeper lay bleeding across the bar with a spent crossbow in his hand.

She flew down to him and inspected the long, jagged cut of a sword across his back, but saw that it was shallow, and his chest still rose and fell with a steady rhythm. She traced the cut with her finger, sealing it shut with his frozen blood, and scanned the area around the fire. The hearth was broken, and coals had scattered around the kindling bark, and were beginning to catch on the wood floor.

She ran to it and covered the area with frost. The coals smoked and sizzled, fighting against it, but she killed them with another wave of her hand.

These hunters were dangerous. Fryn bit her lip, searching for anyone else, regretting ever 'looking for trouble' when this monster was involved.

This would be enough to sow doubt about the hunters' activity in the city. Indeed, she felt Alyra's touch on her mind, with a sharp impulse that seemed to indicate a direction. North.

She nodded to herself and ducked out the back. Grifton was still storming around the rooftop, yelling about clearing the fog, so Fryn flew out the door and followed the street in the direction Alyra had indicated.

Grifton wouldn't stop hunting them, but maybe next time they could have a little help bringing him down.

Looking back over her shoulder, she could see the shadows of two figures within the fog and forced down the guilt over the damage they had brought on the tavern. It was not their fault they had injured civilians, but... they had been hurt because of her, nonetheless.

Her flight was cut short as she flew into another patch of fog and skidded to a halt across the stones in an empty square. She could feel footsteps approaching, and on instinct, she knelt, and wingbursted into the attacker, ramming her fist into his face.

Hatha had predicted her escape, but he hadn't expected <u>this</u>. She followed through with her punch, allowing the infused shard of icy armor along that arm to explode, blasting him back.

He flipped backwards and flew into the air. She followed, dodging another one of his blades, turning her head slightly as another knife scratched her face, and she collided with him in the air, Bloodknife through his neck.

The knife drank in his blood, healing her injuries, and darkening to its folded black state again. He weakly pushed himself off her blade, and he fell with a dull thud to the stones. He was still breathing. Somehow, he had held onto some of his blood, resisting her, so that he lay half-drained in a daze.

Satisfied he was no longer a threat, Fryn flew on. She wasn't interested in killing him, but because his part in attacking the tavern, he deserved what he got.

Was this even enough?

Hatha lay at her feet, his mouth moving with a sly smile and whispered words. Curious, Fryn leaned down next to him.

"Never seen a fae so mad for blood..." he rasped.

Fryn frowned, and feeling slightly guilty, she waved a hand over her blade and watched a portion of the stolen blood flow in a spiraling tendril through the air to partially refill the hunter's veins.

"I may have been too greedy. Perhaps I'll simply take this instead." She found Hatha's license sewn onto his collar and cut it free.

Hatha didn't rise, but he breathed easier as he gave her a ragged laugh. "Not you," he pointed over her shoulder, "him."

She went cold and noticed the slight haze of sand and dust beginning to float up into the air. The fog tasted of the thirst for blood, and without turning to see, she knew his attack was coming. Fryn spun into a low stance, drawing her blade again as she scanned her surroundings. Ice formed into armored plating around her legs and arms, and she rolled to the side dodging as a spear of flaking minerals and stone slammed into the stones where she had stood just moments before.

The spear was as thick as her thigh, and as long as a lamp post, as if... she didn't have time think about that... for she saw where the spear had come from, and as she traced the disturbance in the fog, she scrambled back to her feet and ran toward the figure looming on the rooftop of the buildings to the south.

Grifton watched her with the still posture and stern eyes of a statue, not like the inspiring or harrowing statues of Froreholt, but like the cruel, vengeful, haunting figures the Cherim used to scare away outsiders living or dead. His feet were rooted to the rooftop with cords of stone, and as she swung at his face, he caught her knife with the edge of his Bonesword.

Where were Havrshyk and Alyra?

Fryn met Grifton's membranous eyes.

"So, we meet again at last, Fryn, are you surprised to see me?" he asked her, voice low and gravelly. He raised his free hand, the one that shouldn't be attached to his orphaned shoulder, the skeletal arm that he'd formed from the faeries he'd killed in his quest for revenge.

Fryn refused to look away. She met his bloodthirsting gaze and growled softly, "Just disappointed...!" She wingbursted backwards and spun around his next slash, as she ducked under a swipe of his skeletal claws, and rammed home her Bloodknife into his thigh.

Only, her blade cut through a thin layer of flesh, and then slid off more bone than he should have had in his legs, as if his flesh were being consumed by the ravenous hunger of his marrow.

He kicked her in the stomach, and she was thrown to the ground beside Hatha. Grifton landed beside her, sword coming down in a finishing stab, so she surrounded herself with ice. His blade sank into the ice and held there, and for once Fryn considered her elemental affinity more useful than her Lichform. She shattered the ice in a spray of dazzling shards and thrust her free palm into the soft spot under Grifton's arm pit. As the impact sank in, she threw out a lance of blood-ice, and tried to tap into whatever reserves the bonecrafter might have left. She cut into the soft tendons and sinews, and that was it.

There was no blood left. All he had was wet bone, and marrow, interspersed with hardened crystal lines reminiscent of the veins that had once lined his body.

He laughed, a ragged, hoarse laugh, that seemed to rattle and vibrate through his body. "I am beyond you, Lich. So feared, for so long, but what are you but a brittle body preserved beyond usefulness?" His sword came down in the same moment, and Fryn screamed as her free hand was cut clean off.

It fell to the stones, spinning off into the fog, and though she didn't bleed in her drained state, Fryn could feel the panic mounting. Her heart couldn't beat or accelerate, but her mind was racing. The light in her wings pulsed red and green, and then orange, as she flitted back, and fixed her grip on her Bloodknife.

She'd been surrounded before. She'd fought and killed before… but this… she had never fought a single hunter who could *kill* her before.

Before she could plan another attack, he was already rushing her with a heavy wingblast and a spear of mineral fibers from his outstretched clawed hand. She felt it scrape off the icy armor on her cheek but focused on moving forward. For all his power, Grifton was too confident, and not nearly practiced enough with those powers.

She slid under his next sword swing and cut through the tendons on his sword-arm elbow before rising and kicking him back, as she rolled over her shoulder, and collapsed onto the ground. She re-drained, flooding the stump of her left arm with blood as she reached toward the limp, frozen hand on the ground, and reached with all her strength to remind the limb that it belonged to *her*.

Fryn had reattached limbs before, but she forced that memory away every time it rose from her subconscious. This time though, she let herself revisit the flashes of memory of jaws crushing her, teeth splitting her bones, blood pooling around her… she had been fourteen.

Hairs rose on the back of her neck, and sensing more danger, Fryn rolled away from her hand, unable to reattach it in time, as Grifton's sword sliced through her right leg above her knee and sent it skidding across the stones.

Now, with blood in her veins, Fryn felt the furious pounding in her chest, she tasted the adrenaline in her blood, and her eyes widened to take in the complete view of her attacker bringing his sword down for another strike.

"This is for my brothers!" he shouted, teeth bared in a feral cry.

In that moment, to her eyes, he reared above her like the ermine had all those years ago, sweeping down with deadly claws. Instinctively, she did again what she had done then. She rose, putting all her weight on the stump of her leg, infusing everything she had into the darkest and longest, and sharpest blade she could form, so that she could impale Grifton's heart on his way down.

He grinned, and as he brought his sword down with a confident, victorious swing, she wingbursted up into his attack, under the swing, and slid the hand-and-a-half Bloodsword through his heart.

It was still alive.

She could taste it. All that remained of his blood. Fryn drained Grifton's dehydrated heart completely.

Grifton howled, a hollow, rasping cry, and he recoiled from her.

Fryn retrieved her severed hand, sending fresh blood—courtesy of Grifton—to reattach it to her arm. As she watched him shivering on the stones, confident that she had at last defeated him, Fryn flew back to her leg and held it in place to attach it again.

Then, dismissing Grifton with an eyeroll at his 'revenge' she walked back to Hatha.

"Perhaps you bet on the wrong bird, Hunter," she said, sheathing her now anemic blade.

Hatha looked up at her with bloodshot, laughing eyes. "Don't bet on birds, Lich, bet on the martin, the mongoose, and the ermine..."

There was a soft sound of scraping behind her, almost insect-like, like carapace. Time slowed as she drained everything into her blade and began to shift to her right.

Grifton was still alive. He scratched stones with claws that formed from his natural armor covering his feet, and reached toward her with his clawed hand outstretched, and his sword held back for a swing.

In a breeze of a moment, Fryn was under his attack, and running back into the fog… only, he didn't chase her.

She heard the sickening squelch of his Bonesword hitting flesh, and Hatha's pitiful scream cut off. Through the mist, she glanced back just in time to see Hatha's form dissolve into the sword, and hear Grifton whisper, "That's quite enough, Hatha."

Footsteps and shouts sounded in the direction of the tavern. They'd done what they were supposed to… and she shuddered considering spending one more second fighting that… whatever he was.

Interlude 3

CRUSHING

Gaersheim

Fassen

Earl's Estates

Loren

Vinellin stood at the Earl's elbow, a tea towel draped over the arm bearing a tray with an unopened bottle of wine and a pair of untouched glasses. Beside these, a letter folded into thirds lay sealed with a blob of purple wax, and the symbol of an ermine against a field of stars. Loren reached over to it, fingering the edge of the letter and biting his lip in thought as he summoned the will to read it.

"I never thought it would arrive," he admitted, glancing up at the Zellan butler with a raised eyebrow.

For his part, the butler remained impassive, though the way he pursed his lips and glanced away betrayed his doubt about the veracity of Loren's statement. As always, he was far too observant. Truthfully, he'd known a missive would come, he just worried at the seal with his thumb as he worried about its contents. Finally, the butler cleared his throat and shuffled his wings before commenting, "as your people like to say, 'a bird that refuses to hatch withers within a prison of its own making'."

The Earl's frown deepened, and he flushed. "Mind your tone, Vinellin, I am not the 'young master' anymore. I am the Earl and as such due your courtesy and respect."

"Quite so, sir," Vinellin agreed, and set the tray down on a side table, and trimmed the wax from the sealed cork with a small knife.

Loren waited for the butler to pour him a glass of dark red wine before peeling the seal from the letter carefully to preserve its impression. As he unfolded the letter, his eyebrows rose higher at the delicate, intricate hand that filled the page in large, bold characters.

"My lord Fassen, it was with great surprise and interest that Our Mother received your correspondence. She has dictated her response to me, thirty-fourth of her blood, Eladarin Fhora, as follows: 'my roots shall stretch far beyond the reach of my branches. Though you be the heir of my rival, there was one enemy we chose to face together. So long as you hold true to your word, I will grant you the same right to hold your ancient lands for Waverly. He was ever the honest fool. It was his one redeeming quality, as it appears to be yours.' So spake the mother of the forest, Fhoraena, the Immortal Queen of all lands untainted by Jakaren's Shade."

"I never thought for an instant she would agree," Loren said, "it's... I wonder."

"What, sir?"

"Apparently, we will have the support of the Cherim when we break off from Gaersheim." Loren handed him the letter and took a long draught of his wine. "She has little love for the Gaersyn crown... if only we could have kept the Harvest Crown here..."

Vinellin hummed as he read the letter. When he finished, he set it on the tray and asked, "I thought you were planning to wait until the Cherim invade?"

He laughed. "And they are likely planning for us to cause a distraction as the 'rebel province' so they can claim Rosenkraun when it is ill defended."

"What of Prince Ieffin, my lord, will he assist us?"

"He is so focused on the Commission he has little attention left for other matters. No, I doubt we will have the support of Froreholt until the battles commence."

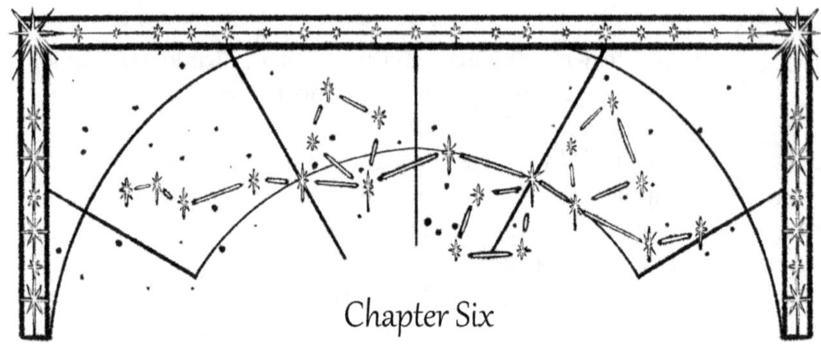

Chapter Six

VINE

Ice Wastes

The Lichfield

Fryn

One week after watching Grifton kill Hatha, consume his body with his sword, and then disappear, Fryn was standing in the entourage of the Prince's wait staff, keeping her eyes moving. The scars on her arm and leg itched, and even though she was so ready for Leif to return, for Havrshyk to leave his body, she was afraid. She was surrounded by the nameless fear of knowing that something would go wrong right before they were supposed to get better.

The Lichfield was a hollow in the glacial flower fields surrounded by a towering wall of natural granite boulders. The ring was unbroken, so they had landed their birds on the stones and then flown down to the unmarked flat clearing dusted only with powdery snow. To the north lay the three resting grounds, three tiers of connected terraces of statues and stone markers, proceeding from the lay nobility and heroes honored by the Crown, then to the kings and queens of Froreholt, and then finally to the highest tier where Yndril's ancient memorial was visible from below—the statue of Arta, lance planted in the ground before him, carrying Yndril with her wings drooping and her eyes closed.

As she dusted off her jacket, wanting to both look the part of a servant, and also not wanting to dishonor the space, Fryn looked over her shoulder to Alyra. The Moraskyn fee wore the dress of a scribe, carrying a writing board and a pen case, so she could document the speech—but she looked out at the Lichfield with reverential eyes and an open mouth. Her wings beat to a strange pattern, and she nodded at Fryn cryptically.

"This place," she said, "is as old as the *lashedyn*... older... maybe."

Aldyr stood beside her, in a stiff coat and a stiffer posture. She could feel the anxious beat of his heart through her bonded link with Leif. Snow fell more heavily outside of this space, but here inside the ring of stones, only bits of harmless dust fell to fill in the places that the visitors disturbed.

Ieffin led the procession up the path, flanked by gravestones and mounds of snow, to the highest level. There, they assembled before the dais with Yndril and Arta's statue, waiting as more of the invited guests arrived behind them. Ieffin stood looking out at the terraces filling with nobles, merchants, and commoners, a random sampling of members of every district—including the outcasts in the Sky District.

The prince watched the gathering with a blank expression, eyes moving to the birds that surrounded them, perching on the boulders above, waiting to ferry home their masters after his speech. A fae in a white cloak and hood went up to the prince, placing a wrinkled hand on his arm, before moving behind him to a podium being assembled by the servants. There, the white robed fae lowered his hood and gazed out upon the faeries assembled on the three levels of the Lichfield, and out into the clearing. He wore a golden crown designed in a wreath of six snowflakes with deep blue sapphires in their centers, and his eyes glowed with a matching light, surrounded in wrinkles that seemed for a moment to match the interlaced snowflakes in his crown.

Havrshyk took in a deep breath, muttering angrily under his breath.

Of course, Fryn thought, the King.

The aged king stood as regal and motionless as the statue behind him, waiting for the last few birds and shuffling feet to still, until a cloud left its occlusion of the sun to allow a burst of wan light into the clearing. King Hyngram Martell of Froreholt raised a hand, and then inclined his head toward the statue of Arta and Yndril. Fryn,

Ieffin, Alyra, and everyone else including Havrshyk all followed suit.

"Today marks the anniversary of Queen Yndril's fall, on the day of Mid-Vine, untold thousands of years ago. Even these stones and statues are young compared to that day, having been carved again and again, recommissioned through the generations that the sorrow, the nobility, and the beauty of their passing may never be forgotten," the king intoned, voice wavering as he attempted to make eye contact with every section of the crowd.

The prince stood before him, at his right hand, dressed in a white and glacial blue suit designed to match the powder and the flowers in the fields.

Fryn's eyes moved up to examine the face of Arta, crossed with worry, and then to Yndril, lying peacefully, appearing to sleep in his arms. The stories never told of Yndril having to hold her beloved from a state of undeath… never told of *her* having to save *him*… but Fryn did. *She* was the Lich; she was the one with the tragic past, and the scars, and the pain, and the hurt, and the lies she told herself that she would never be hurt that way again.

She shot Havrshyk a hateful glance, and then deflated. She *wasn't* Yndril and Leif wasn't Arta, but whatever happened, she wasn't going to let him die.

A shiver ran up her spine, a tingling sensation of inquiry, so Fryn looked over at Alyra, who was watching her concernedly, and gave a fake smile. She mouthed, "keep watching" and refocused on the king.

Hyngram was nearly 80, though he looked much older than that, and as he waved a knobby hand over the crowd, he continued reminiscing about the past.

"Perhaps you wonder why I have summoned so many this Mid-Vine Day to the grave of Yndril and those blessed by the Wing-Giver not to die. Indeed. I had once intended to inter one of our forgotten dead. I will pass on that duty to my son instead. Be aware that times of change, fear, and war are ahead—only my son saw this. Ieffin, come forward."

As Ieffin knelt before his father, the crowd's murmuring intensified, and Fryn found herself holding her breath.

"Ieffin Martell, my son, here in the presence of your ancestors, your citizens, and the forgotten, bow your head."

He did so.

Hyngram shakily pulled off the crown and held it over Ieffin's, and his legs buckled as if he were about to fall, so he steadied himself with a hand on his son's shoulder as he pressed the crown down on his head.

"This weight is yours, Ieffin, in the eyes of Yndril and Arta, take up your crown, and look upon your people." Hyngram pulled him up and stepped aside so that Ieffin stood before the gathering alone in front of the podium, with the crown set slightly crookedly on his head. He straightened it absently, shuffling his wings and adjusting the cuffs of his sleeves before addressing the crowd.

"And I thank you father, for your long watch over our people, and for choosing not to forget the past oft overlooked by us all. Some among you will remember hearing stories about the time the Commission attempted to steal our throne, and how Stanaedre was barred from the Commission for its role in the coup. An event, seventy years ago, should not have much bearing on the hunters and the banks we know today, wouldn't you say?" The prince, (*well, the king*, Fryn corrected herself), asked rhetorically, arms held up for effect.

"That coup was thwarted by one fae." He held up a finger in the air. "And the most recent attempt was stopped by two." He held up two fingers and swept the air with his hand so all could see. "I will not allow a third effort." The attention of the crowd grew tense at these words.

"You see, two hunters unknowingly stopped an attempt to eliminate the heirs of the Crown, perhaps you have heard of these 'renegades' as they are now branded—Fryn Martin, and Leif Aellin, who together defeated one of the most infamous assassins Fhoraena has ever seen. I wonder though, is it any coincidence that one of our saviors should be a Lich, preserved after death for a greater purpose? Isn't it incredible that seventy years ago the Commission's coup was also stopped by a different Lich?"

The murmuring ceased, and a hush settled over the crowd. No wind blew, so Ieffin's lowered voice was easy to hear, though soft, almost conspiratorial.

"You forgot about him. Yndril, Fryn, and this forgotten, outcast Lich were our saviors and yet while we revere them, *him* we imprisoned. When he saved King Imloth, having sacrificed his death for his king, this Lich was betrayed by those he had given himself to save. He was imprisoned alive in the tombs of the dead… not here with those returned by the Wing-Giver, but under a wine cellar where he might never have been remembered…"

A hollow voice rang out from the far end of the clearing. "Who was he?"

Fryn could barely make out the raggedy form of a peddler, likely a Sky Dweller.

She felt a knot in her stomach and looked over at Havrshyk, who was shaking, eyes glazed over with ice, and wings pulsing with purple and green.

"He was one of you." Ieffin's mask of composure cracked, and he wiped away a stray tear. "He was one of us! Aldyr Havrshyk, of the Sky District! He was forsaken, considered accursed by all, but he bought with his death three generations of peace!"

The crowd applauded uproariously, and it took minute for them to quiet again.

"I warn you, though I desire to inter him, to give his body rest, we have need of his strength again," Ieffin declared, "for at the same time as I present his broken body to you, requesting that he be reforged, I must also announce the revocation of the Commission's license to operate in Froreholt. They have assassinated my family, they have attempted to usurp power in our lands, and they have put a bounty on the heads of our heroes.

"At this moment, the Lancers are occupying the bounty office, the bank, the lodge, and they are escorting any hunters in Frorin who will not comply outside of the city. Many of our own citizens obtained their licenses to serve their communities, to those I offer this: turn in your license and join the Lancers." His voice had been rising in a crescendo. "A war is coming," he shouted, "and we must be ready when it does!" He slammed a fist into the palm of his other hand.

The new king took a step to the side, waving toward some attendants at the other side of Fryn's group, and they brought up a table with a body laid out, head resting on a pillow, arm lined up with the stump it was once connected to.

"Aldyr Havrshyk," Ieffin said, lowering his voice, "we should have been grateful, yet we must ask more of you again. Arise." He reached out toward Havrshyk, the one in Leif's body, and took hold of the Bloodsword at his waist. He made a show of cutting his own hand on the blade, and then he stabbed it into Havrshyk's true heart.

Fryn could almost feel the wave of power that flowed through the air, as Leif's body fell limply toward the ground. She caught him, heart pounding as she clung to him, waiting and hoping for Leif to rise up himself again.

Below, the crowd cheered and yelled, as the blood flowed back into Havrshyk's body, as his head reattached itself, and his icy eyes blinked and his fingers twitched.

But Leif...his chest didn't move; in fact, he was almost completely drained, and only a few sparks remained in his liver and heart. Fryn poured in what she had of his blood back into his veins, but it wasn't nearly enough. She sent him what she could of her own blood, but she could only spare so much, and even then, he didn't breathe or move.

Fryn didn't have time to glare at Aldyr, she focused on breathing into Leif's mouth and pressing on his chest.

Leif

Leif had not been able to have a glimpse of the outside world since he had helped Fryn in the Stone Market, but he could feel something was wrong. The skies were the same color as a blood red eclipse, shifting with congealed clouds, and a chill wind bit into his face. Ash and sand shifted over the dunes, swirling in a strange, localized breeze. He sat on the edge of that stone platform, the only object in the heart-world besides the sand, and he dangled his feet over the lip of the stones burying his feet in the sand.

Havrshyk shimmered into the desert as if the sand had decided to take his shape. He gave the rolling dunes, and the cracked stone dais a friendly grin, and finally looked at Leif. "Hello again, Leif."

Leif sat on the edge of the stone, his feet buried in the sand, and he squinted at Havrshyk, outlined against the bright, unmoving eclipsed sun. "What brings you my way, Havi?" he asked, shading his eyes against the red glare.

Aldyr inclined his head to Leif and stepped up from the sand onto the platform. He wore a self-satisfied smile, as if relieved to be in his own form again. As he drew near Leif, Havrshyk placed a hand on the cracked crystal pillar in the center of the platform, where his black sword had once been imprisoned by Leif's heart—a chain that he had shattered when he'd saved Leif and Fryn from the Francis brothers just a few weeks before.

"You know, I thought that physical contact would be enough to cause a spiritual differential and draw me back into my body…" Havrshyk mused, turning his back to the crystal plinth and sliding down to sit against it on the ground. He brushed some stray wind-swept hairs away from his face, but the ceaseless wind just blew them back. "All it did was draw me back in here."

Leif brushed off the dust from his knees and fell back so he could lie down and look at the sky swirling and undulating with so many dark currents. After a minute, he asked, "So, where are you?"

Aldyr's head hung, but he lifted a hand and waved toward the sky, as if brushing aside loose papers on a desk.

The blood swept skies parted around the red sun, and through the haze Leif caught sight of a frozen body, with a crooked head being sewn back on by living tendrils of black blood. The clouds shifted back again, hiding the sun's deep burgundy eye, though it was still detectible in the gloom.

"When Ieffin tied my sword to you, I was still alive. It was not as simple as giving you my power. My will was absorbed by the host. But you see I had a lot of experience consuming the will of those I killed. Normally, when I would stab someone, I would consciously overwhelm their usually meager elemental strength in order to claim their life as my own. When I was left without a vessel, I had no option of claiming you, so I *invaded* you." Aldyr shook his head, looking less and less certain of his plan.

"And…"

"And now we are linked! If I go back to my body, I can't just leave you behind!" he yelled, dragging his hand across his face. Havrshyk took a breath and leaned his head back against the crystal plinth—then his eyes snapped open, and Leif felt a subconscious chill. "If I am to inhabit my body alone, then there can only be one soul to move. I need you, your actual you, to die." Havrshyk slapped the cracked crystal plinth with his hand as he added, "I must destroy this pillar, and force your spirit out."

"No," Leif said, sitting up sharply and spinning toward Havrshyk. "You can't cast me out of my own body!"

Havrshyk avoided meeting his eyes. "I will. You are evicted." He pushed himself off the pillar and extended a hand toward it as if about to smite it with some unknown power.

Leif was already moving. He tackled Havrshyk and slammed a twisting punch into his stomach—tossing him into the air.

Havrshyk stretched out his wings, stopping his fall and he descended with a hard expression. Dark ice formed on his limbs, and chest, in the same way that Fryn had taken to protecting herself since the battle with Mythrim. Havrshyk reached up with a hand toward the sky, fingers taut and held in a grasping posture as he wrenched one of the blood currents down and swept Leif off the platform into the sand.

Capsized in the dunes, Leif spun out of his fall and took to the wing. He could feel another level to the sky, far above the coursing blood of Havrshyk, the power in the blackened clouds that rumbled with his betrayal. Leif sucked in a breath and flew straight at Havrshyk even as he spiraled away from a feinted sweep of Havrshyk's blood and threw a jagged line of lightning at his face. Impossibly, the lightning curved around him and went straight into the sky.

Leif didn't have time to be surprised. Havrshyk was already flying at him, rocketing forward with a lash of the blood current, which he absorbed before plummeting toward Leif.

Leif caught him in an attempted clothesline, but his speed was too great, and Leif was tossed back into the sky. Floundering to right himself, he looked back just in time to see Havrshyk smashing into the crystal pillar.

The desert ground shuddered, rolling with a shockwave that pulsed out from the impact and into the distance. At the impact, the black-red, roiling clouds churned and thundered, as a bolt of lightning descended from above, spearing Leif in the heart and casting him to the sand.

Rolling over, Leif struggled to right himself, feeling drained, weak. As he lifted his head and looked at Havrshyk standing where the crystal plinth had been, he felt emptied, cut loose—untethered. Without that connection to the ground, all his stored power and potential had rebounded onto him, and now he lay smoldering with a glowing hole in his 'self', just a lingering charge with no way out.

He lifted his hand, and looked at his fingers, confused. They shimmered in and out of view, as if he were disappearing. Overhead, the blood-clouds rolled away, taking with them an incredible current of wind, which caught up Havrshyk and pulled him up into the air.

"Havrshyk!" Leif croaked, trying to shout after him.

Aldyr paused in his flight, floating in a clear blue sky beside a small void where the sun was supposed to be, eclipsed by his blood.

"When I first found myself here, Leif, I wanted nothing more than to kill you. Before I go, I want you to know that I wish I didn't have to now. But I am finished sacrificing myself for others, Leif!"

"That's very bitter…" Leif said, pulling himself up onto the cracked and broken platform of stone.

"Justice is *not* rewarding, Leif. We just have to make our way alone as best we can. This is mine." With that, Havrshyk shook his head and stepped into the black sun, vanishing from Leif's heart-world.

The stones vibrated at the severed connection, and though the sun shone above him, warm and fresh, and the sand regained its glow, Leif's connection to his body, his power, to everything he used to have, was gone.

The stones he lay on sunk into the sand, hungry to draw them, to take him, deep beneath the dunes.

Havrshyk had bought his freedom, but at the price of Leif's death.

The sands embraced his body, and he sank beneath an endless blanket of soft warm grains. But… beneath the sands he felt a pulse, a beat, another connection he hadn't known he'd had before. It struggled, rising and falling, in a panic, and as he thought on that sound the sands moved in that direction, swarming and churning—tunneling him through a river in the sand. It was there!

Another dais! Another person connected to him!

As his wings dissolved, and he fell from the sands into bluish black clouds, he landed on a puff of icy dust, in a sweet-smelling glade, surrounded by glacial blue flowers, and dark evergreen leaves. But he couldn't stand. The dusty snow also sank beneath his feet and his wings had already dissolved.

His hands became translucent, everything about him, untethered, until he felt a dragging—no, a tugging on his sleeve.

"Leif, you're here!" Fryn cried, pulling him out of the snow, and dragging him to the pillar of glacial ice in the center of the dais. "I didn't think you'd find me!"

"Of course I'd find you eventually," he said, narrowing his eyes at her, "If it were up to me, I'd never lose you again. It's been so long, *months* in here. Where have you been?"

She smiled kindly at him, as the clouds faded above to reveal a glimpse of Havrshyk's body twitching just a wingspan away. "It's been half that, though it felt like a year. I'm going to show you where to go. I have got a back door; the same one you stumbled through. Now that Havrshyk is gone, it will probably be safe to return."

He shook his head, or tried, as he rested against her knees. "Fryn," he said, "there is something wrong with me, I don't think I can go back." He pointed with a hand at her own similar plinth of ice. "Just as Mythrim stabbed me in my liver for my sparks, Havrshyk stabbed my heart, for my life. I don't think I can make a *new* connection."

Fryn bit her lip. "I had to once, but I don't think it would work the same for you. I doubt with your sparks you could become a Bloodcrafter, and it's not like you're bleeding anyway. It is your mind that was dislocated, or rather, well…"

The view in the hazy sky shifted toward Leif's body, and they watched in amazement as one of his wings began to disintegrate out there as well!

"That's not going to happen to me, Fryn, I'll not be thrown to the sands as a wingless… where's this back door?" He gritted his teeth, and wobbled to his feet, fading in and out like the fog.

Fryn squeezed his hand and pulled him in for a mostly incorporeal kiss before she pushed him into the snow and vanished from the internal world. He was thrown, then shifted and floated down a stream of powder snow, so that he fell from the clear blue sky toward the last few stones of his broken dais the desert hadn't consumed yet. As he landed on the shattered remnants of himself, he felt a lingering spark of strength somewhere deep within, where he had never thought to look before, and gathered it. Leif focused all of his energy, the last of his sparks—a well of power of a type he'd never sensed before—and drew down a lightning bolt from the sky into the last shards of the plinth, and the Viper's fang.

The wave of power hit him with a powerful jolt, and before he was blasted out of his heart-world he saw the crystal forming from the sand itself on the layer of broken stones and sand. It was a translucent green platform of molded glass, with a spike formed around that fang at the center.

Then he opened his eyes.

Lichfield

Fryn

Fryn held onto Leif with frozen tears on her eyes. She could feel the sparks he had left moving through his veins, but his wings continued to disintegrate at a frightening pace. Alyra crouched beside her, one hand on Leif's chest, her eyes closed, as if listening, or sensing.

"He is still there Fryn, somehow, his… he…" she wavered, "his *gellath* has been shattered, though some of his power remains. He must have incredible elemental strength." Alyra drew one of her wingshard blades and pressed the flat against his head, and then her forehead against the other side of it. "Leif," she whispered, "focus your power, do not let it escape."

Before the statue of Yndril and Arta, Havrshyk rose from the table in the same black coat and uniform he had died in not so long ago. He slowly pulled out the sword from his chest and gave Ieffin a long, confused look.

Below, the crowd roared in amazement, calls of "Lich", "hero", and "survivor" echoed in the clearing.

"It wasn't the Commission who killed me, Ieffin," Havrshyk warned in a low voice, "What sort of manipulation is this?" The frozen blood threads he'd sewn his head back on with continued to writhe and tighten their threads.

Ieffin met his eyes. "The honest kind."

"You will keep your word about the Sky District?"

"I will. And I believe the Pine-Martin will also ensure that." Ieffin turned to the crowd, announcing, "Behold, the last survivor of the Stanaedre Coup, restored in our hour of need. This day, I denounce the underhanded actions of the Commission, and declare that we will safeguard our own citizens, invest our own funds, and make our own alliances. Indeed," he added, whipping out a scroll from his coat and letting it flap in the wind with red ribbons sealed at the end, "the clans of Aelaete have also joined our coalition!"

Havrshyk shot Fryn a worried look, as she clutched Leif's body, glaring back with all the hatred she could muster.

As the new king was about to continue his speech, a hawk screeched overhead, scaring away the sparrows and crows of the guests, and a body fell on the dais from above with a sickening crunch. For a moment, silence filled the vale, followed shortly by screams and a flood of faeries trying to find their birds.

Fryn swallowed. That body had no wings.

Even as she watched the body, unsure if it were fee or fae, the air distorted around it, and the body disappeared—replaced by the standing figure of the Moraskyn agent they had fought off in the Stone Market.

He wore deep purple robes, bordering on black, with brilliant yellow trim, and he flexed his hands as he scanned the crowd with ravenous eyes. One hand stiffened into his claw-like posture and a black orb formed before his fingers, and he was already moving before anyone hardly realized he was there. Several of Ieffin's lancers fell with seared holes in their chests or sizzling stumps where their heads used to be.

Alyra left Fryn and Leif on the ground beside the statue, rushing the Moraskyn with her wingshard daggers drawn, and dodged to the side before another figure landed in a cloud of dust on the stones beside the Moraskyn. This one had malformed wings, and skeletal fingers, both its arms lumpy with bony growths, and Grifton's desiccated face looked even more... eroded... as he whipped his head around looking for her.

"Over here," Havrshyk said, standing on the opposite side from Fryn, with Ieffin moving back behind his guards. "It is embarrassing that you survived our encounter back in the Weasel Cairn, Grifton."

Grifton stopped, spun toward him, and then stopped again in confusion. "You're not Leif."

"So, you *are* stupid," Aldyr said, grinning. "I was *never* Leif. I am the Lich Aldyr Havrshyk—perhaps you've heard of me?"

Grifton's wings shifted. "No."

Havrshyk was already moving, rushing under Grifton's confused guard with a fluid grace that outstripped Fryn by a sparrow's flight, sweeping through with a serrated Bloodsword that actually managed to score a cut in Grifton's sword and chest plates. "Too bad you won't have another chance to remember it, but at least you can die knowing it was *I* who left you to die there."

Grifton howled. He slashed out with claws and blade in a one-two swing, but Aldyr merely deflected the hand, and caught the blade as he slipped behind his guard and thrust an ice-encrusted jab into one of the cuts he'd made before.

"So good to be myself again!" Havrshyk yelled, dropping under another swing, grabbing Grifton's foot and tripping him off the dais.

As Grifton fell to the ground level of the clearing, throwing up a cloud of dusty snow, Fryn looked back to Alyra fighting the Moraskyn fae, and she clutched Leif's jacket, fighting back the shaking in her shoulders and the tears that wouldn't stay frozen.

"Leif… Leif… you promised that you'd stay with me. You were the only ray of sunshine in the ice wastes of my life, Leif… the only one." As she curled over his cold body, Fryn pressed her lips against his, breathing in another burst of air, and working to keep his heart moving again.

He didn't have enough sparks.

As she pushed on his chest, moving his blood through his veins, she eyed the statue of Yndril, and ground her teeth. "You were supposed to be my Arta. Leif, I can't be Yndril without you! I shouldn't have to survive like this—I can't bear it!"

Screams sounded below where Grifton and Havrshyk fought in a clamorous duel, and Fryn distractedly noticed another disintegrating orb fly over her head and kill another one of the servants standing at attention out of the fray.

Leif's wings faded away, dissolving completely, and Fryn kept breathing into him, pressing on his heart, and sensing the flow of blood… and she felt the locus of power forming in his heart, and so she grabbed her knife, and held it out, wavering as Alyra was thrown back from one the Moraskyn's blasts, and met her eyes.

"You shelter the exile at your peril, abomination," the fae said, eyes flicking to her Bloodknife dismissively. "Such a power is easy to melt. Is that the right word?"

Fryn set her jaw, crouching over Leif defensively, "Fly off, Moraskyn…"

"She threatens but is a fool," he replied, snapping his fingers, and summoning a spiraling orb of blackness the size of her head. "This will hit one of you, it is up to you which one. You may live if you accept that he is already dead."

Memories flashed through her head of her fight against the light elemental Grass Guard Captain in Fassen, and how she was able to sacrifice some of the blood in her blade to deflect his attacks, perhaps…

The orb flew at her.

And she was shoved aside.

There, catching the orb on his wings was the frail old fae, the former king, Hyngram. At the same time that the orb hit him, he batted his wings and deflected the void into the sky.

The king collapsed beside her, half his wings consumed—no, *erased* by the blast, and Fryn saw his eyes roll back into his head. Then, the second orb flew at her.

Fryn thrust out her blade, snapping it at an angle so that it would deflect… except that it simply *ate* through her Bloodknife, and continued right toward her face. She didn't even have time to blink. Only think.

Leif, I am coming.

Lichfield

Leif

The wave carried him up from the depths, through fire, water, earth, and sky, through stars, and nebula, through deserts… until his eyes flashed open to a pale sky. His head lay on something soft, and comforting, and as he looked up, he saw Fryn's hand around his cheek, and the Bloodknife held out to protect him.

His hair stood on end. The wave pulsed through him from the sky into the ground, and he clutched onto Fryn's hand with a growing realization of what was about to happen.

Leif pulled Fryn back, barely able to roll her away before a black orb flew overhead, and the *greater* danger pierced his belly from the sky.

Sparks. Energizing, invigorating, electrifying sparks flooded his body, solidifying in his wing joints, spreading out from them in a new set of teal-colored wings.

The air was super charged; he could taste it and smell burns as he rolled over and met Fryn's once panicked and now amazed eyes. Standing up, he walked over to her, ignoring the confusion on the Moraskyn's face, and held out his hand. Fryn lay her hand in his with disbelief written on her face.

"I heard you, Fryn," he said, pulling her up and wrapping his arms around her. "I heard you calling my name."

She avoided meeting his eyes, staring past him into the distance. "Leif, the king…"

But he wasn't listening, he turned her chin, put one hand on the small of her back, and slid the other around her cheek to cup the back of her head, as they kissed.

She collapsed into the kiss, and though his legs felt weak from his long time spent locked into the sword, he held her in a tight embrace.

Leif sensed the black orb several spans before it would have reached him, and so he leaned Fryn back as if in a dance, and with a wave of his hand he threw sparks into the dust of the stone platform and a marbled wall of glass divided him from the Moraskyn fae. "No more interruptions!" he shouted, "I have important business!"

Fryn nodded at that, pulling him back into another kiss.

Cries, swords, shouts, and the shuddering use of power surrounded them—but for ten seconds they held onto each other and were alone.

"Leif, your wings… they're changed." Fryn pulled back from the kiss with narrowed eyes.

He gently, begrudgingly, let her step back. "They're new wings Fryn, what did you expect?"

"But…"

"When you first died, what was it that you lost?"

"My blood…" she said, nervously looking through the glass wall he'd made.

"So, that is what he gave you back." He followed her gaze and nodded. "I lost something a little different, a little harder to explain…but, a new connection meant some slight changes to my element."

"Don't think you can ignore me!" shouted the Moraskyn fae, throwing a shock wave at the wall of glass and shattering it. "We cannot allow another wingcrafter, not you, not her. I am the only one sanctioned to use this!" As he said this, one of his six wings dissolved into mist, and another one of his dark orbs appeared in his hands. How they dissolved everything but his hands, Leif had no idea, but what he'd said about wingcrafting made him think that he didn't have to be as concerned about this one as he'd first assumed.

"Fryn, Havrshyk is a weasel—he didn't have a way to bring me back and would rather kill me than stay dead… but go help him anyway. I will take care of this fae here." He put more confidence into those words than he truly felt, but she nodded with a smile and flitted off toward the clearing below. "I have to say, Moraskyn, I did not want to fight you."

"You are still young and unpracticed, wingbreaker, you do not know what you are," said the now five-winged fae, balancing his implosive orb on a finger.

"I broke nothing, stole nothing. I was merely given my wings again. What about you…um…who are you?"

"Pashen, and I have shattered many like you before. You claim to be blessed with the power of the stars, but power like anything else, is something that can be taken." Pashen, the Moraskyn fae, focused on Leif with eyes that darkened to a violet shade. The air fell heavily on Leif's neck, and he struggled under its weight.

"Go back to your country Pashen. Leave this place as you are, or leave it broken," Leif warned, clenching his fists and drawing in sparks from the increased charge in the air. Swirling northern lights formed above him, and even spiraled down to caress his hands, as he drew in the electromagnetic activity of the skies. Leif's hair stood on end, the metal buttons on his coat stuck together, and he could feel a tugging on his wings, as if…as if he could fly *without* them, perfectly weightless despite the increased gravity Pashen bore down on him.

Pashen swore in an unknown language and glared at Leif. "You are too young, too inexperienced to stop *this*!" He lobbed one orb, and then, discarding another wing, he threw another larger ball of swirling void at Leif.

Leif grunted against the combined pressures of the gravity and the pulling of the magnetic forces on his heart, as he twisted his fingers and snapped a snake of aurora light into the stones and also around the first orb, so that he caught it and threw it straight up into the air.

The look on Pashen's face, a mixture of disbelief and horror, strengthened Leif as he rolled under the second, larger orb, letting it collide with one of the kings' gravestones behind him.

Not wanting to lose his momentum, Leif leapt off the platform to take to the skies, and… even though he had wings, he couldn't get them to flutter! He spiraled in a pathetic spin to the ground, where he threw up a cloud of dusty snow. One of his ribs ached, but for the most part, he felt whole.

Fryn and Havrshyk were just ahead, fighting against Grifton and a hunter with a spear. As Aldyr held Grifton's sword edge to edge,

Fryn was frantically shouting at the spearfae as she caught or deflected his attacks.

"Stop protecting him, Jeldon! He killed Hatha just like he killed that Cherim in the city! You mean nothing, you are nothing to him!"

The spearfae ignored her, focusing on jabbing toward her knife-hand, and keep her at a distance.

Leif felt the shift in the air as Pashen floated down to the ground behind him, and he turned to see his amused eyes locked on the hunters battling the Liches, Fryn and Havrshyk.

"He is a simple fae, so powerful, for a faerie born with four wings. But at least he was smart enough to bring enough hunters to depose this king before his orders could be enforced."

"What orders?" Leif asked, dusting himself off and focusing on where he knew his wing joints were, trying to get them to move.

"He wanted to exile the Commission," Pashen said laughing, resting a hand on an amethyst jeweled dagger on his belt. "Even I know how foolish that would be. That is why I negotiated with the President for assistance in tracking and eliminating that exile over there." He pointed up toward where their newest companion, Alyra, was peering out over the ledge at them.

Then Leif saw the other birds.

A few of the birds landing on the rocks looked like the type used by nobility or commoners for traveling long distances, but there were others, large hawks and ravens, offloading mismatched groups of faeries armed with spears, bows, and swords.

"Alyra!" Leif shouted. "Protect the prince!"

She looked at him blankly.

"Ieffin!"

"Oh… the king?" she asked, "I will!"

Pashen tutted at him and shook his head. "You'd send a wingbreaker to save someone? That is like asking a butcher to cut out a tumor."

"Effective? I thought so too." Leif finally got his wings to shift into their correct positions and tested a flutter. Strangely, they felt weak, like they had when he was a child still learning to walk.

The Moraskyn nodded at him with a wry smile, "I am truly sorry I have to kill you. You are humorous, and we cannot seem to keep our jesters alive for very long." He closed his eyes, and the air darkened around him, and a third wing vanished into smoke as the darkness surrounded him in serpentine spirals.

Still drawing on the intense green aurora, Leif pulled it into similar trails of green light that snaked around his arms, and between his feet and back around his waist.

One of the prince's… the king's lancers fell to the ground unmoving with an arrow through his eye, but Leif didn't let himself become distracted, not even by Fryn's desperate fight with Jeldon.

Pashen vanished. He reappeared as a displacement in the electric field that Leif had surrounded himself with, and he was barely fast enough to dodge the searing blackness. As it ate away at his green-infused power, Leif lowered his stance and struck a palm into the ground. A bubble of magnetic energy flowed from him, tossing the Moraskyn into the air where his three wings would be useless for flight, so that Leif could aim an outstretched finger up at his head.

He threw out a bolt of lightning to the sky. Pashen closed his eyes, vanishing out of thin air before the lightning could strike.

Pashen's next strike wasn't infused with power, though it was incredibly strong, as he shimmered into existence at Leif's feet and swept his legs out from under him.

Leif fell rolling reflexively as an obsidian dagger traced through the air where his neck had been a moment before, catching on just the edge so that a shallow cut formed over his throat.

Leif pulled on the static in the sky and gloried in the power that seared through him as another lightning bolt descended, flowing through him into the stones. He stepped back, and found himself back-to-back with Fryn, grinning with confidence. "Jeldon, is it? Fryn doesn't lie."

The spearfae behind him snickered. "You think you're winning? Look up high, Leif, Ieffin's going to fall in a minute, and those last few lancers and nobles are going to break and abandon him. We win."

Fryn hissed. "I didn't beat death just to hear you whine, Jeldon. When Grifton devours you, just remember I warned you. Leif," she said, glancing over her shoulder at him, "how is Ieffin really?" She asked, softly so Jeldon couldn't hear.

Leif could still sense everything around him thanks to the static field, so he spared a moment to look up at the statue of Yndril and Arta, where Ieffin, sporting a bandage on one arm, was waving a silver sword in the other at a group of Lancers rushing a mismatched group of hunters.

"Ieffin's doing fine. Harissa is even there. Oooh! She just killed a hunter twice her size." Leif laughed, and then met Pashen's eyes. "You only have three wings left."

"The fae can count," Pashen said with a dry laugh, and then ran toward them, his obsidian dagger glowing with an impossibly black light.

"One, two, three, five…" Leif counted, folding his green aurora light into the semblance of a blade, one that he didn't even have to hold, "eight…"

"Leif?" Fryn asked, grabbing the haft of Jeldon's spear, and ripping it from his grasp.

"Thirteen." Leif whipped the line of compressed electro-magnetic energy around to catch the obsidian dagger. Sparks flew from the impact, and heat radiated from where they met.

Pashen's worried eyes met Leif's and he focused harder on his blade—one more wing disappearing to fuel the elemental attack.

"Twenty-one," Leif said, sweat pouring down his face, as he compounded the intensity of the sparks he focused into the blade…and felt a tugging at the edges of his wings. He couldn't infuse any more without consuming them—and he'd just gotten them!

Leif and Fryn were blown back toward the empty clearing, and Pashen was thrown against the stone wall of the upper graveyard. Fryn clung to him, and they rolled in flight, skidding to a stop some fifty wingspans away.

If Pashen had hit the stones, the force of that impact should have been fatal but at this point Leif hardly believed it was possible to kill the Moraskyn fae. As he gently disentangled himself from Fryn's arms, and looked up past Grifton and Jeldon, he saw Pashen floating in the air without a single wing to be seen.

He glared at the two with a rage completely divorced from all the amusement he'd shown before. Settling to the stones with a dark fluttering power surrounding him like a shadow, he raised his hands and summoned a spiraling black orb, far larger and more impenetrable than the previous ones. But Leif didn't have time to react.

Grifton was flying towards them.

Havrshyk stood where they had been fighting, arms spread in abandonment and face nonplussed, and Jeldon, too, looked over at them with a confused scowl.

Just as Grifton's dropped down before him, Leif noticed Ieffin running a hunter through with his sword and smiled. "It's not really going as planned, is it?"

Grifton opened his mouth as he landed heavily on the ground.

"You are really stupid, Grifton," Fryn interjected, grabbing Leif by his coat, and pulling him back toward the ground.

Grifton's eyes followed him, rage twisting his face…and the black orb slammed into his back, cutting off whatever he had planned to say. He screamed a ragged, screeching scream as an invisible explosion blasted him over the boulder wall.

Leif held Fryn tightly, watching for another orb, but Pashen was gone. Really, truly gone.

Jeldon stood alone, leaning down to retrieve his spear, but cautious of actually picking it up. His eyes kept flashing back and forth between Leif, Fryn, and Havrshyk. Finally, he simply sat down, pulled a metal square out of his pocket, and threw it away.

Fryn flew over to the little piece of metal, retrieving it with a sneer. "Giving up your license, eh, Jeldon? That's the smart move, and you should be glad you weren't able to kill anyone before surrendering."

He mumbled something under his breath, sitting cross-legged and avoiding her eyes.

"You want to repeat that?" she demanded, showing him his own discarded hunter's license.

"No," he said, sighing heavily.

Ieffin's voice rang out from above, as he shouted orders, and Leif saw birds flying off with the retreating hunters. "This is not over."

Havrshyk walked over, awkwardly looking between Leif and the birds.

"Leif… I…"

"You feel like the double yoke that didn't get to be the bird?" Leif guessed.

"What?"

"Like the twin who never made much of himself when his brother was a huge success?" Leif guessed again.

Havrshyk frowned.

Leif added in a softer tone so Fryn couldn't hear. "You feel like a traitor who has been found out and can't run away?" Watching his face, Leif couldn't stifle a laugh. Lich or no, Havrshyk blushed both in his face and his wings.

"What you did for yourself, I did for her," Leif said, "Sometimes we try to be selfish, and it helps others anyway. Sometimes we try to help others, but we are just deceiving ourselves. Which were you?"

"Leif… I…" Havrshyk's face hardened, "you killed me! You locked me away again, after I had been betrayed, I was *owed* better!"

"And you got it," Fryn said, pointing up at Ieffin. "Leif, you may not have heard the speech, but Ieffin made a real apology to Havrshyk, so for Jakaren's sake!" She turned to Havrshyk, "Accept what you wanted anyway!"

Jeldon muttered softly, "Shouldn't swear by Jakaren…"

Fryn spun toward him, jabbing a finger into his chest. "I've already died once, Jeldon, do you want to say that again?"

Leif caught her shoulder and shot a pointed look at Havrshyk, hoping that he caught the message to discuss his betrayal later. He led Fryn up the steps, over the bodies of nobles, commoners, soldiers, and guards, and then… over the body of an old fae in a white robe and missing two of his wings.

Fryn shook herself free of Leif's arm and knelt beside the body, wings shaking as she searched around herself for someone, or something. She crawled over to a fallen lancer and froze.

Beside the lancer lay Harissa in a black coat, with a red scarf around her neck, her Bonesword drawn and dripping red, her face pale and cold. Fryn choked off a sob and put her fingers against Harissa's neck.

Harissa's eyes fluttered open. "Fryn? Your hands are freezing!"

"You're alive!" Fryn cried, hugging Harissa, and making her gasp in pain. "What happened to you?"

Leif was still kneeling beside the old fae, bowing his head to convey his respect and thanks for the pivotal aid the old king had provided. Leif unwrapped the tan scarf from around his neck and folded it in the ceremonial way of his clan, so that it formed a pillow in the shape of a diamond and placed it under the king's head.

As he did, he felt shallow breath escaping the former king's nostrils, and so he placed a hand on his forehead. "My lord," Leif said, "where are you injured?"

Fryn would care for Harissa; Leif focused on tracing the natural lines of sparks through the old king's body—they were weak, even for his age.

"I know you," the king said, voice wispy and frail, "you will help my son, yes? Make things right?" He wheezed and took in a shaky breath.

Sparks gathered around the base of his skull, as if he had cracked his head on the stairs, so Leif nodded. "Your son will be a wise and honorable king."

Hyngram smiled. "I was so scared to take up the crown. My father was not right in the head, a danger to others, a danger to himself…" he coughed up a foaming red fluid that dribbled from his mouth in a sickly trail, "I never wanted…" he hacked again, "to be a king like him… but too afraid to free the lich who saved him—who saved me."

"He was angry," Leif said, remembering all the times since being linked to Havrshyk he had talked about this very subject, "but deep down I think he would have accepted hearing it from you."

"When Ieffin said he wanted to do this… I knew. He was ready." As he said those words, the king breathed out and didn't breathe in again.

Leif closed the king's eyes and looked over at Fryn and Harissa. "How is she?" he asked.

"*She* will survive, Leif," Harissa choked out, "Fryn just decided to be generous for once and share some of her blood."

"Fryn's always generous," he said with a distant smile.

Fryn shot him a questioning look and a dimpled smile in return, as she quipped, "Don't forget it!"

"I won't." Further up the steps Leif felt the approach of others, and slowly let the static charge around his body dissipate. "Fryn…" he said, looking back at Hyngram, "I couldn't do anything for him. He saved us…"

Ieffin appeared at the steps above them with a pale face, either from the emotional loss or the blood loss, Leif couldn't tell. "Leif. Fryn. Thank you. My father has given his life with honor, and will be remembered with Yndril, Arta, Martell, and in the same breath as Havrshyk and Fryn, and the Viper of the North."

Fryn, one shoulder supporting Harissa, bowed her head. "King Ieffin, I am pleased your father was the one to crown you before this attack." She knelt tiredly, leaning her head against her cousin's. "But you left one name off that list."

Ieffin ignored her, settling on the ground beside his father, holding out one arm so an attendant could clean a slash that ran from his wrist to his elbow. With his left hand, King Ieffin brushed a stray hair out of his father's peacefully resting face, and then bent down to kiss his forehead.

The prince-now-king's blood dripped from the cut onto the strips of his white sleeve, as the young butler uncorked a bottle of ceren and poured it over the wound.

Ieffin held out a hand, and instinctively the butler passed a crystal glass of the ceren, two-fingers worth, to him. The new king opened his father's mouth and let a small sip of the liquid fall into it, and then he lifted the glass to his own mouth and drank the whole glass—wincing as the first attendant pierced his skin with a needle and began to pass it through, stitching up the slash.

Then, after a moment of silence, the king stood and moved over to the edge of the platform where he could look out over the remaining guards, nobles, and commoners gathered; reclaimed birds waited on the rocks. Somehow the faeries knew that they were not done.

"Faeries of Froreholt!" Ieffin shouted in a hoarse, tremulous voice, "even on the day I have been given the Winter Crown, our enemy has attempted to destroy us. They have slaughtered our people, they have slain my father, and..." he pulled his arm free of his servant, who was still trying to finish sewing up the wound, so that a spatter of blood sprayed over Ieffin's tunic, "we will not be afraid!"

Leif swallowed, joining in the applause and the shouts of agreement from below.

"If there are any left who doubted my motion to expel the Commission, let this be a testament to the truth! I will not stand by after this attack, nor will you; and in this hollow where I had planned to honor a Lich, I am going to honor the life and the death of my father the king. There was to be a toast in celebration and welcoming to our forgotten hero, Aldyr Havrshyk, the Sword of the Crown, but in the same sip you take to welcome him, remember the king who sacrificed himself for the next generation—who died with honor protecting his people!"

Havrshyk shifted with a conflicted expression on the next level down, avoiding meeting Leif or Fryn's eyes. Alyra stood beside him, talking softly, one hand on his shoulder.

Bottles of Guldhand Frost, their sweetest floral ice wine, were opened all throughout the clearing as servants and attendants filled a myriad of glasses and passed them around. A flute found its way into Leif's hand, and he was about to give it to Fryn, but she merely burrowed under his arm, and clinked glasses with the one she already had.

"This is for the living, the preserved of the dead, those we love, and those we loved alike. May the Wing-Giver take up our lost, and may he watch over our land as this war begins!" Ieffin pronounced the toast and thrust his bleeding hand into the air, and the crowd joined with him in a silent salute. In the process, he yanked the needle and thread from his butler's hand, and it swung in the air, dangling with beads of blood along the length.

Leif and Fryn sipped the delicate dessert wine, savoring the apricot and honey notes and the caramel essence that lingered for ages, and bowed their heads in the extended quiet. Then, as Leif opened his eyes again, he saw the empty grave where Havrshyk was going to be buried before Ieffin's plan had had to change.

"Fryn, can you drain and freeze the king?" he asked, his voice barely a whisper.

She pulled back and glared at him. "What? Are you trying to desecrate his memory?"

"I am going to preserve it," he answered, drawing on the lingering static charge in the air. One of the tendrils of the far of aurora snaked down from the sky around his body as he passed off his glass to Jaeson, (who was now supporting Harissa), picked up the king's body as carefully as he could, and carried it over to the grave site.

Ieffin turned toward him in alarm, his mouth opening and closing, but without sound.

"Fryn, lay a block of ice in the same shape as that supporting Arta and Yndril over there, and freeze the king so he can look out over the people."

She shivered but held out a hand toward the empty space. "It's not going to be easy," she said.

Havrshyk appeared beside them, matching Fryn's posture, "Then it is good you are not doing it alone."

Together they spread out a veil of mist over the space that coalesced into a deep blue block of ice with tendrils of black, like veins, running throughout. Hyngram stood, frozen into the position he had been when he had taken the blast of that disintegrating orb, arms outstretched, face held in a determined expression, and with two of his wings erased halfway from the joints.

Then, Leif spun the green snake of sparks, and felt the sand and dust on the platform shifting toward his hands. He closed his eyes, envisioning how it should be when completed, and a blinding flash of light exploded from his hands as he slammed them onto the ground.

Glass formed from the impact, running up the block of ice, up and around the body of the king, sealing him completely in a perfectly clear crystal glass that ran out to the tips of where his wings had been—so that from the broken ends, the blue wings transitioned to invisible glass shards. Hyngram's features took on a noble aspect beneath the translucent marbling of raw glass, and a hint of starlight seemed to reside within it.

Leif heard the gasp from the crowd, and Ieffin cursing by Jakaren, of all things, so he turned to him and remained kneeling on the ground. "Tell me now, is there any way that he will be forgotten?" Leif looked up, at the space between Fryn and Havrshyk, and at Ieffin with tears streaming down his face.

Ieffin collapsed, just for a moment, and stood again stiffly.

The butler rushed forward with a glass of ceren, but he pushed it away, and walked back to the ledge. "I begin a new tradition this Mid-Vine Day. No more is this hollow sacred to a few, but it is now hallowed for all our people, from the ancestors who gave their lives to birth our royal line, to the heroes that defended that line, and to the king who died to preserve his people! I invite any who will come next year to lay a snowflake at his feet!" He flicked his fingers and a large crystalline snowflake formed from the moisture in the air, and then he moved to the perfectly preserved statue of his father and set the snowflake in his open hand.

As Ieffin stepped away, Fryn, then Havrshyk laid blood red flakes at his feet, and other faeries and attendants approached one by one so that as they descended the top level of the Lichfield was surrounded by a field of sparkling ice.

Leif nodded gratefully toward Havrshyk, and then pulled Fryn aside, behind the statue of Yndril and Arta.

"Leif, I…" she started, but he didn't let her finish. He pulled her in for a long kiss. "Leif… wait… I…" still he caught her again and held her tight, not letting her talk until they sank into the embrace and knelt on the ground, short of breath.

"You saved me, Fryn," Leif said, grinning and wiping away a tear.

She scrunched up her eyes and froze them clear. Dimples marked her cheeks as she smiled broadly and brushed a lock of hair behind her ear. "I don't want to lose you ever again, Leif."

"You won't have to," Leif said, pressing his lips to a line, "because I'm not going anywhere."

She nodded slowly, and then leaned back with tears breaking free of her icy blockades, as she shook with a silent bout of crying. He wrapped an arm around her shoulders and pulled her close, letting her cry, resting her head on his knees, until she took a deep breath and looked up at him with red eyes and a weary smile.

"Leif… I'm sorry you had to go through that, too…"

"Through what, Fryn?" he asked, petting her cheek idly.

She avoided meeting his eyes as she said, "it happened to me once too—when I died—when I became a Lich. I was a child. And…And…I've never been able to talk to anyone about it, never wanted to relive it…it's…I'm sorry, Leif."

"I'm not." Leif shook his head. "And somehow, I think I had a much better experience than you did. Will you tell me?"

Fryn shivered, curling up her legs and huddling closer to him. "Yes...but not right now…"

He laughed. "Deal."

Fryn sniffed, and then shakily breathed out a sigh.

"This is going to mean war then."

"Most likely," he agreed.

"Where do we fit into all this?"

He picked up her hand and kissed it. "Right here."

On the other side of the statue, they heard musicians playing melancholy tunes, and the soft calls and cries of faeries inspecting the wounded or dead and clearing the space. Over the next hour or so, as the battlefield, the Lichfield, was restored to order, the pile of snowflakes spread all the way around the base of the king's pedestal.

Interlude 4

CASK

~70 Years Ago~

Snow District

Aldyr

Havrshyk spun around the corner of the Frosthall Winery wall, slid across the icy cobblestones, and skidded to a halt in the courtyard. The wind of his flight tossed his white coattails around him, casting stray powdery snowflakes back into the air. Aldyr's eyes drifted over the anemic trail of smoke coming from the chimney of the manor on the north side of the square, and then to the still body on the stones beside the doors of the warehouse to the south. He pressed a hand to his chest, almost as if to claw back the fingers of dread that constricted his heart and knelt beside the body.

His attending members of the Crown Guard landed behind him as he rested a gloved hand on the unmoving chest. Havrshyk closed his eyes, and hissed, "Search the area, he can't be far!"

Two of the Crown Guard split off from the group, one checking the north and the other looking in the warehouse to the south. The one remaining guard stood beside him rigid, and frozen before the body of Master Baesil—Master of the Swordhand Palm.

"Captain," she said, her voice cold and distant, "who could have done this?"

Aldyr ground his teeth, and removed his black leather glove so he could brush Master Baesil's hair out of his eyes, which glared coldly at the blanketed sky. Aldyr gently closed his eyelids and released a long sigh.

"His body is cold, Yala, he died some time ago. The killer has likely already gotten away…" he trailed off as he glanced down toward Baesil's free-hand, which had something clutched in it, like a piece of cloth.

Noticing something else, Aldyr stood and searched around the body, and could find no sign of Master Baesil's signature sword. Seeing no further clues, Aldyr lifted Baesil's hand, and pried the bit of cloth out from his fingers and took in a breath as the light of the nearby oil lamp glinted off the metal plate sewn into the green fabric—a Hunter's License.

"We must bring his body back to the Guardhouse immediately," Aldyr said, pocketing the license, "we'll have to investigate this further then." He shook his head. "Jerrin, Tullod!"

The other two guards returned, sweeping back from both sides in a rush. "Yes sir?" they asked at once.

"Wake the winery staff. Ask around to see if anyone heard or saw anything. Yala and I will carry the Master back to the Guardhouse."

She nodded. "Yes, Captain," she said, saluting him with a beat of her wings and bending down to take hold of Master Baesil's feet. Her shoulder-length dark red hair looked nearly the color of blood, and as she held onto the Master's ankles, she met Aldyr's eyes. He swallowed. Her blue eyes searched deep within, and she nodded to herself.

Jerrin, the tall brown-haired fae with a curling mustache gave him the same salute and flew back toward the warehouse once more; and Tullod, the blond, cleanshaven fae, who had joined the Swordhand-Palm a year or two after Aldyr, nodded deeply with steeled eyes. He didn't fly, since it was a short distance, but merely walked over to the front door and knocked firmly.

Aldyr crouched and lifted the master's head, and with Yala's aid, they flew off toward the Guardhouse with his former Master in tow.

"I am sorry, Captain," Yala said, talking in a half-yell so he could hear her as they flew above the Vineroad.

Havrshyk didn't have the words. He stuffed his dismay and loss deep into his stomach and focused on not dropping the body. It was a quiet flight in the night, as most of the citizens were already asleep in their beds.

They landed at the entrance of the Guardhouse and strode in, surprising the city guards, who had been leaning too comfortably back in their chairs beside the watch desk. The two guards rose to their feet, eyes widening as they saw the cream and blue uniform of the Crown Guard, and the body he and Yala carried.

"Clear a table!" Havrshyk shouted at them, "and go wake your captain!"

The guards hastened to the dining table in the ball room and shoved aside some of the mugs and plates that had been left there from their evening meal. They thoughtfully laid a runner on the table so they could set the body down on something finer than the hard wood.

Yala stepped back, white in the face, and shivering even though she, like Havrshyk, was a frost elemental. "Sir? You said the Master called you out to talk…that it was a matter of national importance."

"It was," was all he replied as he examined the body more carefully in the light of the Guardhouse's starlamps. The Master had been unarmed, and there were no wounds on his chest, face, or hands, so Aldyr rolled him onto his side and found a small tear in his coat.

He laid him back down and then sat him up so he could remove his coat… but he didn't have enough hands.

"Yala, hold him," he directed, and thankfully without question, she supported the body so Havrshyk could remove the long black coat the Master wore. As he folded and set that aside, he inspected the silver and black Sanhas—the mark of the Swordhand-Palm, or more precisely, the mark of his clan—and found there was no sign of blood on the fabric.

Taking a deep breath, Aldyr pulled on the tie at the front of the tunic and loosened it enough that he could lower it and see the bare skin.

There. At the center of the small hollow between his wing joints was a tiny puncture wound. It *had* bled but scabbed over before any blood got onto the fabric. But…as he pinched the skin around the hole, the light flashed off a bit of metal embedded in it. A broken needle.

"Wingless traitors!" Havrshyk cursed, stepping back so quickly that Yala almost lost her balance trying to keep the body sitting upright.

"What is it, Captain? What did you see?" she asked, shifting around so she could look at his back too. "There nothing the-r-r… Wait…there is a…a needle? What does it mean? Was he poisoned?"

"Yes, but we'll need the surgeon to do more tests to determine what kind. And he was holding this." Havrshyk produced the torn cloth with the license and set it on the table. "It is likely from the fae he was meeting with when he was hit with that needle."

Yala narrowed her eyes at that. "Who is it licensed to?"

"It says that it belongs to a Garret Hasworth, out of Rosenkraun. What is he doing in Frorin?" Aldyr asked, but didn't have time to think more, as the door opened again and a groggy, graying fae in a city guard coat stalked in rubbing his eyes.

"What is this all about, Captain?" The guard demanded, wearily moving up beside him to look at the body. He stared for a minute or so, until the tiredness left his body, and a chill washed over him, visible as a wave of frost. His wings faded to a dim blue light, and he muttered a curse. "Someone's killed the Master? Who is it? What do you know?"

Aldyr pinched the hole on Baesil's back and showed him the needle and presented the license, "I know that he was poisoned, likely surprised because of the lack of defensive wounds. I know he was meeting with this Hunter, but do not know if they were involved in his death or if we have another victim out there somewhere."

The city guard captain shuffled from one foot to the other, and ordered under his breath, without even looking at his subordinates, "Go fetch a clerk from the Bounty Office."

Aldyr wasn't watching, so all he heard were retreating footsteps. "Yala, cover him, I need to report this right away."

She laid the body down and draped the coat over it without a word, and Havrshyk took to the wing towards the palace. As he swept by the other guards, who saluted sharply at his passing, he moved through the front door and behind a painting to the same dark corridors he had first entered six years before. Only this time, he didn't go to the throne room.

He went straight to the king's bedchamber. He followed the twists and turns, one hand on the pipe, until he found himself facing a thick stone wall. Aldyr tugged on a pull chain at the end of the corridor and stood with his back to the wall. When it rotated, he found himself standing in a grand room facing a gigantic four poster bed draped with the white and blue colors of the crown.

King Imloth was not alone.

Aldyr discretely coughed and announced himself with a short, "Urgent news my king," and knelt on the circular stone so that the king could pull a lever and send him out if he wished.

The king, grayer than when Aldyr had joined his service, pulled on his robe, and left the fee he had been with so that he could stand before Havrshyk and glare at him.

"Ellisa takes her first vacation in five years, and you have to bring me news tonight, sword?" Imloth asked with a wild edge to his voice. Metal grinding on stone sounded from the cane that the king took from beside his bed and leaned on.

"There has been a murder, my king, Master Baesil…"

The king snorted. "You interrupt my evening for a murder? Let Baesil resolve it."

The fee in the bed whispered something through the curtains, but too softly for Havrshyk to hear.

"Of course, my dear, just as soon as I send this guard away," the king said to her, and glared with fiery blue eyes that shone impossibly in the darkness of his room. Imloth twisted the cane, and Aldyr heard rather than saw, the blade he drew from it.

"That is just it, sire. Master Baesil has been murdered."

The fee in the bed gasped, and the king let the empty scabbard of the cane sword fall in shock.

"Dead, you say? Well, why haven't you killed his murderer? Aren't you supposed to be his successor? What sort of joke is this?" the king asked, falling back against the bed frame, losing his sword in the folds of draping cloth.

Arms reached through the cloths, and folded around the king's chest, sliding under his robe so that they held him tight. The lady whispered so quietly Havrshyk could only hear the slightest swishing sounds as she spoke.

At her words, the king nodded, but his face was red. He looked down at Havrshyk, seething, as his chest rose and fell in faster and faster breaths. "If you are his successor, you must avenge him for me. Who did this?"

Aldyr swallowed. "All I can say is this. A Commission Hunter is involved, and that he was poisoned."

"The Commission would never betray me. They know I have…
I had… the third hand."

"Yes, sire," Aldyr said stiffly. The Third Hand…his personal
agent, the unknown specter was dead…*Wait! Did that mean…?*

"And Master…" The king added, pausing and putting a
reassuring hand on the arm of his mistress.

"Havrshyk."

"Master Havrshyk, the scales of justice balance money and
power on the edge of the sword. You are the sword. Swear that
neither money nor power will sway you in your pursuit for justice."
Imloth practically growled the pronouncement.

The Third Hand… Havrshyk nodded soberly. "I swear it. My
sword will find justice, it will cut through all titles, all powers, all
promises, and mint. I will avenge Master Baesil's death for you."

The floor rotated—the mistress likely having decided that was
enough and pulling the lever to return him to the tunnels—and he
found himself in an even deeper darkness than before.

Havrshyk chose a different exit from before, returning to the
main chambers of the palace through a second flue into one of the
offices in the Grand Assembly.

Not just any office. Master Baesil's.

As Aldyr climbed out of the fireplace, grateful that it went
unused for its traditional purpose, he dusted off a few cobwebs from
his wings and scanned the office. Master Baesil's desk was bare,
cleared completely of all his papers, pens, and trinkets, which had
been swept onto the floor on the far side. The drawers of the deep
brown desk lay scattered around the chair, and the sideboard and
guest chairs were thrown on their sides.

His feet crunched on the remnants of Baesil's crystal glassware,
yet oddly the decanter was untouched, as if the one searching the
office didn't want the liquid to damage whatever it was they were
after.

Aldyr removed the stopper and took a long sniff. Aged sceppe,
with hints of honey and juniper, and… something floral, and
unfamiliar. He put the top back on and was about to return to the
guardhouse when he saw a glint of silver on the ground in the pile
of papers and rubbish.

Baesil's sword, still in its sheath, had been purposefully left
behind. Aldyr picked it up and brought it and the decanter back to

the guardhouse. When he arrived, he wasn't surprised that the clerk had been waiting for some time.

The clerk was a fee with dark black hair and a hawkish face, who fixed him with an impatient glare as he approached. "You know I have a shift in the morning. How am I expected to work without sleep?" Her harsh, quick accent sounded northern Stanaedre. That was common enough; they had been eager to join the Commission when the guild invited them—something about their militaristic culture and individualism.

"You will have more time to sleep if you answer our questions quickly," Havrshyk replied, nodding at Tullod, and passing Baesil's sword over to him.

The clerk snorted and took a seat in one of the chairs, crossing her arms and legs. "You know very well that I do not have to comply, unless there is evidence that a member of the Commission is involved in any wrongdoing. I cannot be harassed."

Yala saw the blood rushing to Havrshyk's face, and interjected before he could. "We just need to know about this Hunter," she said calmly, holding the torn badge so the clerk could see it. "He was at the scene of the murder and is missing…he may be injured, or worse."

"Worse?" she demanded. "Are you accusing a member of our organization of murdering this fae? And even if he did, he likely did it to kill a criminal with a bounty on his head. You should thank him!"

"You ignorant finch!" Tullod shouted, rushing forward with a hand on his side sword. Aldyr held up a hand and stilled him with a cold look. He put the decanter in her hands and reached for a glass. "You're tired, and so are we. Would you like a glass of sceppe? It is a lovely cask."

She idly took the decanter, and pulled the stopper free, and smelled it. "Yes, it is a lovely smell…honey, those pine berries you love here, and… I know that smell, that's rock rose blossom! Why would you want that in there? You know that's poisonous." She narrowed her eyes and scowled.

"I've never heard of or smelled it before," Havrshyk said, "but it is enticing. Go on, have a sip." He took the decanter back and poured a finger into a crystal glass and offered it to the clerk.

"I'm not drinking that! Even in small doses it can cause drowsiness and confusion!" she protested more hotly, shoving back Aldyr's hand with the glass so the contents spilled on the floor.

Some of it got on his sleeve, so he set the glass back on a side table and shook some of the droplets away. Then he leveled a glare at her and gave a pointed look at the guards in the doorway behind her. "Do you know who this is?" he asked, gesturing toward the body on the table.

"A criminal no doubt. Why else would he have poisoned sceppe?" She sniffed and rubbed at her eyes again.

Yala avoided meeting Havrshyk's gaze, as he in turn kept looking away from the clerk. "Tell me, do you recognize him?"

The clerk yawned, complaining, "He's just a… a… *Jakaren's breath*… the Third Hand?"

Havrshyk turned back towards her with a cold smile. Her wings drained of all color and shook anxiously.

"You don't understand, it isn't what it looks like! We didn't do this! We wouldn't!"

"You wouldn't? Then how do you explain this license I found in his cold fingers, and the injection mark on his back where the needle broke off in his spine?" he demanded, stepping closer so that he could stare deeper and deeper into her eyes.

Her knees wobbled, and she collapsed sputtering. "It can't be… but they were never supposed to… you don't understand, it was just a contingency!"

Aldyr waved toward the guards and stalked off toward Yala. "Interrogate her, Yala, and report back to me as soon as you are finished. I am going to the Lodge. Tullod, Jerrin, come with me." He strode out the door and took to the wing, fastening his dead master's sword around his waist.

"What's the plan, Captain?" Jerrin asked, rising to join him above the rooftops, his mustache whipping in the wind.

"We are going to search the Lodge for clues about this 'contingency' the clerk mentioned. The killer may still be there or have left something behind."

Tullod fell in with them to Havrshyk's left, but he avoided looking at Aldyr. "The king, does he know?"

Havrshyk snorted. "He made me swear the oath. Now come. We will not rest until Master Baesil is avenged."

"Yes, Master Havrshyk…" Tullod agreed regretfully.

No matter what the other students may have thought, Aldyr had never wanted the title either. He had done what he'd needed to for his family, not for fame, or loyalty to the crown. He'd done all this so they could live in peace—so his sister could have the medicine she needed.

They had never gained entry into the city, even after all he'd killed and trained for. The last time he had passed through the Sky District gates, he hadn't seen them; but a thin line of smoke spiraled up from their makeshift chimney.

"Havrshyk?" Tullod asked, "we will find whoever did this, right?"

He nodded, banishing all thoughts of home and of Baesil from his mind. As they swept down the Rain Ringroad, he spied light glimmering through the shutters of more than a few of the Lodge's windows. Most nights, only the lobby was lit after midnight, so that hunters arriving late could be supplied with a room.

They landed before the main entrance and stood all three back-to-back to scan their surroundings. The windows were all closed, and nothing moved in the street except for a soft breeze. Overhead, the sky was clear of clouds and the greater moon covered the whole of the Lich constellation. Despite it being the height of winter, it was unseasonably warm.

"It's quiet, sir," Jerrin said under his breath, stretching his wings, and looking around suspiciously.

"It's the middle of the night," Tullod sniffed.

"Keep one hand on your swords and follow me," Havrshyk ordered, stalking toward the bronze-stained pine door to the Lodge. He reached out and hesitated with his hand hovering above the latch.

Aldyr pulled back, and then rushed the door in a fluid Swordhand-Palm charge, kicking it in with one boot and following through in a roll into the lobby. He rose to a knee, and looked to the clerk's desk, which was empty, and heard the others rush in flanking him on either side.

To the right was a small lounge area with a low table and chairs, and a hearth glowing with the last heat of the day's fire. Ahead were the stairs set in a square spiral leading up to the rooms on the upper floors. Havrshyk waved Tullod forward with a purposeful beat of his left wings, holding his right wings still so Jerrin would stay with him.

Tullod stopped at the foot of the stairs, leaning against the last newel post so that he faced them, with his sword drawn partially from its sheath. Aldyr beat once with his right wings, so Jerrin flew forward to the next landing up the stairs, where he took up a position similar to Tullod's, and Havrshyk rushed past him to do the same at the top of the stairs looking out at the hallway of the second floor.

As they'd practiced in other, less urgent missions, he held out a hand over the stair railing, and formed a brittle ice crystal between his fingertips, and after waiting five heartbeats, he let it fall.

Jerrin caught it and tossed it to Tullod, who couldn't catch it from that angle—so it shattered on the wood floor below, signaling Tullod so that he flew up to meet Havrshyk and then partway down the hall to the right.

One more crystal brought Jerrin up and down the hallway to the left, so that Havrshyk stood at the stairs waiting as the other two did a short circuit around the hallways and met back up with him.

"No lights are on at this level, Master," Tullod said jerking a thumb over his shoulder.

Havrshyk kept his sigh to himself, and tossed an ice shard to Jerrin, who went up to the landing, and then he signaled Tullod to go up to the next floor. This time on the third level, Havrshyk gestured for Jerrin to go down the left as he went right down the hall. In the Lodge, the hall turned a corner with the building and circled back all the way around to the stair landing.

Havrshyk kept one hand on the wall as he walked, heel to toe, silently, scanning the crack under each door for a glimmer of light. Just when he thought this floor would prove another fruitless search, he met Jerrin at the farthest room from the stairs, and they spotted a flickering light coming from under the door.

Aldyr put a finger over his mouth and passed a crystal of ice to Jerrin, who nodded and flew back to the stairs. Moments later, he returned with Tullod in tow, and they leaned against the wall on either side, as he took a deep breath and prepared to kick in the door just like he had at the entrance. He paused, and then tentatively tried the door handle. It was unlocked.

He pushed it open, crouching so the others could lean around the door frame and look over him.

The door creaked.

Havrshyk held his breath.

After ten seconds, he released it, and crept into the room, drawing Baesil's sword from its sheath a finger's breadth. Inside he passed a dark washroom and entered the single sleeping chamber. The bed was unused, with blankets still tucked under the thistledown mattress, and beautifully accented with a red and green quilt. A candle guttered in a glass bowl on the desk against the wall, and in a pewter tray lay a pile of ashes, and corner remnants of burnt pages.

"Where are all the Hunters?" Jerrin asked, backing up to the hallway door, poking his head out so he could keep watch.

Tullod moved to the dresser on the opposite wall and checked the drawers. "Empty. Empty. Empty… and empty," he said, shoving the drawers back in with a grunt.

One of the burnt remnants in the tray had a few trace words that looked nearly legible; despite being converted to ash, it hadn't crumbled.

Havrshyk leaned in close in the last flickering light of the dying candle and read the single sentence aloud.

"Third hand cut off. Move on the crown."

All three stopped and shared a look.

"We must get back to the palace. Jerrin, stop by the guardhouse and have them join us there. Tullod, you and I are going straight to the king."

Not wasting time, Aldyr turned to the single window, and scooted the lower pane up, letting in a rush of winter air that snuffed out the candle as he waved the others out.

The three rose above the Lodge, and flew north together since the Guardhouse was on the way to the palace. Jerrin shook his head and flew closer to the others as he said, "What is the Commission doing?"

"It's not enough to control our economy, or to take more and more control of our defense—it seems they want the kingdom as well," Havrshyk guessed.

"No one would just let them take over!" Tullod argued.

He doubted that. "Our guards are good at handling petty crime, but we haven't had a standing army for decades. On the whole, their Hunters are more skilled and experienced than our Guard, they may just be able to take control of the city."

"We'll stop them sir," Jerrin shouted, shifting back toward the west, "I'll bring up the guard and meet you at the palace!"

Aldyr steadied himself and locked his gaze on the Grand Assembly, and the Palace just ahead. "Tullod, do you remember the first tenet of the Swordhand-Palm?"

"Strength comes from the feet?"

"Not today. Dive, and if you catch any Hunter, take off his head."

They dropped from the sky, sweeping down to the towering entry doors of birch painted white and blue; they were cracked open, and the two nightguards lay bleeding on the stairs. Aldyr landed beside one of them, but without even putting a finger on his neck, he could tell by the lack of light in his wings, that the guard was already dead.

He didn't waste time on the bodies but rose and pushed through the doors. Bloody footprints and shouts directed him straight ahead, up the stairs, and toward the throne room.

A hunter in a green tunic slumped over the banister with a silver sword broken off in his chest, the guard who owned it lay back against the opposite wall with a spear holding him down. The blood dribbling from his mouth was fresh, but he was already gone. Tullod kept one step behind Havrshyk as they flew down the hallway in the direction of the shouting, and the clanging of steel on steel.

The air reverberated with a thunderous pop, a flash of light, and then the acrid stench of burnt flesh, as they rounded a corner and saw the doors to the throne room. Eight hunters faced away from Tullod and Havrshyk, approaching the closed, but now unguarded doors. The bodies of three more Hunters and five Crown Guard lay scattered with broken spears, elemental burns, and loose swords.

The Hunter at the head of the group stool taller than the others, and he wore a green cloak emblazoned with a symbolic representation of the Serpent constellation.

When Tullod was about to rush them, Havrshyk grabbed him by the arm and spun them back around the corner out of sight. The door resounded with a loud thud as it was attacked with swords, kicks, and hammers.

"We need to get inside," Aldyr hissed, slapping a painting of an ermine on the wall beside their heads so that it went askew, and a narrow panel of the wall sunk inward and creaked on hinges, presenting a black tunnel.

Tullod grimaced, wings reddening in embarrassment. "I forgot."

Ignoring that, Havrshyk led the way into the tunnel, took a right, and then climbed up, and then ahead a bit, until he found a small panel on the floor with a handhold. He hoisted it up, and then dropped to the floor below.

He blinked, eyes adjusting to the sudden burst of light. Four guards surrounded him with swords drawn and shouts to hold still… shouts that stilled in their throats, and another voice interjected, a gravely, indulgent voice.

"I told you to avenge me, Master, not to incite an attack!" King Imloth yelled.

Aldyr turned to face him, noting that Tullod followed him through the opening and closed the hole in the ceiling. The king sat on his throne with his drawn sword across his knees. The sword was nicked with chips and scratches from all the times he had 'tested' new recruits and bore permanent rust and blood stains from his disposing of those who failed to pass his tests.

The doors shuddered, but the two thick door bars held.

Havrshyk knelt, bowing his head as he replied, "I investigated the Hunter's Lodge and discovered that they are behind this attack, and that Master Baesil was only a preliminary target."

The king huffed, scratching his chin. He stood and looked around to the back of the throne and found his mistress hiding there slumped against the back of it, whimpering. "Useless fee, aren't you supposed to protect me?"

"From poison… and secrets… my king," she answered, so softly that it was nearly inaudible.

He bent over her with his sword hand tightening on the hilt menacingly. "You should have known about *this!*" He spun toward Havrshyk, who still knelt with his head down just enough to be respectful while still able to track his movements with his eyes. "You will halt this attack, Havrshyk." His wings twitched, not moving freely as they should, scarred by so many sword swings over the years.

How ironic. He fearlessly attacked and killed his own citizens when protected by his guard, but when he was truly endangered, he was powerless.

The air carried a tang, and his hair began to stand on end. Havrshyk spun around toward the doors and the other guards, who were pushing with all their weight to brace the doors.

"Stand away from the doors!" he shouted too late.

An intense, blinding light cut through the doors, burning through one of the guards and splitting so that the tongues of the bolt of lightning fractured, chasing metal and arcing to the ground.

The guard struck by the bolt screamed in agony, but stilled as a spear came through the gaping, smoking hole in the doors, catching him in the chest.

"Pull back to me and form up! Dove formation!" Aldyr shouted, drawing Baesil's sword—leaving his own its sheath. He stood at the head of the flying V formation with the other guards flanking him on either side, barring the way as the doors burst open.

Splintered timbers, and broken panels of wood soared overhead, and slid across the marble tiles. In the clearing smoke, Havrshyk watched the leader of the Hunters stride in over the debris and bodies with a long spear topped with red ribbon. He was followed by the other seven Hunters bearing a myriad of weapons: swords, spears, axes, one even held a bow.

The Hunter in the lead had long, curling brown hair and a short beard around his chin. His burning yellow eyes were marked by a striking scar as if he had survived the claws of some terrible creature.

"The stars are aligned for the fall of your king," he declared in the sharp, staccato accent of the Stanaedre clans, "If you welcome us, we will grant you citizenship in this city."

Havrshyk narrowed his eyes. None of his guards replied. The king though, sputtered and yelled back, "I will grant the request of the guard that kills him!"

The guards settled into their stances, one foot forward, their empty hands out to guard, and their swords held back and angled over their heads.

"Not going to listen? Then by the Lich, the Serpent, and the Lost, you will all die this day." The scarred hunter lunged forward with his spear held out and before he could attack, another hunter behind him fired an arrow at the king.

Havrshyk had been watching the archer. He wingbursted up and caught the arrow with a wave of frost, throwing its trajectory off with the increased weight. It spun toward the corner, and he landed just as the lead hunter's spear snapped at his face.

Tullod was already there. He deflected the spear's shaft with his free hand and twisted from the hip to lunge out with his sword, scratching the hunter across the chest.

One of the other guards flew at the archer to stop his next arrow, sword swinging just as the arrow took him in the throat. He spiraled in midair and collided with one of the throne room's scratched pillars.

The melee began. They fought struggling to maintain their flying V formation, as they clashed, shoving and cutting. Havrshyk parried and hacked at the spear's haft to no avail. It was made of one of the densest, strongest types of wood he had ever encountered.

An arrow took down a guard on the opposite end of their V, and one of the hunters fell as one of the guards jumped in to avenge the fallen guard.

The spear spun in a distracting dance, jabbing, slicing, and bashing away Havrshyk's guard. Aldyr put one hand on the flat of Baesil's sword, and braced against another spinning smash, and was thrown to the ground with the sword shattering in his hands. He rolled backwards, tossed the broken handle aside, and drew his spare.

"Defend the king!" came a shout from the doorway. Jerrin rushed in with six more guards, taking down the archer before he could fire again.

The scarred hunter cursed, leaving Havrshyk for the moment so he could fly in a charge, and speared one of the newcomers before they could even join the fray.

Jerrin spun around the fallen city guard still impaled by the hunter and swung his sword toward the fae's neck. The hunter didn't even flinch.

Light flashed again, and another lightning bolt traced a searing line through the air, blinding everyone, as it cut down Jerrin and left a black scar on the wall.

The hunter on the far left of their group had an axe, and his hands arced and tingled with energy.

"No more lightning," Havrshyk promised, pulling back behind his guards, and stalking around the group so he could charge the elemental.

He flew right at him, and felt the hair standing on his head, spinning to narrowly avoid the weaker bolt of lightning and stab the hunter through the heart. He landed on his chest, met the hunter's confused black eyes, twisting the sword before pulling it out and then scanning the mass of hunters and guards.

Jerrin's reinforcements, barely trained city guards, were falling quickly, and his Crown Guard had been reduced to himself, Tullod, and three others. There were still five of the hunters, and ominous shouts coming from the hallway.

"Yndril's Casket, now, Tullod!" Aldyr yelled, calling him over as they flew toward the king. The king heard him, nodding as he crouched beside his mistress. Havrshyk and Tullod, bleeding from various scratches, some minor, some severe, slapped their hands on the ground, and formed a wall of crystalline ice in a pillar around the throne.

Havrshyk rose and readied his sword wearily.

Tullod screamed, but his voice cut off with a gurgle. The leader of the hunters stood with his boot on Tullod's back, and his spear through the back of his neck, regarding the pillar of ice with distaste.

"You delay death by moments," he said, frowning as he pulled his spear free and flicked off the blood with a flourish. It splattered across the white marble tiles in a spray of bright red drops.

Behind him the other crown guards fell, one with an axe caving in his chest, another's head falling to a sword swing, a third caught in the back as he tried to rush to Havrshyk's aid.

Aldyr reset his stance, took a breath, and met the hunter's eyes. The Swordhand-Palm was not designed for defense. He rushed, not just using the power of his feet, he wingbursted forward, slipping under the thrust of the spear as he slammed his sword home through the hunter's stomach.

Under his green tunic, the blade pierced a thin chest plate, and cracked through the other side.

"The Lich is ours," he whispered in the hunter's ear, "she does not aid you. She dooms you."

He pulled his sword free, and moved on past the falling hunter and flew at the next one. *Other guards would come.* He just had to kill the enemies in front of him.

The next hunter he met caught his attack on a metal-plated leather shield and swung an axe toward his head. Aldyr raised his free hand and caught the axe head in an ice-encrusted grip, twisting the weapon around and following with a sword through the hunter's back.

Now there were six hunters. He ducked under the sword swing of the nearest hunter, and jumped into the air to avoid a leg-sweeping kick from another, as he twisted and cut off the head of the fae with the sword. His sword caught on his spine, and it took the extra effort of the wingburst to completely break through.

His sword came free with a large crack forming near the center. The hunter that had kicked at him, rose as he descended, catching the sword between two hammer-fist strikes and breaking it at the center. He followed with a knee strike to Aldyr's gut.

He skidded back toward the throne, still encased in armored ice, radiating with chill, and surrounded by a thin fog. He held out his broken sword, sharp splintered point forward, and felt his strength fading. He had spent most of his elemental energy on the ice surrounding the king, and with the cuts and scratches all over his body, he was weakening with every minute that passed.

He faced the hunter who had broken his blade with a grimace and was stabbed through the back.

Dumbfounded, he looked at his chest, at the narrow spear tip, and the red ribbon that blossomed there, and twisted his head to look over his shoulder at the leader of the hunters, crouching there with one hand on his spear, and the other on his wound.

"A gut wound is fatal, over time," he said, laughing wetly as he coughed up blood. "Break the ice!" he shouted at the others. "The crown is ours!" The hunter pulled his spear free and Havrshyk felt the last of his strength leave him.

He fell to the tiles beside the body of Tullod, unable to move as darkness closed in on the edges of his vision, and he watched the hunters attack the icy pillar. Swords chipped or were deflected, axes rebounded, and the hunter's wrung their hands from the force of the impact, but only small cracks formed—which refroze quickly.

Other guards were coming, but would they arrive in time?

The blood from the hole in his chest flowed around him, sticking to his face, and to his eyes he floated on a blood red sea, surrounded by a bitter frost.

The lead hunter let one of the other remove his armor and bind his wound. He then shoved the others aside and spun his ironwood spear around and smashed it against the pillar. This time, it cracked deeply, and did not refreeze right away.

He did it again, and the cracks spread through the ice.

Again.

Again.

Again.

Blood oozed through the bandage on his stomach, but one more strike and the icy pillar, their final defense, Yndril's Casket shattered in a blinding spray of ice shards.

They settled over him, and as the darkness closed in, Aldyr cried. How had this happened? Why?

The hunter moved toward the king and his mistress, and when he tried to stab the king, she jumped in front of it and screamed in agony.

The scream tore at his soul.

She did not deserve to die for him. He did not deserve to die for him! His blood flowed out completely, and he was wholly drained, and yet his sight lingered on the hunter and the king.

He still felt a reserve of power in his frost, partially restored with the ice from the casket, and time slowed to a crawl. In one moment, he rested in a pool of his own blood, and in another, he lay on the stones of a hillside, looking out over a forest from on high. There was a crystal basin filled with blood, but it was cracked, and leaking, and the blood ran down from the hill into a ravine filled with an impenetrable blackness.

He dragged himself toward that basin, and touched the side that was cracked, willing the last of his frost to seal the wound. Instead, the basin changed, the glass being replaced with ice, changing into a mimicry of the pillar he had shielded the king with.

In the dual space, he watched in slow motion the hunter's spear being drawn back, and the king's eyes widening in terror, a tear trailing slowly down his cheek.

He needed a sword.

Havrshyk grasped the sides of that icy pillar, filled with his blood, and willed the shape to change—to condense, to fold upon itself, and to solidify into black sword with edges sharper than any sword he had ever maintained.

His cloudy vision cleared, and he rose from the dreamlike space to the awareness of the throne room. He held out his hand as his blood flowed up from the ground to meet it, tendrils of it coiling and freezing, and they formed into the sword he had imagined.

All pain, and weakness fled.

He pushed off the ground and just as the hunter's spear was about to snap forward to finish off the king, Aldyr deflected it with a frozen free hand, and sunk his Bloodsword into the hunter's heart.

It drank and gloried in the wealth of life hidden there. The blood refilled Havrshyk's veins and the cuts and scratches, and even the terrible wound in his chest thawed and began to seal closed. Agonizing pain washed over him as the mortal injury healed, and he screamed.

Then, he pushed away the hunter's drained corpse, and raised his black blade toward the others.

They attacked him all at once. When one tried to cut him with a slash, he let it scrape off his frozen chest, and took the hunter in the heart—draining him as well to complete his healing.

When another cut off Havrshyk's leg, he kept his balance with his wings, cut the off the offending hunter's head, and bent down, reattaching the limb with a flush of blood and focus.

The remaining three hunters backed away, looking to the doorway, their faces pale as they faced him and heard the shouts of more guards moving to cut off their escape.

"We will kill the king!" One of them shouted, sweeping around the others to slip past Havrshyk. But as he neared the king, Aldyr spun and threw his Bloodsword with all his strength, smiling as it pierced the hunter in the back and he drained him.

The other two rushed him, probably thinking to kill him while he was unarmed, but he caught the sword hand of one, and deflected it so that the sword cut off his companion's arm, and he stepped around that one's attack, catching the orphaned weapon and stabbing the stunned hunter before decapitating the other.

Thundering feet announced the other city guards arriving, Yala at their head. She stopped in the door and covered her mouth, wings flashing white in shock, and the other guards stopped behind her.

The king was silent.

Havrshyk dropped the hunter's sword and retrieved his new Bloodsword from the body of the hunter who lay at the king's feet, and he knelt.

"Yala, what have you learned from the clerk?" he asked.

She flew over and knelt beside him. "Master, your Majesty, the attack was instigated by a faction within the Commission based out of Estenna. I believe that these were all the Hunters from Stanaedre in Frorin."

"My king, the attack has been rebuffed." He turned to the guards. "Escort the king to his chambers and seal the throne room!"

He got several shouts in the affirmative and tried to slide his new weapon into his old sheath. It was too thick, and the blade too wide to be anywhere near fitting, so he focused, and flooded his veins with the excess blood, and reshaped it so that it matched his old sword perfectly except in color.

The king stuttered and shook as the guards took him by each arm, supporting him on the way out. "…l…l…lich… he is… he is a lich… Oh Arta, forgive me…"

"Yala, do you have the clerk's account?" he asked, taking up a position to the right of the throne and sitting down on the step.

"Yes, Master," she stammered, rising to her feet and fishing out a slim notebook from her jacket. Yala offered it to him warily and moved back a step.

He sighed and opened it to the page she'd saved with a blue ribbon.

"Will they try again Master Havrshyk?" she asked, looking away.

"I will ensure they do not. Go and prepare a bird. I am going to Stanaedre." He rubbed his temple with one hand and rested the other on the hilt of his sword. "They interpreted the stars to portend our king's fall. But they have brought that doom upon themselves."

He stood and strode toward the doors.

"Yala!" he snapped, startling her from her thoughts.

She rushed to follow him. "I'll prepare a bird right away, sir," she said, avoiding meeting his eyes.

"Good. Because you are coming with me."

She yelped but nodded ruefully.

More softly, he added, "I am not going to kill you."

Yala nodded but didn't look convinced.

For now, that was enough.

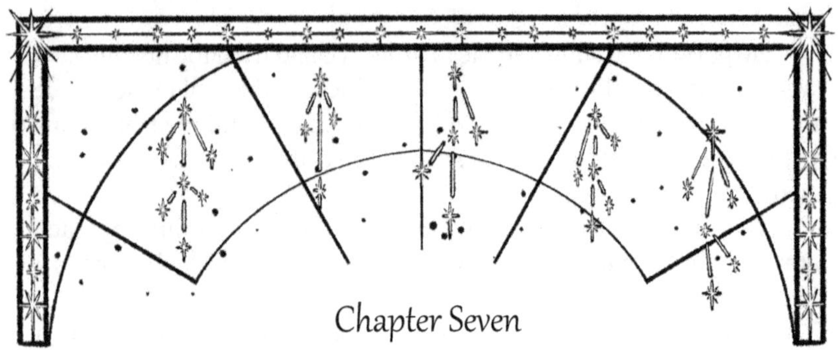

Chapter Seven

FOREST

Gaersheim

Rosenkraun

Windleaf Inn

Savis

Princess Savis woke early the day after Trel and Yarrow's private wedding ceremony. True to the name of their inn, she heard the wind rustling peacefully in the branches of the grapevine across the river from the crack in her windows, portending another temperate, tranquil day. Savis resisted the urge to snuggle deeper into her duvet, instead getting out of bed and moving to the window, where she threw open the lilac-colored curtains and pushed out her windows. The wind rushed around her, tossing her hair, and causing her wings to flutter subconsciously as she held onto the edges of her night robe to keep it from flying away. Last night, two of her most trusted companions had been happily married—yet her thoughts circled around her own canceled engagement.

She took a deep breath and closed her eyes.

In the end, she was… she felt… above all else… relief. Her arranged marriage with the Duke of Wellsey had been planned for two decades, and now he had gone and married some unknown commoner. Everyone Savis spoke to extended their condolences, speaking at length about how disgraceful it was for the duke to marry beneath his station, but inside she envied him and found pride swelling there as well. Nodding to herself, she opened her eyes and drank in the view. Sparkling sunlight on the grapevines reflected in pristine colors in the slow-moving river below. Not a single cloud in sight.

A wild finch flitted down from the azure sky and landed on one of the many perching rods sticking out from the windows of the inn, where bowls of seeds enticed them to provide a charming atmosphere for the guests. The golden finch chirped and turned on its feet as it regarded the full bowl of seeds.

"It's not really a rejection, is it?" she asked the bird, sitting on her windowsill with her arms wrapped around her body to keep her gown closed. The wind continued to flow by, flicking strands of her long blond hair up and down again, as she waited for a response.

It sang cheerfully, chortling as it chomped down on a beak-full of seeds.

"You're right," she agreed, resting her chin on her hand as she reclined, watching him, "It's not sweet, but it still tastes good. Bitterness is often nutritious." With a sigh, she rose and moved to the closet where her traveling wardrobe was packed into a suitcase and a half. They were leaving in the afternoon, and by a quick glance at the sky, she could see it was still mid-morning. Even so, she had decided to get dressed and pack up her things. These included the dress she'd worn to the Harvest Festival, a white blouse with a pale blue skirt, and her ambassadorial uniform—a blue blazer, tulip bell skirt, and matching vest. Not wanting to offend, she decided to dress in the blazer and skirt. One last visit to the king before leaving, no matter how rude and indelicate he was, was expected of her.

She tied her hair back with a blue ribbon and a pin decorated to look like a white gold crown. Then, having dressed and packed, she took her satchel from the coat pegs, patted it to be sure the Harvest Crown was still safely inside it, and made for the dining hall.

The inn was situated on a spit of land where the river snaked in a curve around it, and the dining hall was placed on the eastern end of the inn so that it had a nearly panoramic view of the vineyard, river, and quays. The sounds of dishes clinking and servers chatting greeted her as she entered, and she spied Trel and Yarrow sitting at the table in the corner laughing and drinking tea as Lia covered her mouth in dismay, and Nora stood on top of her chair with her hands on the windowpanes.

"There's a bird right there mama!" she declared, taking only a moment to glance back at her mother before looking back out at a massive wren. It was standing on one of the perches, eating all the seeds the bowl held—the metal perching rod bending beneath its weight. At this, one of the cooks bustled out with a pan raised menacingly, red-faced, making for the balcony doors.

"Get off that, you beast!" The cook yelled, shoving her chef's hat back so it settled in the right position on her head, if a little smashed. Her green-lined wings beat to the rhythm of her words, flashing red with anger.

The wren paused as she approached, but went right back to eating, so the cook shoved her way through the doors and tried to bat the wren away with the pan.

It balanced on the rod, dodging her attacks, with an amused sort of warbling sound, ducked and scooped up the last seeds, and then shoved off the rod into the sky. The rod broke free of its brackets on the stone wall and fell to the mossy lawn below.

"And stay away, you menace! Or it's the knife next time!" The cook shook her head and did her best to ignore Savis and the others as she returned inside muttering something about how to roast a bird.

Savis covered her mouth, laughing quietly. Nora joined in, and in a moment the whole table had lost their composure. The princess shook her head, finally calming, and smiled cheerfully at her companions.

The chair at the head of the table, the one with the most direct sunlight, remained empty, so Savis seated herself and folded her hands on the table. Before she could say even a word to the others, a teacup full of the Windleaf's proprietary tea blend was placed beside her hands, and several servers arrived bearing plates loaded with finch-egg omelets and chopped sprouts salads.

At this, Nora—who had still been looking out the window mournfully since the wren had been shooed away—turned around and let out a cheer at the arrival of the food.

Lia motioned for her to sit down and put a finger over her mouth.

Nora sat down obediently, and only then noticed Savis. "*Linella søran helay*, Princess!"

"Good morning, Nora," Savis replied gently, "everyone."

Trel smiled warmly at her and held out her hand to summon another server, "More tea, if you please."

The server was a fee in a white dress and green apron. Her brown hair was tied back into a bun with a gold pin decorated with a cluster of grapes. She gave Trel a polite smile, and flitted back to the kitchen, returning moments later with another full pot of tea, and set it down on a trivet in the center of the table. Then, nodding, she left. The teacups, saucers, plates, and tea pot were all of the same white bone china, decorated with a light green detailing of grape leaves and clusters.

The two veteran hunters, now formally married for one day, no longer wore their rugged uniforms and coats. Instead, they were still clothed in their robes over silk pajamas. Though the servers were embarrassed, Trel and Yarrow could not have been more comfortable or relaxed. Yarrow cut a bite of his omelet and chewed on it with a calm smile, and Trel drank her tea with one finger in the air as if that were what proper faeries did—in all the circles Savis had frequented, however, that was no longer common.

They ate quietly, not chatting until everyone had eaten as much as they wanted. Nora leaned back in her chair with her hands on her stomach, falling in her seat so her bright yellow floral dress got rumpled and rose improperly high. Everyone ignored that however; she was just a child. Savis was just relieved the girl was not running all around the room like yesterday, flapping her wings and arms trying to imitate bird calls.

"I mean to visit the king once more before I leave town," she began, setting her fork down on her nearly empty plate. "We have had this same conversation several times now over the years, but today I believe it is most appropriate. You are not bound to accompany me any longer than you wish—especially so soon after your wedding. If need be, I will take a Gaershawk up to Artell, and then return by sparrow."

The adults at the table stared at her in shock, or disapproval, but Nora gazed up at her with wide, excited eyes. "By yourself?" she asked, seemingly impressed.

She gave an awkward laugh and continued, "I am nearly thirty, Nora. I would manage just fine, especially if I were to travel anonymously."

"Amonynously," she agreed, chewing on the word.

"Anonymously," Lia corrected.

"That's what I said!" Nora declared, stealing a bite of Savis' omelet that she'd left untouched.

"You said 'amonynously' dear," Trel explained, "It's a hard word. It means 'unknown', you see."

Yarrow coughed into his hand and gestured for Savis' attention. "You have asked us this question many times over the years, and never has it ever been phrased properly as a question. As always, our answer, put incorrectly, is simple. We had planned on it." He winked.

Savis suspected the sentence was more complete than he intended. "Which is to say?" she asked.

He shared a look with his wife and held out a hand for her. She took it and they both looked directly at her. "We will accompany you as long as we wish, whether we are welcome to or not."

The princess laughed heartily at that, and then shook her head, and finished her tea. "Then you should probably get dressed. I am just about to visit the king."

"Not much time then," Lia said, "but I must ask—we still need to travel anonymously,"

"Amonynously," Nora corrected, wagging a finger at her mother.

"Amonynously," Lia said with a smile, "and were hoping you would continue to provide us with your protection."

Savis had expected they would stay with Trel and Yarrow, but hadn't said anything. "If you join us, we will provide you with all the protections of my house. But I must obey the first law of nobility: obligation." She hesitated, and then put a hand on her satchel. "Are you certain I should go through with this?"

Lia nodded. "I would be relieved to have that matter behind me."

"After this you may not need my protection." The princess nodded and stood, scooting her chair back as she did so. "I am heading over there now. Yarrow, if you would ready the carriage and meet me there, just send a message with a porter and I will rejoin you—please do not tarry too long—the queen is a vain and simple fee, and I would prefer to read in the carriage than to listen to her gossip."

"As ever, my lady," Yarrow promised, bowing his head, "may you enjoy your time all the same."

Savis nodded gratefully and returned to the hallway. She followed it to the stairs and flitted down a few flights to the ground level and out into the lobby. The owner of the inn, Jean Windleaf, the proud fourth-generation proprietor of the establishment, waved to her as she left.

"Good day princess!" he called, lowering his news sheet as she went by.

She ignored him and flew down the street toward the palace at the height of the bluffs north of the inn. Rosenkraun was arranged in a different fashion from any city Savis had visited. Frorin was centered on its seat of government, Fassen on the crossroads of trade, with the palace at the base of its iconic vine, Artell built similar to Frorin, and Gaerlin centered on the docks…but Gaersheim had no center. It was arranged as if four hamlets had grown large enough that their borders ceased to matter.

The Rosenkraun estate was built on the northern edge of town beside the river, looking out at the vines on the other side that supplied the town with grapes, wine, and lumber, and immediately around that estate were more common residential areas with taverns, merchants, and rows upon rows of townhouses. The borough immediately to the west of it was similar, in that it was built around another estate—the Commissar's Quarter—as it was commonly known, with housing for hunters, banks, and offices; suffused with trade and economic business, it was also flush with residences interspersed throughout.

Savis paused at the busiest intersection in the city, Diamond Square, the intersection of the roads that connected all four boroughs of the city's west bank. Eight roads, centered perfectly on the eight cardinal directions, met here in a roundabout with a fountainhead monument in the center. Moss lawn surrounded a pool decorated with a towering statue of King Gallett Rosenkraun, a memorial of his sacrifice in the last Cherim War 80 years earlier.

Her inn had been situated on the northern end of The Quays Quarter, and finally, as she looked down the road to the southwest, she considered that The Forest Quarter was likely only named so that it could be recognized as being different from the others—it was the section of the city most similar to the Hill District back home— a place for common folk and common wares, where life was focused on simple pleasures, and domestic problems. Its southern section was almost entirely devoted to the farming of flax for fiber, however, so the forest title was inaccurate.

Moving northeast on the diagonal road to the palace, Savis flew around wagons and carts loaded with goods bound for the markets, for there were markets in every section of the city, and kept one hand on her bag, which bulged with the bulky object she had stuffed inside it. This had been her idea, but she worried. The king was erratic, and she never could rely on him to have a calm response to anything—even news that dinner was served.

She passed by shops and the markets, decorated with bunting and ribbons for the Midharvest Market, and flew up the ramparts to the palace on the bluff, which stretched across the rocky outcrop in a spectacular u-shaped estate with grounds and gardens extending all around it.

At the crest of the hill, she was stopped at the open gates of the red granite walls surrounding the palace grounds. Two of the Grass Guard minded the gates, though there was no one passing through, or even on the road. One leaned against the wall with his arms crossed, watching her suspiciously, and the other, with the twin bars of a captain on the collar of his padded uniform, held her up with a raised hand.

"Hold, miss," he declared, "entry to the palace grounds is allowed only during tours, proclamations, or by appointment."

Savis frowned. She had been through this gate a dozen times in the past week, and she did not recognize him. His eyes flicked over his shoulder to the open door of the gatehouse and he reached over to close the door. Were the off-duty guards taking a nap? For a moment she'd seen one lying down on a cot.

The princess shook her head and resisted rolling her eyes. Gaersheim hadn't seen a threat within its borders for nearly a century, and between its Grass Guard, and the Commissar's Quarter, it was arguably the most secure city on the continent. To the guard captain, she crossed her arms and said, "And what about foreign dignitaries?"

He looked her up and down, in a way that made her skin itch, and then he frowned. "What dignitary?"

Savis sighed, shoving the urge to groan in frustration deep down, "I am Princess Savis Martell of Froreholt—Ambassador to Gaersheim!"

"Sure you are, miss, do you have proof to back that claim?" asked the guard leaning against the wall.

In truth, she had left her documents at the inn, packed away in her bags, since she had been on a first name basis with all the guard captains—or so she thought. "Is Captain Edwin here? He can vouch for me."

"He took the day off," supplied the captain.

"What about Captain Mordane?" she asked hopefully.

The other guard snickered. "He wasn't feeling well so he went home."

"Then who are you?" she asked, growing exasperated.

The guard with the captain's uniform bowed sarcastically and presented a hunter's license from a pocket. "I am Lystadt Derron, filling in by commission, as it were."

"Well, go get someone who knows and bring them here!" she demanded, crossing her arms, wings flashing red.

"Fine then, fine," the hunter in the captain's uniform said, "but he won't be feeling well." He stepped into the gate house and returned a few moments later with another Grass-Guard-uniformed fae whom he supported as he walked out. "Someone gave the guards a cake yesterday, but it doesn't appear to have sat well with them, see? So, they contracted out for the small things."

Entry to the palace grounds was a small thing? Savis rolled her eyes and directed her attention to the green-faced fae leaning on the hunter. "Pardon me, sir, but I am Princess Savis of Froreholt—this hunter will not let me through. Will you grant me passage?"

The sickly captain regarded her with swimming eyes, and then he promptly vomited on the ground. Savis smiled as she noticed some of it got on the hunter's boots. "Princess?" he asked, seeming to notice her for the first time, "Yes, stars above, let her through." He coughed weakly and the hunter led him back to the gatehouse.

The other guard, obviously also a hunter from his lack of concern and decorum, waved her through the gates lazily, and returned to chewing on a nail.

She stomped up the walk to the steps of the palace, surprised by the lack of gardeners and attendants working the grounds, until she remembered that it was a holiday—the anniversary of Gallett's death. That did not excuse the lack of servants to mind doors and announce her entry.

She felt a growing disquiet as she tugged on the excessively tall vinewood door and slipped inside the foyer of the palace. The clock in the corner chimed ten, and at this time the king would normally be taking lunch in the windowed balcony, where he could enjoy the sun and views in the morning looking down on the river without the irritants of wind or insects. The halls were still as she took to the wing, flying silently toward the east end of the palace—not wanting to make any noise to disturb the quiet.

A minute or so later, she alighted on the stones before the open doors to the balcony and saw that the king and queen were seated at a table enjoying their news sheets and tea. Savis rapped a knock on the windowed door and coughed purposefully.

"Your majesty?" she asked, staying outside just in case he refused her.

The king paused with a slice of toast halfway to his mouth and eyed her suspiciously. "Princess?"

His wife, Queen Melyse, chattered happily and swallowed a mouthful of her breakfast. "Come in, come in! Sit beside me, Savis, you will *never* believe what happened yesterday."

"I am sure I will not," Savis said, entering what she could not decide was more properly a balcony or solarium, and taking a seat beside the queen. "Good morning to you both, I hope you will pardon my intrusion."

The king took a breath and nodded as he took a large bite of toast, seemingly mollified at her interruption and apology. He wiped some crumbs from the corner of his mouth with his forest green napkin, replaced it on his lap, and fixed her with his keen brown eyes. "You know, Savis," he said, waving away his wife who seemed about to interject with a comment, "not now dear," he said, continuing to wave, "it must be so embarrassing to be rejected like that."

Melyse laughed awkwardly, glaring in his direction.

This so soon? "I am proud of him," she said, smiling as a butler entered with a cup of tea and set it before her. She had already had plenty of tea, so she took a sip to be polite, but didn't plan on doing more than that. It was slightly bitter, but she didn't bother asking for honey.

"Proud?" Melyse asked, nearly choking on her food.

"Our parents had arranged the wedding, years ago, but we had never truly connected. When he confessed to me that he had found someone else he wanted to marry at the risk of all else, I told him that we had known each other for long as cousins, and could continue our relationship as such. I fully intend to maintain cordial relations with Wellsey and invite the duke and duchess over for dinner when I return." Savis was relieved to get that out and let out a breath. The hard part was done.

"I do mean to return home," she said, continuing with a false frown.

Melyse nodded seriously.

The king also looked somber. "It is just terrible, I heard just this morning—I imagine you must return." A servant refilled his and Melyse's tea, and the king took a long gulp, before grimacing and adding honey. "Amateur substitute servants," he complained.

Savis raised an eyebrow and moved onto her next topic, as she opened her bag and took out the crown. "Yes, well, I wanted to bring you this, which I recovered in Fassen at great personal risk."

The king's eyes fixed on the Harvest Crown, and his mouth stopped moving.

"It was taken you see, so that you would be embarrassed in front of all the lords of Fhoraena."

"A Waverly exile stole it," he said, putting down his napkin and looking anxiously to his wife, "how did you get it back?"

"She was extorted, and the story is far longer than I have time to tell you. I obtained it, and I meant to return it to you before leaving. I am going back to Frorin tonight." It felt good to say that— to plant the seed of the truth in the king's ears.

He took the crown, set it on the table, and rang the bell for the butler to return. "Savis, I am grateful for this act of kindness…generosity, I am not sure what the act is to be completely honest, but it is overshadowed by my dearest condolences to you for your father's death." He fiddled with the crown, avoiding meeting her eyes.

Savis felt the hairs on the back of her neck standing on end, and a cold flush fall on her wings from head to toe. "My father is dead?"

"He passed last night. He and your brother have banished the Commission… and we had suspected you of stealing the crown to ruin us… meant to capture you… but Savis…" he looked up at the butler with a confused look, "Where is Derrick?"

The butler who came to his bell ring was not the same butler who had come before but was the dark-eyed hunter from the gate. Not the captain, but the one who'd lounged bored and uninterested as she fought to get through.

She couldn't move, her fingers tingled and her muscles slow to respond, as the hunter pulled a knife from his apron, and his eyes locked on the crown. "So clever, Princess, you nearly undid a century of work. I am sorry, sire, but today is the perfect day for you to become a martyr. This crown is going to have to disappear—it doesn't fit the narrative that your murderer would return your crown." He shot her a look. "Besides, you have been a fungus in our roots for too long, and the President wants Ieffin to pay for what he did."

Savis swallowed. She twisted and fought, nerves afire with panic and energy, twitching with lethargic strength as if she were paralyzed, half awake and half in a dream. As she struggled to move, the hunter's hand caressed the queen's paralyzed and panicked face, he tickled her with the edge of the blade, and then carelessly slit her throat.

Blood sprayed across the white table linens and china, droplets spattering across Savis' face, and she watched in slow horror as the hunter rounded the table and stabbed the king in the chest.

Savis' fingers were still closed around the crown, and somehow, she found the strength to break through the paralysis and pull it to herself. She shoved it back in her bag and fell backwards in her chair.

The hunter skewered the king against the ground, leaving the knife planted in his chest, and his body frozen but for the tears streaming from his immobile eyes. Then he stood—looking at Savis with an eager smile. It sent another chill through her body.

"Candor," a voice from the doorway announced, "the carriage for the princess has arrived, what do we do?"

The hunter looked away from her for a moment to glare pointedly at the voice. "Kill them!" he shouted, turning back toward her and rolling his eyes. "Obviously…"

"Right away," the voice replied and footsteps trailed off in the direction Savis had come.

"Now princess, it wouldn't be right if you died looking like a victim," the hunter said, laughing as he bent over her, "but first, give me that crown."

She blinked through her own tears, shaking her head. Her heartbeat thundered in her ears, but all she could think of were Trel, Yarrow, Lia, Nora, and the deaths of Leif and Fryn.

"We're going to get rid of that, and then we're going to stamp out your brother. We're going to kill those cursed traitors Leif and Fryn, and then we're going to kill them again!"

The princess, tears still streaming from her eyes, narrowed her eyebrows and examined him. He talked about Leif and Fryn as if they had somehow beat all the odds and survived? She clutched onto her bag more tightly and gave him the most purposeful, determined look she could.

"Fancy yourself a fighter, too, eh? Well, let's just see how much you can." The hunter dove over the table at her, so Savis kicked at him with her feet—finding that somehow the paralysis was gone—and knocked him back onto the table, which broke under his weight and shattered the plates in a shower of porcelain. She edged towards the doorway, chest heaving as she tried not to panic completely.

The hunter, Candor, the other had called him, groaned and rose to his feet, pulling a sliver of one of the ceramic plates from his cheek. The groan turned into a growl, as he ripped the dagger from the king's chest.

She struggled, trying to remember her lessons from childhood, and was startled when the hunter rushed her. He didn't use any sort of stance, or style, he just moved with a purposeful energy, bloody dagger in hand. The hunter slashed at her face, so she backed up into the doors, which were closed, and though the blade swished through air, he followed through, turning on his heel and kicking her through the glass solarium doors.

Savis was thrown in a shower of glass down the hall, landing in a sore, splintered, bloody heap. She lay there dazed, aware only of the pain stabbing into her from every side, and rolled over just in time to see the hunter bearing down on her with a malicious grin.

"Time for regicide number three!" he shouted gleefully, pouncing on her with the knife held in a back hand grip.

Savis caught his arm and struggled, rolling from one side to another, as he stabbed it into the wood of the hallway floor, and then she held it back as he tried to stab her through the neck.

"I am going to kill your brother, too," he hissed, "regicide number four! It won't stop there!" He laughed maniacally and then calmed himself as he focused, hissing as he sank the dagger into her shoulder.

Savis screamed, cutting off as he pulled out the knife and attacked her again.

So far, she had avoided a fatal blow, but he shifted his weight unpredictably, forcing her to edge the knife down where it would sink into her chest. If only she had a weapon!

He twisted again, and the knife slammed down into the wood floor, and she had a flash of inspiration. She let go of his knife hand with one hand, and reached into her bag again.

Sensing weakness perhaps, he straddled her and gripped the knife in both hands, bringing it down with all his weight, as she swept the Harvest Crown out of her bag and sank the sharp edges of the alloyed grass blades into the side of his neck.

Savis closed her eyes almost instinctively as a spray of hot liquid came from the puncture wounds when she pulled back on the crown.

He let out a strange wet gargle and slumped over on top of her.

Savis lay there, frozen, for nearly a minute, until she remembered what the other hunters had said. She rolled the body off of her and rose on shaky legs. As she made for the front door, blood dripping from her fingers, and clothes, and the crown she clung to; she passed the bodies of servants and Grass Guard alike, until she arrived at the door askew, attached to the jamb by one hinge, and saw the melee in the drive.

Trel stood on top of the carriage, Bloodbow firing black lines of semi-solid fluid through the bodies of hunters and mercenaries, as Yarrow stood on the stones before the carriage, stepping through sword stances and strikes, clashing with one and then another, engaging any who tried to go after his wife.

"Princess?" asked a small, wavering voice.

Savis used her sleeve to wipe her eyes and looked around. Hiding against the wall, just inside the doors, Nora looked up at her, holding onto her mother's arms, as Lia watched around the corner.

"Nora?" she asked.

"Come hide," she said, making a 'sh' gesture with a finger over her mouth, and then waving her over.

It wouldn't be much use to hide, the courtyard was full of guards and hunters. Even though six bodies lay on the ground, Savis estimated that there were ten more trying to engage the duo, with more far off specks flying in from the distance. Still, she moved over to Lia and Nora, and slumped against the wall. The rush of adrenaline created a powerful, exhausting effect, and now the blood leaking from her shoulder wound and scratches, the sheer amount of energy she'd used in fighting the hunter, left her immobile.

"She's hurt, Mama," Nora said, looking up at Lia. "What do we do?"

Lia glanced over and then sputtered, *"Geletoalan Jakarenin,"* then covered her mouth and added, "Don't say that, Nora... we need to clean the wound and bind it up."

Her vision swam, but Savis recalled well enough what she should do. She closed her eyes and let her perception focus on the cuts and stab wounds, directing her frost to seal those areas with ice. It would provide a double effect—staunching the bleeding and numbing the injuries.

The pain faded slightly, and the fog in her mind dissipated with it. She crawled around the two and looked out at the courtyard again. Fifteen bodies lay scattered around the carriage, but the dark specks were getting closer.

"Yarrow! Get in here!" Savis yelled, motioning for both to join her inside.

The final guard turned to fly away, but a threaded blood arrow speared him through the chest, and he fell twitching to the ground as Trel drained him and spooled his blood into one of the empty vials on her belt.

They rushed in through the doors and knelt before her, Yarrow looking gray and anxious, Trel looking vibrant, if worried, despite her recent infusions of fresh blood.

"My lady, the entire city is stirring like a hornet's nest. What happened? Did you anger the king?" Yarrow asked, closing the doors behind him with one hand as he searched her eyes.

Savis held up the blood-stained crown and smiled weakly, "He was grateful...it was going so well..." Tears streamed from her eyes. "The... the Commission has turned against us. A Hunter killed them right at the table... They killed my father, too."

Trel gasped. "Princess," she said seriously, still looking out the window with her Bloodbow in hand, and spirals of black-red liquid flowing around her arms, "we must get out of this city immediately. There is no time to go back for bags, or to take the carriage. We need to fly."

Savis put a shaky hand on the wall, rising to her feet on wobbly legs. "I know."

"Somehow, I knew that they were doing something big," Lia said, "when they went to such lengths to make me steal that crown, but overthrowing the government?"

"It's not the first time they've tried," Savis said, walking back down the passage toward the hallway that would take them north to the Royal Aviary. "I am just surprised that after the Stanaedre Coup they were allowed to operate at all."

"More guards and hunters are arriving in the courtyard, hurry!" Trel warned, rushing up beside Savis, "Princess, I haven't time to warn you or ask permission, but you are weakened and in need of healing." She flicked her wrist and pointed at Savis, so that one of the flowing ribbons of blood shot like an arrow into her, filling her depleted veins and removing some of the exhaustion she'd felt.

"I am not able to completely heal your wounds, so keep them frozen over, but at least you won't be suffering the effects of blood loss. This way!" Trel shouted the last part, and the group trotted after her down the hall.

As they neared the northern end of the estate, after passing empty corridors and rooms, they turned a corner and were faced with a barricade of turned over tables and a trio of hunters at the head of five more Grass Guards.

"She killed the king!" One of the hunters yelled, "Do not let her escape!"

The Grass Guards rushed around the hunters, who hung back guarding the hall, as they flew over the tables and right at her! Trel was quick to fire off a blood-arrow into the neck of one of the guards, and Yarrow distracted one by darting up and locking blades with him, but three still flew in fast.

Lia growled, and seeing the windows leading outside, she grabbed a vase from a side table and threw it through the window, taking Nora and Savis by the hands and shoving them toward it. "Get outside!" she ordered, spinning on her heel to kick high and toss one of the flying guards into the ceiling.

"I used to be a Hunter," she said over her shoulder, "I know a thing or two about staying alive."

Savis paused at the window, and Nora hovered outside, calling her to come out too, voice shaking.

"Protect my daughter, Princess!" Lia said, twisting again, with a rush of elemental-enhanced wind as she flew up toward the guard slowly falling from the ceiling, and punched him in the throat. "I will join you shortly!"

Savis swallowed and climbed out the window.

Outside, she could see a steep drop from the bluff toward the window, and a narrow walking path for the gardens that meandered along the cliff edge toward the Aviary. That would be watched.

"Nora," Savis said softly, "your mama is really strong, isn't she?" She took the girl's hand and led her on the wing down below the edge of the cliff.

She nodded seriously. "She is the strongest!"

"Yes, she is, and she will join us after she has beat up those bad fae. Do you want to pick out which bird we fly on?" Savis asked, continuing to guide her around the edge of the bluff where guards and hunters up above would not be able to see them.

"Really, I can?" Nora asked excitedly, voice no longer shaking.

"Just make sure it is big enough for everyone."

When they had rounded the bend, Savis carefully led her up the slope so they could peer over the edge at the western side of the Aviary overlooking the river. Sure enough, it was unguarded, and there was a small service door into the large glass dome that housed the king's birds.

Even so, they crawled up to the door, and through it to hide behind barrels of birdseed, and saddles. Savis heard voices.

"Our scouts report they should arrive in another minute, sir. Trel and Yarrow are a formidable team—it is regrettable that they chose not to join us." This voice was young, and serious, with a Soranil accent. Had Stanaedre returned to the Commission?

"I did not ask them to, Hasfel. Those two are too focused on their ideals to consider the long-term benefit to our goals." That voice, that stern yet paternal voice, was President Hans of the Commission! Had he come to oversee his coup in person?

Meanwhile, to her right, Nora was peering through a hole in the boards, spying out the birds. "There is a big blue bird over there with feathers on his head… I want that one."

"A blue-jay? They are fast, but not very friendly." Still, fast was probably what they needed if they were going to outfly crows. Savis saw a small space they could crawl through that would keep them along the outer wall of the Aviary and behind cover so they could get closer to the bird. She waved to Nora for her to follow and began crawling along the channel to the blue-jay.

"Hasfel," the president's voice said.

"Yes, sir,"

"When we encounter them, try your hardest to keep the princess alive."

"Why the change?"

The president sighed. "I want to bring her before the gates of Frorin and take off her head."

Savis shivered, and a cold rush of frost coated her skin…and she kept crawling.

Just then, the doors at the other end crashed open with the sound of shattering glass, and Hasfel let out a gargle. Savis could only guess that Trel had shot him with one of her arrows—the uncanny blood-arrows that she could partially manipulate even when loosed from the bow.

"President Hans himself," Yarrow declared, "how gracious of you to endanger yourself here."

Trel snickered at that.

"And you only have five guards… well four now…" Trel added.

"Is mama there?" Nora asked Savis.

Savis risked a peek over one of the crates, but only saw Trel and Yarrow in the entry facing off the Hunters. "I don't see her yet…"

Nora didn't respond.

"She is strong. Now come, let us get that bird ready for her. She will be tired when she gets here." Savis came out of the tiny corridor of crates and bales, into the blue-jay's enclosure. The large stable's floor was covered in clean hay, and the blue-jay sat on a rod halfway up its enclosure where it basked in the afternoon sun.

Excitedly, Nora waved to the bird, and said softly, "Come on down, Bluedy!"

Surprisingly, the bird noticed her and hopped from one perching stick to another as it chortled and came down to the ground. It bent over to inspect her and ruffled her curly hair as it sniffed her.

Seemingly satisfied, it bowed its head to her, and so she scratched its head around the ears and cooed at it. Seeing it was distracted, Savis found the saddle—a gigantic leather monstrosity that was somehow light enough for her to move—and pulled it over the back of the bird.

She didn't know the first thing about saddling a blue-jay. So, she focused on making the belts and buckles connect. Hopefully it wouldn't slide off while in flight, but as far as she could tell, the forward belt would not slip back over the flapping wings.

A hand touched her on the shoulder, and she nearly yelped, except Lia whispered, "Good choice" and moved to the other side to help her.

"Mama, you found us!" Nora said, causing both Savis and Lia to "sh" her.

Fortunately, the sounds that now came from the other side of the enclosure's walls would have drowned that out. Swords clashed, and the twang of Trel's bowstring and the strangled cries of its successful strikes were hopeful sounds.

"Hans," Yarrow said, grunting from an impact, "I challenge you to single combat."

"You fool, even if you were to best me, my Hunters would not let you escape. Besides, you and I have dueled three times now in the Grass Blades, and in all three I have won."

"No reason for you to turn me down then."

"Yarrow, no," Trel's voice shouted, "we take him together!"

Sounds of regular fighting continued, and as they finished readying the bird, Lia, Savis, and Nora climbed up into the saddle, and they could just see over the walls of the enclosure. Trel fought against three of the hunters, and Yarrow against Hans and one other.

Trel ducked under a sword swing from one guard, fired an arrow, and grasped the blood-line that trailed behind it, pulling on it as it flew in a spiral, through the neck of one guard and then loosened her grip on it so it spiraled back out and impaled the other guard fighting Yarrow.

That guard fell, drained to the ground, so Hans faced Yarrow alone, while Trel fought two others.

The two raised their blades in salute, Yarrow's stained red, and chipped from the countless fae he had killed along the way to the Aviary, Hans' blade pristine and honed.

They rushed each other, swords clashing and flashing in a flurry of blows and parries, lunges, and feints. Trel let her blood bow dissipate and fought the two hunters attacking her with her blood flowing like whips around her. She used them to tie one down as she turned and disarmed the other with a careful spinning kick.

Yarrow dodged a feint, lunging simultaneously as his sword snapped out and scratched Hans' cheek, and he flitted back a step to avoid the backslash from the President's feint, also earning a scratch along his arm.

"You are as direct as ever, Yarrow," Hans said, breathing deeply and glancing over at Trel, "you never could learn to attack your opponents where they are not expecting it."

As Trel followed through with a blood arrow forming in her empty hands, she stabbed it into the chest of the disarmed fae, and President Hans threw his sword.

It spun end over end, timed perfectly, so that it pierced her heart. She gasped, and the flowing ribbons of blood she'd used to protect herself lost their buoyancy and fell to the ground.

Yarrow howled, rushing the president with a lunge, but right as his blade neared him, Hans tapped the sword with his hand, deflecting it, as he stepped into Yarrow's lunge and kneed him in the throat.

Then, kneeling on the prone dazed body of Yarrow, he aimed his hand at Trel, and snapped his fingers. A flash of sparkling energy shot from them into the hilt of the sword, and it flew back to his hand, where he stabbed Yarrow through the heart.

Savis screamed.

Yarrow, Trel, the president, and the hunter looked in her direction.

"Get her," the president ordered, and the other hunter—now free from Trel's tangling blood—flew toward their enclosure with an axe at the ready.

Trel held a hand to her chest, tears flowing from her eyes as she yelled with all her remaining strength, "Fly! *Jakaren's breath*, fly, Princess!" She looked down toward Yarrow, and bit her lip. Blood flowed freely from her chest, and it resisted her obvious attempt to control it. "How…?"

Hans eyed her, and a wave of sparks washed out from him, tendrils of lightning rising from the ground. "It is all physical science. I canceled out your influence." He watched her with a smug, satisfied expression as she crawled to Yarrow and put her hand on his face.

He mouthed something to her, and they both closed their eyes.

Heart shaking, and tears once more streaming from her eyes, Savis realized they had no way out of the enclosure. As the hunter burst through the doors, Savis threw her hand back and focused on launching as large a shard of ice as she could through the exterior glass.

It was massive.

She tore a hole in the side of the Aviary, and Lia was quick to pull the blue-jay in the direction of the opening. In seconds, they were out in the air flying down the bluff to gain speed on the cooler air above the river, and they left the hunter, the president, and the bodies of her friends behind.

They rose into the clear blue sky, the northerly wind buoying them as they flew in the warm sunlight.

Savis wept and clutched at her chest. "I shouldn't have any tears left..." she wondered, and cried all the more as Nora held onto her.

Biting her lip, Lia shouted over the wind, "We will not make it to Frorin in one flight, but this bird should be able to reach Fassen. The Earl will help us."

Her hands shook as she reached into her bag and held up the bloody Harvest Crown. "Will he?"

Lia looked over her shoulder at Savis and smiled wanly. "My people have long believed that we will be restored. Not to live in shame and guilt, not forgotten, but renewed to a greater glory than we had before the Fall of Waverly. He will see it, too. This is the time to shake off the hold of Gaersheim and stand once more on our own."

She hoped he would.

But for now, the loss of her friends was still more than she could bear. She clutched onto the crown, grateful at least to hear that Leif and Fryn had somehow, against all odds, survived.

Froreholt

Frorin

Crown District

Havrshyk

Aldyr stood in the foyer, looking up at a painting of King Imloth hanging beside one of the hidden levers he once used to navigate the Palace. Since his revival, he had not seen a single servant, or guard use one of the many corridors that crisscrossed the estate like veins connecting so many organs in the body—he guessed that when the Swordhand Palm had been disbanded, that knowledge had died with it.

King Hyngram was too young when Imloth killed himself, so he had not been informed of the secrets and sins of his father, and that was probably for the best. He had, to all accounts, grown into a good king. Still, seeing this portrait of King Imloth standing in his throne room with a sword in hand, and green-garbed attackers coming in to attack him from the borders made his stomach twist. The placard beside it titled it "The Stanaedre Coup" and he resented the fact that the king was portrayed as a lone hero when he had hid behind his mistress.

His wings flushed purple, and he started when one of the servants coughed politely to attract his attention. "The king is ready to see you, Master," she said uncertainly.

He supposed that, ironically, the title fit. He was truly the last of the Swordhand Palm and had even been appointed as their head. Aldyr regarded her with a tired smile, one hand resting on the pommel of his Bloodsword, as he gave a slight bow in response. "Thank you, shall I follow you now?"

She bobbed her head, avoiding his eyes, and led him down the hall to and through the same doors he had once defended with his life and death into the Throne Room. "King Ieffin apologizes for making you wait so long and wanted me to explain that the Assembly's demands on his time were pressing, so that the Commission could be quickly ousted from Frorin and their assets seized."

Havrshyk didn't respond to her, and she seemed pleased with his silence. Despite the passing of seventy years in the catacombs, the fear and mistrust faeries had for Liches was just as prevalent today. Perhaps slightly less since they now had two of them. He smiled thinking about Fryn and how, finally, he had the comfort of knowing that his was not a singular existence… but that was soured when he considered that he had forced her to cooperate with him, and readily betrayed his promise to return Leif to her.

Leif had survived, miraculously, but that did not change the fact that he had chosen himself and consigned Leif to die instead.

Fryn knew… and she was not one to forgive so easily.

Prince…King Ieffin was not sitting in his throne when Havrshyk entered. Instead, he was at the ground level, leaning over a table with his hands pressed out on a map of Fhoraena, decorated with pins, pieces, and tiny colored flags. Across the table stood one of his messengers, still wearing their old Commission's Messenger uniform, though it was decorated with a white snowflake patterned sash.

Two guards stood beside the doors, silver lances held crisply in salute, and they nodded at Havrshyk as he passed.

"Thank you for bringing me this message. I will need to draft a response immediately, so now change birds, eat something, and return in an hour," the king said to the messenger. Then, noticing Havrshyk approach, he waved Aldyr over and showed him a letter he had pinned on the table beside the map.

Havrshyk read it, narrowing his eyes, and then taking a breath as the immensity of the news hit him.

Brother,

You may have heard, or perhaps word from Gaersheim has been cut off, but I have narrowly escaped the city with my life. I was returning the Harvest Crown to the king, when the Commission staged a coup, and killed the king and queen right before my eyes. They tried to kill me too, but I escaped with the help of my good friends Trel and Yarrow… who died at the hands of President Hans himself.

We fled by bird to Fassen, and even as I write this message, we are watchful for the spies of the Commission. I was fortunate to recognize this messenger, and send word by him, for he saw me in my wretched state, covered in blood, and wounds, and did not even ask for payment as I sent him to you with this letter.

I believe that the Commission is watching the city closely, and as we are searching for a way to get inside, we are wary and do not know who to trust.

But tell me, is it true? Is Father dead?
Are Leif and Fryn alive?

Ieffin, I don't know what to do…
Please send help.

And be careful, Hans says he is coming for you. Frorin must stand, or the Commission will control everything north of Cherim. If only they would strike at the Commission as they did before the Stanaedre Coup.

~Your sister,
Savis

Havrshyk swallowed. Another coup? Rosenkrauns dead? He looked up at Ieffin and saw the uncertainty plainly on his face. "I am going to ask Leif and Fryn to go to her, but… if they could kill one Bloodcrafter… they may not be able to stop two. Will you go with them to look after my sister? Get her somewhere the Commission can't touch her?"

"Who is going to protect you?" Havrshyk found himself asking.

Ieffin's eyes flicked over to the doorway, and the soft clicking footsteps that approached.

"I will," Harissa said, tapping the ground with her Bonesword cane.

Aldyr looked back at Ieffin nodding to himself. "I need you to do one thing. You must enfranchise the Sky District, as you promised."

King Ieffin met his eyes and gave a determined smile. "I was not meeting with the Assembly just to close down the Commission and take control of their resources, but to lay out the proposal the Pine-Martin brought to me."

Harissa added, "Trade will be impossible with Gaersheim under Commission control. They will strangle us, and deprive our markets of food, cloth, and many other necessities. But have you heard of the strides Norenan has made in traversing long distances safely in their airships?"

He hadn't. Aldyr shook his head and waited for them to continue.

"Harissa wants to replace the Stone Market that you helped destroy with something more open, and less… corrupt… that brings in a wide array of goods from far off lands via airship. Even if we do not have these ships ourselves, building the infrastructure will invite them to come to our city and bring more tourism and trade even with the Commission blocking roads through the Forest of Grass," Ieffin explained.

"That sounds well and good, but to build this market and the walls needed to defend it, what will you do with the population and the houses you will need to destroy?" he asked, tightening his jaw.

Ieffin looked at Harissa.

"I have connections with many in the Sky District, and for years they have reached out to my family for aid and protection. In my proposal, the families living there now will be granted citizenship, and have the option of receiving one of the new houses we will build or fair payment for the land they currently occupy; and they can find housing in whatever ring they can afford.”

“What of the homeless and the poor?”

“As I mentioned, we are building blocks of housing, much of it townhouses with limited rooms, that will be available for those faeries. The ground is being broken on this project tomorrow, and the Alderleaf Tower will be the pride of the Sky District, accessible through the new gate along Pine-Martin Road.”

Havrshyk felt lightheaded and pinched his temples. “Ieffin… if you follow through with this, I’ll take your sister to Moraskyr if that is what it takes. But… do not fail. The Sky District is my home, and I remember their mistreatment at the hands of the citizens of Frorin. Be a king who cares for his people… or I will have choice words for you.”

“Threatening the king who is asking for your help is hardly appropriate,” Harissa complained, tapping her fingers on the handle of her cane.

Ieffin shot her a stern look, and then returned his focus on Havrshyk with a thin smile. “I understand, Havrshyk. I found the vow of the Swordhand Palm Masters… no titles or mint, or power will stand between you and justice, right? I will prove a more just king than the last. Now, please, hurry.”

“Leif and Fryn are waiting for you in the courtyard,” Harissa said, “I’ll go with you to explain.”

Ieffin sighed with relief, as he turned to her. “Thank you, Harissa, I will send this message ahead of you.”

Harissa is full of surprises, Aldyr shook his head, bemused. She was already walking to the doors, the tails of her long black coat swishing with her wings. “Harissa,” he said, moving to one of the wall sconces, “there is a faster way to the courtyard.”

“Use the passages,” he suggested, and when he pulled down on the starlamp sconce, a section of the wall slid inwards with a scraping of stone, revealing the black maw of a narrow, unlit corridor. The faintest light reflected off the brass guide rail, just as it had seventy years before. “This one links up with your chambers, Ieffin, and with an escape route to the courtyard. Harissa, keep one hand on the handrail, and follow me to the west.”

She gave the tunnel an amazed, if suspicious look, but followed him anyway. “How long have these been here?”

“Centuries.”

"And they haven't been dusted in that long?" she asked with a sniff.

He shook his head and led her out.

"If you are going to watch him, and watch over the Sky Dwellers, I will hold you accountable, too," he added.

She sneezed behind him and muttered something under her breath.

"What was that?"

"I said I still needed to hold you accountable… you stood me up once."

He scratched his head, and chuckled.

"The Sky District is mine," she added, "and no noble or king is going to take them from me."

"Good."

Froreholt

Frorin

Crown District

Leif

Three days, was that all it had been since he was freed? Leif sat on a bench in the courtyard of the Crown District, where he had a pleasant view of the entry to the Palace and the Grand Assembly across the way. He leaned back against the wall, soaking in the warmth of the guard post fire at his side, where one of the Crown Guard sipped tea before his shift. Leif's arm was around Fryn, who sat on the side of the bench further from the fire, and he gave her shoulder a squeeze.

She glanced over, eyes refocusing on him, as she gave a small smile, and then she looked back at her hands in her lap. Fryn had been like this ever since he returned, sometimes present and excited, the rest of the time, anxious and distracted. His attempts to stir her from her reveries, granted, mostly involved teasing and annoying, but even then, she just wasn't really there with him.

"What are we going to do, Leif?" she asked him, not looking away from her hands.

He pursed his lips. "The Commission has been kicked out and I'm back—and very glad to see you—but the truth is Fryn, we are free to do whatever we wish."

She hesitated, wings pulsing a confused yellow and blue. "What if I don't know what I want to do?"

Leif held in a sigh. He could not shake her free of this, so he stated his thoughts honestly and hoped that would be enough. "My people have a saying, 'If you want to know which way the wind is blowing, fly away from it.'"

"What?" Fryn asked, giving him a raised eyebrow. "What does that mean?"

"It means," he said, "deep down you know what you want to do, but you're avoiding it."

She nudged him in a half-playful way and then put her chin in on her hand and sighed loudly. "I can't bear waiting here for the Commission to make a move. I want to be *doing* something."

"Looks like something might be about to happen, Fryn," Leif said, pointing toward one of the stones in the courtyard. It wobbled and rose into the air, and was slid aside onto the ground, and from the hole beneath it, Havrshyk rose and dusted himself off before reaching down and lifting Harissa out. He slid the stone back into the hole with his foot and looked around until he spotted them.

He walked toward them lazily, but through some lingering remnant of his connection to the fae, Leif knew that he was ashamed. Leif gave Fryn's shoulder another squeeze and rose to meet the two.

"Where's your Moraskyn friend?" Harissa asked, brow furrowing as she looked around.

"Alyra?" Fryn confirmed, then jabbed a thumb toward the guard post where the fee was huddled close to the fire with a cup of steaming tea in her hands.

"Could you have the meeting over here?" Alyra asked, shivering as she pulled back her hood to greet them.

They moved closer, and while the others held back at the outer edge of the post, Leif happily stood closer to the warmth of the fire. "Ieffin summoned us, right? When do we get to go in?" he asked.

"I am afraid that he received urgent news that ultimately means a delay in your meeting with him," Harissa said, frowning as she looked at Havrshyk. "Perhaps you should explain."

He gave her an inquiring look, but shrugged and added, "Princess Savis sent a letter, she was attacked while meeting with the king of Gaersheim, and reports that though she escaped with her life, the king, the queen, Trel, and Yarrow, have fallen to the Commission. She is now searching for a way to enter Fassen and seek the aid of the Earl but needs help. The pr… the king has asked that we go to her and get her safely out of the reach of the Commission."

Alyra's teeth chattered a little as she asked, "Fassen? I need to go there."

Leif met Fryn's eyes, and when she nodded slowly, he said, "We will go."

"Poor Trel," Fryn said, putting a hand over her breast, "and poor Savis, she traveled with them for years… she must be terrified!"

"She was able to escape at least," Harissa said with a dark expression, "It was likely a closer thing than she suggests from her letter."

The others all shared a nod.

"There is a bird waiting for you. Fly to Fassen, locate Savis, and kill any Hunters who get in your way," Harissa ordered, "but first, your licenses."

Leif felt a chill that went down to his stomach. They truly were done with the Commission. He and Fryn handed their licenses to Harissa, and in the same motion that she took them, she placed plaques in their hands to replace them.

Leif held his up to the light and whistled. There was a small likeness of his face stamped into the steel, and in bright blue enameled lettering, his name, and surprisingly his title. "Viper" of the Silver Lancers of Frorin.

"Ieffin offers these honorary titles, so that none within the borders of Froreholt may deny your lawful inquiries… but he does not require your service in his regular forces. You are independent agents of his Lance." Harissa pocketed the old licenses, and then gave Fryn a firm hug. "I have so missed you, Fryn, but please, see her to safety, and when this whole mess is over… come home."

Fryn wiped away frosted tears and hugged her cousin back with all her might. "We will."

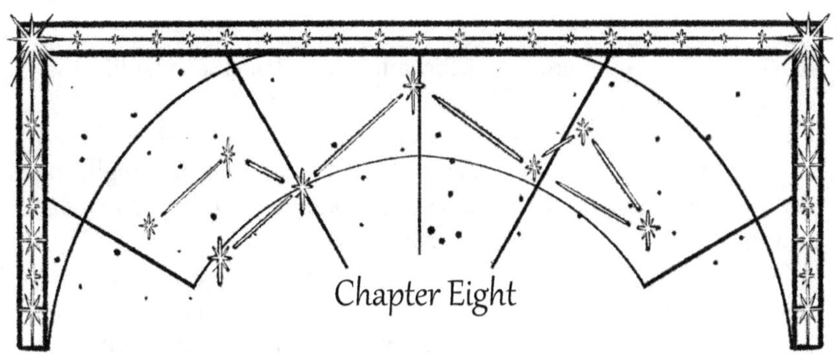

Chapter Eight

Mountain

Ice Wastes

Grifton

A dull ache permeated his body, reaching deep into his marrow as awareness returned to him. Tendrils of sinewy bone were knitting his flesh back together with a mind all their own, and Grifton mused to himself that the involuntary nervous system was more mysterious than he had ever realized. The air, the powdery snow, and the hard ground radiated cold—yet strangely, he was as unaffected by it as by the warm sun overhead.

His skeletal right arm and the superior replacement limb flexed and clawed at the frozen earth. He opened his eyes and stared at the pale sky laughing uncontrollably.

Grifton only calmed down after his breath ran out, and he sat up. He was in a snow drift with his back to the ring of stones where he had fought, what, days before? Looking at his chest, he could see the hollow where his organs used to be, now undulating with twisting fibers of bone and marrow, knitting together replacements for what the Moraskyn fae had disintegrated.

Where was all the material for those sinews coming from anyway?

He rose to his feet shakily, nearly falling over from the change in his center of balance and searched in the snow for his sword... but it was gone. Completely. He could sense it, suffusing his body.

233

It had all been converted to keep him alive. But that wouldn't be enough.

There would be plenty of weak, useless hatchlings he could kill to rebuild his armor and weapon along the way as he sought his revenge. He scanned the horizon, and found the mountains where Frorin sat, like a fat, decrepit monarch on his couch.

Grifton grinned, cheeks tearing at the sides where what remained of his skin peeled away, and he began to march.

"Just a little farther…" he rasped, voice hoarse, and gravelly, like a bird imitating a fae. "I will grind you both to dust…"

Forest of Grass

Festival Grounds

(north of Fassen)

Savis

Savis had never been accustomed to camping outdoors, nor being on the run like a criminal, or being without her friends to cheer her up or protect her left her feeling hollow. She huddled under the wing of the blue-jay they had flown there, arms hugging her knees to herself. The Harvest Crown sat on a small, bundled tarp before her, blood flaking off between breezes.

Nora and Lia had gone to their old house during the night to "steal" supplies, and narrowly avoided notice from the Grass Guards stationed at the unmapped hamlet. Thankfully, that had supplied them with a few luxuries, such as a couple blankets and dried fruit, but even with that, her stomach growled, and she had dark bags under her eyes.

Savis wiped her raw eyes and sighed. It was still early, and Lia and Nora slept on the other side of the blue jay, huddled under that wing. Savis was surprised the bird didn't seem to mind their use of it for cover. Weary from crying and hiding, she picked up the crown, and climbed out from under the bird's feathers. Not entirely sure where she was going, she crossed the clearing to the raised section that had once held the tables where the king and queen of Gaersheim had hosted the Harvest Festival, and where not long ago she had given one of the toasts.

In her mind's eye she could still see the streamers and lanterns, crisscrossing the clearing from one bundle of grass to another, and she walked along the edge of the long, imagined table, and stopped at the spot where her chair had been. There, she closed her eyes, and focused on forming a layer of frost over the ground there. It clung to her as well, flaking away like bits of ash with every gust of wind.

The grass rustled all around her in the breeze, and somewhere deep within the Forest of Grass, she heard the singing of crickets, and further away, the distant croaking of frogs. It almost sounded like the music played in the pavilion, and the movements of the grass like the swishing of dresses and dancers' wings.

Savis clutched the crown in her hands and using the pain of its blades pressing into her fingers as a focus, she whispered into the air. "Trel, where do I go?"

"Wherever you wish," the wind seemed to say, echoing one of her last conversations with the Hunter duo.

"What if I don't know what I wish?" she asked, opening her eyes.

Savis started.

There was a fee standing before her on the next step below. She wore a green shawl over a white cloak, but her green-fringed hood was up and shadowed her face. Her wings pulsed with a tentative yellow flash, and she raised her hands to her hood, lowering it with a jingling of her brass bracelets.

The fee had a weathered face, somber wrinkles around her mouth and eyes, and a sharp nose over thin lips. She fixed Savis with solemn violet eyes and held up one hand to silence the princess. "I heard you were here," she said glancing over her shoulder toward the bird where Lia and Nora still slept, "and I have come for that crown in your hands."

Savis tightened her grip on it. "I am not giving this to you," she said softly, voice shaking, "I am giving it to a friend."

The fee nodded patiently, brushing a stray bit of grass-down from her cloak. "Lord Fassen, I believe."

She bit her lip, uncertain.

"He is not ready for the crown, child. I will keep it safe until he is ready for it."

"Ready?" Savis asked, wings shifting uncomfortably.

"Yes. You would have him keep it to protect it, but we believe rather that he should wear it," the fee replied, smiling, and holding up a hand. "Be a dear and help me up."

Savis held the crown away as she used the other hand to help the stranger up onto the top level, who sighed and sat on the edge, dangling her feet.

"I don't understand," Savis admitted, sitting down stiffly beside her, with the crown on her lap.

The fee leaned back and looked at the sky. "Neither do I, child, but it is time. What was *fassen* will be no more cast off but will be preserved and nurtured into a thriving people again. Yours is the generation to see it, but we have waited for a long, long time."

"Who are you?" she asked, examining the last few blood stains on the crown, and rubbing them clean.

"My name is Alesaeja."

The princess frowned. "But *who* are you?"

"An old lady," she replied cheekily with a laugh, "but no, to answer your question, I am the one who remembers and instructs the children of Waverly. Loren may be all grown now, but even he had to sit at my feet sometimes to know his past."

Savis waited.

The wind changed directions, blowing the sweet scent of grapes from the city to the south, and the bird cleaned its feathers. Finally, Alesaeja continued.

"It is time for our people to stand on their own. No Gaersyn king, no bankers or mercenaries, just a city spared one disaster after another. Loren is not ready to be king, but he will be soon. This crown belongs to him."

"It does?"

"Indeed. The tradition of the Harvest Festival dates back to before Fassen was annexed by Gaersheim, you know. They allowed the festival to continue but put their king in place of the Fassen lords, and the crown of Fassen was given to the king of Gaersheim as a symbol of their sovereignty." The old fee held out a hand to Savis. "May I see it?"

Reluctantly, yet intrigued, Savis handed it over. Alesaeja turned it over in her hands and clicked her tongue at the bent blades and blood flakes. "How fitting that the crown stolen from our people was the weapon of our vengeance."

The story-teller turned the crown over in her hands and stared at it longingly for several moments, then her shoulders slumped and she reluctantly handed it back to Savis with a sigh. "We know that it was untold years ago, and that no one is left who counted the days. It is simpler to tell it this way:

"A thousand years ago this day, when the mountain broke, and fire and ash covered the Forest of Grass, a few of us survived. They'd flown away to the south, to the farthest reach of Waverly. Cast away, exiled, but preserved to repent—our grandfathers, mothers, and ancestors wept for their arrogance." Alesaeja closed her eyes and turned her face toward the sky as she spoke, reciting the story with an air of solemn nostalgia.

"In the days that followed, as more and more survivors arrived, the last Lord of Waverly gathered them beneath the branches of a wild grape vine and divided the labor of clearing out the ash, and building shelters from the incessant storms that followed the eruption. The sky was blackened for days, and even after weeks, smoke still rose from the mountain. Hopeless and forsaken by the Wing-Giver, the remnant of Waverly languished in the desolate remains of the land. But hope remained."

Savis, listening intently, noticed that the wing of the Blue Jay shifted as Nora and Lia came out and walked over to hear the story. Lia sat one level down, cross-legged, and Nora climbed into her lap, and folded her hands.

Alesaeja smiled and continued. "Weeks after the disaster, as the people were starved for food and hope, a watcher from the vine spied a lone figure walking across the barren plains. Hooded and cloaked, they avoided him, as he strode up the dirt path to the foot of the vine and collapsed before Lord Fasset.

The stranger lowered his hood and looked up, revealing the emaciated, scarred, and dying face of Darsin, the last prophet. "Lord Fasset," he said in rasping voice, "you have been *Fassen*, cast off, a symbol of disgrace for all nations." At this, Lord Fasset knelt before him, and all the people wept. Why, after all they had been through, would they be preserved? It would be better if they had fallen in the fires of Mount Waver.

Nora took in a breath, and Lia hushed her gently.

"But..." Darsin added, weakly grasping his sleeve, "do not despair. As you are a symbol of judgment, you are a symbol of restoration as well. Though you are cast off, you are thrown as seeds into the ground, a replanting of your people. Take what gold you have and weave it into a circlet of grass blades, and with it, restore the House of Waverly. In time, even this will be washed in the waters of the Wing-Giver and your restoration will be complete."

Alesaeja paused, pointing a delicate, wrinkled finger at the crown in Savis' hands. "But they were weak, and even when the city of Fassen grew around the vine, invaders from the south took all they had—including this crown. The exiles of Waverly were forced to live under the power of a strange land, longing for the restoration of their crown. That time is near, nearer than it has ever been, but is not yet. We must safeguard the crown until that time… and you will be the one to carry it to the mountain and wash the blood from it in the Wing-Giver's pool."

Lia gave Savis a confused expression. "What mountain? Waver?"

She shook her head. "It is far, far from here, and I do not know its name. But in the stories, there are hints. If this is truly the year of our redemption, then you must seek the adviser of the current Fassen Lord. He will know this mountain and will help you keep this crown safe."

"How are we supposed to get into the city? There are Grass Guards everywhere!" Lia interjected, wings flashing an anxious blue.

"I will show you the forgotten path, there is a way through the boulder wall unknown to the guards, kept safe by my people. If we go now, we should arrive by nightfall." Abruptly she stood and gave the bird an odd look. "I would advise setting him free, as he will only draw attention to us." She walked up to the bird and tapped it on the beak. "Go home blue jay," she said kindly.

It chirped and looked at Savis and then back at Alesaeja.

"I will watch over them, now go back to your hay and seeds." At that, the blue jay whistled, and took off back toward Rosenkraun.

"We have to *walk*?" Nora complained, trailing behind her mother as the story-teller led them down a trail in the grass.

Savis slipped a satchel of dried goods and a blanket over her shoulder, and flitted after her, and Lia carried the rest.

Nora's mother clicked her tongue, and answered, "I don't think it is wise to fly above the grass right now child, besides, flying with this much baggage is pretty difficult."

Alesaeja had not been exaggerating—the sky overhead was dark, and the stars glowed in a spray of white on black. The greater moon covered most of the Vine, and the two lesser moons were barely visible as a couple of slowly moving pinpoints of light.

Savis, Lia, and Nora followed their guide along a wandering path, ducking into bunches of grass whenever the beating wings of Grass Guard crows flew nearby. Then, finally, the shadow of the eastern edge of the boulder wall of Fassen loomed over them.

Their trail, which was hardly recognizable as a trail, snaked around the bunches of grass all the way from the festival grounds, and was marked only by the appearance of tiny green stones used to mark the path from one cluster of grass to the next.

"Our people have struggled, and been impoverished under the rule of Gaersheim," Alesaeja explained, "so having our own, untaxed passages into and out of the city helped preserve us. Even so, the Eastwall District is the poorest and most crowded of the districts."

She paused under the eaves of one of the boulders, holding up a hand for them to stop, as a bird flew by overhead. Moving forward again, she found a narrow crack cut into the boulder, marked on the outside by a green pebble on the ground, and squeezed through it.

Savis followed her, with Lia and Nora right behind. Her satchel complicated the squeeze, but she somehow scrambled through at an angle, and found herself stepping out from behind a tapestry into a long hallway lined with stalls lit by lantern light.

The boulder's smoky interior was carved into the cavity of a geode and filled with a warm light that was colored and filtered with amber and amethyst. The path forward was paved with more green pebbles, and the shops were all manned by faeries in Waverly cloaks, with caramel-colored eyes. Whispers in Waverly echoed just beyond clarity in Savis' ears, so that though she had studied the language, she could not understand what they said. Two fae stood just beyond the tapestry, wearing brass breastplates and wrist guards to complement their cloaks, with bronze spears in hand. They bowed politely to Alesaeja, and the one on the right spoke readily to her.

"We have closed the doors of the boulder market to all as you requested, Lore-keeper. Were you successful?" he asked, fingering the tassels of his spear.

She nodded, bringing Savis forward with a cryptic smile. "I have," she replied, "are you ready to escort us?"

"Of course, come with us," he turned to Savis, "welcome to Fassen, Princess. We have one more journey ahead for you."

"Do we have to walk?" Nora asked sourly.

The guard laughed, startling one of the shopkeepers. "No, child, this time we will take a carriage."

He led them down the empty pebble stone path, and through a set of vinewood doors into one of the wider streets of the Eastwall District. There, a carriage emblazoned with the symbol of the Gaersyn Grass Guard awaited them, surrounded by more guards in the traditional garb of the Grass Guard, though with Waverly brass arm-bands and hair that flowed in long red-blond waves over their shoulders, both fee and fae.

"No one will accost you now, my lady," the guard explained, "even up to the entrance of Lord Loren's estate."

Alesaeja thanked him and held the door of the carriage open so that Savis and the others could enter. Savis gave the tan hare hitched to the carriage a look, and then climbed inside.

Her feet ached, and her wings felt weak, so she slipped off her flat shoes as they settled in. The carriage trundled up the road toward the south-western side of the city, splashing in potholes, and rocking over the uneven road. Savis was utterly exhausted… but mostly, she was surprised to have survived, and marveled that she had made it inside the city at all. Using her satchel as a pillow, she leaned her head against the wall of the carriage so she could still look outside the tiny, circular window, and she dozed in and out of sleep.

They rode past the Commission's offices, the estates of the low lords, and back and forth through the switchbacks to the base of the vine. The journey likely took nearly an hour, but the scenery and her awareness of time had slipped as she slept.

The guards at the gate did not even stop them for questioning and they rolled straight into the courtyard before the Earl's Estate, and before Savis could even sit up, or slip her shoes back on, the door of the carriage opened, and a tall fae with graying black hair, wearing a black and white uniform, presented a white gloved hand.

"Princess Savis," he said, "we have been waiting."

Savis awkwardly put on her shoes, and took his hand, stepping out into the dark, unlit courtyard. Lia, Nora, and Alesaeja came out a moment later, looking around, surprised by the lack of light—since the grapevine blocked a view of the stars.

"We?" Savis confirmed, more than a little confused.

"The Earl and I," he glanced over his shoulder in the direction of the gates. "I am Vinellin. We have met before, but first let us go inside."

Rubbing the sleep from her eyes, Savis yawned and asked, "Vinellin? Oh…" she yawned again, "I was supposed to ask you about the pool in the mountain."

He guided her up the stairs and shot a confused look at Alesaeja. To Savis he said, "we can talk more about that later." He opened the doors to the estate and guided them into a rush of warm air and welcome light, where Loren stood waiting in the foyer.

"Welcome Princess," Loren said cheerfully, quieting at a look from his butler, "to Fassen… come, right this way."

He turned and led her up a flight of stairs and down a corridor to a private wing of the estate, where bookshelves lined the walls, and a set of couches faced a hearth. He scooted over an armchair and waved for them to sit down before the fire and seated himself. He held out a hand, and within a moment or two, Vinellin had opened a cabinet set between two of the bookcases and passed a glass of wine to the Earl.

Three more glasses followed, one each for Savis, Lia, and Alesaeja, and another smaller glass of juice for Nora.

The girl eyed it warily. "This isn't bad juice again, is it?"

The butler chuckled and shook his head. "No, it is not."

"Gaersheim has fallen," Savis said, accepting her glass of wine. She took a long swallow and then a breath of relief. "The Commission killed the king and queen while I was visiting them, and Hans tried to have me killed as well… I barely escaped… Trel and Yarrow did not."

Loren set his wineglass down on an amber-colored side table, steepling his fingers and narrowing his eyes. "The Commission has already informed me of several drastic changes coming to our region, warning that we should join their coalition against the evils of Frorin and to hold true to our long-standing kinship with Rosenkraun. Fools…" He took another sip of his wine, watching Savis carefully. "They moved against your brother too quickly. With Ieffin king of Froreholt, and their assets seized, it will come to a long, drawn-out conflict."

"Not if they hold Fassen," Savis countered, finishing her glass, and glancing at Vinellin for a refill. "If they control this city, they will be able to run supply chains, and aerial attacks on Artell, and from there mount a siege against my home. But to control Fassen, they would need the same legitimacy that Gaersheim claimed against you."

Savis removed the crown from her bag and set it on the low table before her. The light from the peat fire shone off its blades in a dazzling, flickering display, and she left it there as she took the refilled glass from the butler.

"Loren," Alesaeja said, glancing at the crown, "do you remember?"

He met her eyes and seemed to shrink slightly, "I remember all the stories you told me."

"You must stand alone," she said, pointing to the crown, "until this crown is returned to you. Do not bow to the Commission."

"My brother will help," Savis added, "if you were to fall, we would be endangered. I should write to him, tell him what has happened!"

A chair scraped against the ground, and they all looked sharply as Vinellin, the butler, sat down with a glass of wine to join them. "A fine vintage indeed my lord. Princess Savis, I suspect you will have another journey after this."

She examined him with a raised eyebrow over the rim of her glass.

"The mountain is in my homeland, quite a way from Aizora, in the very center of Elin," he explained. "My people speak a language loosely related to Waverly, so I will recommend you get a copy of the Elifor Dictionary when you pass through Norenan."

A pit formed in her stomach. "Norenan… Elin…"

Alesaeja smiled sweetly and put her hand on Savis' knee. "This is vitally important, child, you must take the Harvest Crown to the top of the mountain, wash it clean in the waters there, and return to us."

"Why must *I* do it?" she demanded. "I need to return home!"

"No," Loren said carefully, "if you return to Frorin, the Commission will send another assassin to kill you both, and your line will end. When you tell Ieffin you are safe in Fassen, he will probably tell you to stay here. I cannot protect you if my gambit is to succeed."

"Gambit?" Savis snapped, nearly spilling her wine as hurried to set her glass on the side table. "What are you talking about?"

Loren met Alesaeja's gaze and recited in a hard quiet voice, "and so those who were cast aside, to hang forgotten in the web of the spider, shall find succor in the spinner's eyes."

Alesaeja nodded. "Cobwebs are only called such when the spider who formed them is dead. Alive forever, mother of the many, shall bite the neck of the oppressor and distract him from the truth."

Disturbed, Savis grabbed the crown and shoved it back in her bag. Then, not wanting to wait, she shot Vinellin a glance and said, "I need to draft a letter. Do you have a messenger who can get word past the Grass Guards?"

Loren smiled slyly. "Most of those in the Grass Guard stationed here at Fassen are locals, all of whom are loyal to their homeland. They will let my messengers pass. Of course, I will not be able to openly declare myself your ally until Fhora's army leaves the forest."

"The Cherim?" Savis asked incredulously. "They hate the Rosenkrauns nearly as much as you do, but how do you know they will not thank Hans for killing them?"

"Because he will not accept her claims over the 'Forest of Grass' and bend his knee." Loren said. "I can only hope for your sake, and for your homeland that she does not delay in sending her forces."

Savis swallowed.

Nora finished her glass of juice and then looked up at Vinellin and asked plaintively, "Is there any dinner left over?"

The tension melted away, and Lia laughed. Savis felt her stomach rumbling as well—wine was only so welcome without food to settle it.

Vinellin jumped up and bowed slightly, "How remiss of me, of course. I will return with stationary, and dinner."

"I haven't eaten yet either," Loren complained, eyes alight with mischief.

"You just didn't want to eat alone," Vinellin corrected with a smile, "but I will bring enough stew and bread for all." He ducked out the side door, and Savis turned her face to the fire.

Despite having a frost elemental affinity, she welcomed its warmth, and the heady scent of the moss burning. After such a long journey, she had somehow survived, and was safe at last.

Minutes passed, and Vinellin returned with a cart bearing dishes and a whole pot of stew, with several skinny loaves of golden, crusty bread. "Typically, I scold the earl when he tries to eat anywhere besides the dining hall, but I hesitate to make you all move again when you are starving."

Vinellin laid out napkins on the low table between the couches and armchairs, with spoons and knives, and a small bowl of grape seed oil mixed with herbs and salt. Then, he ladled a rich brown stew into wide bone china bowls decorated with the vine of Fassen and set them on the table beside the cutlery. The loaves of bread, he set down in the center of the table beside the oil. Finally, he caught Savis' eye and patted a small vinewood box and pen case and left them on the cart before seating himself.

Loren cleared his throat and uncrossed his legs, leaning forward and resting his elbows on his knees as he smiled and said, "You have traveled far, and through great dangers, to come here tonight. May the food of my table fill the void, and displace the fear, and anxiety that filled it before." He motioned to the food, and took one of the loaves of bread, breaking a small piece off of it, and dipping it in the oil. "This has always been a favorite snack of mine—if Vinellin allowed me, I'd just eat the bread."

Nora laughed and took a piece of bread and tried to mimic him. A drop of oil fell on the tabletop, but though the Earl noticed it, he didn't complain. In fact, he chuckled and used another small piece of bread to pick up the oil spot and then dipped it in his stew.

Savis picked up her bowl, and breathed in the rich, spicy scent. Hare, sage, and wheat berries, and a myriad of other spices and herbs in a thick broth made her stomach rumble and her mouth salivate in anticipation. Eagerly, she dipped bread in the oil and then in the stew, and, blowing on it with her frost slightly, she took a bite and savored the smoky spices.

By the time she finished her stew, she had eaten more bread than she should have liked; she understood how Loren could overindulge in the crusty breads. When broken open, the loaves were filled with numerous, wide air pockets, perfect for absorbing and holding oil, sauce, or broth... and it was chewy.

After dinner, slightly more relaxed, Savis took the pen case and stationary, and sat down to draft a letter to her brother... the king of Froreholt. She had been attacked and nearly killed, but to have been so far away when her father died—that was the hardest thing. She froze her eyes slightly, not wanting any tears to drop on her letter to smear the ink.

> *Ieffin,*
>
> *I have found a way inside Fassen, and even now am safe from the Commission's eyes. There is a new wrinkle in Hans' plans I need to share with you.*
>
> *He wants the Harvest Crown, even after taking control of Gaersheim. I cannot imagine why he still seeks it, but I will not allow him to have it. If you have found Leif and Fryn, send them to me. Without Trel and Yarrow, I cannot think of anyone else I would trust to protect me.*
>
> *I... believe I am meant to take it far away, even to Elin! I would feel more confident with Leif and Fryn beside me. A part of me hopes that I can rest there until all this blows over—except I believe that there is something the Wing-Giver has given me to do.*
>
> *Help may be found even in the shadows of the darkest forest. Perhaps I may find aid for our people therein.*
>
> *May Setfjeø cover you with his wings.*
>
> *Savis*

Blowing on the paper, and blotting in a couple places, she only hoped that Ieffin would understand her hints, and know that he would not truly face the Commission alone. Savis sealed the plain white candle wax with an imprint of her signet ring and passed the letter over to Vinellin, and the butler stalked out.

"Now we wait," she guessed.

Loren chuckled dryly. "Now you rest. Vinellin will show you to your rooms, and after baths and blankets, and a full night's rest, I am sure you will feel much better tomorrow. Then perhaps I will give you a more proper tour of my city."

Savis noticed then that Nora had fallen asleep on her mother's lap, and was snoring softly, and even Lia was leaning back against the couch, eyes closed.

"That sounds..." tears fell from Savis' eyes, no longer frozen over, "that sounds good..."

The earl stood, and went to a bureau beside the hearth. He opened one drawer and then another, and not finding what he was looking for, he took his pocket square and handed it over to Savis.

"It may be rougher than the spider-silk you may be used to, but I hope it will suffice."

His pocket square was woven from fine linen, dyed a deep green, even darker than the Grass Guard. He was not exaggerating. As she took it and wiped away her tears, the coarse fabric took her mind away from the shock and stress and focused on the tactile sensation of the textile. "I never spent as much time with you, Loren, since I was sent as an ambassador to Gaersheim…"

"And you were engaged to Duke Wellsey," he added.

She raised an eyebrow, "I never spent much time with him either. But I am sorry to say that the opinion of many was that Fassen was merely a waystop on the path to more cultured cities. Despite that reputation, somehow your estate reminds me of home."

He smiled at that. "Fassen has always been of little importance, isn't that right?" He looked over where Alesaeja had been sitting, but she had vanished. "Always used to do that," he muttered, "sometimes in the middle of the story."

Savis laughed, dabbing away a stray tear with his pocket square.

"Come onto the balcony for a moment and look up at the vine," he suggested, helping her up and opening the door for her. They stepped out onto a small balcony, large enough for a private table or two, and he pointed up at the trunk and branches of the vine.

It twisted about itself, climbing up and then knotted into a bulb before branching in eight directions. From below, they could see light from the windows of the offices, and from the lanterns hanging along the branches' lengths.

"I have always wondered, even since I was a child, why we did not have the Harvest Festival here at the estate. How marvelous it would be with the lanterns strung across from the estate to the wall, and all around the vine. Even the old story tells of my people gathering beneath a wild vine to rebuild." He spoke wistfully, hands resting on decorative brass railing.

"Is it so the people could see how they started? With nothing?" Savis asked, idly pocketing the linen square in her blouse pocket in case she needed it again.

"Possibly, but I rather think it is because either my ancestors didn't want the common people crowding the estate, or because the kings of Gaersheim did not want to connect the tradition to the people of Waverly. They wanted us to assimilate. Well, they didn't succeed."

Savis sighed and rested against the railing.

The door opened behind them, and Vinellin joined them at the rail. "I have sent the letter, Princess, but you must be exhausted. Come and I will show you to your room. A hot bath and a long night's sleep, and you will feel much better, I promise."

She let him lead her away, but she smiled at Loren as she left. Savis had never associated with him when they were younger because he had been unimportant and ridiculous, yet somehow, he'd grown into a serious-minded and capable ruler, and she realized she had misjudged him. He was a gracious host and kind, and she regretted the times at balls and festivals when she was younger when she and the others in court would mock him.

The queen of Gaersheim had always singled him out, making sport of his amber eyes, and blond straight hair, since they were the opposite of the king she was trying to court. Their gossip and rivalries from just a few years ago seemed so trivial now—now that the world was changing, and Savis had killed a fae with her bare hands and a crown.

She hated the thought of leaving, especially when she had finally gained a chance to rest, but it was not safe to return home just yet.

Fassen

Earl's Estate

Leif

Traveling to Fassen had been quicker this time around. Where on the first trip they had taken a leisurely route to attend the Harvest Festival, now they flew quickly on one of Ieffin's birds. The young king did not keep many, but for this flight the Aviary-keeper had allowed them to ride the hawk, which could soar higher and longer distances than any other bird available. Even now they circled the city, watching the crows of the Grass Guard below.

Fryn sat beside him, one arm around his waist as she leaned over the rim of the saddle. "Do you think they can see us?"

He was about to answer when Alyra cut in, "I can feel their anxiety. At the least, the crows know we are up here." She was sitting in the row behind them, with Havrshyk aloofly staring at the horizon beside her. He hadn't been able or willing to talk to Leif in private since his return; Leif could tell he felt guilty.

As a cloud slid across the sun, dark and full of unproven rain, their guide brought the hawk into a dive, straight for the vine below. Leif and Fryn, grateful for the belts securing them to the bench, felt the tug of gravity in their stomachs and the wind ripped at their hair as they flew straight down.

Within moments, the hawk swooped and leveled, landing in the courtyard with a rushing wind, and a cloud of dust. Unbuckling, Leif tossed their bags over, and flitted to the ground. He was joined by Fryn, Alyra, and Havrshyk, and their guide swept right back into the air.

Guards in green, with brass breastplates and arm guards approached them from the estate, encircling the group with spears held at the ready. They wore hooded cloaks over their faces, with copper thread embroidery around the hem. Their leader, a fae with a cluster of grapes woven into the shoulders of his cloak, approached them with his spear lowered and his hood down.

"Hold there, strangers, what business do you have at the Earl's Estate?"

Havrshyk stiffened, gripping the hilt of his Bloodsword, so Leif swiftly put a hand on his arm and replied, "*Helay,* guardsfae, we have come from Frorin to bring word from the king."

He eyed Leif at his use of the Waverly word, and then examined the rest of the group, Fryn and Havrshyk with their black blades strapped to their hips, and Alyra with the white and gold daggers on her back. "She said the blood of our brothers would be guided by the blades of the dead. Is that you?"

Leif shot Fryn a look.

"Savis said that?" Fryn asked, drawing her Bloodknife and showing it to the guard. "We are friends and have come as she requested."

He frowned. "We require proof that it is truly yours, that you are who you say you are." With that, he signaled one of the other guards, who promptly raised a crossbow and fired a bolt into Fryn's neck.

Havrshyk drew his sword, and Leif settled into a fighting stance, but Alyra held them back with a hand. "Peace," she said, "they don't mean to harm us."

Fryn ripped the bolt from her neck, freezing the wound so that none of the blood stained her clothes, and tossed it aside. "There are better ways of doing that, Alyra," she said, voice gravelly as her vocal chords repaired themselves. The guards stared in amazement, and horror, as she rolled her neck and stretched. Leif could feel the intense pain radiating through their bondtf and pressed his lips together, impressed at her ability to hide it. Anytime she healed a wound, the frost helped deaden some of the pain…but she could never truly avoid it.

Soft clapping sounded from the stairs leading up to the entrance of Loren's estate, and as Leif looked, he saw Loren descending the steps with Vinellin at this side and Nora running ahead of him. She charged Leif and flew into an embrace.

"Hello, Nora!" he said, ruffling her hair and making her squirm to be free.

"*Helay,*" she corrected, and then rushed over to Fryn, and was about to hug Alyra and Havrshyk when she scrunched up her face and glanced back at Fryn for confirmation.

"You haven't met them before," Fryn explained, "This is Alyra, and this is Aldyr. They are friends we have made since we last saw each other."

Leif went up to Loren, meeting him at the foot of the steps, and clasped his hand. "Quite the welcoming party," he said, jerking a thumb toward the guards.

Loren nodded seriously and frowned. "It is necessary. I am sure you've heard what happened in Rosenkraun—I cannot rely on guards not directly in my employ."

Fryn joined them, nodding to Vinellin, and asking, "Are you going to expel the Commission as Ieffin did?"

He laughed. "Not exactly. I won't have to. Fassen has such a small Commission presence; most of the staff were locals who jumped at the opportunity to be independent. The Grass Guard were the same, they immediately donned their cloaks and swore to Fassen... but I am not ready for Hans to know about that just yet. Besides, I want to know his plans."

Vinellin shook hands with them, nodding to Alyra and Havrshyk as they approached. "It must have been a long flight. Come, we have lunch ready at the Vine."

He continued down the steps along the path to the foot of the Vine and waited for a lift to be lowered. Soon enough, the rest joined him and at a pull of a lever the platform rose up the trunk of the grapevine to the office level.

It was as busy as Leif remembered from a few weeks before. If anything, it was more frenzied as faeries bustled about with orders, inventories, and worked on allocating shipments to wineries and markets. He paused to watch the head clerk berate some poor courier, ample belly shaking with the vigorousness of his argument, and Leif hid a smile as they continued on to the stairs leading to the platform on the canopy of the vine.

The dining area had been cleared, and they stepped out onto the deck with a view of the city, dark clouds drifting eastward and the sun shining overhead, to see Savis and Lia sitting alone at the gazebo's bar sipping tea.

"Princess!" Fryn called, flitting to the gazebo. She perched on a stool beside Savis and put a hand on her arm, staring into her face with concern.

Leif could sense now, through the link Fryn had forged between them, Fryn's earnest heartbeat, and relief at seeing the princess alive. The wind stirred around them, bringing with it the rich dry scent of the Forest of Grass, and the sound of rustling leaves.

As the others went to join her, Leif moved to the balcony railing where he could get a view of the mountains in the direction of Stanaedre. In the distant haze they were visible as a series of jagged shadows marching toward the southeast, misty purple and white, dappled with sharp silver lines. Clouds broke over them, vanishing in the direction of the Shadelands beyond the mountains. Havrshyk followed him, looking eastward with his jaw set on edge, and his wings flicking.

"You've got a choice Aldyr," Leif said, tapping on the vinebark railing. "When you returned to your body, you did it knowing I would die."

"You didn't," he said defensively.

"I should have," Leif said evenly, "When you were trapped in that sword I listened to you, I sympathized, and while what was done to you was cruel and wrong, it takes all the resolve I have to even consider forgiving you for trying to kill me." He allowed a moment of tense silence to lengthen between them before breathing out a sigh and continuing. "But everything is changing. Kingdoms fall, friends die... and the future has never seemed so unknowable or unpredictable. I only want to make sure we get through this." Leif glanced over his shoulder toward Fryn and Savis, and avoided meeting Aldyr's eyes as he resumed looking out toward the horizon.

"You *did* listen to me," Havrshyk admitted, shuffling his wings, as he shoved his hands into his pockets. "And I didn't want to kill you."

Leif bit his lip.

"Yet you were so focused on getting revenge that you allowed that to justify hurting innocent people," Leif said. "Do you really want to become what you hate so much in others, Aldyr?"

Havrshyk growled softly. "What, and you're so righteous? All you care about is getting your way with…" he shot a look at Fryn, and then wisely cut his statement short.

Leif breathed deeply, letting the breath cycle from his wingtips to his heart, following the meditative path he'd learned from Master Yarl years before, so that when he looked at Havrshyk he was calm, and not at all defensive. Instead, he turned, leaning his back against the railing, and pointing at the group forming at the gazebo. "And like you I am aware that there is a right and good way to pursue what I desire. Havrshyk, the three of us, perhaps all four of us in some way, have died. We have given up pieces of ourselves for others—sometimes for those who do not deserve it—but even so, it shows we are prepared to pay that price to do what is right. I think right now you are conflicted because you know neither what is right nor what you want anymore."

Aldyr stared at him, and his face frosted over momentarily as his expression turned from bitter, to contemplative. He nodded, more to himself than to Leif, and said quietly. "I want my people, the Sky Dwellers, to be treated fairly, and provided the same opportunities for security, prosperity, and happiness as those in the inner rings."

Leif smiled, "And I want you and Fryn to be freed from the shadows of your deaths. You can live for yourself, and if you choose to use that life to serve your people that is good and noble, and if she accepts my offer, and chooses to live her life with me, that is my joy—but none of our goals will succeed while the Commission is after us."

"Leif!" Fryn called from the bar, "Come greet Savis!" She turned to the princess, muttering something about his manners.

He waved to them and turned to Havrshyk once more. "I've decided to forgive you, Aldyr, but it isn't easy being betrayed." Leif tapped his head with a finger and added, "This decision is made here, but…" he said, dropping his hand to his chest, "it takes time to sink in here."

Havrshyk laughed sharply with a pained expression. As Leif walked back to Fryn at the gazebo, he replied softly, "That is the same for me, Leif, with Ieffin." As they approached, Vinellin offered them glasses of water and a tray spread with grape slices and toasted wheat berries.

"Princess Savis," Leif said, bowing deeply with a flourish, "I am relieved to see you well. Ieffin said you killed one of the hunters yourself! We might have to give you your own license. Or perhaps count you among us as honorary lancers."

She laughed, smiling widely, as Nora climbed onto her lap and slammed an empty glass onto the bar.

"More juice!"

"Nora!" Lia exclaimed, her face pale and wings flushed in embarrassment, "Ask him politely!"

"More juice… please…" she said, giving the butler remorseless, begging eyes.

He resignedly brought up a bottle from under the bar and refilled her glass. The child hopped off the princess's knees and ran off to jump from stool to stool at one of the nearby tables, sloshing her juice as she went.

Savis turned back from watching her and her cheer faded as she looked between Leif and Fryn somberly. Fryn sidled up beside him, putting an arm around his back and scratching at one of his wing joints as they waited for her to speak.

After a long moment, Savis pulled out a green pocket square from her blouse pocket and wiped her eyes. "I am so glad you are alive," she said, "I was afraid that everyone I knew was dying, or already gone."

"I am so sorry to hear about Trel and Yarrow," Fryn said, wings drooping and fading as her strong front wavered, "they were a wonderful pair, and the world is dimmer for their loss."

"But it is all the brighter with your return," Savis replied, "I thought you'd died at the Weasel Cairn."

"We nearly did," Leif admitted cheerfully, "a friend saved us. Princess, this is Aldyr Havrshyk. At one time, he served your grandfather. At another he helped Mythrim, and in the end, he helped us."

"And this is another friend," Fryn added, "Alyra of Moraskyr."

Havrshyk's bow was stiff and awkward, despite once serving as a Captain of the Crown Guard, and Alyra inclined her head without a word. She likely sensed that Fryn had more to say.

"We have come at the request of your brother, to protect you. Doubtless, the president will not want you to escape, or for word of their coup to spread." Fryn was about to continue, but Savis opened her mouth and closed it quickly, as if she wanted to speak.

"They don't just want my head," Savis clarified, "they want this." She held up the crown Leif and Fryn had fought so hard to collect. "Apparently, it will help legitimize their control of Fassen, and the northern plains if they have it. As it stands, Haryn and Rosenkraun are fully under Commission control, and the other duchies are likely going to join them. Fortunately, I was able to tell Loren here the truth."

Loren waved, chewing on a bite of grape, and clapping as Nora twirled on a spinning stool.

Alyra nodded toward the butler, "is it true you are from Elin?" she asked.

"I am from Aizora, the Cottonwood City in Zella on the west coast of Elin. And to think I've traveled a great distance… you have come from the other side of the world, not just a neighboring continent." He took her hand in one of his, and then patted it with the other. "It is a pleasure to meet a fellow traveler."

Her mouth worked for a moment, as if rehearsing her sentence before saying it in a second language. "It is." She smiled and glanced down uncertainly. "Vinellin, is it… I mean to say I have heard… on Elin there is someone there…"

He smiled knowingly. "You are correct mistress, there are many on Elin." The butler's smile widened into a facetious grin.

Savis glanced over at their conversation and mused, "the storyteller said it was important that I take the crown to Elin."

"Elin, Elin…across the ocean Elin?" Leif asked, "Why?"

"I need to protect this crown, and if I go over there the president can hardly get to me. I am sure Ieffin would approve, and even if he doesn't, I don't answer to my brother." She crossed her arms and looked off toward the mountains.

Leif supposed it was more likely Ieffin, and perhaps Loren to some extent, would welcome a chance to protect her from the chaos and bloodshed. Froreholt would need her if the young King died, since he had no heirs, or betrothed.

"I should just kill him," Havrshyk said with a sigh, and as the others shot him confused and concerned looks, he clarified, "I should kill the president, but that would only unite the other kingdoms against us. Stanaedre has returned to the Commission, and we encountered agents of the Cherim wandering beyond the forests."

While they talked, Leif mulled over the events, and leaned in toward Vinellin. "Can I have a glass of your good wine?" he asked softly.

As he did, Fryn's tapping on his back informed him that she wanted some too, so he held up two fingers for the butler. Without complaint, as usual, the butler retrieved an unlabeled green bottle from under the bar and poured out three glasses. Two he passed to Leif, and the other he held out toward Loren. The Earl made a meaningful gesture, tapping the glass with two fingers and smiling.

After taking a sip, Leif tuned out the political conversation Fryn, Savis, and Aldyr were having and asked the butler, Why is it really so important that she go to Elin?"

Vinellin poured a fourth glass for himself and swirled its contents for a moment before answering. "There is a prophecy that she needs to fulfill. Waverly collapsed as a nation, but it was not the first to fall to the curses of the Wingless." He took a sip and inclined his head toward the mountains. "Beyond Stanaedre lay the Shadelands, the blighted remnants of a land that once boasted a prosperous and cultured civilization—one that surpassed and rivaled that of the Cherim, Arta, or Waver. Their glory was built by the blood of its slaves. Our legends tell that any crime was punished by the cutting of a wing. Repeat offenders lost further wings and segments. Rarely did this ever lead to the docking of all four wings."

Leif listened, nodding to himself. Some of this he had heard before, but small details had not made their way to Aelaete. He noticed that slowly the other conversations halted, and they began to listen in.

Dramatic as ever, Vinellin drank deeply from his glass and put both hands on the bar. "The caste made up of those criminals accumulated members and power with each generation… some even gaining incredible elemental abilities that they had never had before their punishment."

"…never told me this story before…" Loren muttered to himself a few stools down the bar.

Alyra rested her elbows on the bar beside Fryn, who still had her arms around Leif, and spellbound they all waited for the butler to resume his story.

"It is said that the kingdom, whose name is long forgotten, finally collapsed five thousand years ago. The Prescians hold that it was really about three and a half thousand, but regardless, long before the rise of the kingdoms of Elin and Orel, Jyakarn the Wingless started a revolution. Over the centuries that the broken caste was being enslaved and oppressed, they had started their own cult."

"The wingless cult?" Nora asked, jumping down from one of the tables and coming to join the group.

"Yes," Vinellin replied, refilling her cup of juice, and gesturing for her to sit with her mother, "Some of those who were broken, or punished, gained great power. And among them, the most powerful were the murderers and psychotics. These were afflicted with multiple wings cut off with an axe—often intended to be a fatal punishment if the axe cut into their flesh. Some of these would survive the impossible injury, and those were venerated among the poor. Wherever they worked, they were strengthened and empowered. They came to believe that they had always deserved and held this power and that the wings were shackles put on their backs to humble them. That the gift of flight was a beautiful lie meant to distract them from the loss of their godlike powers. Deep within the quarries of the Shadelands, these cultists cut away the wings of their followers, killing and creating new priests and agents, until members of their cult were employed in every institution, at every noble house, and industry.

"The signal for their revolution was to be when all three moons eclipsed the Lost Constellation, and in the hour they aligned, the Wingless Cult slaughtered everyone holding an office. All others, they turned upon, all the merchants and artists, the craftsfae and farmers, even their own followers—an axe to sever all four wings at once."

"If that really grants power, it probably wasn't a good idea to give it to their enemies," Havrshyk said, and then shut his mouth as Fryn glared at him.

Leif smiled to himself as he noted that this conversation with Vinellin had lulled the talk of politics to silence.

"You are correct," Vinellin nodded and fingered his chin. "You are the second Lich I have met; surely having held the powers granted by Death Himself, you would understand the chaos these cultists unleashed by spreading their powers among all people?"

Aldyr narrowed his eyes.

"Let us say, a group in Frorin decided to create an army of Liches, gathering children, training them, and killing them, in the hopes that a small percentage would become immortal soldiers in their games?"

Fryn shivered on Leif's arm, and he could feel her discomfort like an icy chill that washed into his veins through their bond.

"That would be horrible," Savis said, "we would never do such a thing!"

Havrshyk swallowed. "Long before my time, the Third Hand did pursue such an experiment."

The group quieted at that, and Leif nodded. "My clan also keeps records of the past, and one of the stories tells of a great war with Froreholt, when the clans allied to defend their freedom against an invasion of immortal soldiers made of ice."

"When?" Fryn demanded, sounding more concerned than disbelieving.

"Three thousand years?" he guessed.

Vinellin's eyes sparkled at that, as if Leif had proved one of his suspicions. "Chaos indeed filled the land. Division, bloodshed, upheaval, and confusion reigned. Those who gained power and survived hated the Wingless Cult, and the war ripped the land apart. Terrible storms, earthquakes, floods, and fires came in waves, as each faction became entrenched in a protracted war.

"Cities crumbled into ruins, the land became barren and sick, trees bent and twisted, and a horrible blight infected everything that remained. After one final conflict, with lightning storms, and a tearing of the land in two, the Wingless Cult was finally defeated. Those who survived, though wingless themselves from their battles, deserted the Shadelands and rode on the backs of migrating turtles, who bore them to the shores of Elin and Orel."

"Turtles!?" Nora demanded, then more softly she whispered to Savis, "They're real?"

Savis shrugged.

"There were hundreds of survivors, and when they rode the turtles to new lands, the turtles went wherever they wished. The survivors were scattered, wingless, unable to fly from the land where they arrived. Their settlements were founded on new principles, so that such a calamity would never transpire again. One of these, after whom the land is now named, Elin of the Waters, had gained an incredible power to control the seas, and it was because of his power that the survivors did not drown on their voyage. He was delivered to a land far from the others, lost, and lifted his eyes to the towering mountains in the center of the land. He longed for and sought the guidance and forgiveness of the Wing-Giver for the sins of their people: oppression, wing-breaking, and enslavement—and climbed on foot to a valley high in the mountains.

"He swam in the waters of the mountain, and its crystalline purity washed away his sorrow, and restored to him his wings. Impossibly, his enhanced elemental powers did not decrease but were further strengthened. He lived atop the mountain and guided many on pilgrimages of repentance and helped many reclaim their wings. Our legends say that even after all these millennia his spirit guards the path to the Wing-Giver's Pool."

Savis sat up straighter and put her hand on the bar. "So, how did she…?"

Loren smiled wanly. "Alesaeja? She calls herself a story-teller, but my people have known her for what she is for as long as she has been telling stories of our past. She sees, she knows, many impossible things, and has been called the First Prophet since Darsin. I do not know how necessary it is for you to wash that crown in the pool on Elin, but I do believe that if she says you need to go there, then it is important that you do so."

"I can't go riding turtles," Savis said with a frown.

"You take an airship," Alyra suggested, "Isn't that how you got here?" she asked Vinellin.

He grinned. "It is, my Moraskyn friend, and it is far safer than trying to hold onto a turtle's back for two weeks. The ships were invented decades ago in Norenan, but they have not deigned to share their knowledge with anyone else on Fhoraena or Elin. The Council of Aizora has been able to negotiate for regular trade with the machinists of Norenan, so you will likely be able to book passage."

"The Commission could send hunters on the next airship after us," Leif said, "Is this really the best way to keep you safe, Princess?"

Savis' nose twitched as she considered. "Yes. It is. Norenan is very insular, and if I tell them I am fleeing the Commission, and tell them everything that has happened in Gaersheim, they will likely close their borders."

The Earl stood and leaned over the bar toward his butler, whispering and pointing in their direction, before sitting back down.

Vinellin didn't reply to him, but instead looked at Leif and said, "It would be remiss of me not to send a letter to my family asking them to orient you to the land. And Princess, it may be good to pack your bags for a long journey. This business with the Commission will not end quickly, and a trek along the Pilgrim's Path is arduous. Invest in making connections in Elin."

He looked like he wanted to say more, but he pursed his lips and shook his head. Alyra nodded to Fryn and then waved the butler over to the other side of the gazebo, where they talked quickly, in voices too soft to be heard.

"You've got a lot to catch up on, Leif," Fryn whispered to him, "I doubt Alyra has had time since your return to talk with you, but she is not merely running away. Apparently, the last heir of her homeland was once the youngest of many and was given to the study of history and religion. His travels brought him to Elin, where he was safe from the reach of a coup that destroyed her country and she wants to bring him back."

Fryn wrapped her arms around him from behind, so he patted her arm with his hand and whispered back. "I heard more than you'd likely expect when I was trapped in that sword, but I can't help feeling like these disasters are timed conveniently at once."

She nodded, resting her chin on his shoulder. "Isn't it funny how that happens?"

"You don't think the Commission… they couldn't possibly have something to do with the politics on Moraskyr?" Leif asked.

"That would be a little surprising." Fryn noticed Savis leaving her stool to go play with Nora and the Earl, and swept into the seat. She set her wine glass down and watched its deep violet liquid swirl like a miniature vortex. "Do you remember the day we met?"

Startled, Leif looked away from the vortex, and focused on her. "It feels like so long ago, but it's really only been a season."

She picked up the glass and raised it to her lips, taking a long sip and savoring it. When she set it back down, she gave him a sideways look and smiled wistfully. "I was just thinking of the wine thief, who drank away the goods and nearly cost me my commission on the bounty."

"Have you considered a life of crime?" Leif asked, winking as he remembered the thief's advice to him about not having any good bounties to pursue.

Fryn laughed, and nudged him with her elbow. "You had to use every opportunity to flirt with me… with every fee who had wings!"

He scratched his head. "Well, you see training with Master Yarl in a remote place, where the only fee I'd see every few weeks was my sister… perhaps you'd be flirting with every fee at that point."

She sighed dramatically. "What? If it had been Camilla from the Pheasant you met first, would you have fallen for her?"

"No, Fryn," he replied seriously, taking her hand, "I think when I met you, I saw immediately that beyond the surface professionalism and strength there was a woman who wanted to laugh."

She raised an eyebrow. "I could tell right away that you were always good for a laugh, and very fun to laugh at," she said, poking him in the side. "If you were any more ridiculous, I'd never believe your stories."

He shifted his wings, watching the Earl sweep up Nora and toss her into the air so she could fly from one table to another, laughing all the while.

"Your scars are really horrifying, Leif, and there is something in there that my blood does not like."

He rubbed his arm where the broken fang had formed a lump in his bone. "I was fortunate. Despite my naive confidence I survived an encounter with a sand viper and defeated it—a feat unheard of in my time. But it was Mythrim who showed me that arrogance only brings embarrassment, and that if I don't think too highly of myself, I can find a way to defeat any opponent."

She hummed and met his eyes. "I think I learned the opposite lesson. Mythrim taught me that if you are paralyzed by fear, your fears come true—but if you face them—there is a chance to defeat them."

"And you're pretty capable," Leif added, "I mean pretty, and capable."

"That's better," she agreed with a laugh. She glanced around and seeing that everyone else was involved in other conversations or games, she leaned in and gave him a kiss. "And don't go flirting with anyone else."

He kissed her again. "I'm too occupied flirting with you and danger to add anyone else to the mix."

"Good." She went for another kiss, but he stopped her with a finger on her lips.

"One thing bothers me," he admitted, "the stories we tell about the Wingless Cult all seem slightly different."

"I didn't hear anything too different from what they say in Frorin," Fryn said.

He took a sip from his wine and said in a soft tone, in the same cadence his sister used to use by the fire before he had ever gone to study beneath Master Yarl. "In the first days of dawning, when the world began to breath, twelve stars fell from the heavens and landed in the sands of Linaera. Syrin and Janu fell into the waters and swam their way to shore. Yndril and Arta in the snows where they cultivated the flowers in the wastes, and Fhora and Avess planted forests in the sunlit, rich lands of the south. Rhora, Noren, Mora, and Askyr, settled further and further from the others. Silvi wandered the mountain lands alone."

Fryn motioned for Vinellin to refill their glasses, and Leif noted with a measure of satisfaction that the butler remained nearby, listening with interest.

"The Wing-Giver caused them to sprout wings. These first, grew four wings, the next grew six, but Silvi alone had two massive wings. While the others appreciated the beauty of the land, the forest, fields, and waters, Silvi traveled higher and higher in the mountains to draw nearer to the stars. Her great wings allowed her to fly longer and higher than all her siblings, and she began to see lights on the surface of the moon, like the reflections on the surface of the lakes below, she marveled at the lakes above. Eventually, she gathered the strength and courage to fly all the way to the Moon. The bright green light it shed on the lands below was the green of beauty, and life, and a world covered with towering trees and vines. Flowers of white, pink, and red shed a floor of fragrant petals onto the ground all year round—a place of permanent Summer."

Vinellin hummed to himself but did not interrupt, and Leif suppressed a blush as he noticed the rest of the group regathering around him.

"For years, she wandered the moon, until she began to miss the fellowship of her siblings. She could see them building great gardens and see their children learning how to fly, and a great loneliness and longing filled her. It was then that she heard a fae singing in the forest and came upon him, pale, with black hair, and wingless as she had been before the Wing-Giver granted her wings. His voice was beautiful, and he cultivated flowers of myriad colors, and shaped the land of the Moon with the same level of power and ease as she flew through the air. He welcomed her, and they spent many years together, until she begged him to come with her to visit her home in the mountains of the world below, but he could not fly, and try as she might she could not carry him."

"What happened then?" Nora asked.

Leif remembered asking his sister the same thing.

"She begged the Wing-Giver to grant him wings like her own, so he could visit her lands, but he refused. Jakaren was there to cultivate the Moon, and not to leave it. She had her wings so she could visit him and move between the worlds. That was enough. So... she accepted this. Jakaren lost interest in his flowers, and spent the evenings watching the world below, and every time she went home without him, his bitterness grew. One day, as she prepared to fly from the height of his vines to return to the mountains, he could bear it no more, and using his pruning shears he cut off her wings hoping to keep her there forever."

Fryn shifted uneasily beside him, and Loren whistled.

"Instead of remaining with him, she died from the shock and he went mad. He fused the wings into his flesh and jumped from the highest point to attempt to reach the world below or draw the attention of the Wing-Giver to restore her. He flew, and in the glory of flight he forgot his guilt and sorrow and descended toward her mountains. The Wing-Giver had seen what he had done and struck him with light from the heavens. His stolen wings shattered, and he fell, forgotten, to the world below."

Alyra considered him with a serious gaze before saying, "I have heard a similar tale in my homeland, Leif. How then did he start a cult?"

"He was jealous of all who could still fly and wanted the power to retake the skies and to return to the Moon. He has tried many times throughout the ages, for he continued to steal the life and power of others, in his endless pursuit, corrupting others and catching them up in his wake all the while."

"Do you think the moon is really alive?" Nora asked.

Fryn nodded. "It is, Nora, but if Leif's story is true there would have been no one to populate it."

He shrugged. "Nor do I claim our children's tales contain the truth. I was merely surprised that compared to others, we claim Jakaren is as old as the land of Fhora herself."

Loren shifted in his chair and took a long pull of his wine. "Yes, well, thankfully, we do not have to contend with Wingbreakers and Cultists... just enterprising capitalists."

Interlude 5

FAE

~70 Years Ago~

Crown District

Frorin

Aldyr

Havrshyk had died just weeks ago yet here he was against all explanation, sitting in the gatehouse between the Crown District and the Snow District, sipping a cup of pine-needle tea. He drank it unsweetened and held the fine bone china cup with both hands, draining the heat so he could drink its contents more comfortably. It was decorated with the snowflake of the royal crest and speckles of gold dust that sparkled under the wan light of the starlamp in the sconce by the door.

Yala sat across from him, resting her elbow on the table as she savored her plum blossom tea. Steam rose from her cup, but the scone on the plate beside her elbow had stopped steaming ten minutes ago. She presented a perfect example of the regulars, though with the passage of time, her red hair had grown long enough that she could tie it back with a few small braids and a bun. Her white uniform was pressed, ironed, and wrinkle-free.

"It's going cold," Aldyr said, pointing at the scone.

She wore her captain's snow-stars on her collar, brilliant crystal blue on white: the king's colors. Her face was obscured by the news sheet she read from the Winter Herald, featuring a headline that read

263

"Expelled from Commission: Stanaedre Coup Ringleaders Mysteriously Found Dead." Her blue-lined wings' shifting was enough to signal that she heard him.

"I can fix that," Yala said cheerfully, not meeting his gaze as she set aside the paper and examined her scone. As her dark blue eyes focused on the pastry the air shimmered and steam rose from the top of it.

Outside the gatehouse, a snowstorm blew in gusts against the courtyard-facing door, and Aldyr found himself longing to slip outside into the brilliant white, to become invisible, and lost, even for a short moment. Just as he was about to stand however, the door pulled open and a hapless guard slipped through the crack and slammed it shut. This was one of Yala's newer recruits, brought in from the city guard, but he could not remember the fae's name.

"It's colder than an ermine's ass in winter, isn't it?" the newcomer asked, slipping into an empty chair at their table. He looked at them with a foolish grin, one that melted into a horrified frown as he recognized them. "Captain… Master… oh my… good morning."

To her credit, Yala merely nodded, busily chewing on her scone. "It is rather, cold, I mean," she said after washing it down with some tea. "Do you mind climbing the tower?" she asked, nodding in the direction of the spiral stair.

His forehead wrinkled in confusion and he stared.

"We're having a private conversation," Aldyr explained, "now go upstairs and warm up with some tea."

The guard paled when Havrshyk spoke to him, and promptly flitted up the stairs. Aldyr shook his head and turned a suffering glance toward Yala. "Was he that embarrassed?"

She avoided meeting his eyes again. "He's not, well, they aren't, you see it isn't…" she gave a frustrated huff and looked him in the eyes. "You frighten them, Aldyr. It's not natural," she explained, using her half-eaten scone to poke at him, "you died… or rather should have died."

He brushed a crumb from his jacket and narrowed his eyes at her. The tension showing in her shoulders and face told a slightly different story. "I frighten *you*, Yala? Why?"

She shivered and set her teacup back on its saucer, and whispered, "I was there, you know, I saw what you did, how you came back together like an…a glass shattering in reverse, and you killed them. You slaughtered them all!"

Havrshyk nodded. He wanted to shrug it off and move on, but if he was truly honest with himself, he had to admit he wasn't at all comfortable being the first Lich in recent history. "I came back to save him." It was an excuse… despite his honorable intentions to save his king… it wasn't the galvanizing factor that had preserved him. Noticing the conflict in her expression, he added, "I am not going to hurt anyone." He stood, drank the dregs of his tea, and set the cup on its saucer before moving to the door. His hand hovered there, as he decided, and then he braced himself against the door to push it open. "Alas, it is early yet, but the king's summons cannot wait." He waved regretfully to her as he heaved the door open and stepped out into the courtyard and into the wind and snow.

As the door closed, he barely heard Yala's soft reply, "I hope you don't."

In the below freezing temperatures of the storm, the snowflakes were smaller, yet more jagged, and they buffeted him as he strode toward the palace. As he climbed up the steps, one of the snowflakes cut across his face, and he instinctively froze it over and sent blood to the wound to heal it… only instead of an icy scab, the cut closed, and healed completely by the time he grasped the pull of the palace doors.

The entry was as empty and silent as a tomb awaiting a corpse, and the irony of the thought tickled at him as he realized that he was that corpse—and the space had been waiting for him to fill it. He strode over to the stairs and slid his hand along the banister as he ascended to the next level where a few steps down the hall and a choice wall sconce brought him into one of the many secret passages in the palace.

He closed his eyes, following his hand on the rail inside the corridor to an intersection where he could flit down a chute to a lower level and then to a dead end. He stood on a semicircle of stone identical to the one he'd used to access the king's bedchamber just weeks before, but instead of triggering the wall with a sconce, he pressed a specific stone in the wall till it clicked, and lowered his hand quickly before the rotating wall could snap it off against the wall.

As the wall clicked into place again, Aldyr was assaulted by a wave of steam and hot mineral air. The cavernous walls, uncut, natural stone, slick with moisture and sweat, marched in a squat, oval shaped tunnel down a steep incline like an enormous esophagus. Instead of steps. He descended the eddies and ridges formed by the natural sediments, and within a few minutes stepped out into the main chamber.

This space widened and the ceiling rose in a vaulted dome, with stalactites dangling above like the arrows of the guards in the alcoves of the throne room.

King Imloth awaited him, robed in a simple white towel and sitting on a stool in the middle of the shallow lake that bubbled with steam rising from the deep. One of his servants stood at the edge of the water, comfortably dry, though with a fogged monocle, while another servant bent in the water applying a soapy brush to the king's feet. His son Hyngram played in the pool naked, hair lathered to a foam, and wings flapping as he made the water splash.

The child was only seven, and he ignored Havrshyk as he stepped out onto the water, freezing it beneath his feet in small footsteps so that he could tread on the surface and keep himself dry. The small pillars of ice he left behind steamed and melted quickly as he approached, and knelt on the surface of the water, covered in a persistent frost—the heat washed over him, but he deflected it, and resisted the discomfort.

"I have come, your majesty, how may I be of service?" he asked, lowering his eyes.

The servant's wings flickered with an alarmed flash of red, but she ignored him, and lowered the king's foot into the water as she soaped up the brush and began working on the other foot.

The king grumbled to himself and waved the servant away. "Tend to the child," he ordered, and fixed red, shadowed eyes on Havrshyk.

It wasn't commonly known, but after the queen had given birth to a single daughter, she hadn't been able to have another child. Hyngram was the son of the concubine who'd died that day weeks ago trying to protect the king.

"I have heard a disturbing rumor, impossible tales of death and terror in Stanaedre," he began, lowering his soapy foot into the water and rubbing away the last of the suds himself. The king kept a wary watch on Aldyr, who still knelt on a shelf of ice above the water. "There are tales of chieftains, priests, and masters of guilds all throughout Estenna, and Soranil, a terrible being impervious to all magic and blades."

Havrshyk smiled. Impervious was not entirely accurate, he'd earned some scars the last few weeks, that even his enhanced regenerative abilities could not heal completely.

"They call him "The Splinter of the Lich", a star that has left the constellation to terrorize them tenfold for their attack on our country. They sent envoys begging for me to forgive them, to send this star back into the heavens—and I have seen it myself through the telescope… one of the stars has gone out. The left eye." The king's hands shook momentarily, and the servant moved Hyngram further away to play closer to the exit, shooting hateful eyes at Havrshyk.

"It is true that I have killed many throughout their lands," Aldyr said, "I did it to prevent any future attacks, to show that underhanded attempts at conquering our nation would only result in their destruction. We cannot allow any nation to embarrass us like they did… that day…" He added the last statement with an edged tone, looking up and meeting the king's eyes.

The king's cheeks quivered as he spoke, and his slippery wet wings flapped momentarily as he pushed himself out of his seat and glared at Havrshyk.

"You should have died!" he shouted, face pale, eyelids dark and baggy, as he pointed at Aldyr forcefully and continued in a wavering voice, "I should have died… all these faeries, guards and kings, and priests, all these innocents… Merrin died… she fell before my eyes, Havrshyk! Her blood dripping in my eyes!" He wobbled and fell to his knees in the water, tears streaming down his face.

Aldyr hesitated, shaken by the outburst, this display of weakness and loss from the mad king who'd slain countless potential servants just to gauge their worth. He did not move, not wanting to offend the king, and knelt in the same posture as before on his ice floe surrounded by wavering lines of steam. "She saved you, your majesty. If she had not jumped before his blade, I would not have been quick enough to protect you."

The water bubbled around the king, as if responding to his emotional distress. His shoulders shook, but only a solitary tear dripped from his eye.

"Without her death," Aldyr added, "your son would grow up an orphan king."

The king did not look at him, kneeling in the water with more tears following the first into the steamy pool. He curled his fingers into fists, and added stiffly through clenched teeth, "I command you to cease your attacks. You are to act and to kill only when I command it."

Havrshyk frowned, shooting a glance over his shoulder toward the exit. "As you command, your majesty… though I had already completed my list."

"How many?" he demanded, rising and standing firm again, "how many did you kill?"

The list had the names of twenty important figures throughout Stanaedre—including the ones who had planned the coup. Beyond that, there were guards, servants, and witnesses. "Forty-three," he replied.

"Not one more, Havrshyk."

"As you wish, sire."

"Now leave me!" King Imloth ordered, throwing up his hand and waving him away with a disgusted twist to his mouth.

Aldyr rose and turned on his heel on the platform of ice he'd maintained. He stalked across the surface of the water back the way he'd come, disturbed by the king's emotional state. Distracted, he wound his way back through the hidden tunnels to the palace and exited a disguised wall panel into the hall atop the stairs.

He could still hear the storm raging outside, rattling the stained-glass windows decorated with the white crown of the Martell line, and as he descended the grand stair to the foyer, he was startled as the doors opened suddenly and Yala burst in.

She slammed the door shut behind her, and fell back against it, one arm on either door, as she looked around the room frantically and spotted him. "Havrshyk!" she yelled, "it's not good."

He lifted an eyebrow at her and used a handkerchief to polish a spot of water from his scabbard. "What dreadfulness could occur in a blizzard, Yala?"

She eyed the scabbard and sword he cleaned suspiciously, and then shook herself. "There's been another murder."

Who else is there to kill? he thought idly. "Where?"

She flitted up to him, just a few steps down, and gave him a soft smile. "Your involvement is no longer required in these events, Third Hand, you have more important matters to consider."

He lifted the other eyebrow and watched her carefully. "You wouldn't come here to tell me if it didn't concern me."

She took the steps up to him and leaned in toward his ear, whispering, "The body is no one important, just a Sky Dweller," she said.

He stiffened.

"The alarming thing is how the body was found. Completely drained of his blood." She turned slightly and stared deep into his eyes. He met them and ground his teeth.

"I was with the king."

She narrowed her eyebrows suspiciously and pursed her lips. "With a bloodless corpse it is impossible to determine the time of death… especially during a blizzard."

He took her arm and leaned in closer, keeping her eyes locked with his. "Yala," he said in a low voice, nearly a growl, which caused her to pale slightly, "I would never harm our people. And I would never kill a Sky Dweller."

She blinked. "Sky Dwellers are the perfect victims to refill…"

He shook his head. "I will not allow anyone to harm *my people*."

Yala closed her mouth and shook her arm free, wings pulsing yellow in confusion. "Your people?"

"<u>My people.</u>" He put his arms behind his back and stood still in a resting position as his eyes dragged away from hers toward the doors. "I am going to find who did this."

Stuttering, Yala followed him down the stairs, "A-aldyr, he's not worth it, he doesn't matter!"

He pulled the door open, letting in a rush of snow and cold wind, glaring over his shoulder at her. "We matter, Yala! My parents, my sister, my friends… everyone I left behind to protect! They matter!"

She stumbled down the last couple steps and halted before him and the rushing wind, worried eyes looking out toward the storm. "I was worried about you!"

He looked away, slipping out into the storm, barely hearing her last words.

"Y-you m-m-matter, Aldyr…"

The door slammed shut behind him, and he flew up into the snow. He had no idea who had died, or where they were, but he knew the Sky District better than anyone.

The guards had left the body out in the snow, no one caring to give the old fae a proper burial. Not in a blizzard. Not for a Sky Dweller.

Havrshyk toiled in the storm to claw out a hollow in the shale of the foothills with his Bloodsword taking the shape of a pick or a shovel when he needed one and buried him in an unmarked grave. When he finished, the winds had died down, and the sunrise rose red on the horizon.

He knelt at the grave, looking up and soaking in the light of the sun, and time passed slowly.

Crunching in the snow announced the approach of someone nearby, so he looked over his shoulder and saw Yala walking toward him through the snow. She carried a pitcher that steamed from the top, and couple teacups hooked by her lower fingers.

She sat on the snow beside the dirty mound and raised an eyebrow at him. "You weren't supposed to get all that on your uniform…" She hesitated and poured a cup of tea for each of them and handed one over. She bit her lip, glanced away, and brushed a stray bit of red hair behind her ear. "Did you know him?"

Aldyr sighed deeply, accepting the tea as he looked up at the sun.

"No."

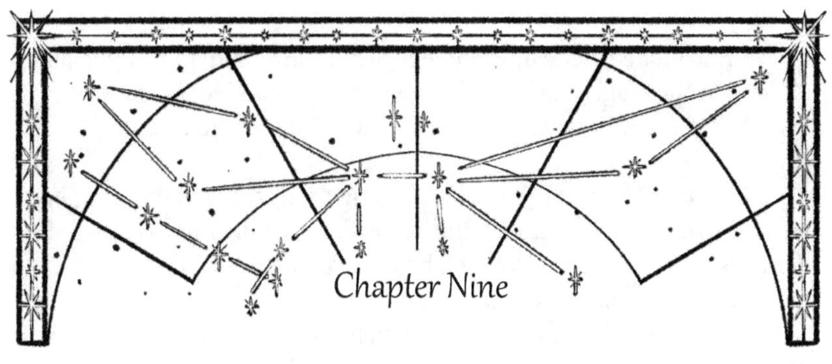

LICH

~Ten Years Ago~

Ice Wastes

Fryn

Fryn danced on the outstretched leaf of a glacial flower, stepping through some modified Soft-Point Fist movements she'd adapted for the dance. Through the steps she advanced linearly toward the stalk, cutting through idle snowflakes with frost-hardened hands. As she finished her dance, she swirled and knelt in a crouch, one hand cupping a snowflake she'd palmed from the air, and she bowed at Pyran's applause.

Pyra stood on the snow-powdered ground below. She gave a loud "whoop" after the performance, smiling gleefully with rosy-tinted wings. "Very well done, Frynalin!" she cried, using one of the many nicknames she'd given Fryn over the years they'd been friends.

Fryn swept down from the leaf, landing beside Pyran with an awkward, non-dimpled smile. "Do you think it will be good enough for the ceremony?" She asked, scratching the back of her neck.

Pyra laughed, a single sharp bark, and shook her head. "I think everyone will be impressed."

"I guess," Fryn said, unconvinced. "It's your turn," she added, jabbing a thumb over her shoulder toward the 'stage' they had chosen to practice at in the Ice Wastes.

Pyran tucked her chin between her thumb and forefinger and examined the stage with a critical eye. She "hmm"ed and sighed.

"What's wrong with it?" Fryn asked, "It was good enough for me…"

"I need a flower," Pyra said, nodding to herself and crossing her arms. "Your dance is about the snow, and well, mine is not. My dance is more about the flowers, beauty that is beautiful not because of what it is for, or does, but by itself."

Fryn frowned, more playfully than seriously, as she replied, "What, and my dance is not beautiful by itself?"

"Not really, no," Pyra answered cheekily. Her brilliant eyes flashed as she said it, so Fryn guessed she was not supposed to be offended. "Your dance converts something deadly into something wonderful, and hopefully, my dance will do the opposite."

"Convert something harmless into something deadly?"

Pyra sighed. "To make something beautiful into something dangerous."

Fryn sighed as well but not for the same reason. "Good luck finding a glacial flower at the right stage to bring in for the ceremony tomorrow." She crossed her arms and watched as Pyran flitted into the air, hovering to survey the fields filled with glacial flowers. Fryn tapped one foot on the powdery ground, with a suspicion that as soon as she flew into the air, Pyra would descend to the flower she had already conveniently found when she arrived. She waited another thirty seconds and kicked off into the air in a cloud of frost.

Pyran laughed as Fryn hovered beside her and pointed a little way north. "Do you see that massive flower up ahead? It must be ancient! My dance will be much better there." The shifting of the northern lights cast a shimmer of green and gold across her face, and her wings glowed as if in response… or as if drinking in the light. Before Fryn could respond, she was off again, diving forward through the sky like an arrow loosed from the sun. Her long black hair flapped in a tail, and her wings trailed white lines with the speed of her flight.

Fryn took a breath, smiling ruefully as she followed her to the flower that towered over the field. Though all of the flowers rose high over her head when she stood on the ground, with a spray of long silvery green leaves like so many snaking tongues, and wiry tuberous roots that stretched across the snow to mingle with the roots of their neighbors, and long stalks that rose to tulip shaped pale blue perennial flowers—this one presided over them all.

She sailed through the air, angling to the side so she could get a view of the pile of husk leaves the flower had shed over the years, through which roots as thick as her body wrestled with the barren, cracked stones beneath. The leaves were twice the width and length of the lesser flowers, and instead of the singular blossom the others bore, this one sent out a spray of five gargantuan flowers that radiated as if endowed with starlight.

Her friend swept down to one of the long stretches of interwoven leaves and walked the breadth of the new stage with her hands on her hips and a gloating grin. As Fryn descended to the leaves, Pyra waved for her to stand back and observe. "Behold, Frynalin, this is my new dancing ground!" she declared in a voice that echoed through the field.

Fryn nodded as expected, and smoothed out the wrinkles in her training Sanhas, a grey and blue unadorned uniform made of the more durable nettle fibers. It was folded in the front and tied around the side with a blue ribbon. Like Pyra, she wore the traditional black undershirt and shorts, and a pair of ankle high gray boots and knee-high black socks.

During the formal advancement dance tomorrow, they would be dancing and fighting in these same uniforms in order to earn their new Disciple's Sanhas.

"With a leaf blade this wide," Fryn said, "you shouldn't have a chance at falling this time." She gave Pyra a cheeky, dimpled smile and folded her arms.

Pyra stuck out her tongue. "That was a fluke, we all know my grace and skill are inborn."

"If you got any of Master Bersari's skill, you only got half of it, right?" Fryn teased, counting on her fingers.

"At least I have…" Pyra said, leaning forward and pointing at Fryn, before she thought better of it, and corrected, "half…"

"Very good then, let's see if you got it this time." Fryn took a few steps back to let Pyran have the full width of the level section of leaves.

Her wings flicked a few times, as she pursed her lips and narrowed her brow. Then, she centered herself, and stood in a perfect meditative stance with her wings folded behind her back, her feet shoulder width apart, and her hands at her sides. She took a deep breath, and the raised her hands into the Soft-Point Fist stance, with her forehand held up like a blade, and her back hand by her waist in a fist.

She quickly raced forward in a low stance, rising with a swing of her 'blade' hand, followed by a gut punch in the air. She flipped and landed in a crouch, springing off the stiff but bouncy platform of leaves back the way she'd come with a shadow block and slash.

Fryn nodded to herself as she watched Pyran slide from one movement and form to another, aglow in the northern lights, surrounded by clear skies and a haze of the glacial orchid's aroma. The 'floor' bounced and shook under her feet as Pyra danced, and trembled as she landed at the end of her performance in a crouch, and then she wobbled to a stand and ended in the meditative position she had started with.

Despite her wasted, flowery movements, Fryn saw an elegant strength in each imaginary attack, and awareness as Pyra scanned her surroundings, not just the next place she would be moving. Her practice was perfect.

The tremor in the leaf settled as she stilled, and Fryn applauded the performance with a loud cheer. "That was perfect, Pyra! If you can do that this well on a moving floor, you'll smash it tomorrow!"

Pyran blushed. "What, nooo... I stumbled through several movements there. I swear the leaf kept moving before I would land." She walked over to the edge of the leaves and sat down, dangling her legs over the side, and looking out at the Ice Wastes.

Fryn walked over and patted her on the head before sitting down beside her. "This was a good idea Pyra, practicing out here where no one can watch or judge our performance."

Pyra nudged Fryn and laughed. "The boys are probably not going to advance quite yet, they're too distracted looking at you..."

It was Fryn's turn to blush. "What? No... they are not."

"I suppose they have been told not to get ideas about me," Pyra said, shaking her head.

"But there's no problem if they harass the orphan?" Fryn asked sourly.

Pyra nudged her again. "If they think that, they have no idea how much danger they are in." She grinned. "If I have half my dad's skill, then yours is all your own."

Fryn laughed, looking away and wiping her eyes. The last six years had not been easy to say the least, but Pyra had adopted her more than her parents had. Master Bersari had brought her in to train her and help her family make inroads in the Snow District. He never patted her on the head, encouraged her, or did any of the things Fryn remembered her father doing—like reading stories. He was a teacher.

It was a wonder Pyra's mother tolerated his loveless marriage; the only thing they seemed to have in common was the centrality of Pyran's importance.

"You're doing it again," Pyra said, waving a hand in front of her face, "Are you still in there?"

Fryn nudged her back and laughed. "I'm just thinking about tomorrow."

"Hey, you want to go visit your family after this? Go to the Pine District?" The wind rustled the flowers and the sunlight glowed through the auroras across Pyra's face.

"Didn't your dad forbid us last time?"

"*Pppbbh*," Pyra scoffed, "Who's going to tell him? He thinks we are out training on the training grounds in the East Sky Shelf."

The sun was beginning to slide down the sky. It was early afternoon, but it would be setting soon. During the month of the Lich, it often set around three. Though Fryn was used to the cold, she could feel a change in the air, a growing chill.

"Well, come on then, we'd best head on over before it gets too late," she said, standing and looking back toward the city on the southern horizon. As she stood, she felt the leaves shift and wobble, and nearly lost her balance.

"It's alive!" Pyra joked, flitting up and then jumping back onto the leafy platform in a mock attack.

The flower trembled under her attack, and all five of the blossoms overhead swung in the air, absent of a breeze. Then it shook again… a tremor that traveled up from the base, shaking the whole plant.

Pyran held her hands out to the sides and splayed her wings as she struggled to balance and stay on the leaf. She looked at Fryn worriedly, biting her lip as she waved her over. "I think there really might be something out there Fryn."

Fryn scrambled to her and knelt in a low crouch. She put her hand through the slits of her Sanhas' skirt and drew her knife—a chef's knife she had taken from the kitchens to practice forms and strapped onto her thigh.

Pyra smiled, also pulling out a knife from her leg. Hers was a traditional Soft-Point Fist folded steel blade the length of her forearm with a bone handle. "Should we try our routines on it?"

Fryn frowned. "We don't know what it is."

"There's rats, cardinals, and well, it's still daytime so I doubt it could be an ermine," Pyra replied, edging over to peer at the ground. "I don't see anything, just snow powder and dead leaves. Oh! The leaves moved." She slipped over the edge and flitted down to hover above the giant root bulb, blade held out in the ready.

"Pyra, what are you doing?" Fryn demanded, leaning over the edge on her hands and knees, wings shifting with discomfort.

Pyran didn't answer verbally, instead she put a finger over her mouth and waved for Fryn to come down too. Fryn swallowed, and flew down to meet her, so that they watched the ground in two directions.

"Ooh!" Pyra said, pointing at the base of the flower. In the direction she indicated, Fryn saw the shadow of a burrow under the flower. The opening was ringed with roots, and a trail devoid of dead leaves marked the entrance of the subterranean home of some creature. "Look at the size of that hole! It must be the burrow of an arctic hare!" She relaxed, laughing.

Fryn couldn't shake the feeling that they were being watched. She spun in the air and flew in a circuit around the flower. Neither of them saw any more sign of whatever had rustled the leaves. "It must have been a hare," Fryn agreed, landing on the ground at the base of the orchid, so she could peer into the void of the burrow.

Pyran landed beside her and sighed. "I would have liked to see it. They are all white and supposed to be really soft." She sheathed her knife on her leg and then nodded to herself. "Let's head back!" She took to the wing with a laugh, Fryn right on her heels, but a white blur passed between them and Fryn found herself being knocked back into the air spinning end over end.

Pyra let out a yelp and crashed into the interwoven leaves she had used as a stage. Fryn caught herself by grabbing onto a passing blossom and shot back to her friend. She skidded to a stop beside her and anxiously looked over the edge.

The flower shook, so she pulled back.

"What was it?" Pyra asked, her face pale. She had one hand on her face, and a trickle of blood ran down her cheek under her fingers. Her wings shivered, and her skin prickled.

"I didn't see it," Fryn whispered back, "Pyra, you're bleeding! Freeze it!"

Pyran took a breath and closed her eyes. When she took her hand away from her face, the narrow cut on her face had been sealed over by a thin layer of ice. "Fryn, have you ever heard of a hare attacking people?"

The leaves shook again, and below they heard the telling chattering cry of an ermine. Fryn and Pyra shared an anxious look and slid back as close as they could to the center of the flower, where they could hide behind some of the leaves.

"I thought they only came out at night," Pyra complained.

"Shh…" Fryn shook her head, and then nodded. "They do. But you woke him up during his nap!"

"*I* woke him up?" she demanded, voice rising.

Huddled together in the shadow of the orchid leaves, Fryn growled at her. "Was I dancing and shaking the whole flower?"

"Point taken." Pyran hugged Fryn and groaned. "We need to get out of here Fryn."

"It might think we've left if we just wait it out or…" she said under her breath, and was going to say more, when the entire plant shook and the leaves they sat on bent under the weight of something massive landing on the platform they had been using before.

A sniffing nose prodded at the leaves beyond them, and Pyra let out a low moan. It pawed and struggled to dig deeper before it started to wriggle in toward them.

We're going to be trapped. We're going to be trapped! Fryn thought in alarm, pulling Pyra a little deeper toward the center of the plant where they fell through the last leaves toward the central bulb.

They tumbled in shock toward the ground, and stared up at the impenetrable wall of leaves around them with only a small circle for the sky overhead. Thick stalks rose around them, with bulbs and blossoms rising from the heart of the orchid.

To the side, Fryn saw a tiny hole that looked like it had been chewed into the bulb, and a tiny ermine head poked up through it, watching them with bright blue, blinking eyes. It chattered excitedly, and a louder cry sounded from above in response.

"Oh no-no-no-no…" Pyra pulled Fryn back from the baby ermine and tugged toward the sky. "Up, up, up, Fryn!" She flew straight up beside the stalks of the flowers, glowing in the light from the unopened bulbs and the radiant blossoms at the top. Fryn followed, and they landed on top of the flowers, nestling into their petals to hide as they looked out toward the city again.

The sky was darkening, and the greater moon appeared through the fading light with the head of the Lich Constellation peeking out over the top of it. Supposedly it used to have two eyes, but as long as Fryn had known of it, it had just the one red eye.

The wind caught their flowers and they swayed precariously. Pyran held onto her flower desperately but grinned at Fryn. "We'll certainly have a story to tell about today! I think we're high enough to fly off now, let's go!"

The northern lights shimmered around them, and Fryn felt an indescribable anxiety. The green and orange light glimmered in the darkening sky like the fire encroaching on her room as a child.

"Now!" Pyran yelled, and they both dashed into the air, kicking back on their flowers to gain speed. Pyra laughed, victoriously as she soared upwards.

The white blur returned.

Pyra's smile faded into a terrified, horrified scream. Time slowed as Fryn watched the jaws of a massive ermine close around Pyra's body and sink its teeth into her chest. Its brilliant blue eye watched Fryn with an intelligent monstrosity that sent a chill down her spine.

Pyra fell with the ermine at the end of its momentum, and Pyra screamed and cried out in agony until it gave her another firm bite and her voice was suddenly cut off. Fryn hovered in the air, perfectly still, not believing what she was seeing. She slipped through the air toward the ermine and Pyra's body which lay on a bed of dead leaves. The ermine watched Fryn, and rested one of its paws on Pyra's chest, digging its claws in.

Tears streamed from Fryn's eyes, and she charged the ermine with her kitchen knife in hand. She slid under a swing of the creature's paw and stabbed it in the chest.

It pulled away, taking the knife with it, and growled at her with narrowed eyes. Fryn moved to Pyra and used her frost to freeze over the puncture wounds and slashes, relieved but pained as she saw that Pyra's chest rose and fell slowly in a ragged motion—likely with one collapsed lung.

"Hold on, Pyra… I'll bring you back!"

Fryn grabbed the knife from Pyra's leg and stared down the ermine once more. "You can't have her!" she shouted at it.

It watched her, seeming almost amused, as if its dinner had simply come to it asking to be eaten.

"…F…Fryn… fly…"

"Yes, we'll fly back together."

"…I can't…" Pyra's voice wavered, and her eyes rolled, with pained tears trickling into the dried leaves.

Fryn growled. "I'm not going to lose you too, Pyra!"

Pyra let out a breath, and her chest did not rise again.

Fryn screamed at the ermine and charged it. This time she dodged its swipe to the side, and then used a wingburst to narrowly avoid a bite as she stabbed the ermine in its eye with Pyra's blade.

It let out a roar and backed away, sweeping a tail at her.

But Fryn kept her grip and chased it.

It rose on its hind legs and fell at her in a smash, knocking her to the ground, and followed through with a bite that cleanly took off her right leg at the knee.

Flush with adrenaline, the pain was dulled, but it took all of her training to freeze the stump and to use her wings to avoid another swing of its paws. This time, she flipped through the air around its blinded side, and stabbed at the other eye with a yell.

It twisted as soon as it saw her and her blade sliced along its face, but its eye remained fixed on her, unharmed. She landed on its head, sliding back so it couldn't bite her immediately, and tried to stab its brain.

The knife stuck in its bone, and it shook her free, sending her rolling back toward where Pyran lay.

Fryn's eyes settled on her leg, laying on the ground before the ermine which glowered at her with blood matting the fur of its face around the punctured eye and the cuts she had inflicted. Pyran's knife still poked in the top of its head, stuck in the bone.

They both growled and charged. Fryn flew over its attack and into its blind spot again, and as she flipped, she formed a hammer of ice in her hands, and swung it down on the butt of the knife.

It sank in.

The ermine let out a cry and its good eye rolled back. Fryn landed on one leg before it, absently picking up her dismembered leg and looking from it to the ermine then to Pyra, before shaking her head and flying over to Pyra.

Save only what you can! she thought, tossing her leg to the ground and struggling to lift Pyra's body and fly. It wasn't as easy with one leg to lift her from the ground, but she managed to get upright and flit a foot up into the air before falling in a heap with Pyra on top of her.

Pyra wasn't breathing. Her heart wasn't beating. Her face was fixed in an expression of terrible pain, and Fryn lay on the ground feeling the ache in her leg and a terrible ripping in her heart. Her parents, dead. Pyran dead…and now, as it was getting dark, she was going to die as well.

Fryn rolled over and balanced awkwardly on one leg. It was odd how the loss of the other made her feel so off centered, like a poorly weighted blade.

A chattering cry sounded behind her, and a shadow loomed over her head, blocking the light of the auroras and the moon. The young ermine, the one from the burrow, caught her body and arms in a crushing bite.

Fryn felt her ribs cracking and piercing, their broken sections stabbing her lungs and heart. She spat up blood and felt a moment of complete disassociation. In the one moment, she was there in the ermine's mouth, but in another she was standing with both legs beside Pyra, watching herself get eaten by the ermine.

The pain was hardly real anymore, and with the dusk she was cast in a surreal glow of starlight, moonlight, and northern light. Fryn stood on a mound of stone, surrounded by an empty field of powdery snow, with a small glacial orchid struggling to gain purchase on the rocky outcropping. Its tiny roots clung to the stone and stretched toward her and the dripping rivulets of blood that seeped from the stones.

Fryn turned back toward the baby ermine, which had flung her body back towards Pyra, seeming frustrated it could not swallow her whole.

As Fryn's body slid up against Pyra's, the tiny orchid on the stone mound drank of her blood and its tiny bud blossomed in a shower of crimson petals. Fryn walked toward it.

She had used her ice to make a hammer before, but she really needed something sharp, something she was trained to use. Both of the knives they had brought with them were embedded in the larger ermine's body, but there was plenty of iron in blood…She knelt before the flower, scooping up from the puddle of blood at its base with her hands cupped.

It wasn't just hers. The blood shimmered with frost, but it seemed to be shifting in distinct currents, almost dancing.

It's Pyra's! Fryn realized, looking back toward her body. If Pyra was bleeding again she must have unfrozen the… ice…

A translucent shadow of Pyran stood above their fallen bodies, arms akimbo, and a chagrined expression on her face. "I can't do it, Fryn," she said in a voice that resonated on the wind.

She bent down and closed her own eyelids and moved her hand to hold Fryn's. "It's such a riddle and I never liked those. No wonder no one ever becomes a Lich. I'm already fading, and I don't have time." She held up a ghostlike hand to stop Fryn from interrupting. "Kill it!"

Fryn held up the cupped portion of blood, trying and failing to freeze it into a blade.

"And Fryn…" Pyra added, "survive this." Her translucent form faded into a haze of sparkling light, like reflections on dry snow, and vanished into the night.

Fryn shivered. Even as a spirit she shouldn't be cold! Angered, she grabbed onto the stalk of the red flower and ripped it free.

Her world shifted.

The stars glowed overhead, and now she stood on a platform of worked stones. Where the orchid had been, now a stone pillar rose and blossomed at the top with leaves and multiple blossoms of the crimson flowers.

Below the platform, she saw a vast field of snow and in the distance, flowers… and she saw no sign of her body, or Pyra's, and the flower in her hand was now a shard of black ice.

For her part, Fryn liked riddles, but this was no test, it was a matter of effort—something Pyran had never appreciated in her own training since her skills came so naturally. Fryn closed her eyes, but could still hazily see her ethereal surroundings through the lids, and focused on the shard of ice in her hands.

It wriggled and twisted in her hands, over and over, about itself like a starved worm eating its other half. It condensed and hardened, growing darker and blacker, and heavier with each second.

Fryn could see the small spring and pool of blood around the base of the pillar sinking, nearly emptying, as she forced all of the blood she and Pyran had combined into a folded blade with a keen, jagged edge. It was roughly the same length and shape as Pyran's knife.

The pool of blood bubbled as if still emptying even though Fryn had stopped filling the blade. Through her closed eyelids she got a shadowy view on the other side, where she could see her arms shifting into the correct alignment, a rib that had been poking out of her breast sinking back under the skin, and scratches freezing over with black lines.

In a moment of panic, Fryn opened her eyes and saw once more from the viewpoint of her own head. She lay sideways on the ground, completely frozen, with a knife in her hand formed from her own blood.

She reached over and struggled to grab onto her dismembered leg, fingers slipping off it a couple times before she could snatch it and hold it against her stump. Instinctively, she let some of the blood from the blade recede, and it flowed to the wound, freezing the limb back together.

Being completely frozen, the pain of all her healing wounds dulled, and she watched the ermine approach with one hand on her leg, and the other held out warding it away. "You can't have me," she said in a hollow, cold voice. "And you can't have her!" she yelled. Feeling the final stitching of bone and sinew in her leg, she launched herself at the beast.

It spun, slashing at her with claws and tail, catching her on the side, but she ignored the injury. She froze the slashes over with black ice, and slid under the beast's guard, slamming the blade home under its chin.

It let out a pained cry and recoiled, lowering his head to bite at her. Fryn slashed, cutting its teeth with a satisfying tug. It was sharp, incredibly sharp! She sprang forward in the charge perfected by the Soft-Point Fist, deflecting one of his paws with an ice encrusted fist, as she lowered her stance and kicked upward using all the power her legs and wings could provide to thrust the blade into its chest.

The knife sunk to the hilt and the beast shivered.

On the other side of the blade, in the plane she had stood observing her own death, Fryn felt the creature's hot, roiling blood and resisted pulling it in. It would not be good to heal herself with *that*.

Instead, to ensure it died, she drew out the ermine's blood and focused it into a crystal in her other hand. She drained it completely and condensed the creature's blood into a massive stone the size of her head, and let it fall to the ground.

It bounced on the dead leaves and snow and rolled to a stop beside Pyran. The dead ermine seemed frozen, and did not fall on Fryn immediately, so she dropped her knife and fell to her knees. She put her head in her hands, fell over and curled up into a ball. Her wings shivered and her shoulders shook as she wept.

After a good half hour of lying there, she uncurled herself and looked over at Pyran's body, lying there bloodless as well—since she had given everything she had left to help Fryn transform. She idly slipped her Bloodknife into the imperfect sheath at her leg, and crawled over to her friend, and brushed her hair out of her face.

Tears still trickled from her eyes, and one of them fell on Pyra's face. Wherever Pyra's soul had gone, whether to the Wing-Giver's Sky, or someplace far more mysterious, Fryn had watched her soul disappear. She picked up Pyra's broken form and hugged it close for a few minutes before looking around and realizing that it was completely dark.

She might have defeated two ermines, impossibly, but more would likely start to prowl. Fryn put her arms under Pyra's form and was relieved that bloodless she was noticeably lighter than before. Still, try as she might, Fryn could not fly while carrying her.

Instead, she put her friend on her back, marked the stars, and started walking south.

All around her in the forest of glacial orchids, she was surrounded by an unearthly glow of the radiant blooms, pale blue like ice. The green and gold northern lights and the moon's powerful glow provided enough light to see by, and she walked between the lesser flowers easily.

Fryn shifted Pyra slightly on her back, sniffling as she carried her friend's body to her home in a field of silence.

Once, while looking up to check her directions, she noticed that she could actually see two eyes in the Lich's constellation, but one was just a faded white. And then it moved, swinging in front of the greater moon. It must have been Fee, the dancing female moon, so small that it looked like one of the stars.

Fryn shook her head and continued south.

She walked for hours and didn't feel tired. She felt drained, emotionally exhausted, but her body was numb, and she kept going because that was what she did. Everyone died around her, but she kept going.

Finally, she walked into something, and found herself bouncing off of the city gate and falling into the snow.

"…you hear that…?"

"…heard nothin'…"

"I'm sure I heard something!" The first voice said more loudly.

"Then go take a look!"

The single-person door cut into the city gates creaked as a city guard in a blue and white uniform peeked out of a crack in the doorway at her. Golden lamplight flowed out in a stream, and he blinked at them. "Children?"

The other guard's voice, gruff and disinterested said, "Well, bring them in, you dolt!"

The guard in the doorway didn't move, he shouted over his shoulder, "But what if they aren't citizens?"

"Do they look like Sky Dwellers?"

The guard in the door looked back at Fryn, and then as he examined them, his face went white as the snow on the ground. "Wing-Giver preserve me, I think they're dead!" he shouted, slamming the door shut and sliding a door bar into its brackets.

The commanding voice gave a sigh Fryn could hear on the other side of the door. "There is no such thing as ghost-walkers, Hadi. Give me that lamp." The door bar slid again and this time the door opened all the way to reveal a guard with a narrow, handsome face, and combed blond hair. He was tall and thin, and he looked down on Fryn with a disappointed frown. He walked out onto the snow, adjusting his coat as he held the oil lamp in one hand and reached out toward Fryn with the other.

"Come along, children," he said, keeping his gaze locked with Fryn's.

The other guard anxiously watched from the doorway. "Are you sure they aren't Sky Dwellers?"

The blond guard shot him a look, "I'd recognize their uniforms anywhere, Hadi. These are students of Master Bersari!"

The other guard relaxed. "That is a relief that they both returned alive, Alan… er… Captain…"

Fryn allowed the captain to help her up but did not set Pyran down. She carried her through the doorway and over to the guard post. There, at the captain's insistence, she let him take Pyran and lay her down on a cot, and he unfolded an extra cot for Fryn.

"Thank you, Captain…uh…"

"Hartlin, child," he said, putting a hand on her head. "Lie down and get some rest. We will inform the Master you have returned."

Fryn did not use the cot Captain Hartlin had brought out for her. She nodded tiredly, yawned, and climbed onto the cot beside Pyra, and hugged her till she fell asleep.

She vaguely noticed when the captain brought a blanket to cover them and remembered his confused expression when he saw the black blade on her leg.

When Master Bersari and Pyra's mother, Yuli, came, they were red eyed and red faced; Yuli, a beautiful fee with golden hair and bright round brown eyes dressed in green. She wore her hair in a series of braids, studded with silver ornaments, and another silver medallion around her neck. She had a brilliant violet scarf around her shoulders.

Master Bersari wore a ceremonial Sanhas, embroidered with gold thread on a white cloth, with the same violet sash as Yuli's scarf. He had paired his silver dangling earrings with the silver in Yuli's hair.

"How was the dance?" Fryn asked, rising from the cot, and bowing respectfully.

Yuli rushed past her and bowed over Pyra's body, weeping, and shaking as she sobbed.

Master Bersari approached her stiffly, and in a strange moment of genuine emotion, he picked her up and hugged her to his chest. He shook gently as a quiet cry sounded in the back of his throat, and his tears dripped onto her face.

"Thank you," he said, choking out the words, "for bringing her home to us."

Fryn nodded, nestling deeper into his embrace as she began to sob anew. "She... she saved me..." Fryn whispered.

Captain Hartlin appeared beside them, offering steaming cups of tea. "We should move inside," he said shivering.

Master Bersari covered his eyes with frost and fixed a cold gaze on the captain. "We are not bothered by the cold, Captain, perhaps you should head inside first."

He looked about to argue, but Bersari added, "We would wish to be alone."

"Of course, Master," he said, inclining his head in a gentle bow. "Hadi come inside and give them privacy."

The other guard continued to watch Fryn warily, so the captain had to pull him away by his sleeve.

"Tell me what happened," Master Bersari muttered, "so I can explain it to Yuli."

Fryn nodded. "We wanted to practice for tomorrow," she said, prompting a pained groan from the Master, "She said that the Ice Wastes were the perfect place, and safe during the day."

How could she explain what happened? Did they need to know there were two ermines?

She wove a tale of desperation and danger, and how Fryn was knocked out after a failed charge, and how when she came to it was dark. She found the ermine dead and Pyra fallen beside it. She said nothing about herself, her knife, or the experience of becoming a Lich.

Master Bersari nodded, but still looked like he half-believed the story. He simply said, "Can you stand? I don't think Yuli can carry her."

She nodded and he let her down, and then went to scoop up Pyran's body. Not knowing what to do, Fryn took Yuli's hand, and they all began the walk back to the academy.

The advancement ceremony would be canceled.

They would hold the funeral in a few days.

Fryn put her free hand where the Bloodknife rested on her thigh under the flaps of her Sanhas and froze her eyes over so she couldn't cry.

If Pyra was gone, Fryn was going to do her best to fill her place in the academy, and in the Master's family. She would master the style and become the next heir of the school.

That evening, as she dressed in a ceremonial Sanhas, charcoal gray with deep blue scrollwork and trim, with a matching ribbon tied in a careful bow at her waist, she slid the fingers of one hand down her arm to smooth out any wrinkles with frost. It... clung to her in a stiff way, crinkling and shedding a fine icy dust as she brushed out wrinkles in the front, and shifted her wings in the slits of the back. This had been one of Pyra's garments, and half in memory of her friend, and half to step more fully into her shoes, Fryn took up a bracelet of small black marble beads and slid it over her left hand.

No one called to inform her dinner was ready. When she met Yuli and Master Bersari at the table, the food was laid out, and their goblets full of wine. Both were red-eyed, and Yuli sniffled as she opened her arms and invited Fryn into an embrace.

Yuli wept into her shoulder, but no tears came to Fryn's eyes.

She felt numb.

~Present Day~

Frorin

Sky District

Grifton

Grifton Francis stood in a forest of bone. White trunks stretched toward the sky all around him, spreading their arms into a spray of sinewy leaves and marrow flowers. It was humid, and a warm fog filled the space around him. Here, he raised his hands and saw they were as they once had been, flesh and blood, both of them. His wings were as normal, glistening and dappled with dew.

It was peaceful, and he was tempted to breathe in the warmth of the air and let his soul move on.

But he could not rest.

Not until Leif, Fryn, and that other Lich were dead. He grinned. They thought they were immortal, but they still had their flesh and bones—they had material that he could use to absorb their essence and annihilate their existence!

Grifton closed his eyes, and opened them, and saw that he was once more standing in the road leading up the hill toward the gates of Frorin. Ramshackle houses and sheds were scattered around the hill without a hint of organization, as if built there by mistake. He spat to the side, satisfied that though so much about his body had changed, he could still perform that action in this place for these faeries.

This frostbitten wasteland inhabited by a forbidding folk long abandoned by history, they had remained irrelevant and forgotten for too long. Grifton laughed as he considered what he would do to bring the city to its knees—just as soon as Leif and Fryn were dead.

As he climbed the hill, his road meandered around the hill to the south side of the city, to the same main gate he had used to enter Frorin the last time. In the dawning light, he saw a full squad of guards bearing the silver lances Ieffin had brought back into rotation, five guards on the right, five on the left, with an officer up in the parapet above the gate. They all wore the new uniform, white tunics with pale blue trim, polished breast plates emblazoned with the Snowflake Crown. They didn't wear capes; those would just hamper their flight. Instead, they wore a pale blue skirt that was cut from two flowing panels with a pattern in white chained snowflakes.

Grifton rounded the bend and approached them with gritted teeth. Even without his Bonesword, these guards would not stop him from entering the city.

A hare drawn carriage rolled through the gates, and the guards crossed their lances barring the way as he drew near. Several of them shuffled anxiously, murmuring to each other.

"Hold there!" Called the officer from the parapet above. He leaned over the battlements and squinted at Grifton with a superior air. "What business do you have in Frorin?"

Grifton sighed, but found his license in his tattered jacket pocket, and unfolded a copy of the bounty for Leif and Fryn. He held these up as if the officer could even read them from there.

"I am a Hunter of the Commission, tracking the movements of the wanted criminals Leif Aellin and Fryn Martin," he replied in a gravelly voice. The skeletal fingers of his left hand held onto his license, knuckles shifting impatiently as one of the lancers approached to examine his documents a wingspan away.

"Hunter? Commission? Begone, stranger, you are not welcome in Frorin. You are not welcome in Froreholt! Go back to your traitorous organization and do not return here again!" The officer cried, sneering at him for good measure.

A gathering of faeries on the hill to the right stopped their work, staking out lines and strings to mark new construction, but Grifton ignored them. Instead, he ground his teeth and rushed the guard before him. He grabbed the lancer's neck and sunk his claws down until they met spine, and he *drank* in the marrow and bone, letting it coalesce into a narrow blade, leaving an empty set of clothes.

He tested the blade, frowning at its meager size, and then eyed the others. "You think you can stop us?" he taunted, and then charged.

All around, he raised a cloud of dust, flakes of stone and dirt that occluded the movements of the lancers, and through which he could sense every single one.

As two rushed him in a wingbursted attack, he stepped between them, slashing and cutting the left one in half at the stomach, and then stabbing the other in the back.

The other guards pulled away, and he used that moment to absorb the bodies of those two to strengthen his blade, savoring its weight. He cackled, and raised his empty hand to form a shower of stone shards and flung them at the other group of guards just beyond his reach. Three went down, and the remaining four circled him with lances pointed inward.

The officer descended from the parapet with a lance over his shoulder. "So, it's you, eh?" he asked. "I thought you died in the debacle at the King's Grave." The officer brushed his unkempt brown hair out of his face and fixed Grifton with a glare. His fingers trembled on the handle of his lance, and Grifton drank in the fear that filled the fae's eyes.

"You cannot kill the mountain," he replied, looking back, and pointing two fingers at one of the other guards. His fingers shot out in a flare of sinewy tendrils that speared the guard with a cry, and then he absorbed them as well. "You thought a Lich was something to fear?"

He spun slashing the air and sending a shockwave of dust and debris outward, that tossed one guard into the gates with a sickening crunch, sliced off another's head, and threw the final guard into the group working on the construction project.

The captain avoided getting hit with the blast, using his arm guards to block the debris from hitting his face. He cursed, stumbling back toward the gate in a panic.

"Where are the criminals?" Grifton asked again. "Surely you know?"

"They…I…not sure…um…" he stuttered, and then fell backwards over the body of the guard thrown before. "I don't know! They flew! They flew away!" The last part he screamed desperately, dropping his lance to hold up his hands.

"Where did they fly?" Grifton leaned over him, thrusting his blade into the stones beside his face.

The officer cringed, and tears leaked from his eyes. "No one knows!"

"No one?" Grifton prompted, gently placing his clawed bone hand on the captain's chest. "Surely someone knows."

He whimpered. "Maybe not…"

"Surely your king knows…" Grifton said, stabbing the captain in the chest with his fingers and sucking out his life. After a few seconds of sloshing and slurping, all the organic matter that had once been a faerie was gone, absorbed through his hand.

He rose and started toward the gate once more. As he reached the gates, he saw a figure standing in the courtyard, a fee with black hair, in an elegant black dress, leaning on a cane.

"I'm afraid you'll need to stop right there, sir," she declared, staring at him with a red cast to her green eyes.

He narrowed his eyes at her, and indeed he saw the same floating haze of dust surrounding her that he had around himself. He grinned.

"Where did they go, Pine Martin?" he asked, lifting his blade in salute.

She twisted the top of her cane and drew out a narrow sword lined with red veins. The Pine Martin stepped forward into an unfamiliar stance, one foot behind the other, with the blade outstretched. It was reminiscent of the Rosenkraun Grass Blade style. "I'm afraid your journey ends here, oh Fang of the Mountain."

He laughed. Why worry about using stances anymore? "You think you can stop me?" he asked, drawing closer and filling the air with their colliding debris fields.

She grinned. "It doesn't matter who you kill, no one is giving you the information you seek."

At that he charged. He rushed her with all his might put into a powerful overhead swing, and though she sidestepped his attack, he shattered the ground where she had been standing, and scratched her cheek with displaced stone flakes.

She stepped around the attack, rapping the knuckles of his fleshy right hand with the bone sheath as she thrust the blade through his bicep.

Pain.

He roared, pulling away as she sheared through the muscles and left them splaying, and he growled… sword forgotten for the moment. Though his autonomous marrow fibers reknit the arm, it hung useless for the moment, and he spat in her direction.

He grasped his sword with the bone hand and twirled in a massive spiral slash. She bent under it, and stabbed him in the foot, eyes alight in the thrill of the contest.

He felt it too.

He reached out despite the flare of pain in his foot, and grabbed her arm, wrenching it back, crushing it with his impossible strength. She screamed *so* satisfyingly, and he pressed his advantage, kicking her back against the wall of one of the nearby shops.

Passersby watched transfixed, muttering amongst themselves and he grabbed her by her hair and lifted her up. "Where are they!!!" he demanded, roaring in her face.

To the side, he noticed a group of children huddling under the bench on the porch of a shop.

"She's our princess!" one shouted angrily, "Kill him, Pine Martin!"

Harissa growled in the back of her throat and used her blade to cut her hair under his grip so that she fell to the ground coughing, and Grifton was left with a handful of silky black hair.

"I'll kill you next, child!" he shouted at the boy, and then looked around the courtyard.

A crowd gathered in the street, surrounding them, chanting quietly at first and then more loudly, "Pine Martin! Pauper's Princess!"

A sword slashed, and he watched in disbelief as his flesh arm fell lifeless to the ground. He gripped his sword in his skeletal hand and swung hard, but Harissa had already moved. His momentum carried it into the wall of the building, and it *stuck* there in the stones!

She gripped her blade in both hands, and screamed as she brought it up in a leaping, wingbursting strike through his skeletal arm, and he felt his connection to the bones themselves being severed.

He backed away, stumbling in shock toward the gate.

How could she cut through bones? He focused on her cane, and saw the marrow-like tendrils that knitted its length and realized, they were the same.

He roared, using his will power alone to order his ribs to stretch out like fangs, in a splaying attack toward her. She leapt into the attack, spinning the sword as she sliced all the bone shards off at his chest, and then she kicked him back out of the city.

"You," she declared, cutting off one of his wings, "are not," she cut off another, "welcome," and another, "in my city!" She sliced off his last wing and booted him to the ground.

He fell in a heap in the gravel, and looked longingly at his wings and arms, and the sword stuck in the building so far away, and as her sword descended toward his neck, he rolled away and wobbled onto his knees. Then, gathering his strength, he ran forward, and caught the handle of his sword in his teeth and continued down the craggy slope.

Harissa swore behind him, and he drew on the essence within his sword, regrowing his bone-limbs and wings, and fled between the broken shacks of the Sky District toward the forest below.

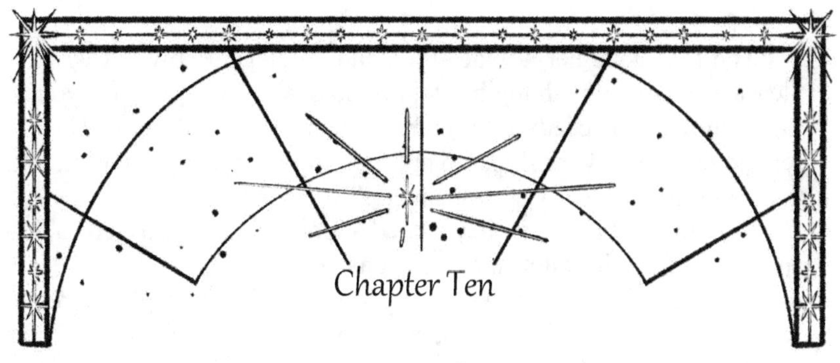

STAR

Fassen

Earl's Estate Courtyard

Fryn

Fryn stood with the others at the foot of the stairs before the main entrance of the Earl's Estate. Faintly she heard the working calls of the grape harvesters overhead in the boughs of the vine, and the wind carried the scent of rubbed oil and burning peat from the Earl's armorers refitting the newly renamed Fassen Crows.

Alyra and Havrshyk stood beside the hawk, looking through bags and verifying that everything on the list had been packed. Fryn smiled as Leif moved up beside her, slipping his arm around so that his hand rested gently at the small of her back. Fryn leaned into him, watching as Savis stepped onto the lowest step and looked nervously up at Loren, Vinellin, Lia and Nora. They all stood at the top of the stairs, but Nora clung to her mother's dark green dress, and buried her face so she wouldn't have to say goodbye.

"Loren, thank you for taking us in during the night, and sending us safely on. Yours is a very hospitable house," Savis said, looking slightly away from him. Her hand rested on the bag that still contained the Harvest Crown. "Tell my brother I am well, and... be wary. If the president was willing to go in person to conduct the assassination in Rosenkraun, there is nothing he will not do to kill his enemies."

The Earl gave her a wide smile and an elegant bow. "It was a pleasure to have you in my house, Princess, and I will pray for your safe journey and speedy return. We have contacts in Elin, so I will send letters with every ship. Do not fear, together we will not fall to the Commission. An army of bankers!"

Fryn nudged Leif and they shared a look. Savis took a step back and joined in their doubtful expressions.

"Bankers that took down a kingdom," Leif countered, "Loren, keep your eyes on your borders, and choose your friends wisely."

The Earl nodded, stepping over toward Lia so he could pat Nora's head. Her wings fluttered and flushed with a sorrowful blue light. "I have made some lovely friends here, Leif, and they will keep better company than you could," he teased, then, more seriously he added, "I was surprised to hear your story the other day, Leif. More surprised to have it corroborate something Fhora said." He patted a folded letter that protruded from his waistcoat. "If you are pursued, do not hesitate to lead them toward the Cherim. I suspect they will, for once, be willing to help you."

Lia fidgeted and Fryn shifted her weight from foot to foot. Havrshyk glared at them, climbing into the hawk's massive saddle and waving for Alyra to toss bags up.

"Hopefully, we will not need to invite such risk. Regardless, I'll write as often as I can," Savis said, stepping back and flying up to the saddle.

Fryn and the others followed, settling into the two rows of seats. Aldyr had held the reins on their last trip, and once more he rushed to the forward singular seat to hold the reins.

"Maybe I should have a go," Leif complained playfully, pulling away from Fryn though she tried to tug him back. "Why should you get to do it?"

Havrshyk raised an eyebrow at him. "For one thing, Leif, I have actually flown to Norenan before. They still tell stories of the last time I visited Stanaedre." He shrugged off Leif's hand on his shoulder and focused ahead. "Up!" he cried, flicking the reins, and launching the massive hawk into the air.

Leif stumbled back into Fryn, and though she caught him, he fell on top of her, with his face right next to hers. Her heart raced, and he kissed her on the cheek before sitting down properly beside her.

Fryn looked away, blushing despite her efforts to drain more blood into her blade. He settled into his seat and folded his wings, putting an arm around her shoulders again as he whispered, "I can't wait to board an airship."

The hawk spun in an arc around the Fassen vine and streaked through the air toward the southeast. Fryn adjusted her coat against the wind, holding it perfectly in place with a thin layer of frost, and shaded her eyes against the sun.

"This is going to take us close to Rosenkraun, Havrshyk," she cautioned.

He scoffed. "There are so many birds flying out of Rosenkraun, no one is going to even notice us unless we land." He turned in his seat and noticed her concerned face, and added, "Besides, this bird can fly high enough that no one will even see us." He faced forward again and went quiet.

A hand patted her shoulder from behind, so Fryn turned and saw Savis bending closer so she could speak over the wind. "I'd rather we didn't get within a day's flight of Rosenkraun, Fryn… I only just barely escaped with my life."

Alyra sat beside the princess, eyes closed, as she interrupted in a voice just loud enough to be heard. "Unless they have another faerie with a mental affinity, Princess, no one will notice us."

Fryn nodded at that.

"Mental affinity?" Savis asked, putting her hand over her breast, "I didn't know that such a thing existed!"

"I have only met a couple," Leif said, joining the conversation and turning so he sat backwards on the bench to face the other two. "In Sendra, we have a sage. Faeries from all over bring their disputes to her, and she negotiates the price of reconciliation and ensures that nothing is hidden.

"I also had a fellow disciple in my school who had the same affinity… but he died in a strange accident… and I think that someone wanted him out of the way. It was right before my master was put in prison!" he added excitedly.

Fryn smiled, it was rare for him to talk about his homeland. For so long, he'd been absorbed with the thrill of seeing new places and learning about other cultures, now she finally had a chance to hear more about his. She put a hand on his arm and asked, "Wasn't that right before your final test?"

His eyes narrowed in thought, and he absently took the small sandalwood box with the serpent crest from his pocket and started rubbing the metal with his thumb. "It was. Now that I think of it, they sent me to a different region for my test than all the previous students."

Savis clapped her hands excitedly, wings shuffling. "Where did they send the other students?"

Leif frowned as he looked down at the box in his hands and opened it. Inside the pearly white fang of the viper he'd slain rested on a layer of velvet. "They sent the other students to the eastern desert, where the vipers are smaller, younger, and usually less venomous."

"And you?" Fryn asked, sliding her hand down his arm to take his hand and interlace her fingers with his.

"I was sent into the heart of the Aelaete and told to meditate until one came to find me."

"You beautiful fool," Fryn said with a sigh, "you should know not to go into the farthest reaches of the wilderness."

"I know that all the better from what you told me about the Ice Wastes," he replied with a shiver. "Ooh, your hands are cold Fryn..."

She smiled, allowing some blood to flow back into her fingers. "Better?"

He nodded, looking out toward the vine retreating into the distance. "We should be taking the fight to Hans," he said softly, so that only she could hear him.

Fryn bit her lip. Her instinct was also to face the problem directly and try to correct it as soon as possible... but their foe wasn't some bandit, or beast. Their enemy had coordinated a string of events that granted him enough legitimacy and power to redefine justice however he wished.

"Even if we killed him, there would still be a war," she replied, leaning her head against his shoulder.

Leif raised his free hand and brushed a stray lock of hair behind her ear. "We should be helping in the fight then."

She looked up and met his eyes. "We are helping our friends have the freedom to fight. We are distracting our foes and escaping the traps they have set for us."

His brow furrowed in thought, and after a minute he said, "I am excited to see new things, and grateful to help protect our friends, but leaving everything unresolved as we go into this indeterminate exile...? I feel sick, guilty."

"I'm glad, Leif," she teased, poking him in the side, "but you know what?"

He stared back at her hopefully.

"The first thing I learned about fighting more than one opponent is to maneuver the terrain so I only face one fae at a time. I think this flight is something like that. We are not fighting individuals but must maneuver nations and powers, so they do not all come together at once." Fryn turned eastward toward the mountains. "On the other side, lie the ashen ruins of the Shadelands. Without our distraction, perhaps our homelands would resemble them?"

Leif's arm around her back tightened as he pulled her closer. "May it never come to that."

She nodded, still watching the swath of thin clouds rising from the mountaintops like wisps of smoke, as if the Shadelands on the other side were still afire.

Gaersheim

Sky above Rosenkraun

Leif

Their northern hawk flew with all the grace and haste the legends ascribed to them. He dove and soared through cloud and sky like a salmon in the rivers of the Aelaete. Mulberry, the magpie, they had left behind under Harissa's care, as she rushed the work on her plans to build the Sky District wall. It would doubtless appreciate the rest, and occasional hopping flights Harissa would need it for as she surveyed the irregular shelf the Sky District occupied outside the city of Frorin.

Six hours had taken them from Fassen to Rosenkraun, and the sun was beginning to edge toward the horizon—though there were still a few hours till sunset. On the eastern bank of the river that cut through the city, the grape vines spread their arms in a traditional rectilinear arrangement, creating lines and boxes that interconnected the vines, and all around the city they saw birds flying, and small figures moving down the streets.

"There's more crows about than I expected," Havrshyk commented dryly.

Indeed, two of the black birds that circled the city started to get larger as they wafted up on warm currents and approached. Leif looked over his shoulder at Savis, and she held her hands clasped with white knuckles, and her jaw was set in an anxious expression.

The crows drew up on either side, and Leif noticed that the riders on wore the green, fibrous armor of the Grass Guard. To their right, the rider lifted a cone and shouted at them.

"I am Captain Horin of the Grass Guard, representative of the commissioned government of Rosenkraun. All birds passing through Gaersyn skies must pay tariffs on all goods and passengers by order of the Archon!" he declared, veering closer so they could hear him over the wind.

"What tariffs?" Havrshyk yelled back.

"The tariff on all mercantile cargo shall be no less than 12 percent of the appraised value, and every faerie shall pay a fee of 50 mint. Descend immediately to the Commissar's Quarter for customs!"

Leif shared glances with the others on the hawk and then he interrupted Havrshyk to shout back, "We are on a matter of diplomatic urgency! We will not descend!"

The captain on the bird narrowed his eyes at him, pulling a short stick with a red cap from his saddle bag. He maintained his gaze, eyes locked with Leif's, as he rested the red cap of the stick against the rough textured elbow-length cuff of his gauntlet, and scraped it in a quick motion, throwing the stick over his shoulder so that it fell toward the city below.

Leif broke eye contact with the Grass Guard captain and tracked the stick's descent. It burst alight in a crimson flash, and as it fell, it trailed a long blood red line of smoke.

"Hold onto the saddle!" Havrshyk yelled at them, pulling on the reins, and bringing the hawk up to put the sun behind them. "We're going to have to out-pace them!" He tugged the leads, and their hawk arced toward the south, putting the cloudless afternoon sky behind, and the mirage-like green haze straight ahead.

Fryn did not listen to Havrshyk's advice to hold tight, instead leaning over the saddle to watch the two crows trailing in hot pursuit. "There are three more birds rising from the city, Aldyr!"

Savis sank deeper into her seat, holding Alyra's hand in a white-knuckled grip. "I thought they weren't supposed to notice us?"

Alyra used her free hand to pat Savis' knee. "I am sorry Princess. If they were lax, and not watching the sky carefully, I could divert their attention… but such motivated guards cannot be easily distracted."

Leif shaded his eyes, ignoring the two crows that closed in on them, as he focused his gaze on the hazy line of trees to the south. The wall of brown, green, and wisps of mist, was formed from an incredibly massive, and overgrown forest. Though the mysterious heart of the realm of the Cherim lay deep within the forest, the very trees radiated an aura of menace and chill. His wings shivered involuntarily, and he suppressed a gulp as they drew nearer.

"I don't care what Loren said, are you sure flying into the Immortal Queen's forest is a good idea?" Leif asked Havrshyk, loosening and tightening his fingers into fists as he considered the idea.

"I'm immortal," he replied, jabbing a thumb over his shoulder toward Fryn, "She's immortal," and then he leaned back and met Leif's eyes, "and somehow, to whatever degree, it seems so are you. So, stop complaining and we'll see if the fear of the evil forest queen keeps the Grass Guard from following us."

Alyra shook her head, now squeezing Savis' hand as hard as Savis held onto hers. "No… no, not there, Havrshyk… there is something *terribly wrong* with that forest. It is *ashenarel'e…* corrupted… If we go in, something will see us… just as I see the minds of the riders giving chase."

His facade broke slightly, but the mask reappeared quickly, as he replied in a confident tone, "I don't care. She can see, you can see—as long as it gets the Gaersyn fools out of our feathers I'll be as happy as a fern in the Spring."

One of the crows swept up beside them, its rider aiming a small one-handed crossbow in their direction, firing a bolt that shot past Leif's face and sunk into Fryn's shoulder. She grunted at the impact and ripped it out with a grimace.

"I'll deflect this one," she said, pointing to the opposite side of the saddle, "Leif, you guard the other side."

He didn't need to nod, merely putting his back to hers so that their wings touched, and stood precariously with one foot on either side of the bench seat.

"Keep your head down, Savis!" Fryn added, "I'm not sure what Ieffin would do to me if you got hurt, but locking Liches in graves isn't off the table, I am well aware." Havrshyk clicked his tongue as she said it.

The Princess gave a little yelp as the second guard flew up on Leif's side and fired a bolt right at her. Leif, still trying to get used to his new elemental abilities, swept through the air to grab the bolt, and could not quite reach it.

Savis ducked just in time, as an arc of lightning leapt from Leif's outstretched fingers and pulled the bolt into his grasp. His hair stood on end, and the minute amount of dust on the bird and saddle rose in the air around him in the charged air.

The hawk squawked in annoyance as some of the energy zapped its feathers, but it maintained its flight toward the forest of Renholt.

Leif twirled the iron bolt in his fingers, and instinctively he drew back and with a burst of sparks that trailed from its length, he cast it back at the guard. A thunderclap rolled past him as it screamed through the air and cleaved through the forehead of the offending guard with impossible speed.

The guard slumped in the saddle, his hands loosening on the leads of his crow, and he fell forward against the bird. No blood flowed from the hole in his head, with the edges seared and cauterized by the intense heat of the electrified bolt. The crow cawed, locking angry eyes with Leif, before falling back toward the city.

"Too much," Leif said under his breath, making a mental note. He could feel that he had used perhaps twenty percent of his accumulated sparks to send the bolt back.

Over his shoulder, Fryn raised her Bloodknife toward the other guard and whispered, "Leif, stay here," before flitting across the distance to turn aside a crossbow bolt with her blade as she kicked the rider in his face. She regretfully sank the blade in his neck and tossed him pale and bloodless from the saddle.

Leif looked at her with a raised eyebrow, but Fryn merely settled into the saddle and tugged on the reins. "I won't have any trouble with you, will I?" she asked, pulling the crow's head back so he could meet her gaze.

It made a kind of purring croak in its throat, so Fryn nodded and then turned it around to face the other riders ascending from the city.

Leif flicked his wings, ready to join her, but Savis looked up from under the bench and held onto his lower wingtip. "Don't go!" she pleaded, pale, and wings shaking.

Instead, he watched Fryn fly off behind them, and guide her crow into a swooping attack, so that the crow grabbed the rider of another bird in his talons, and tossed him into the air, before she leapt from her bird and flew right at the hapless, hovering guard and stabbed him in the chest. She completed the maneuver, falling easily into line with her crow's descent, landing evenly in its saddle. She guided the crow into a chasing pattern, as two more of the Grass Guard closed in on the hawk.

"*Ermine's breath*," Havrshyk said, cursing under his breath, "here we go…"

Suddenly they were not in the open skies of Gaersheim.

Massive tree trunks flashed by on either side. Leif took in a breath, barely able to make out the details of the towering cedars and hemlock trees that now surrounded them, towering over the grassy plain like spears or teeth from the ground below. In fact, they had not even needed to make a descent to fly into the forest. They stood hundreds, perhaps thousands of wingspans tall, and their thick limbs sprouted horizontally in all directions, enshrouded with a feathery mask of needles and cones.

The hawk gave an alarmed cry, pulling in its wings and diving under a branch, and Leif had to cling to Havrshyk to avoid falling off. Savis screamed, and Aldyr cursed at him, and as they descended under a snarl of branches, Leif watched one of the following crows fly directly into a branch with a resounding 'crack'. The bird bounced back and fell limply from the air with a dazed rider.

Leif cheered, and Havrshyk brought the hawk up and around one of the ancient trees and guided it to a perch on one of the branches facing the direction where they had entered the forest.

It settled down and clamped onto the branch with what Leif considered a nervous tension. They could not see the ground clearly beyond a green haze. Mist, or fog, filled the space at the foot of the trees, and only hints of moss and ferns gave them a clue to what lay below. The air was thick and humid, yet somehow so fresh, and alive, it was both stifling and invigorating. His store of sparks churned and refreshed as they waited, far more alive in the forest, than out in the sky.

Alyra peeked over the edge of the saddle, still holding Savis down so she would not be exposed. She shaded her eyes and grinned. "Fryn approaches!"

Havrshyk heaved a sigh of relief.

"Anyone else?" Leif asked, hoping that she'd say 'no'.

She closed her eyes and took a breath. Even as she focused, the hairs on the backs of his arms and neck stood on end, and he felt like they were being observed. Birds cried out in alarm deeper in the forest, and the creaking of the trees in the wind made him feel less and less comfortable.

Alyra shuddered, opening her eyes, and pointing toward a branch above them at a neighboring tree. "They are here," she said, narrowing her eyes at a trio of faeries in black. They were arrayed on the branch with one standing at their head, another crouched just behind with a bow drawn and aimed in their direction, and a third flanking the leader by sitting on the edge with legs dangling.

Looking more closely, Leif was surprised to notice they were all fee. The leader had long black hair that was pulled into a tail that trailed behind her back, and she rested her hand idly on the pommel of a sword at her waist. Her bright golden eyes examined them suspiciously, but her gray-lined wings remained still, betraying no emotion.

Fryn flitted down beside Leif, no longer in the company of her stolen crow, and put a hand on his shoulder as she turned to examine their watchers with a raised eyebrow.

After nearly a minute of silence, the fee at their head addressed them in a proud, imperious voice. "Strangers, trespassers, and the unholy... none of these are permitted to enter the Realm of the Cherim and her queen. You appear to be all three of these things. Be warned that Our Mother's anger does not relent, nor can it be diverted with gifts or words—no matter how gilded."

She focused on Havrshyk, then Fryn, then Leif, and her eyes widened as she noticed Alyra poking her head above the edge of the saddle.

"Her curiosity likewise is insatiable. What could have caused her enemies, Liches, and worse, to come within her borders?" The fee pivoted on her heel and looked at them sideways, as if considering, and used one hand to shift her fringe out of her eyes. She wore an intricately carved golden ring but was too far away for Leif to tell much of the design.

Savis stood, rising from under the bench she'd been hiding, to give the fee an appraising look as she smoothed out the wrinkles from her dress. "These are my escort, agent of the Cherim, and we were harried and diverted into your forest by Gaersyn forces against our will."

The agent's eyes widened as she looked at Savis, and flew closer, hovering in the air before them. Fryn's hand rested on the handle of her knife, and Havrshyk likewise did a poor job of looking relaxed with his hand gripping the hilt of his sword and glaring at her.

Perhaps it was the changes to his elemental affinity, but Leif only detected inquisitiveness in her movements. He crossed his arms, and watched her in return, relaxed.

"The princess?" she asked, mouth hanging open for a moment as she considered. Then, she waved the other two away, and by the time Leif looked back at the branch they had vanished, though likely they watched from a hidden perch elsewhere.

Savis narrowed her eyebrows as she recognized the agent, and she gave a small smile. "This is interesting…Masie, wasn't it, when you served on my staff at the embassy?"

The fee's smile widened, though she shook her head. "My true name is Eldarin," she replied, "and I am pleased you survived the coup. Where are your usual guards?"

The princess bit her lower lip as she met the Cherim agent's eyes.

"I see. I must warn you, Princess, my mother does not look kindly on trespassers in her forest, extenuating circumstances or not. When I infiltrated your embassy, I expected to have better access to information about the world at large—but even I was surprised by the Commission's move to usurp control of the throne."

"Masie... er... Eldarin," Savis said, wings twitching anxiously, "I am being escorted away from this land. We are all of us going into exile to Elin. Our friend, Loren of Fassen suggested that you might allow us to pass through your forest to lose the scent of the Commission. Please let us be on our way before more Grass Guards come after us."

Now that she was closer, Leif noticed Eldarin's ring had been carved into the shape of an Ermine with a backdrop of stars. Her eyes held a flicker of something.

She was not happy to be back in the forest. Rosenkraun had been an exciting adventure, and now the world was changing and the Cherim had no access to information.

He coughed lightly to get Savis' attention, and she nodded so he could interrupt. "Eldarin, was it? My name is..."

She glared at him, "I know who you are, Viper, let the fee talk."

He shut up and then raised an eyebrow to Fryn.

"His contribution to the conversation may be of use," Savis said delicately, "despite his reputation for being flippant."

Leif shot her an offended look, but continued as the Cherim agent crossed her arms and looked at him dubiously. She raised her chin as she said, "The worker bee may be unimportant, but has firsthand knowledge of the flowers..." likely a local proverb.

"In Aelaete, we have only heard the name of your people and queen whispered in tales, but in those tales we see a kinship. Yours is not the only kingdom that has been attacked by the Liches of the north, and your mistrust of them is not unfounded... however... we are leaving this land, and going across the sea where we will not be a threat to you, your queen, or this forest. We share a common enemy and are no threat to the Cherim."

"The only access to Elin is by the airships of the Norenan Trade Guilds. We have tried and failed to infiltrate their vessels or send agents abroad. How do you expect me to believe they will simply take you away?"

"I have connections there," Savis said, fidgeting and looking back North toward the plain. "This is no time to isolate, to hide from the world without knowing what is happening beyond your borders. The Commission will seek retribution against my brother, and work to seize control of all of Fhoraena. I urge you, and ask that you convince Fhora, to not stand by while the Commission destroys everything beyond the forest."

"Eldarin smiled. "My mother has had a special dislike of Gaersheim for many years, ever since they burned back the forest to expand their vaunted 'Forest of Grass'. She will already take action, my dear, but what can you offer us in return for passage through our lands?"

"I will agree to a treaty solidifying our borders and agreeing to an alliance with the Cherim against the Commission," Savis suggested, hands clasped before her earnestly. "We will lay no claim on the lands south or east of the Artell River, and I invite you personally to be an ambassador in Frorin and open an embassy therein." Her wings shifted between blue and pale white light.

Leif nearly piped up again but got a nudge in the ribs from Savis' elbow. "Let me speak," she said quietly, "the Cherim are a matriarchal society and do not heed the words of fae."

Eldarin considered the suggestion and tapped her chin. "That sounds agreeable. I will bring this proposal, and a letter signed by you to my mother, who will negotiate with your brother further. That should suffice to grant you passage through our lands. Your companions... Wingbreakers and Liches, are a greater concern—our standing orders are to behead such on sight."

Savis paled.

"I believe a compromise will be for them to remain in your company, not loosed upon the world. One day the branches of the Immortal Queen will cover the earth, and all shall be nurtured and safe beneath her arms." Looking at Leif and the others, she added, "and it is by her forbearance that the nations exist. You may go."

Havrshyk did not need any further prompting; he jumped into the saddle and Leif and Fryn followed soon after. Just before they took off, Eldarin locked eyes with Havrshyk and added, "We are pleased to see that some Liches can change."

The hawk rose into the air, and they sped eastward through the forest. The bird's feathers were fluffed and he croaked under his breath as if he had been just as nervous as all of them.

"What was that about, Havi?" Leif asked.

"Eldarin is nearly as old as I am, Leif. She was stationed in Stanaedre when I went to avenge the king seventy years ago. I could not absorb her blood. Do not presume you are safe around the daughters of the queen. She has many children, but few survive to adulthood. Those who do possess strange and powerful abilities." He glanced over his shoulder toward Alyra. "It is a lot like what they did to you, Alyra."

The Moraskyn fee shivered, absently moving and patting the hilt of one of her crystal daggers. "Wing breaking, death defiance, these are not a science. It is sacrifice. Only the worthy are empowered, and the innocent die."

Havrshyk shook his head. "It shouldn't be forced on anyone..."

In another hour, the hawk broke through the barrier of trees, and out into the clear sky once more. The sun was beginning to set, and to the east long shadows clung to the skirts of the purple Stanaedre mountains.

"Norenan will be easy to spot at night," Havrshyk added, "their industry never stops because it is night, they just rotate shifts like the guard."

"Let us hope then, that the airships operate similarly." Savis wrapped a cloak around herself, more for comfort than concern for the cold since, like Fryn, she had an affinity for frost.

"Indeed," Havrshyk said, leaning forward to scratch the hawk's feathers near its ear.

Foothills of the Stanaedre Mountains

Outskirts of Norenan

Leif

Havrshyk brought the hawk into a circle in the air above the city. Norenan glowed in the night like the embers of a charcoal fire, nestled in the arms of the hills on the slopes of the southernmost reaches of the Stanaedre mountains, climbing from one ring to the next like a caterpillar. The hawk drifted in the black sky, far above where anyone could see them, shadowed as they were from the moons' light by a blanket of portentous clouds.

Wind buffeted them as they rode the turbulent currents rising off the river and rebounding off the mountains. Below, the scrubby trees swayed with a loud rustling of dry leaves, visible only as faintly shifting shadows cast across the land.

A flash of lightning lit the sky, and moments later, thunder rolled over them. The hawk's head snapped in the direction of the light and stalled in midflight. Frightened by the storm coming in from the south, it tucked its wings and dove toward the ground.

Leif held onto Fryn as his stomach threatened to jump out of his mouth, and his heart raced at their quick descent. Savis hid under her seat, and Havrshyk cheered, stretching out his wings to feel the wind as the hawk darted down toward the sparse trees, and found a squirrel's den to hide in.

It pounced inside and huddled against the far wall of the den, feathers fluffed and his voice croaking in irritation.

The hair on Leif's arms and head stood on end, then fell, as another flash of lightning and an immediate burst of thunder followed outside. "This makes it awfully difficult to get to the city, doesn't it?" he ventured cheerfully, giving Fryn's shoulder a light squeeze.

The princess, lit only by a passing flash of lightning gave him a distressed and confused look from under her bench, but said nothing.

Havrshyk dismounted, waving for Leif to toss bags over the side of the saddle as he whistled a light tune. They'd had to travel light, one canvas bag for each passenger, and a waxed sack of provisions which was now nearly empty.

"We'll need to make the approach on foot," Havrshyk announced, lining up the bags by the opening of the den. "Unfortunately, the ship Vinellin rode to Norenan crashed in a thunderstorm years ago, and he doesn't know another captain or airship to recommend, so we will have to ask around on our own. His only advice is not to board one of the Diad's ships. This leg of the journey will likely be the most tiresome, so I suggest we find an inn and start asking around in the morning."

"That's not unfortunate," Leif said, chewing on a piece of hare jerky. He tugged on the meat, and it snapped, as he worked at the bit in his mouth. "I had hoped to sample some of the famed Norenan wines and take Fryn on a tour before we fly off into exile."

Fryn sat down on a broken acorn shell and rested her elbows on her knees and chin in her hands as she closed her eyes. "No, Leif, we don't want word of our movements making it back to the Commission. We were lucky to lose them in the forest."

As he ate his jerky, Leif turned and leaned his back against the hollow wall of the tree, shifting so he could watch the princess and Alyra, who worked to unbuckle the saddle from the hawk and scratch his head. The fee from Moraskyr cooed at the bird, resting her forehead against its massive beak, and humming as she ruffled the feathers under its chin. Savis let the saddle slide off the hawk's back and promptly settled it on the ground and slid back onto one of the benches, reclining with her head nestled on her satchel.

It couldn't be comfortable for the princess, with a hardwood bench for a mattress, and a pointy crown for her pillow, yet she bore it with a patience he hadn't expected. Outside, the wind howled and whistled through the branches, and thunder rolled through the night sky.

Fryn shifted, shoulders slumping, and she rested her face in her hands. Frost settled around her, forming a sparkling membrane over her wings, face, and surroundings. She wore the shroud of frost like an aura of melancholy made visible, so Leif hefted his piece of jerky and walked over. He crouched in front of her and proffered it, wagging the piece of meat temptingly. "You need to eat something, Fryn," he whispered, "I can't imagine the blood of a few guards does anything except heal your wounds."

"I'm not hungry," she said, sighing and sitting up with her brow furrowed and her teeth clenched. "It's just this, all of this, I thought I was going somewhere, building a career, a life...discovering the world...meeting you...but the Commission just took everything I worked for, and turned it on its head."

"Fryn," Leif said, staring into her eyes.

"We were going to be a dynamic duo, Leif, like Trel and Yarrow! But they died!" she said, balling her hands into fists and looking away.

"We are," he said, noticing that Savis turned onto her side facing the back wall.

"I wanted to bring you back and *fix* my stupid family...but everyone keeps dying...everyone but me, Leif!"

Leif nodded, leaning in closer, taking a deep breath as he took the sandalwood box out of his jacket pocket. "I have something I've wanted to give to you, Fryn. We've known each other for only a short time, but I am not going anywhere. This is my promise to you." He opened the box and from it he removed a pair of earrings he had carved himself from the second viper's fang—the sibling of the one that was now fused with the bones in his arm. They were smooth teardrops of bone which dangled by two silver rings and a long hook. The narrow point that hung at the bottom had a faint violet coloring to it from the venom it had once contained.

Lightning flashed outside the opening of the tree, illuminating the earrings in his hand, and Fryn's eyes fixed on them in surprise.

"Leif..."

Thunder rolled in the seconds that followed the light, and in the darkness that followed, he felt her lips on his.

"Even in exile, Fryn, being with you means more than any of the other dreams I had," he said as she pulled back and put on the earrings.

She laughed and wiped away a stray bit of ice from her eyes. "Perhaps my new dream is better now than the ones the president took away." She looked hard at him and even in the darkness he could see a reflection of faint light off her frosted glacial blue eyes. "I know what this means in Aelaete," she said, standing and pulling him up so she could wrap her arms around him. "You have to wear these too."

The lightning flashed again, and it revealed a pair of earrings formed from her frozen blood in the exact same design as the ones he'd made for her minus the silver rings. They looked like crystalline fangs of blood.

He grinned.

His ears were not pierced, but that would not be an issue. Fryn reached up to one ear and stabbed it through the cartilage in the upper part of his ear. Its radiating chill numbed the pain within moments, and he didn't flinch as she set the other one and pulled back to review her work.

"The inns will be closing soon, Leif," Havrshyk complained.

"No, they won't," he replied, "all hours, remember?"

Aldyr huffed in annoyance, looking back out toward the mountains from the lip of the den.

Fryn wrapped her arms around Leif and hugged him close as she whispered, "I think I see now why this is your tradition," she said, looking up at him which caused the silver to clink. "Rings on your fingers are a liability when fighting or working with your hands."

He chuckled. "That's not it at all, Fryn, the tradition predates wearing rings. It symbolizes that I will listen rather than speak, wait before acting, and consider before I make assumptions. It is about trust... though I suppose it is similar to rings in that it makes it very easy for others to recognize that you are not available."

"That's not everything, is it?" she asked softly, turning away.

He suppressed an awkward smile. "In Aelaete we have two weddings. The first involves only the couple, and the second involves their celebration for the clan...giving and bonding the earrings is not simply a betrothal in Aelaete, Fryn."

"I thought so," Fryn said, settling deeper into the embrace, "but I am going to ask we do our second wedding in Frorin when we return."

He nodded, and said, "I predicted you would."

Fryn stepped away, grinning in the next flash of lightning. "I love you, Leif, but you need to know, I'm not from Aelaete. I'm not ready to call you my husband until there's been a ceremony."

"I understand. I wanted *you* to understand that my commitment now is as binding, and devoted, as if the ceremony had already happened." He gave her hand a light squeeze. "I also understand that this is really fast, so I am not assuming anything beyond this truth: where you go, I will follow, and when we return, we will make it official."

Havrshyk groaned behind them, but his groan turned into an alarmed yelp as he stepped away from the mouth of the hollowed-out knot in the tree.

Alyra, who had been quiet at the back, comforting the hawk, called out. "Something's wrong! Look out!"

Leif looked up toward the entrance of the den, but he couldn't see anything besides the shadow of a faerie against the dim light of the stormy sky beyond the tree. It seemed darker than even the darkest corners of their enclosed space, like a fae-shaped void in the night.

Immediately he drew on the heightened potential in the stormy skies and pointed his finger at the shadow. Lightning leapt from his fingertip, arced through the air, and scattered against an invisible barrier around the fae. The white-blue sparks caught on the dried tinder of an abandoned nest, and on either side of the intruder yellow flames licked at the edges of the den.

The flickering light revealed the gloating face of the Moraskyn agent, Pashen, very much alive.

Leif growled.

"Bare your fangs, Viper," Pashen sneered, "I have fought many such wingbreakers as you!"

Fryn pulled out of Leif's arms, and in one smooth motion both she and Havrshyk leveled black blades toward the intruder. Leif pulled inward, tugging on the power of the storm, building a more powerful charge.

If he gathered enough sparks, it might be enough to burn through the light-bending power the Moraskyn fae wielded. Footsteps scraped on stone, and out of the corner of his eye, Leif saw Alyra racing towards them with her crystal daggers drawn. Her eyes were narrowed, and her teeth clenched, as she gave a wingburst and slid across the ground toward him.

He nearly panicked as she darted under his low stance, pulling in her arms and legs so that she shot between his legs and then righted into a sprint toward her foe. Somehow in the flickering light, Leif felt an intense pressure coming off of Alyra, and deep down he knew.

Savis was their priority.

He shared a look with Fryn, and they ran back to the saddle. As Havrshyk and Alyra danced around the Moraskyn fae, with those black spheres of disintegrating powers flying about, nearly invisible in the night, they found the Princess curled up in a fetal position with tears streaming down out of her eyes and down the side of her face.

Savis clutched at the satchel which held the crown, and held her eyes closed as hard as she could.

"Fryn?" Leif asked, hoping she understood.

Fryn pulled the princess to her feet and Leif swept her into his arms. He flew toward the exit, sending a farewell glance toward the anxious hawk as he approached the opening to the stormy sky.

Wind whistled through various holes in the tree, created by the strange powers of the Moraskyn agent, and Fryn carefully deflected one of the orbs that had been sent on an intercepting course with him and the Princess.

Somehow, the agent held off the attacks of both the Lichblade and the wingbreaker, Alyra, who danced around attacks as if fully knowing where they would be directed.

He didn't wait.

Ducking under a heavy blade, if indeed that sweeping void could be called such, he flew out into the night. Behind him, Fryn cursed and spiraled after. The old tree creaked under the strain of the stormy winds, and the various weaknesses created by the fire, and the consuming orbs. The hawk cried, and flew out after them, vanishing into the dark. Leif hoped it would find its way back home.

Savis buried her face in his tan scarf, so he whispered through the wind, "You can't see it now, Princess, but we are so close to the city. I am drifting, a little awkwardly I suppose, but we are gliding all the way down to the main gates."

Lightning flashed at his words, but it was far to the east now, and the thunder that rolled over them was subdued, delayed by a good fifteen seconds. His new wings, still not used to the effort of flying, wavered when he was only a span above the road, so he fell the last bit and scrabbled to a rough landing before the gates of Norenan.

From above, the city had glowed like the embers of an old fire. On the ground, it rose like sheer cliffs ringed with bright lanterns. The gates, massive wooden doors that towered all the way to the height of the thirty span stone walls, were shut fast and unmanned at road level.

Fryn settled easily beside him and stalked up to the gates. She shouted something towards the gatehouse up on the northern side of the wall, but thunder drowned out her voice.

Leif carried Savis, whose now gentle, regular breathing told him she had likely fainted during the descent, and walked up to the small faerie-sized sally-port cut into the main gates. It was banded in black steel and had a large ring-shaped knocker. He inclined his head to the door, so Fryn gave the ring several heartfelt knocks.

When no answer came after a few seconds, she rang the knocker a good five more times, until a voice shouted from the other side.

"Why all the fuss? I'm coming, just settle down now," a gruff fae's voice declared. A tiny door at eye level opened and a graying, bearded fae glowered at them. "What's the meaning of this, so late at night, and during a storm?" His eyes scanned Fryn, then Leif, and then Savis in his arms.

"We are seeking shelter," Leif answered, "our companion here is not well, and needs water and rest."

The fae fingered his beard as he adjusted a heavy metal cap on his dark curly hair and burped. His yellow wings twitched awkwardly. "Pardon, the…" he hiccupped "rudeness of my tone, my good travelers. Uh… what business…" His eyes drifted over their disheveled forms, and then flicked in the direction of a distant flash of lightning. He thought better than to finish his question, and after some fumbling with the locks, he pulled the small door open. "Please come in. Welcome to Norenan, travelers."

Fryn pulled up her hood as she entered, and thoughtfully did the same for Leif, helping tug his hood up and over onto his head. "Thank you, sir, but we are tired, and our bird did not fare well in the storm. We barely survived the lightning. Where might we find an inn, a quiet one that is not too busy, where our companion can rest without too much commotion," Fryn asked, dusting her shoulders off.

He hiccupped again. "Pardon, miss," he excused himself, "but most inns in Norenan are going to be very lively places, especially tonight."

Leif shifted Savis in his arms, which were getting *really* tired of bearing the extra weight. "Is there an inn that specializes in sleep, rather than ale?"

The guard laughed. As he did, the metal buckles of his hauberk rattled over his large belly. He tugged on the cuffs of his massive gloves and was about to answer the question before diving right back into another fit of laughter. The smell of wine was strong on his breath.

Leif ground his teeth.

Over his shoulder, he could hear the creaking and the crash of the top of a tree falling in the night.

The guard wiped tears from his eyes. "You northerners are all alike, sleep, and quiet… this is not Estenna, friends. This is the city that never rests. I assure you, each inn has rooms on levels where the drinking is done for the night and the crews sleep at their tables. Go try the Gallstone, just down the road north from the square." With that advice, the guard shook his head, muttered under his breath, and returned to his guard post—a tiny room with a chair that was far too small for him, with a large green bottle of *something* on the desk before it.

Leif sighed but followed Fryn up the hill toward the square he'd indicated. It appeared that Norenan was a city of extremes. The walls and gates had been equally impressive, and on the other side of those, not one of the buildings was shorter than three stories. In fact, there was not a bit of space between buildings either. Where other cities had alleys, this one had tunnels either built or carved between sections, so that the buildings formed contiguous sections of buildings that were all interconnected.

He nodded toward Fryn, and she helped transfer the princess so that he could carry her on his back, and they trekked up the slope toward the first square.

"I got a good look at the city as we descended," Fryn said, a few steps ahead of him, "it is arrayed as a sequence of circles, almost like beads on a necklace."

"A necklace?"

She shrugged with her wings, not turning around as they climbed up the hill. Over her shoulder she added, "each circle looks to climb the slope of the mountain a little higher than the last."

The street climbed a steep slope, and on the right-hand side of the road ran a long set of iron tracks. As they ascended to the first square, they stepped out of the claustrophobic street into a courtyard ringed by towering buildings, with a series of permanent market stalls occupying the center. Yellow and gray bunting was strung up between the rooftops, so that the sky above the square was crisscrossed with a tapestry of banners and dangling starlamps. The space glowed nearly as bright as the day, and under the banners they could barely make out the sound of the storm.

Fryn gave a low whistle and shaded her eyes against the glare of the glowing lamps, scanning the stalls. Conversation bubbled everywhere; merchants bartered, workers laughed over ale at one of the outdoor dining carts, and children ran practically underfoot… or sometimes overhead on their wings.

A ball bounced off Leif's forehead and fell flatly on the pavement before him, sewn in a pattern of green, red, and yellow triangles, and felt like it was stuffed with seeds.

Before he even knew what to make of it, a flying child scooped it up and threw it at one of the children hiding behind the posts of a market stall.

Leif took a step to the side, narrowly avoiding getting barreled into by another child, as he raised an eyebrow to Fryn. "I thought we could find an inn to wait for the others but… we might be in more danger here than out there!"

She gave him a small smile, resuming her search with one hand shading her eyes, and the other resting on her hip. "There! I see an inn!" Fryn pointed to the right, toward the edge of the square where a large square arch formed an entry to a smaller courtyard, and an ornate iron banded sign ironically proclaimed the presence of the 'Silversmith's Inn'; an irony that seemed more than a little appropriate to him.

"It can't be worse than the 'Gallstone'," Leif commented.

They shied away from the chaos of the First Square and ducked under the arch. The private courtyard was occupied by a scattering of small tables, and was lined with planters of climbing moss, which ascended the walls all the way to the level of the awnings above. Thunder rolled dully through the air, and they followed the path from the archway straight toward the entrance of the inn at the end, ignoring the looks of the patrons of the inn who sat at the tables in hushed conversations.

The faeries of Norenan wore more varied colors than Leif had ever seen… and he was born in the Aelaete which was known for its cultural use of bright dyes and paints. At one table he saw a fee barely into adulthood, with her short hair dyed three colors! It was not even broken into sections, but faded from one to the next, at her roots her hair was dyed a vibrant red, and shifted into violet, then florescent green at the tips. Her clothing was also styled in the same way, only her sleeveless tunic looked like it had been dipped into a random spray of the same three colors. The other patrons had similarly eclectic styles—but Fryn tugged on his arm and led him through the doors into the inn.

"Yes, yes, welcome to the Silversmith's Inn, no, I do not make jewelry anymore, and no, I *will not* pierce your navel…" came the well-practiced greeting from the proprietress as the doors swung shut behind them. "Oh…I don't make coffins either," she added with a frown, looking at the princess and pursing her purple-painted lips.

Leif was grateful that Fryn took over. She stepped in front of him and smiled tiredly at their potential hostess.

"She is not dead, just tired after a long evening," she explained, jabbing a thumb over her shoulder toward a rowdy tavern area Leif hadn't even noticed before. A wave of laughter seemed to come just as she gestured.

"Need to sleep one off, eh?" the proprietress asked, crossing her arms over a plain brown linen apron, and fixing Leif with an angry glare of her dark green eyes. "I also don't appreciate any shady business…"

As Leif and Fryn shared a confused look, the proprietress laughed.

"That's why I got out of smithing! The name's Merill. Now come along upstairs and we'll get her a room." She shook her head, and lifted the folding counter that separated her entry booth from the foyer. "The stairs are this way, travelers," she added, flying into a doorway just around the corner.

She guided them up three flights of the spiraling stairs, and then down the hall to one of the last rooms. "It's always a party on a stormy night in Norenan," she explained, "for those fools who believe the stars are watchin', it's the perfect time to let loose a little underneath the blanket of clouds."

"Yes, ah…um," Leif replied, as she put a brass key into the lock and swung the door to the room open, "How much for the room?"

The Silversmith, Merill, made a fist and pretended to conk herself on the side of the head with it, "Oh yes! See, I'm one of those sillies who lets loose a little in a storm, right? I forgot. We'll settle up in the morning—not before noon, got it?"

He swallowed and nodded.

"Good. I'm going to need to sleep after a busy day like this too, now get in there so I can go back downstairs." She started back down the hall, and Leif found his mouth working but no words coming out.

"We have some friends," Fryn shouted, "A fee with curly black hair and white wings, and a fae with short black hair and an evil aura might come by. Please send them up."

"Evil aura, black hair… you got it, missy!"

She was gone a moment later, and Leif was more than ready for the quiet that descended on the hall and pervaded the room he entered. Inside, he found a long couch in front of a fireplace, with an artificer's false fire already glowing, and a separate bedroom off to one side.

He nudged the door to the bedroom open and set the princess down on top of the green and crimson quilt. Fryn put her hand on his shoulder and nodded her head toward the door, so he retreated to wait on the couch.

He sat there and scratched his head looking around at the room. It was as chaotically decorated as he might have expected after the sight in the square, with a mixture of poorly done paintings of flowers, a bland knitted wall hanging that clashed with the colors of the room, and of course, the yellow upholstered couch itself. The false fire didn't even give off heat, just light that varied in a soft reddish orange glow.

He waited a few minutes before Fryn closed the door to the bedroom and settled onto the couch beside him. She released a long sigh and snuggled in closer, intertwining her arms with his.

"How is she doing?" he asked gently, finding her hand and interlacing fingers.

Fryn let out a slightly smaller sigh before answering. "She is still afraid, but the quiet and the comfort of being in a bed helps."

"How are you doing?" he asked, giving her hand a light squeeze.

She laughed. "Besides stressed, you mean?"

He met her eyes.

She looked down and nestled her head against his shoulder. "I'm very, very tired."

"Me too…" he replied, too anxious to let his muscles relax.

"You better believe that Havrshyk is going to kill that Moraskyn fae, Leif," Fryn said, "he's got too much bitterness to go and die now."

He laughed softly. "I spent a long time tied to that fae, Fryn, and I think he'd surprise you… he's done a lot of thinking and maturing lately."

She stiffened. "He tried to kill you, Leif!"

"He's failed at that a few times before," he replied, yawning, "but I have a feeling it was the last time he'd try. You let me sort that out and give him a chance."

She muttered something under her breath, but his eyes were already sliding closed. He rested his head against the top of hers, and within a few moments, fell asleep.

Outskirts of Norenan

Aldyr

A flash of lightning shattered the remnants of the treetop's crown as Leif and Fryn escaped. While the crumbling remains of the oak tree fell through the air in slow motion, flames licked at the edges of the hollow that was once the nest of a squirrel. Black sky peered through the splintered remnants of the tree above, and before him, Aldyr held out his sword, panting, and his eyes shifted, never quite settling on the void like figure in the night.

He was surprised to find himself panting, since he did not often exert himself this much while in Lichform.

"Pashen, was it?" he asked, sidestepping to put the fire at his back, flaring his wings and willing a layer of frost to coalesce around his form.

The Moraskyn agent stepped closer to the light, but it slid around his body like water around an oiled blade. His face was invisible, and his voice resonant, as he replied darkly, "Your attempt to buy more time is as effectual as a single spark in the winds,

Lichblade. You are not the first so-called immortal to fall by my hand."

Havrshyk made eye-contact with Alyra and flicked his lower wings. He only hoped she could read the thoughts he tried to push in her direction. She seemed at least to read the *emotion* behind his gesture, and moved across from him, so that the Moraskyn stood between them.

Through the shadow of his form, Havrshyk could see Pashen raise a hand and summon one of his spheres of power, and flick his fingers, launching it directly toward his face. Aldyr ducked, reaching up with a frost covered hand to try to deflect the sphere. It grazed across the ice on his fingers, disintegrating it in an instant, just a knife's edge away from his flesh.

Best try something else… he considered as he tumbled into a roll and rose to the balls of his feet. Of course…there was already a second orb on a direct course to meet his face.

He kept tumbling. He rolled over his shoulder, beat his wings, and leapt into the air so that he landed feet first against the inner wall above the flames. The dried grass, bark, and leaves gathered into the burrow blazed with heat, getting hotter and hotter as the wind fed its fury through the cracks and holes caused by their fight. In one bound he was off the wall, encased in ice, barreling through the fire directly toward his attacker.

The Swordhand-Palm specialized in linear attacks, especially up close, but one of his greatest strengths, and innovations on the style, was to develop techniques for closing the distance between himself and his opponent. From his weeks of observing Leif and Fryn's fighting, (not their embarrassing romance), he was gratified to see that his techniques had been preserved in the new, sterilized Soft-Point Fist.

A sword would always be better than a spear or lance—if only the new king understood that—because the blade ran the entire length of the haft and sacrificed only slightly its reach.

With a yell, Havrshyk split the flames, spinning in the air between two of the dark spheres, and hit the ground in a wing-powered sprint, leaned into a lunge, and cast forward with the point of his Bloodsword.

The tip scratched off an impossibly hard scale-like armor, as black as the orbs he threw. It was angled slightly, seemingly formed of overlapping scales of condensed *something* invisible because of its all-consuming darkness, but it caught on the edge of the next scale and he drove the point into Pashen's shoulder.

He felt the blood rushing into the blade, and heard with relief a startled, disbelieving scream from the Moraskyn fae, as he began to absorb his life.

"Havrshyk! Back away!" Alyra warned, with a voice that crashed through the euphoria that came with the influx of fresh blood in his veins.

He furrowed his eyebrows and shifted his focus to the tugging sensation that came from *within* the fae. All that blood began flowing back! Havrshyk's blood rushed forward to fill the void, nearly into the wound itself!

Aldyr instinctively froze the puncture wound and fell away in a backwards roll, panting not just from exertion, but from a deep concern.

Pashen laughed. "A-ha-ha-ha-hah! You are just like all the other bloodcrafters I have fought, Lich! Once your sink your fangs you foolishly believe I am at your mercy! Hah!" The darkness bled into color slightly, and for the first time during their encounter, Aldyr saw his face. His narrow jaw, pursed lips, and confident eyes. "I will praise you for surviving that time."

"Praise *this*!" Alyra shouted, spinning into range behind his back with her crystal daggers flashing. One slash caught him on the back, casting a shower of black shards into the air, and the other missed.

He ducked the second blow, chiding her with a clicking of his tongue. "You foolish child… the very light and darkness tells me where you are." He was about to continue talking, but he had to duck another slash. "Now stop it!" he shouted, stepping under her guard and reaching out with a black sphere forming under his fingers.

Aldyr realized, belatedly, as the color leeched back into Pashen's body, that he was *wingless*. How could he be using his powers to this extent?

Ignoring the concept for the moment, he thrust his Bloodsword into Pashen's unprotected back, and resisted the urge to drain him.

Pashen grunted in pain, and the black orb puffed away in his hand against Alyra's chest without effect.

"You berate and instruct the young," Havrshyk commented, rising with an ice-encrusted chop at the Moraskyn fae's shoulder, "but you are *young to me,* Grandpa!" He followed through with a powerful kick that sent Pashen over the lip of the den.

Alyra stared at him, and then glanced at her chest, and released a pent-up breath. "You saved me!" she said, bewildered.

"I've got a lot of experience avoiding and preventing death my lady," he said sarcastically. "Now, let that wingless rock fall to the ground and we, fly off to Norenan."

Thunder rolled, and lightning flashed again, this time simultaneously, as a bolt struck the roots of the tree. It vibrated underfoot, shuddering, and listing to one side. Alyra stumbled, catching herself on his arm, and meeting his eyes with a worried look. "He didn't fall."

She spun in the air with her eyes closed, deflecting two dark orbs into the sky with a flash of her wingshard blades.

Once again, the dark shadowy form clawed its way up over the edge and faced them in the firelight. Pashen's face was still visible, black armor fading to a translucent violet color, and blood dripped from a scratch above his eye and from the corner of his mouth.

"Ooh, I am not going to leave the two of you. Lich, I may have been satisfied with only her life at first, but *you have earned my wrath.*"

Havrshyk shivered, sword held out warding.

In ninety years, he had faced warriors, assassins, even other bloodcrafters… yet somehow the hair on his arms stood on end, and his wings flushed a deep purple color.

Alyra edged closer, put one hand on his, and whispered, "Do not be intimidated."

"I'm… I'm not afraid," he said, doubting his own words.

Pashen held both hands above his head, fingers straining in the air as he summoned a massive orb of dark power that swirled, drawing in tongues of flame and gusts of wind, growing, and growing to the same width as the tree itself!

Havrshyk shrugged away from Alyra and wingbursted forward. He could not redirect that disintegrating power, but… but conventional injuries could do it for him. He roared in midflight and cut Pashen across his chest in an angled slash from one shoulder to the opposite hip. Dark shards and a spray of blood flew into the air and were sucked into the vortex.

Pashen's focus was not swayed in the slightest.

"Aldyr! Catch!" Alyra shouted, and as he looked towards her, he saw her two daggers flying through the air directly at him.

He grimaced, stabbed his sword into Pashen's back, caught the crystal daggers, and stabbed those directly into his spine.

No scream of pain came as the black sphere dissipated, and Pashen fell to his knees, twitching.

"Hah!" Havrshyk laughed, kicking the body onto his stomach. He looked up to Alyra, but she also slumped onto her knees, holding her head in her hands, groaning, and muttering under her breath. Aldyr swallowed, and walked towards her, giving the body one last kick for good measure. "Hey, what's wrong?"

She gasped. "He's struggling to fight his death. I am walling him in, but he is fighting to come back!"

"I'll just stab him again." Havrshyk turned back to the body, and as his fingers brushed the handle of her dagger, he got a flash of something, a view of his internal spirit world. A land of varied, pungent flowers.

"Stabbing him won't kill his soul," she replied.

Havrshyk grinned.

"Fortunately, I know how to do just that." He pulled his sword out of Pashen's kidneys and stabbed him through the heart—only instead of draining him of all his blood, he poured in his own, and invaded Pashen's mind.

Just like when he invaded Leif, he found himself immediately standing in a foreign land. Unlike Leif, this was no barren desert with a lonely dais of stone, but was a vibrant jungle filled with bird calls, wind through vines, and the humid pungent scent of heady flowers.

Yellow, purple, and orange flowers dangled like grapes from vines that climbed around the roots of massive trees above a warm sea, and he stood not on stone, but on an earthen outlook staring out towards a setting sun.

The Pashen who stood at the farthest end of the root above water was not dark, or even old. He looked tired, and weathered, but closer to his thirties than fifties. His wings were broken off at the joints, and the crystal pillar that Havrshyk had come to accept was a part of each soul, was cracked with what looked like years of abuse.

The Moraskyn fae turned and met his eyes.

"I'm not going to let you evade death this time," Havrshyk said, walking down the length of the lichen covered root.

The fae merely spread out his arms to the sea. "You may not have to Lich… it appears my elemental affinity is not suited to either blood or bone crafting."

Aldyr knew better than to trust that statement. He examined his surroundings. "I'll be here to ensure that is true."

Then, he felt the tugging, and had a horrible premonition. Could he, could Pashen be trying to steal *his* body?

The waves rose and crashed against the base of the tree, tossing Havrshyk into the air. Fortunately, he was no stranger to these kinds of battles, and he drew even more on the blood from his sword, so that his dark black currents blotted out the sun and roiled in the sky. Rather than hail, he drew down black spears of ice from clouds to seas, freezing everything.

The blood spears dissolved before the black void spheres in Pashen's hands, and he charged at Havrshyk with a desperate fury.

The pointed ends of white-gold daggers dipped through the clouds of blood, and Alyra's voice broke through. "His power wanes, do not let him invade your soul."

"Easy," he replied, tugging on a current of blood from above and dragging it down to sweep Pashen off the root into the sea. "Try swimming now!"

As Pashen swam towards a shallow clump of smaller roots to climb out, Havrshyk scratched his head. "Why can I hear you?"

"Focus."

He shrugged, and rather than facing his foe head on, ran down the length of the massive root toward the crystal pillar that he considered the link between one's soul and body. Havrshyk raised an ice-encrusted fist and punched the pillar, grunting as his blow rebounded uselessly.

Pashen slunk up behind him. "You cannot kill me, Lich… this is hardly my first body."

"Well, it will be your last," Havrshyk replied, raising a hand, and summoning his Bloodsword fully into the realm. It formed in his hand from tendrils of blood out of the darkening sky, and frost clung to the blade and on his skin.

Before Pashen could say anything else, he swung, slicing the pillar of crystal in half—a half second later, both the upper and lower section fragmented and scattered into wind as an impossible number of glittering shards.

The jungle shuddered, and the water began to rise.

"Fool!" Pashen growled, searching for the way out, frowning as he began to realize.

"Yep." Aldyr crossed his arms and let the water rise to his hips. "This sword is stuck in this dying body, and I am already holding it. My physical form is quite separated. I'm afraid you are going to evaporate here soon."

The Moraskyn fae screamed; the weather churned in a panicked rage, or something else, and he rushed Aldyr in the water. It rose about them, up and up from waist to neck, and neck to sky, and Aldyr let himself sink deeper and deeper into the dark.

Pashen swam, struggling to keep his head up, but eventually, his limbs weakened, and the shadow of his form in the waters above wavered, and vanished like mist in the sun.

"Still in there, Aldyr?" Alyra's voice asked, reverberating oddly through the water.

He nearly tried to talk, but realized he couldn't.

"Not to worry, I can understand what you want to convey."

In that case, he thought very clearly about taking the sword out of Pashen's body and—not ruining his new jacket—stabbing his real body with the Bloodsword again.

The process took mere moments.

One second, he was beneath a dark sea as warm as blood, and the next, he was staring up into Alyra's concerned face, with his head on her knees, and firelight glowing behind her dark curly hair. He swallowed, suppressing a blush...

She smiled. "I will pretend I never saw that vulnerable side of the dangerous Lichblade."

Aldyr let out a sigh and sat up, glaring at the body of the Moraskyn agent with a sense of finality. "I can't imagine what you mean."

She laughed, sounding free, relaxed, and at ease. It reverberated in his ears reminding him of someone long ago, whose warmth and presence had brought him so much joy and consternation. That brought another shiver.

"Let's go find the others," she suggested, offering him a hand up to his feet.

He accepted it and then slid his sword back into its sheath, watching her with unease as she drew her daggers from Pashen's back and cleaned them on his jacket. As she did so, she found a pouch at his belt, and nodded silently to herself.

She pocketed the pouch and slid her daggers into her own sheaths and met his eyes.

"Yes, let's do that," he agreed, walking over to the lip of what had once been a towering tree with a warm burrow… but was now a decapitated, splintered, on-fire wreck. "I'd rather leave before we burn with him."

Alyra laughed cheerlessly and kicked his body closer to the flames. "I am just relieved that both his body, and soul, are finally dead." With that, she jumped into the air, and after taking a moment to retrieve their bags, Havrshyk followed after her.

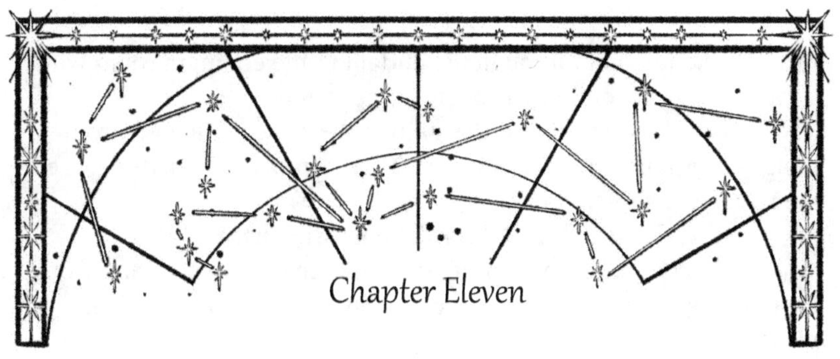

Chapter Eleven

LOST

Norenan, First Circle:

Common Room of the Silversmith's Inn

Savis

Steam hovered in the air of the common room, blasted out of brass pipes in the walls that served, among other arcane purposes, to keep the building at an intolerable temperature. Savis sniffed, blew her nose in her handkerchief, and rested her chin in her hand, and her elbow on the table, as she sighed deeply and examined her surroundings.

Leif sat across from her, playing with a fork in one hand, twirling it around his thumb much as she had seen some secretaries do with their pens. Fryn leaned against his shoulder, eyes closed, looking thoroughly exhausted, and with her hair frizzy and untamed because of the steam.

All around them, leaning over tables, draped over the ends of stools and chairs, even strewn across the floor, a myriad of garishly clothed, dyed, and tattooed faeries slumbered off the alcohol from the previous night.

The Silversmith, Merill, yawned loudly from the kitchens, and then cursed as she stumbled over something and caused a clatter of pots and pans.

"*Jakaren's bloody stumps*, Teem! Why'd you gotta sleep on the kitchen floor?" she shouted angrily, but she didn't get a response.

Instead, she idled out through the curtain to the common room with a tray bearing several bowls of steaming… mush.

Savis swallowed back the saliva she'd accumulated from a hungry morning, and immediately felt a clammy chill settling over the table. She shivered.

"*Egads*, Frorin!" Merill hissed, "put away that chill!"

Sure enough, a layer of frost was expanding outward from Fryn's limp form, and soon the fog in the air condensed into a pleasant coolness.

"It's Fryn," the hunter replied, opening her eyes, and shooing the proprietress away with one hand, once Leif had swiped the tray of food and set it on the table. "If you're cold, Norenan, there's probably a fire in the kitchen."

Merill scratched her head and shrugged with her wings. "All the same to me, miss," she burped and pinched her forehead between two fingers. "I need to down a bit more water and call it a night." She stumbled over a snoring patron on the ground and slipped back into the kitchen.

With a sigh of relief, the princess raised an eyebrow toward Fryn and accepted a steaming bowl of the unnamed food. Like everything she had seen in Norenan, the clay bowl was emblazoned with a swirl of varied and conflicting colors. Bright opalescent white swam in a spiral of violet, radiant pink, and pale green. Though each bowl was different, the careless swirl pattern seemed to tie them into a set as matching as two napkins dropped into the same puddle of soup.

She leaned over her bowl of mush, sniffed it, and surprisingly smelled… nothing. It was simply a bland, unadorned, and unflavored wheat goop.

"It's not great," Leif mused, frowning, as he stirred his brass spoon in the sludge. He chewed and stared off toward the arch that led to the entryway and stairs. "You think Alyra and Havrshyk are coming down soon?

Fryn nodded, but didn't reply, grimacing as she swallowed purposefully.

Savis took a small bite herself, and chewed the mixture, first on one side of her mouth and then the other. She chuckled and gave Leif and Fryn a look. "This is hardly as horrible as you two made out. It's just a hot cereal, really, this is quite a common dish."

"Without honey, or salt?" Fryn asked.

"Yes, even without honey or salt," Savis replied, "and I even imagine that this sort of gentle food is the best sort of meal after a night of extremes such as these faeries indulged in."

Leif's nose crinkled in disdain as he lifted another spoonful in front of his face. "Honey's gentle," he complained.

"Expensive, too," Merill commented, reentering the room with a copper pitcher of cool water, coated in sparkling beads of condensation. "The cereal comes with the room, but honey is an extra mint each."

Leif and Fryn had a coin flipping into the air even before she finished the last word, but Savis shook her head.

The proprietress with the multicolored hair and tattoos running down her arms swiped the coins out of the air and tucked them into a hidden pocket of her brown apron. "Very good, hunters, I'll return with a ladle each."

Savis' mouth hung open, how had she known they were hunters? Merill had already vanished, and when she returned, she set down a tiny ramekin of honey before each of them. Her varied colors were not limited to her choice of green shirt, brown apron, yellow belt, and hair; even the tattoos on her arms ran around her forearms in the seven-colored array of the rainbow.

"How is one mint expensive?" Savis asked, hoping that question didn't betray her wealthy heritage.

Merill laughed, slapping her on the back. "How? It's expensive when you have it every day! Think about it, at the end of one year, if you spent an additional mint per breakfast that would be an additional 400 mint spent just on breakfast!" She jabbed a thumb at Leif and Fryn, "'Course that means nothing to bounty hunters, they just kill someone, steal their mint, and collect the money on their head."

"*Former* bounty hunters," Leif corrected, "and how did you figure that anyway?"

Merill, looking a bit more awake and refreshed in the cooler air around Fryn, took a breath, pointed toward the wall beside them, and laughed. "There's job postings, bounty marks, and even news clippings right here, and roughly half of them are about killing you two!"

Fryn examined her food with a critical eye.

"But you're not going to harm us," Savis guessed.

"*Psh*!" Merill shook her head and pulled up a stool, nudging a sleeping patron with her foot so he'd roll over and make room for her to sit. "Norenan's *not* a part of Stanaedre. We don't care a wind or a wingshard about the Commission, or whatever they've become. You're free spirits, entrepreneurs! We like faeries like you. Welcome to Norenan!"

"Entrepreneurs?" Savis asked.

"Sure, whatever," Merill insisted. "Now here's my question, what business brings two renegade hunters, and a fee who looks like royalty to my humble establishment in the First Circle after a storm?"

Leif shifted uncomfortably in his seat but didn't answer. Instead, a voice from the archway announced the arrival of Havrshyk. He answered her question in a chill, soft tone that seemed to cut through the steam. Savis shivered as he entered.

"The kind of business that involves the death of kings," he replied, stalking in with a wave of frost that shoved back the steam even more powerfully than Fryn's microcosm of autumn. He met them at the table and, seeing no chair or stool, he eyed the floor and a pillar of ice rose from the ground to the correct height. He settled upon it, resting his elbows on the table and locking eyes with the proprietress. "No need for honey, or heating my food, Merill."

Her eyes widened and shifted to the hilt of his Bloodsword. "Stars above… it's all true…" She shook herself and stood. "I'll be right back."

She scrambled away, knocking over her stool in her retreat to the kitchen.

"That was unkind, Aldyr," Alyra said, flitting in and taking the recently vacated stool. "I can feel her fear even from here."

He grunted.

True to her word, Merill returned quickly with a bowl for Havrshyk, and noticing Alyra, she flew back to the kitchens for another one. Once deposited, they ate in relative silence, everyone seeming to hold their breaths, waiting for something.

Finally, squirming in his seat, Leif asked, "Where do we go now?"

"Before that," Savis replied, "I want to know Havrshyk. Are we safe?"

"Safe?" he snorted. "We're not going to be safe till the Commission is dismantled… but in the short term? Yes, we killed him."

"That's convenient," Fryn commented, gesturing toward Havrshyk with her spoon, "you killed the Moraskyn, and he killed Grifton, I think that means we're in the clear unless the Grass Guard come after us here."

Savis bit her lip, setting her spoon back into her empty bowl. She had dreamt all through the night, tossing and turning in her quilts, running downstairs and corridors with shouts, daggers, and screams chasing her till she had awoken early in the morning drenched in sweat clutching the harvest crown in a tight grip.

They ate, paid Merill her fee, a surprisingly low 10 mint each for lodgings and food, and exited into the courtyard into the bright morning sunlight.

Aside from a gentle breeze, the cloudless sky foretold a pleasant day for the end of Harvest, and the complete lack of faeries out and about left the city with a feeling of quiet unease. Or was that a hangover?

Leif carried Savis' bag in addition to his own, and took up the rear of the group, walking with Fryn. Havrshyk strode ahead, out into the main market circle, and Alyra stayed with Savis, leaning in closer to whisper.

"I asked around, Princess," she said, scanning the empty market stalls, closed off only by curtains, "The eighth circle is said to be the location of the ironworks and airship docks."

"Are there any ships going to Elin?" Savis asked, taking a slow breath, and holding up the hem of her dress as she quickened her pace to keep up with the impatient Lich.

Alyra radiated irritation, glaring at Havrshyk for a moment before she returned her attention to the conversation and muttered "We'll see if he senses *that*." She gave a self-deprecating smile and answered, "Despite the fact that airships have been a groundbreaking invention for decades, there is little organization here at the docks. Captains own their ships and they come and go freely on the winds pursuing whatever aims they wish. There's no registry showing where they are going."

Havrshyk actually slowed, wings shifting through several shades of purple before returning to their iridescent blue. He coughed into a fist and continued at a more leisurely pace.

Savis covered a laugh and felt some of the tension from the previous night begin to sublimate under the calming light of the sun. The city slept off its night away from the storm, but out here on the empty streets, in the gentle caress of the wind, she breathed out a relieved sigh.

Further up, she heard the cooing of pigeons in their various aviaries and allowed a smile to break free of her worries. They walked up the road, which snaked between the circular districts of the city like beads on a necklace draped over the cascading folds of a dress, from the foothills to the slopes of the mountains.

The path from the base of the city ran straight through the first circular district, and then up a long rampart to a second circle rounded by a wall as tall as any in Frorin. Even as they passed under the worked stone arches, there were no guards between districts, no checkpoints, just the silence of the "city that never sleeps" finally catching up on its lost hours of rest.

The Second Circle was arranged just like the first, if slightly larger across because of the wider shelf it occupied on the hillside, and its towering buildings, all interconnected, made it appear as if one section was really one segment of a tower that had been sliced into so many circles and tossed against the hill.

Climbing the road to the eighth circle took about an hour, and as they stepped up through the archway from the rampart to the highest level of the city, Savis put a hand to her lips and gasped.

Unlike all the previous circles, this uppermost section was spacious, open to the sky, and comprised of a ring wall around the border of the Circle and a series of towers spaced evenly throughout. On either side of the archway, offices and warehouses were built along the wall, which had one tower that presided over all the others by nearly a hundred spans! That tower rose from the craggy shoulder of the mountain beside the Skydocks, and a brilliant starlamp shone from its pinnacle.

In the center, twelve shorter towers, built of iron and stone with steps, and pulley-operated lifts, stood ready for airships to dock. Five of these were in use, with long oblong airships ranging from wood and canvas contraptions to ornate ships fashioned out of a silvery metal with something of a charcoal cast.

One of the more rustic crafts was already lifting into the air and angling toward the north. This one appeared to be more hot-air balloon than airship, and it disappeared over the wall and shrank into the sky far more quickly than she expected.

Unlike the lower levels, the Skydocks were a bustle of activity; faeries flew and ran, loading and unloading airships, talking with warehouse staff, and shouting down from the decks of their ships.

Of these, the nearest one bristled with ballistae, and its occupants all wore the same cream-colored uniform with gold trimming and embroidery. These had only two massive wings, rather than the four of the native Fhoran faeries, or even the six of the Moraskyr. One of these wore a large, angled hat, also bordered in gold, and he had a stern, hawkish face. His amber eyes passed over them dismissively. His crew shouted back and forth in an unfamiliar tongue. All of these had skin tones ranging from a pale green through a faint blue, though all had long white hair.

Savis turned from the ship, which was designed like an arrow with ropes attaching it to a narrow "balloon" and started across the dockyard.

"I never expected to see *them* here," Alyra commented, still keeping pace with Savis.

Distractedly, Savis nodded. "Where do they come from? Who are they?"

She shrugged. "Even in Moraskyr we heard stories of their passing. Supposedly, they are from a land even further north than your Fhoraena, we call them…" Alyra considered for a moment, "in our language the name translates to 'children of the moon' but we do not know anything about their language or people."

They continued past unused docks, and towards a group of three airships. These all appeared to have the same general design, made in the shape of a long lower section shaped like any river-going ship, with chains and ropes connecting it to a hovering narrow balloon, all made from the same dark silver metal. These varied only in the depth of their hulls, and their lengthwise span.

The nearest of them was the smallest, with a shallow hull, and a short length, and only a small crew of garishly clad Norenan faeries. Savis ignored this one and looked down between the other two. The furthest was wide, but shallow and also with a short length, perhaps some kind of short-range transport? The middle one was long, deep, and narrow, and its red-lacquered wood trimmings, black etched metal hull, and its richly dressed crew made a good impression so she immediately started in that direction.

"You sure you want that one, Savis?" Leif asked, pointing toward the retracted lateral masts and the black banners that were carefully rolled up to be inconspicuous.

Alyra glared at him. "What's wrong with this one?"

"Black banners are usually used by bandits, raiders, or pirates," he replied.

"You afraid of pirates now?" Havrshyk asked him with a cheeky tone.

He fell silent, but all the same, she walked toward the docked airship examining the crew unloading barrels and crates with care. Their fine clothing all spoke to their wealth and success, whatever their business, but she noticed that each one bore a black cloth tied to some part of their body. For some, it was around their wrist, or upper arm, for others it was tied around their forehead, or in their long brightly dyed hair, and for some few it was tied around their neck like a cravat.

While several of the crew raised a platform loaded with barrels and crates up the lift, a dark-skinned fae in a long gray coat with a white billowy shirt and his black tie done in the cravat style observed them approach with an unreadable expression. His blue eyes scanned each of them in turn, and he moved toward the gangplank to the tower's top to meet them as they flitted up.

Savis swallowed subconsciously, shared a look with Alyra, and then inclined her head toward the fae who likely operated as the ship's captain.

He flashed a calculating smile of shimmering white teeth and bowed graciously with a flourish of one hand; the other resting discretely on the hilt of his sword. "Good morning, and my yes, it is indeed a good morning, my lady. What manner of business brings you to my humble ship at this early hour?" He met her eyes as he straightened, ran a hand through his short, combed, thick green hair and grinned.

Her wings shifted awkwardly at her back, but she put on a smile, and returned his bow with polite nod. "Greetings, ah, Captain," she said, eyes flicking toward his ship and the crew moving the last few barrels of goods from the lift to the hold.

"Captain Navarro at your service," he agreed pleasantly, waiting.

I've spoken to nobles across the whole of Fhoraena and <u>now</u> I get nervous? she thought to herself and took a small breath. "Savis," she said, "out of Frorin."

"Ah yes… the runaway princess," he smiled more widely, "I do believe we have some matters that would be wise to discuss, pray come aboard." He turned on his heel and shouted toward the deck, "At the ready! Stand by and clear the deck!" He returned his attention to her and flitted onto the gangplank. "Right this way princess… though I must say, the confines of my office are small, so please bring only one of your attendants."

Savis closed her mouth, looking over the others, uncertain who to choose.

"I will attend the princess," Havrshyk said, shaking his head at the others. "Come along then, let's see what this pirate has to say."

She followed Navarro aboard the ship, ducking under the ropes and chains that crossed from one side of the hull to the opposite side of the balloon, and down the deck toward the main cabin at the stern. It was a small room built at the back, and on each of the four sides it had circular windows that looked in toward an office of maps, and a wheel unlike anything she had seen before.

The captain held the door for her, letting Havrshyk go inside first, then her, before following them inside.

The Lichblade scanned every corner of the room, his eyes lingering on the strange wheel, and then he settled at the corner beside the door with one hand resting on the hilt of his Bloodsword.

It was hardly a typical office. Captain Navarro didn't have a desk or a chair anywhere in the room, instead he had maps pinned to the walls between the portholes and a thermometer and barometer hanging from the ceiling above the wheel. Savis leaned back against the ornately carved, red lacquered wheel, and was surprised when it shifted backwards. The wheel was designed so that the support shaft could angle forward or backwards, and the wheel of course spun easily.

"Pray do not disturb the wheel, Princess," Captain Navarro asked, moving so that he, Savis, and Havrshyk stood equally spaced in a triangle. "I said there was something you should know," he added, pointing at a space between portholes where instead of maps, a series of bounty postings had been pinned directly to the wall.

She walked over and examined them. Leif, Fryn, and somehow even Alyra and Havrshyk all had bounties now… and so did she.

There were other bounties she didn't consider notable, but in the center of the arrangement was a bounty for Captain Navarro himself.

Compared to the former bounty on the Venomsword, not so long ago, Leif and Fryn had risen to shocking levels of notoriety. The bounty on Leif, dead or alive, was fifteen thousand mint, and Fryn wanted only dead, had a bounty of twenty-five thousand. Alyra's bounty was less clear, without even a name, just a sketch, with a reward for a thousand mint, and Havrshyk, the Lichblade, was wanted for a reward of a shocking fifty-thousand mint!

Then she saw hers. Savis, alive, eighty-thousand mint…

Her knees felt weak, so she fluttered her wings to take some of the pressure off and examined Navarro's bounty.

He was wanted for a hundred-thousand mint, with part of the reward posted by the "Diad" and the rest fronted by the Commission.

"You're more renowned as a pirate than I expected," Savis said with a low whistle.

The captain bowed. "Apparently you are nearly as dangerous as I, Princess, but I should correct you on one fine point. I am no pirate. I am a privateer, with a letter of marque authorized by the Guildmaster of Norenan himself…who, you may not know…is Ellador Finewright, the inventor of our modern airships."

"I am not as keenly aware of the politics of Norenan," she allowed, "but I did not think Norenan had any enemies—why would they need you?"

He snorted. "Why do you think the city has remained independent? The privateers are the reason the eight circles remain as free as they are, and we, the freest of all."

Savis shook herself. "I…I had hoped to book passage."

"I figured as much, but we don't fly by Froreholt. There aren't any good Skydocks there." He leaned back against the wall and crossed his arms. "So, this is the old Lich's Eye come down from above, eh?" He met Havrshyk's eyes with a challenging look, and after a few awkward seconds of staring, he averted his eyes. "Yes well, I can see his reputation is earned."

"We are not returning to Froreholt, Captain," Aldyr interrupted, a smug smile on his face after winning the staring contest. "A war is coming that will splinter this land into pieces. King Ieffin wants his sister out of harm's way when that happens."

Navarro's eyebrows furrowed in thought. "Then why aren't you talking with the Diads' captain? They can take her far enough away that none of the *lesser*-winged faeries could come after her."

"We must go to Elin," Savis blurted, ignoring the comments about the Diads, "I have matters there I need to attend to." Her fingers tightened on the strap of her satchel around the shape of the crown there.

Navarro laughed. "Elin? Skies above, Princess, why didn't you say so?" He shook his head, sharing a look with Havrshyk before adding, "Go get your friends. We are taking off shortly. My price is simple, and one you will doubtless be willing to pay. If we are pursued by the Diads, your escorts will assist in the defense."

"Done." Savis opened the door and rushed down the gangplank. Grinning, she waved Alyra, Leif, and Fryn to join them. "We're in!"

Norenan, Eighth Circle

Skydock

Leif

Alyra ran up the plank first, meeting Savis and Havrshyk on the deck with a relieved fluttering of her small wings. Fryn waited beside Leif, her arm still looped through his, and she leaned in to kiss him on the cheek. "You'll be relieved to set those bags down, I can imagine," she said as she pulled back and unlinked arms.

He nodded, walking instead of flying with the baggage he bore, and joined the group on the deck of the airship.

"Welcome, welcome aboard the *Silvermist*!" Captain Navarro declared, gesturing to those of his crew on the deck. "We will be taking guests with us on our next voyage, across the sea to Aizora."

A fee in a uniform coat matching his flitted up from the below decks, accessed without a ladder or stairs, and landed beside him. She slipped a hand into his and interlaced her fingers. She eyed them suspiciously, her green wings flicking in annoyance, as she stuffed her free hand into her coat pocket. Instead of a nondescript black cloth, she wore a black lace choker at her neck, and her shoulder length pink hair accented the look surprisingly well.

"No captain is without a mate," he explained, "allow me to introduce you to Chall." He shared a look with her and added, "Our guests are nearly as notorious as we are my dear, and their swords will prove useful if that fool chases after us."

"We don't need the help of outsiders," she hissed softly, but loudly enough Leif could still hear.

"Chall allow me to introduce Savis Martell, Princess of Froreholt," he began, earning a shocked expression, "then the legendary Lichblade, whose thorough work in the Stanaedre clans instigated the massive cultural changes of the last century, and of course, Leif Aellin, the Viper, and Fryn Martin who surprisingly doesn't have a title yet. Our Moraskyn friend here is Alyra, but despite her small bounty, she has evaded the Commission for nearly a year and killed more than a few hunters herself."

Chall grumbled something under her breath, but smoothly looked at Savis with a smile. "If you will join me this way, Princess, we will assign you quarters near the stern, where the sailing tends to be less turbulent."

Alyra and Havrshyk took their bags and followed her down the square opening to the lower decks, and when they had vanished from sight, Captain Navarro regarded Leif and Fryn with a thoughtful expression.

"The Princess says she has an important task on Elin, I've been that way many times, and I must say it is an unforgiving land. The inhabitants are even more so. Where are you going?"

"What did she tell you?" Fryn asked diplomatically.

He grunted. "Not much." The captain led them toward the wale and examined the elegant ship nearby crewed by the faeries with two wings. "But if she is risking traveling across the ocean in Harvest with us... it must be important."

Ignoring him, Leif asked Fryn, "Do you think the Cherim will really aid in the fight against the Commission?"

Fryn nodded seriously.

Navarro sighed loudly, hands gripping the railing as he shook his head. "I became a privateer for the freedom it entailed, but everything is unsettled now. Gaersheim is gone, and the Commission set to dominate the whole of Fhoraena."

"There aren't that many hunters," Leif said, moving up beside him.

"It's not the hunters I am worried about. The Commission, even as an organization has the largest economy in the world. They can simply buy the weapons, armies, and power they need. And if that fails, they can fund the creation of their new empire through their stranglehold on trade." He took a breath and faced his crew. "Decrease ballast and take off! Raise the sails when we are above the lighthouse and mark our heading due east!" He flew off toward the upper cabin, likely to check his maps, and the crew ran about the deck.

None of the privateers bothered Leif or Fryn, and she moved up to join him looking out toward the city. Pulleys spun, ropes creaked, and timbers shifted. The lateral masts rotated out, locking into place with arms reinforced by steel brackets, and sails still furled as the ship began to lift slowly away from the dock tower.

This time, Leif sighed with relief melting from his shoulders to his wingtips, and he pulled Fryn closer, wrapping one arm around her waist as he kissed her gently on the lips. She melted into the embrace, and the gentle kiss became firm, and desperate for a few moments before they finally pulled apart.

She took a deep breath and her flushed cheeks cooled instantly. "I've decided, Leif," she admitted.

"Me too."

"I hate leaving this land. I hate having to flee our home, family, and friends, and put our plans on hold."

He gave her a chagrined smile. "I was actually agreeing to something else."

"I'm not done." Her dimples rose on her cheeks as she avoided meeting his eyes. "I am going to treasure and enjoy every moment spent with you, even if that time is spent in exile."

"Now I agree with you," he said, kissing her on the forehead. "I am not going to let anyone, or anything spoil this day."

Overhead, the sun blazed with a rare late harvest heat, and the clear skies spoke of smooth sailing. Her bloodshard earrings still left his ears numb, and he smiled even wider as his hand moved up to her ear and he examined the earrings he had given her. "You know why I love you?"

She met his eyes and raised an eyebrow. "I suppose it is because I am beautiful?"

He chuckled. "That's true, but that's not why I love you."

Fryn made a mock hurt expression, pouting playfully.

"It's because you take me seriously even when I am at my most ridiculous. I've never felt more known."

She blushed, and this time didn't try to suppress it. "I love you because you know when to be ridiculous and how to laugh even when the world is a horrible place, and even when you stare death and injustice in the face."

"Well, let's laugh this one off then." They looked out on the Skydock shrinking away below and burst into laughter. The crewsfae around them gave odd looks, but continued their work, slowly beginning to unfurl the sails on the lateral masts.

A breeze blew past them, and Leif sighed. "It is indeed a beautiful day. Nothing can go wrong now, right? We *made it*."

"Yes, yes," Fryn said, "which is exactly why you shouldn't ruin the moment by talking." She leaned her head against his and they watched the crew set about their work.

~70 Years Ago~

Sky District

Frorin

Aldyr

It seemed like so long ago, that he had chased down the merchant to buy one mint leaf for his sister's care. Now, as he wandered between hovels, he felt a growing ache in his stomach, a disquiet that urged him onward long after dark.

Three weeks had passed since they had first heard about the body drained of its blood, stabbed in the neck by a cross-shaped blade, and there had been a new one found each week, always on the same day. If that pattern held true, he'd find another bloodless body out here tonight. Maybe this time, he'd catch the killer in the act.

Aldyr paused beside one of the dilapidated houses, putting his hand against the wall and peering around the corner. Though it was now very late, between the ethereal fog and the light of the greater moon in conjunction with the Lich constellation, the alleys between dwellings glowed with a soft light, and nothing moved.

Then he heard the scream.

Not far to the northeast, the echoing cry of a young fee reverberated in the mist, and Aldyr's heart stopped beating. You couldn't truly recognize a voice through a scream, but in that moment of panic, he feared it was Selina.

He took to the wing, flying over one house and between the lean-to shelters built adjacent to another set of shabby hovels, as he twisted and dove horizontally in the mists.

He forced his heart to beat and stopped in a hover at the base of a higher shelf of the hillside. Shale broke through the dirt like blades sliding across each other, eerily reflective, coated in a thin layer of frost.

In a bound he settled on the outcropping of shale shards and closed his eyes. Blood flowed through the body evenly, though with his excitement high, it focused on his lungs, heart, and wings. That was not helping him find the victim.

With a single concerted thought, he redirected the blood flows to prioritize his ears, and drew on the immense amount of blood he'd accumulated in his sword, pouring it in excess into his veins so that his heart thundered in his chest, struggling to pump the increased volume through his body.

There… just beyond the beating of his heart in his ears, he heard a stifled whimper… to the east.

Aldyr jumped off the rocks and glided over the buildings until he found a circle between abandoned dwellings. A shadowy figure hunched over the figure of an adolescent fee, whose legs twitched on the frozen ground. With a loud cry, he landed beside them, shattering the frost flowers that had formed on the natural stone path.

His prey wore a dark, hooded cloak, and was nearly invisible beneath it with a black mask, tunic, and trousers. He held a metal pick, shaped like two thin blades fused along their centers to form a perfect cross—a weapon designed cause wounds impossible to close—a match to the weapon used to kill the previous victims.

The hooded fae's head turned in his direction, but the shadowy figure didn't move. He waited, crouched as he was with the dying fee in his grasp, reclining almost reverently over his knee. Her blood spurted fitfully from a stab wound in her neck, gathering in a shallow puddle on the shale before trickling into the dirt.

She wore the raggedy garments common to the Sky Dwellers, a tattered brown canvas dress that had been crudely sewn together with rope. Her messy blond hair was pulled back in a practical bun, and her green eyes fluttered open and closed in shock. Slowly her legs stopped twitching and stilled altogether.

Havrshyk drew his Bloodsword, leaned forward into an instantaneous stance, and charged.

The killer deflected his first neckline slash with a flick of his fingers, which were black as basalt, and hard as steel.

No words passed between them.

Aldyr switched to a spin into a thrust, trying not to further injure the fee as he brought his deflected weapon back under control and aimed for the fae's chest.

His attack skidded off a dark stony coating over the surface of his tunic, and slid past the attacker's head. The blade nipped his ear, and Havrshyk tasted his blood for the tiniest instant. The fae rose to his feet, allowing his victim to fall carelessly to the ground in her own blood, and jabbed at Havrshyk with his cruel dagger.

Aldyr stepped around the thrust, drawing his blade up and across in an effort to catch him under his arm pit, which he hoped was less armored.

Sparks flew from his attacker's hands as he caught the slash, stabbed him in the arm with the dagger, and with a twist ducked under his countering chop, and rose again with a powerful fist under Havrshyk's chin.

Havrshyk resisted the force of the attack, letting his body freeze, so that the impact crushed his jaw from below, but he still kept after his assailant. Blood flowed to his injury, knitting his bones back together, and a wave of pain was quickly numbed by his frost.

They danced back across the exposed slate shelf of this lowest level of the Sky District, so that they parried and fought beside a drop that descended to the base of the foothills, a good two hundred spans.

Aldyr pressed his attack, launching forward with a powerful overhead swing, seeking to slice his opponent from shoulder to hip, but the fae leaned back over the edge, caught the Bloodsword between two fingers, and slipped around the slash, falling toward the darkness that even the moonlight didn't reach.

He fell into the night.

Heart pounding, Havrshyk stared over the ledge, struggling to decide whether to pursue the attacker or save the fee. King Imloth didn't care about the life of one Sky Dweller, he'd want the threat dealt with. Then again… he thought of the guilt behind the king's eyes during his last audience and looked back over his shoulder toward the fee.

His jaw still had not finished healing, as he turned on his heel and flew back to her. He slid across the stones, dragging his sword across the frost hardened pool of her blood, and drank in what he could before collapsing to the ground beside her.

Her brown canvas dress had a yellow flower embroidered skillfully at the shoulder, and he couldn't shake the feeling that she could just as easily have been his sister. Her cold skin was clammy, and the star-shaped hole in her neck no longer dripped with blood; only a red stain remained where her life had gone.

But he was not going to let her die. Not this time.

Aldyr took up his Bloodsword, tapping its tip to the wound, and when he closed his eyes, he saw the network of veins flowing out from the sword, and he flooded it with her blood, his own blood, and the blood he'd collected and assimilated during his quest for revenge in Stanaedre. He filled her heart and sealed the hole in her neck with a patch of black ice.

He waited, but she didn't stir.

With a groan, Aldyr tossed his sword aside, and took off his coat. He folded it, set it under her head, and brushed her cheek with one hand as he considered. No one cared for the Sky Dwellers… he was the only one who tried to save them.

Aldyr opened his eyes again and put one hand on her chest, right above her heart, and tipped her head back, opening her mouth slightly so he could breathe into it and force her heart to move.

He gave her one short breath, and tried to replicate a calm, steady heartbeat, pushing on her chest at an even pace. That didn't seem to do anything, so he gave her another breath, and tried a faster pattern of applying pressure, and repeated the process, once, twice… five times… till she finally coughed, and her chest rose on its own.

She didn't stir, but her breathing brought such relief that he didn't even see the guards gathering around until Yala spoke.

"Havrshyk… what are you doing to that fee?" Her voice shook with alarm as she drew near, one hand on the hilt of her sword. Her blue eyes darted between the fee on the ground, and Havrshyk leaning over her. Just beyond her, more guards approached, forming a circle with their swords drawn and held out in quivering hands.

They surrounded him, Crown Guard and City Guard alike, glaring at him with mistrust, revulsion, and fear radiating like a thick miasma.

"I'm glad you're here, Yala," Aldyr said, rising to his feet and meeting her eyes. "I got to her just in time. Her attacker escaped…"

He smiled, flushing as he considered, how her red hair coated in frost seemed to glow with its own light. She was so beautiful!

Havrshyk suppressed the thought and added, "I think I have her stabilized."

As if reading what he was thinking, Yala also blushed, wings shifting yellow, red, and blue, in a constant state of confusion. "You better have a good reason to be here, Aldyr," she warned, voice quivering.

"I noticed a pattern in the attacks," he said, looking around at the suspicious guards.

One of them spat to the side. "So, it's a coincidence you were wandering the Sky District each time?"

A sinking feeling settled into his stomach as he swallowed. "Yala tell them, I have been patrolling the Sky District every night since the first attack! Of course, they all happened while I was out here."

Another one of the guards, this one in the white and blue uniform of the Crown Guard, snorted. "Don't trust the Lich Captain."

Havrshyk glared him down.

"Bring the witness," Yala ordered, and the circle parted to reveal a fae with a sparse circle of gray hair on his otherwise bald head, and with the tattered brown robes of the Sky Dwellers. He shivered, rubbing his arms as he was shoved forward and then he shrank back against the guards as he saw Aldyr.

"I-I-it's him!" He quailed, "I *saw* him attack her and drink her blood, ah… I… please, you said I would be safe…" He skittered across the shale and vanished behind the group and then around the next building, running it seemed all the way up the hill.

Aldyr's eyes narrowed, and he put himself between the unconscious fee and Yala. "I was *not* drinking her blood, Yala, I was resuscitating her after she was attacked."

As he stared into her wide eyes, he saw her doubt. Her skin paled, and her mouth worked for a few seconds as she drew her sword and settled into a defensive stance. Her wings flushed red, and her horror shifted, and her face twisted, enraged. "You said they were *your people,* Havrshyk! How could you do this?"

"They *are,* Yala, you can't possibly tell me you believe that I had anything to do with this?"

She gestured to the guards, and the circle tightened around him. "All the bodies had the same injury, the same method of being drained. A cross-shaped cut in the neck. Isn't it interesting that there is such a weapon at your feet?"

Aldyr felt a chill. *How?* "I have nothing to do with that, the killer left it behind."

Yala shifted, angling forward, and moving into a ready stance, as she held out her sword toward him. "I don't believe you!"

"What?" he exclaimed, "I was saving her, Yala! She was bleeding out so I froze the wound. She's alive!"

The fee on the ground turned her head, eyes flickering open and darting around in confusion. They passed over him, Yala, and the guards before settling on the dagger-like weapon the stranger had stabbed her with, and she let out a pained whimper before fainting again. The dagger was right beside his boot.

"You're coming with me, Havrshyk," Yala said, nodding to the guards, "but we're going to have to make sure you don't resist."

Just as she charged him, two of the other guards slashed with their swords toward his back. Aldyr leaned backwards, flitting in a spiral between their attacks, and slamming an ice-encrusted chop at the back of one guard's neck so he fell unconscious, and he then scooped up the fallen sword, and deflected a following attack from the second guard.

Before he could counter the attack, Yala ran him through the back. His stomach tightened around the blade, and he froze it through, twisting so that the blade snapped right at the handle.

Where was his Bloodsword?

He rolled across the stones, heedless of the damage to his internal organs from the blade shard still impaling him, as he dodged the attacks of the other guards and searched. It was *gone*. The sword contained all the blood he had left, and through his link to the weapon, he felt it was getting further and further away.

He roared, attempting to run through the guards in the direction he could feel the sword going, and succeeded in slamming one against the ground with a wet "smack" and launched the other back toward the wall of a hovel nearby.

If he was captured, or killed, the king, the Sky District, would be in danger. Whoever set him up would not simply stop there.

He kicked one of the guards around the head, and twisted, punching another one in the gut, so that the two fell away opening up an avenue for his escape. He took to the wing, rising several spans in an instant.

Something stabbed him in the backs of his legs as he made to fly off, and he lurched backwards toward the circle of guards. Tethered arrows pierced his legs and the guards tugged on the ropes pulling him inexorably back toward Yala, who now held a new sword.

"Bind his hands… and gag him," she ordered, gesturing to one of the other guards forward.

As the guard forced a cloth in his mouth, tying it at the base of his neck, he also shoved a bag over Havrshyk's head. "The lich is secured, Captain," he said, stepping back.

Aldyr wondered if they'd release him when the fee came to, so he stilled, and allowed his arms to be bound.

The sword got far enough away that it might as well have been in another country, and as he weakened, slumping toward the ground in a haze.

"What do we do Captain?" One of the guards asked.

Yala replied with a bitter tone. "We do what the King demands." He heard her kneel closer and whisper beside his ear, "Maybe… maybe it would have been better if we hadn't survived. You wouldn't have become…a monster…and I wouldn't have to kill my friend." Her voice choked, and she walked away.

Aldyr felt the ropes in his legs tugging, and soon enough he was dragged into the air. The flight was not nearly as long as he had expected, so they couldn't have arrived at the palace. Where were they taking him?

He was tossed to the ground, landing in a heap on the hard worked stones of the city roads, and promptly dragged roughly down a few steps and inside a building. A hush surrounded him, and he grew more and more alarmed, and less and less aware of what was happening. His sword, his blood, it was all being stretched to the point of breaking his soul.

Footsteps on wood, creaking hinges, and another fall onto hard raw stone brought him into a cold, still place. Even through the bag on his head, it all felt dark, and peaceful. Rest could help, right?

Focus.

Stone ground upon stone, and anxious voices argued in soft unintelligible whispers. He was heaved one last time, and felt his body being shoved into a narrow chamber, barely large enough for him to turn over on his side.

Yala whispered, "May you find rest, and Wing-Giver forgive us, farewell, Aldyr." She sniffed and retreated.

There was one last loud grinding of stone, and a booming *thud* before the talking ceased entirely. Though his hands were bound, Havrshyk had just enough strength to feel with his fingers, the jagged chiseled out hollow of stone in which he lay. The lack of air, the closeness, the darkness all weighed on him and he felt half awake, and half alive.

He had a strange moment of clarity sometime later, as he felt his sword being brought near and fixed on the outside of his chamber… but he couldn't tap his blood.

In his head he screamed, but the gag prevented any attempts to vocalize his rage. There would be no trial, no evidence, no opportunity for him to defend himself.

They simply put him in a tomb.

And forgot him there.

Weeks passed, and Aldyr's heart slowed to the beat of one beat per hour, then one beat per day, one beat per month… and he supposed it slowed to once a year. In the haze of passing time, he burned with rage, his mind drifted through entire lifetimes of how things could have gone differently, and he believed those to be real, until he found himself spitted on Yala's sword and shoved into the stones to rot.

Slowly, in the decades that followed, he imagined and planned his revenge, and during one of his rare moments of clarity, he tried scratching at the stone sealing him inside. Every time he woke, he scratched, wondering how long it would take to erode.

His world shattered with sound, though he was still bound, gagged, and blindfolded, and the stone crumbled away from his tomb. Air rushed into the hole, and Aldyr's awareness faded in and out, and he fainted from the exposure to such *rich* air.

Hands worked on his blindfold, and lowered the gag, and Aldyr found himself looking up in the bright flickering light of an oil lamp, at a blond fae with keen eyes and a playful smile. He wore a captain's uniform and held a red sword in one gloved hand.

"Hello," the captain said, "I heard a rumor you might be down here."

Havrshyk reached out weakly with one frozen hand and touched his anemic blade. What blood remained flowed from it into his veins and his mind cleared further, and he focused on his face. "Who are you?"

The captain's eyebrows furrowed and he nodded to himself before replying, "I'm the one who's going to help you settle an old score. We're going to kill a king, you know."

Havrshyk wobbled as he tried to stand, and the stranger reached out a hand and helped him up. "That's not nearly good enough…"

The stranger grinned at that and picked up his lamp. "I think then you'll be pleased to learn what else I have planned."

"Thank you," Aldyr breathed.

"Yes, yes, I'm sure you'll be asking me "Who are you?" again so here it is. You understand code names, yes?"

Havrshyk nodded.

"Just call me Mythrim for the duration of this operation." The blond fae laughed to himself, as if it were an inside joke, and only he was on the inside of it.

"How long?"

The stranger, Mythrim, regarded him with a serious expression. "You likely would rather remain ignorant of the answer to *that* question."

"Mythrim…" he growled, "how long?"

The stranger in the captain's uniform shrugged as if to say he brought this emotional shock on himself. "In the neighborhood of seventy years, friend. Now come with me and we will get your blood refreshed, or whatever it is liches need."

Seventy years!? Havrshyk felt his rage building, and frost settling on his hands as he stumbled and leaned against the wall of the catacombs. He was too weak even for some well-earned anger?

"Imloth, you worm, if you're not dead yet, I am going to kill you. And if you're already dead," he wheezed, taking a dusty breath and struggling to follow Mythrim down the corridor, "I'll die and kill you again."

The airship angled eastward slightly, rotating in a gentle arc as it swung around, revealing a breathtaking view of the city to Leif and Fryn. As the *Silvermist* rose higher and higher in the air, the massive column of stonework comprising the lighthouse streaked by during their ascent. It took longer than he expected before they finally rose above its pinnacle. Caught up in the moment, Leif leaned in a gave Fryn a kiss on head, and whispered, "See? It's perfect."

She hummed in response and breathed out a contented sigh. "It's not so bad."

Of course, right then they heard a loud *twang*.

A ballista bolt streaked past them, and skidded off the metal housing of the balloon, sending a shower of sparks on top of them. In a panic, Leif leaned over the wale and scanned the ships below. The airship with the two-winged faeries was still docked, stationary, and not able to fire at the correct angle, so he looked around, heart pounding as he spied a figure at the top of the lighthouse.

The airship drifted idly a good twenty spans above the lighthouse, and they were close enough that the brilliance of the blue starlamp's glow at its peak was so intense that Leif had to shade his eyes. Below it, the uppermost platform was ringed with ballistae. One faerie stood, arming the ballista facing them, and the forms of two dead guards lay on the stones behind him. It was all blurred and indistinct because of the blue glare and haze the lamp cast over everything.

The faerie arming the ballista was tall, and broad shouldered, that much he could tell. As he looked up from cranking the ballista, the faerie shouted at them. "I'm not letting you escape, Viper!" He raised a sword in their direction, it looked like a tangled, sinewy mass of vines, or roots braided into shape. Leif made a circle with his forefinger and thumb, and with the powers he still so poorly understood, his sparks combined with the dust in the air to form a lens of shadowed glass. He peeked through it at the figure, and felt his mouth go dry. His malformed wings, and skeletal arms revealed the stranger's identity in an instant.

"It's Grifton!" Fryn exclaimed, putting a hand on Leif's shoulder. "I thought he was dead!"

"That's funny," Leif said quietly, letting the piece of glass fall toward the city and scratching his neck. After a moment, he smiled and bellowed in return, "Good luck with that, Grifton! See you never!"

The next shot of the ballista again flew over the balloon, and Leif could barely hear him cursing on the tower. He laughed again, a true honest laugh, and patted Fryn on her head. "We're free anyway!"

"Finally," she agreed, sticking out her tongue at the hunter.

Savis appeared beside them, "What are you looking at?" she asked, following their gaze, and looking at the tower. She covered her mouth in alarm when she noticed Grifton arming the ballista again. "Watch out!" She yelped, ducking down below the wale.

"Don't worry, Princess," Leif said, pointing and laughing once more at the figure on the tower, "He can't catch up to us on those mangled wings."

The princess didn't reply, but frowned and shuffled her feet.

Another bolt fired over them, this time though, it trailed a long sinuous cord, and the form of a faerie streaked through the air behind it. The shadow of Grifton Francis centered on them, as he cut the cord and free-fell directly toward them from above. Hearing footsteps, Leif yanked himself out of Fryn's arms, noticed Havrshyk approaching behind them, and grasped Savis' shoulders and pushed her towards the newcomer.

Havrshyk's eyes were up, but he took the princess by the hand and started back toward the hatch to the lower decks.

"Keep her out of sight, Havi!" Leif ordered, "I think this time he's here for me."

The lich nodded, ignoring the nickname for perhaps the first time, as he replied curtly, "Try not to destroy the ship."

Grifton unfurled his wings, heavy and misshapen as they were, and angled with the ship. He seemed to descend too quickly, and with great strain.

Fryn drew her Bloodknife and stood at the ready on the deck a few spans away, and Leif began gathering sparks at his center.

The so-called Mountain Fang slid down the curve of the metal balloon with a cascade of orange sparks, leaving a black scar behind him, and he fell to the deck in a crouch. His landing caused a palpable shudder to course through the airship, and the yelled commands of its crew announced their surprise.

Chall poked her head out of the navigation cabin door and retreated inside when she saw them.

Grifton rose to his feet slowly. He stood in a veritable fog of flaking bone and his own stone elemental fragments. His face was barely recognizable now, so woven together with marrow and bone that it appeared to be a mask worn *over* his face… except this mask moved when he spoke, revealing teeth like fangs, and mad, black-brown eyes.

"At last," he said, voice low and gravely, "I have caught up to you. True to your title, like a Viper, you are skilled at slithering and running away."

Leif raised an eyebrow at Fryn. "It shouldn't count as running away, Grifton, if I was pretty sure I had already killed you... What happened to your other arm?" He shrugged. Any moment spent drawing on the greater potential in the sky helped build up his reserves for the fight to come. "Well, I'm surprised you managed to find us." He wrinkled his nose. Whatever transformation Grifton was going through, the remaining flesh he had on his bones that hadn't already been converted into a ghastly array of sinew and marrow-threads seemed to be rotting. The pungent stink of death hung around him in a visible, disgusting miasma.

Grifton's rusted eyes moved independently, one watching him, and one watching Fryn, as he made the gesture of licking his lips. He didn't have those anymore; he didn't have a proper tongue either. Instead, a tongue-shaped organ woven from marrow-threads darted from behind his fangs and brushed them clean.

Stray tendrils of marrow-thread hung from his scalp in place of his hair, but despite the wind against the bow they barely moved. Leif had to suppress a shiver as he stared this *creature* down.

If Fryn had survived her death to become a lich to bring word of her friend's death to her family, and if Havrshyk had sacrificed so much to save an unworthy king, their transformation had been beautiful, and noble. Grifton's transformation and survival was twisted by his selfish desire for vengeance, uncaring about the worthiness of his commission, and apathetic toward the innocents he harmed. Perhaps for the first time, he understood Vinellin's story about the Shadelands and how good and evil have equal access to powers holy or unholy.

"Fryn," Leif said, eying her carefully, "as much as I want to declare that I will take him on myself, I'm pretty sure I'll need your help."

She sniffed, but despite her reaction, he saw the honest dimples on her cheeks. "Handsome and self-aware," she said, "I'm very fortunate indeed."

Grifton bared his teeth in what was probably supposed to be a smile and raised a skeletal hand toward Leif and his sword toward Fryn. "That will just make it easier for me to kill you!"

Fryn sprang into motion, bursting forward on the wing, low against the deck in a crouch to gain speed and power as she kicked off and raised her Bloodknife in a two-handed grip. In a carefully timed lunge, she darted around his downward swing and rammed the blade into his side, right between the joints of some hardened bone plates. It sank into the soft spongy substance beneath, causing a spurt of sickly, tan ichor to spill around her hands, but he didn't even flinch at the blow.

Grifton raised his sword again, further exposing his side as his sharpened claws slashed in toward her neck.

Leif was there in an instant.

His body tingled, alive with sparks coursing through his veins, his hair standing on end. Tendrils of blue energy ran between his wings and from his body to the various points of metal on the airship. He rushed Grifton, and twirled in a spinning kick that dislodged the sword from his hand,

As he landed, Fryn had already retreated, and was circling around their prey. The Bonesword skidded across the deck and caught on the wale.

Leif clicked his tongue. "That's a shame, I'd hoped it'd fall off."

Grifton ignored the fallen sword and stretched his claw like fingers as if itching to grab onto his flesh. He was so close, with his claws barely out of reach of Leif's chest. "I can still do *this*." The claw points on his fingertips extended, slashing out like swords and stabbed him through the shoulder.

They burrowed through his skin, and then the muscles of his shoulder, as if seeking the bones within, and as one of the claws scratched his collarbone, a lance of searing pain pierced him to his core. Leif couldn't contain the agony and screamed.

Fryn caught Grifton in the leg, slashing through his vestigial hamstrings, and as he released a shocked grunt and lost his balance,

Fryn dove forward, pushing Leif off the claws and tugging him away.

Leif's shoulder ached, and his hands trembled from the intensity of both the initial injury and its lingering effects. He flexed his fingers and tightened them into a fist again, testing his strength as he adjusted to the pain.

Fryn stood before him protectively, and as she spared him a concerned glance, Leif gritted his teeth and nodded to her. She bit her lip and refocused on Grifton. The misshapen Bonecrafter trudged over to the wale, bending awkwardly around the stab wound he had received from Fryn's first attack, and dripping more of the viscous, yellowish fluid as he picked up his sword with his skeletal replacement limb.

He appraised it with a disinterested expression, with one of the few muscles in his face twitching as if trying to smile as he closed his eyes with a sigh. "Yes... I can nearly taste it, Viper," he said slowly, looking over with his eyes closed, and as he opened them, they didn't dart around as if unfamiliar with his surroundings, but they were already dead set and meeting Leif's gaze.

Leif shivered. A phantom tingle of pain lanced from his neck to his fingers.

"You have fine bones."

He attempted to shrug off the comment, and replied uneasily, "You could make a fae blush with compliments like *that*... but alas, I am already madly in love with someone else."

His 'someone else' shot him a quizzical look, but she didn't say anything, she just tightened her grip on her Bloodknife as if she could sense what he was about to do.

She likely *could* sense it through the accidental bond she had forged between their hearts the day they killed Mythrim at the ball.

Leif did not give Grifton more time to bandy words, but in a focused charge, powered by his sparks-enhanced speed, and a powerful wingburst, he launched himself directly toward him. Even as he twisted from his torso, curled through his good arm, and extended forward with a palm strike at Grifton's torso, he focused his nascent powers through his hand and it exploded outward from the impact.

With the shower of sparks, a spray of green glass shards scattered in an arc around the strike, and Leif's palm *sank* into the attack with a disconcerting crunch of bony plates cracking underneath his fingers.

Grifton skidded back toward the wale, far too heavy to make his feet leave the deck, and with a grunt, he saved himself from falling off the ship by plunging his sword into the wooden planks.

The tan ichor dripped from Leif's fingers, and the wound in Grifton's gut sparkled with a sickly light from the green shards of glass embedded in his fleshy carapace. He coughed blood and bile through sharpened teeth, and glared back, perhaps for the first time taking Leif seriously.

He didn't wait long.

The broken bone-plates shifted, stitching themselves back together, and sliding into a new arrangement reminiscent of fish scales. He pointed his skeletal hand toward Leif, and the haze of dust and decay coalesced into a trio of spikes, roughly an arrow's length. They flashed, fusing all the dust and particles into bone shards like teeth, and he closed his fist.

The shards shot toward him quick as a crossbow bolt, and though Leif ducked under one, and deflected a second with a backhand swipe, the third struck him in the arm.

The first bolt flew out into the sky, and the second skipped off the deck and followed soon after, but the third didn't just bite. It *sliced* across the back of his forearm, not just cutting, but absorbing the flesh down to his bones.

Leif screamed, and his right arm hung limp from his shoulder, a mass of pain. Blood sprayed across the deck from the open wound in the on and off pattern of his sparks-quickened heartbeat.

He fell back against the wale, vision swimming in pain, and looked at Fryn, who seemed to vanish from the air before him.

No, it was… it was him losing consciousness.

The air was as cold as the Ice Wastes as he passed from the waking world to the strange internal dimension of his soul.

Skies of Fhoraena

Aboard the Silvermist

Fryn

Leif collapsed against the railing in an agony so intense she could feel it through their bond. Fryn knelt beside him, laying down a layer of frost on the wound, and drained his blood through their link into her blade so he would be preserved until she had time to devote to his recovery.

Grifton laughed, or tried, but between his mangled throat and crushed stomach, it was more of a strangled, punctuated gargling sound. He spat more of his disgusting tan blood onto the deck and pulled his sword from the wood with a jerk.

She took a breath, and… was interrupted.

An arrow flew past her face. One of the sailors leaned over the lip of the deck hold with a bow drawn horizontally, aiming down the shaft with one eye open. The sailor had bright blue hair, dyed with a diluted blue effect that reminded Fryn of the colors of a sunset over the water.

The first arrow slid off his armored wing and spun into the air. The wind caught it, and it sailed by harmlessly into a darkening sky.

Odd, Fryn thought, *It's still morning, why is it getting so dark?* She spared a glance over the wale toward the ground below and was shocked to see that there wasn't any ground beneath them—just the white-capped cobalt blue of the ocean with a blanket of charcoal clouds above.

The weather had been amazing before. Did Leif do something?

Captain Navarro threw open his cabin door, likely deciding that this attacker would require greater efforts to be defeated, and aimed a miniature handheld cannon at Grifton.

"Cast off the stowaway!" he ordered, shouting just as a low rumbling thunder sounded further to the east. "Tam, get below and muster the crew!" As he pulled the lever, he made an expression bordering on, "I hope this works", and a powerful report resounded from the weapon like a thunderclap.

Fryn diverted extra blood to her ears to lessen the ringing it caused and was surprised that she barely even registered the flight of the miniature cannon ball as it crashed into the bony plates of Grifton's shoulder. They sprayed apart like the carapace of a giant beetle being struck by an arrow, with a yellow splash of oozing liquid. His cry of pain was drowned out by the sound, and he slumped, stunned.

The captain was masked by a thick cloud of smoke, and he ducked back inside the cabin, presumably to reload the device. The archer disappeared below the deck for a minute, and Fryn thought she was yelling, but couldn't hear with the ringing in her ears.

Moments later, the archer reappeared, drawing another arrow and loosing it at Grifton as three other members of the crew flitted up onto the deck with swords drawn. They edged around her and surrounded him with their blades held in an unusual stance—held back-handed and held back behind their wings in a crouched stance designed to maximize footing on an unstable surface.

Grifton batted away the arrow with one of his bony wings, and towered above them, unconcerned as his eyes tracked two of them independently, sword angled toward one, clawed hand toward the other. The skeletal fingers stretched and the knuckles popped in anticipation, as he breathed a poisonous fume in their direction.

"Just what I needed," he said, resting his hand over the injury Leif had caused him, "fresh flesh." He laughed hollowly and feinted a sword strike toward the foremost privateer, twirling preternaturally quickly, and grabbed the one he had *not* been watching in a cruel grasp, claws sinking into the bones of his face.

He sighed to himself as he *devoured* the privateer, absorbing him through his fingers with a horrifying sound not unlike noodles being slurped. The other two backed away, and the archer yelped at the sight of one of her friends being consumed.

Fryn stuck Leif to the deck with a layer of ice and rose to her feet with a grim expression. "Do not let him touch your exposed flesh," she warned, pointing with her dagger at the privateer's empty clothes that had fallen to the deck, clean as if they had never been worn. "We need to knock him off the boat into the sea."

Grifton bellowed a laugh, flexing his fingers and swept his sword across the chest of a second privateer, which cut cleanly through his uniform, flesh, and bone, leaving a terrible scar unlike anything a sword should be capable of dealing. This one screamed and fell back against one of the bound cable masts that linked the center of the ship's deck to the armored balloon above.

Fryn flew forward to help, and watched in slow motion as Grifton twisted around, impaled the other privateer, and absorbed him, before turning on the third—who clung desperately to the cables, kicking and screaming as Grifton dragged him back by his foot. She closed her eyes. Once more, that terrible sound echoed in her ears, but before she could cry out at him, the archer screamed hysterically and notched two arrows on the same string and leapt out of the opening. The archer slid across the deck on her back, and stopped directly beneath Grifton as she fired the arrows into his throat. Tears streamed down her cheeks, and she drew her bow in another attack with a wordless cry.

Unperturbed, he ripped the arrows from his neck, splattering her face with his disgusting, yellow blood, and sunk his claws into her chest.

It had only taken half a minute? Four of the privateers were consumed, and empty clothing was all that remained. Fryn felt a chill, like when she had faced down the ermine after Pyran died. Grifton met her eyes and grinned.

"I'm going to take him first," he said, lazily flicking one eye toward Leif while the other remained locked on her, "make you watch as I devour him until nothing is left."

Fryn ground her teeth and hissed, "I won't let you…"

She focused on infusing her ice with her blood, armoring her limbs as best she could while maintaining her mobility.

Grifton lurched forward, sprinting across the deck toward Leif as he lay unconscious, ripping holes in the boards as he went. Fryn launched herself with a powerful wingburst to intercept him, placing a hand on the ground and coating it with ice before he could advance too far, and flipped over to a crouch atop it, facing him down as he drew up. By now, the injury from the miniature cannon had been completely healed, but she could still see the strange glow of the radiant glass embedded in his stomach where Leif had struck him.

He struck her with a backhand skeletal fist and followed through with an overhead smash with his sword. She ducked under the first, and caught the sword on edge with her Bloodknife, resisting his weight as he tried to crush her into the deck, growling and wheezing through his torn throat.

Then, to her surprise, his bone-plated boot kicked her over the edge and into the winds. She felt this intense moment of disconnect. She had been fighting and standing on solid ground one second, and the next instant she was out in the sky with cracked ribs aching despite her being in a full Lichform. She righted herself and flew desperately to catch up with the swiftly flying ship. She thought that he would advance on Leif, but instead he turned to the square opening to the lower decks and was about to drop down when he was blocked by a wall of ice.

Havrshyk! Good. She swept down to the deck beside Leif, put a hand on his chest warmly, and watched Grifton stumble backwards.

Havrshyk flitted onto the deck opposite Fryn, and without even sharing a look, they readied their blades and attacked. Aldyr stabbed out with the point of his Bloodsword, a deep black blade which shifted with nearly imperceptible red eddies.

Grifton parried the jab, and swept through a wide slash, causing a secondary blast of foul wind to buffet him backwards a step, which left his back open to Fryn's attack. In their previous encounters, she'd learned that slashing attacks were ineffective, so she dropped to her knees, slid under his backhand swipe, and rose again with her knife aimed right where Leif had struck him before.

He caught her blade on the bony fingers of his prosthetic hand and held it in a firm grip. Grifton grinned wickedly, and as he swung his sword down toward her neck, the claws on his other hand stretched forward scratching the icy armor on her arms searching for her flesh.

Gritting her teeth, Fryn encased her left hand in a blade of blood-infused ice and caught the Bonesword edge to edge, struggling once more to resist his *weight*. With three cracked ribs, it was much harder this time.

He pressed closer and closer with bone blade and claws, his breath a stinking fume, as he whispered hoarsely, "You can panic now, Lich, I'm going to give you a permanent death."

She strained against the pressure of the blade, wilting against the deck as she fought to keep both his sword and claws at bay.

Once more she heard the cabin door slam open, and simultaneously with a flash of lightning she heard the roar of Navarro's hand cannon. The wind shifted, bucked the airship, and for a moment the direction to her right became '*down*' and then it was the *left*. Boneshards shattered on the back of Grifton's sword arm, and as the deck shifted in the turbulence, he fell away from her.

Fryn clung onto the balusters of the wale, climbing back along its length like a ladder on its side, and she barely reached Leif before he could break free of her ice and fall. Swallowing, she grabbed onto his leg, and let all the blood she'd taken from him flow back.

"Wake up, Leif," she said, closing her eyes, "I'm going to need some support here, even if both your arms are injured, you need to use that power again."

His eyelids fluttered and snapped open, and he shuddered from the cold rush of blood through his veins. Leif sucked in a breath at the pain in his arm and shoulder and clutched onto the rail desperately. "Do not let him cut you, Fryn…" he hissed. "That sword doesn't cut… it *eats*." The airship rolled to a level, wobbling as the thunder rolled in the sky, and light flashed in the depths of the black clouds. His hair stood on end, and he clenched his teeth.

"Can you use that power again, but more of it?" Fryn asked, nodding toward the dark clouds surrounding them. "Can you strike him with the storm?" She rose to her feet, stabilizing her footing to the deck with a coating of ice.

In a similar manner, Grifton steadied himself and locked onto the deck with stone fibers digging into and between the boards like roots. He didn't bother speaking. He raised his Bonesword toward her in challenge.

Fryn flew toward him, jumping free of her footing, sending a shower of ice shards into the air as she charged.

Grifton readied his sword, sweeping it back into a guard stance, and casting a spray of water droplets into the air as he met her glare. He growled, slammed his free hand onto the deck, and sent a ripple of jagged stone spines outward from his skeletal palm.

Fryn spiraled in the air, her jaw grimly set, as she touched down on one of the spikes. It pierced her through her boot, but she kept running. She ducked under a scythe-like sweep of his sword, tore her foot as she pulled up from the spines, and stomped down onto another.

It sent a tendril of pain all the way up her leg, but she ignored it, and continued through the ruined, jagged deck of the ship toward him.

She barely noticed Havrshyk holding back the princess through a hole in the deck and continued on.

Thunder rolled through the clouds, and though the wind bucked the ship, she did not see a subsequent bolt of lightning. Was that Leif's doing?

Havrshyk raised a hand from below and *threw* his Bloodsword!

It twirled through the air, end over end, and Fryn caught it with her free hand, confused. It was light, pale, and obviously weakened after his fight with the Moraskyn agent and now Grifton, so she raised her knife toward him and gestured with the sword.

It shrank, reforming into a denser blade about half the length, and only slightly longer than her own. Then, regaining her speed, she tore through the stony spikes and caught the Bonesword on the edge of both Bloodknives.

"Alyra!" Fryn yelled, not turning away from Grifton's enraged eyes.

His mouth moved, but his jaw was split, broken and wriggling with orphaned tendrils of marrow threads. One of them shot from his cheek straight toward her face, and she felt it strike her ice-encrusted armor and break through to her flesh.

Her wings flashed red in alarm…and the sky shuddered with light and sound!

Imprinted on her retinas, Fryn saw the glowing afterimage of a jagged line of light coming from the dark clouds, across the deck, and piercing through Grifton's torso right where Leif had struck him before and exiting out his back. The light seemed brown, and yellow where it exited, but no… that wasn't the light… that was the brown and yellow of Grifton falling with it.

She rubbed her eyes, and still could not see much around the line of white except for the shape of Grifton sliding away from her with broken stone-fibers left abandoned on the deck. He clung onto the wale, one handed, as one of his skeletal replacement limbs seemed entirely disintegrated by the lightning, with the glow from his broken humerus fading from an incandescent white to a simmering red.

She had to shade her eyes again, but through the bright white light, she saw Leif's shadow approach him, saw his fingers work at the hole in his right arm until he drew out the broken tip of the Viper's Fang, and stabbed it in Grifton's neck. Then with a twirl in a wingburst-empowered spinning kick he dislodged his bonelike finger from the railing and sent the Bonecrafter spiraling into the sky above the sea. Leif screamed in pain, or victory, or something, and the thunder rumbled all around in response, sending lightning like rain simultaneously in all directions *except* the airship. One bolt after another hit the body as it fell, and they arced toward the waves below, where Grifton vanished into the deep.

Fryn slumped against the wale, dropping hers and Havrshyk's Bloodknives, and she breathed a long sigh of relief. The door to the

Captain's Cabin opened and Navarro poked his head out with obvious trepidation.

Clouds dispersed, and sunlight was shunted through a break in the dark sky across the deck so that everything glowed with new light, sparkling, and… horrendously damaged.

"He's gone?" The captain asked, venturing out with his hand cannon held at the ready. "What happened to Tam and the others?"

Leif stood before the railing looking down at the water, blood dripping from his arm and shoulder, arms hanging limply at his side—and yet he stood strong, and magnificent against the light of the sun, tingling with the vestiges of his sparks dissipating.

"They're dead," Leif said, turning around and locking eyes with Fryn and then the captain in turn. "And I do not think Grifton will survive this time. Even if the lightning didn't kill him, that venom should finish him... and if not, he will drown in the deep."

Havrshyk joined Fryn on the other side of the deck, scooping up their blades, and Alyra and Savis were close behind. The princess bit her lip and looked westward toward her homeland.

"Captain, I think it would be best if you spread the word of this attack in such a way that your ship, your attacker, and your passengers were all lost in a terrible conflict in the storm. If the president thinks we are dead, and that *he* succeeded if at great personal cost, then we will be able to pursue our goals unhindered by further attacks."

Navarro nodded, frowning, but agreeing, nonetheless. "We'll have to break out the gold ribbons. Believe it or not, we are prepared for that eventuality."

"You're welcome for saving the ship," Leif said tiredly, collapsing against the railing again with a groan.

"Thank you for endangering it with your presence," the captain replied tersely. He folded his wings and assumed the posture of someone who had not been hiding in his cabin a moment ago. "I am pleased, however, that you lived up to, if not exceeded, your reputation."

Fryn ignored their conversation, crossing the deck to kneel beside Leif, and put a hand on his shoulder, freezing the wounds closed with her blood, and then his other arm. He sighed with relief at the numbing effect, and then gave her a concerned look.

"Do you have enough to heal yourself?"

She shook her head. "This time perhaps, I am content to heal like anyone else, though I suppose I can cheat a little and ice the worst of it."

His hand shook as he raised it to her face and pulled her into a kiss. "Today is still perfect," he said.

She agreed.

Interlude 6

SUNLESS

~Eight Years Ago~

Frorin

Snow District

Fryn

Fryn caught the unsharpened dagger of her opponent edge against edge, and they struggled against each other to push the other back.

"One step, one point!" Master Bersari declared, as another pair of students completed the challenge. One student succeeded, one failed. Those two filed out of the line so that Fryn and her opponent were the last two still performing the contest.

Koen, a male student one year older than she was, glared at her through haughty green eyes. He gritted his teeth and pushed, but she let the pressure slide past her shoulder so that he stepped forward, and she was able to shift her blade under his chin.

"Excellent!" Master Bersari declared. "This exercise is all about redirecting forces. It does not go to the strongest, the fastest, or most experienced. It goes to the one who understands their own body and understands their opponent."

He dismissed the students, allowing them to file out of the training room, and Fryn followed the two other female students out the side door to the main hall. Jemma and Sule were the same age as her, sixteen, but both came from wealthy families who were still

361

alive and neither stayed at the Academy full time like she did. They were taller, fuller, and talked about fae more than anything else.

Fryn... was not interested.

As she turned down a side corridor and followed the stairs up to the private level of the Academy, the Bersari Residence, she shook her head at them. They were more interested in impressing Koen and the other male students with their elegant maneuvers, than they were in minimizing wasted movement, or expertly defeating their opponents. The male students were similar. They wanted to show how *strong* they were, using their greater weight and muscularity to gain notoriety among the small female population. It was all so ridiculous.

She pushed open the door to the residence and was about to turn left in the entry to go toward her room, which was right next to Pyra's room—they had never touched a single thing since her death and it sat waiting in case she ever miraculously returned. The entry stairs ran up to the private sweet of Master Bersari, and his wife—Fryn's adoptive parents. They were arguing again.

Silently, Fryn flew up the stairs and pressed her ear against the crack between door and frame, and she closed her eyes.

"...she hasn't grown *at all* since then!" Yuli complained, sounding more afraid than frustrated.

"Fryn has not been eating well, Yuli," Master Bersari replied—he sounded frustrated.

Fryn frowned. They were talking about her?

"The other fee are growing, maturing, becoming adults but Fryn remains a child! What are we doing wrong?"

"She is a child," he insisted, "surely you don't expect her to ever have the proportions of a lady of leisure, do you? She is a tiny, athletic fee, it is just how she is built." Master Bersari always found a rational reason for everything. Fryn smiled at his words. She couldn't help how she was, did Yuli really want her to be an ungainly buxom mess of a fee?

"It's more than that...I don't know, but she's so cold, and sometimes I'm not sure she isn't just an apparition. She looks at me, and sometimes... it's like she isn't even there."

Fryn backed away from the door, freezing back the tears as she shuddered. *She wasn't sure she was even here, living all this, sometimes.* Ever since Pyran had died, all of this was just a routine, doing what was expected, pretending that nothing had changed. Pretending, in some small way that she was Pyran.

She caught sight of herself in the mirror at the top of the stairs beside the door and gasped. Looking at herself, she saw it, the white powdery snow, could smell the glacial flowers, and feel the chill of her blood seeping from her wounds.

Fryn fell to her knees and scrambled back against the wall holding her head in her hands as she relived the attack, Pyran's death… her own death… over and over again.

How long she sat there, who knew?

The door opened and Master Bersari stopped at the top of the stairs. He knelt beside her and put a hand on her head, and recoiled, before taking a breath and putting his hand on her forehead again.

"Cold as ice," he mumbled, "Fryn… can you hear me?"

She could, but she didn't answer. All she saw was her reflection in the mirror behind him. Hollow, cold, the eyes of a corpse.

"Pale as the grave," he whispered, "but beautiful, unchanging throughout the ages, a queen forever. Yndril's breath… Fryn, what have you done?"

She refocused on him, and… those were not tears of relief. He *resented her*.

"Where has your blood gone, Fryn?" he asked gently, with a kind tone belying the bitterness in his eyes.

She clutched onto something, a black-red dagger forged from her blood, hidden behind her back. She shakily brought it out, showed him and felt something break inside as his bitter eyes locked onto it and darkened.

"Here," she said in a hoarse whisper, "I had to fight."

"You don't just become a Lich, Fryn…" a tear leaked out of one eye, and he brushed it away.

She nodded. "You die."

He nodded as well. "Thank you for bringing her back to us."

Yuli joined him in the doorway, hand to her lips as she took in the Bloodknife and Fryn's blood-drained skin. Then she went back into the room, slammed the door, and started weeping.

"I believe that every Lich is brought back for a reason," he said, examining the knife, "and I will teach you how to use it." He gave her a grim smile and handed it back. "However, you are going to need to stop living in the past and let your body grow."

"I'm not…"

"You are. Consciously or not, you have frozen your progress to that of the girl you were two years ago. Well, it is time for you to take ownership of the life you were given." He stood, cleared his throat, and then pointed down the stairs. "Wait for me in the training room. You will begin training against sharpened blades from now on. The first test will be resilience."

She shivered but stood. The weight of her guilt, of being the one who lived, pushed her as she went to the training room and settled down to wait. She rested the Bloodknife on her knees and hoped that the training would be painful.

Master Bersari did not disappoint her.

Epilogue

Elin

Aizora

Leif

Two weeks after their climactic battle against Grifton, the *Silvermist* was nearly completely repaired. Despite losing four sailors, Captain Navarro's crew had ripped out the broken boards and replaced them with spares from their cargo hold. The ship's carpenter, a thirty-something fee with amber and purple hair, and an ample belly, had told him through a mouthful of nails that good Orellian timber was hard to come by, and they tried to have some on hand for these kinds of repairs. After more questions, he found out Orel was the island just north of Elin, covered in lush forests, and sundered by terrible storms that felled trees for the inhabitants every year.

He currently reclined against the railing at the bow of the ship, watching the land approach. They crossed over the last blue edge of the sea, drifting above golden sandy shores, and vibrant green-gray leafy forests. Amid the trees one forest giant towered above all the others, a monstrous cottonwood with leaves just beginning to change colors to a brilliant yellow gold. Lights glittered from the myriad of buildings and houses built along its ancient branches.

As they got closer, Fryn stepped up beside him, and put a hand on his shoulder. It was still sore. The bone and flesh disintegrating attacks Grifton had inflicted did not repair easily, even with Fryn devoting most of her blood and recovery to healing him. She leaned her head against his and he wrapped an arm around her waist. Under her jacket, she was bound with bandages and her own ice for the ribs Grifton had broken when kicking her overboard. She breathed shallowly to lessen the pain and pointed toward the highest branches.

The canopy of the tree, no, the city, was strung with starlamps and beautiful houses built on top of and attached to the side of the branches. The bustling sounds of a cheerful, industrious city traveled toward them, and the ship angled down toward one particularly hefty branch that shot out nearly at a right angle from the trunk and seemed apart from the rest of the tree. There, at various cut off stems, five airships were docked in a line.

"Marvelous, isn't it?" Chall asked, pausing beside them with a notebook under her arm. "Aizora is wealthy with trade, and renowned in Elin for their mushrooms and mycelium leather goods." She said this with a mouth full of dried biscuits. Crumbs fell from the corners of her mouth and were blown away in the wind.

Fryn narrowed her eyes, pointing at the lower branches that drooped and seemed to have the fewest houses. "It's vibrantly lit and well-inhabited up here, but why are the lower branches so… empty?"

Chall coughed on a mouthful of her biscuits and had to take a pull from her canteen before she answered. "The Deadfall? Take my advice and stay away from the lower branches, Fryn. You come from a higher class, right? They're condemned branches, the tree will shed them sooner or later so only the poorest of the poor or criminals live there."

Fryn didn't meet Leif's eyes. "Fryn…" he warned softly.

Down at the base of the tree, a different kind of light, an almost organic luminescence glowed amongst the roots, and between the hundred or so discarded branches littering the ground. He could just make out the shapes of old houses still mounted on the shed branches.

She swallowed.

"Yeah, don't go down to the Roots either," Chall added, having regained her chipper attitude. "Only mushroom farmers and outcasts live at the bottom of the tree." She moved on, yelling through crumbs at deck hands to throw lines toward the faeries waving them into dock.

"I'm getting tired of being told to ignore faeries because they are poor, outcast, or worthless," Leif admitted.

"Here it is the Roots, in Fassen the Eastwall District, and in Frorin the Sky District—which Harissa is trying to rectify. What do the Aelaete clans do with misfits and criminals?" Fryn asked.

He scratched his chin. "They usually just start their own clan and move on. In a bad case, maybe a bandit clan, but a generation or two later, they usually start to get along with the other families. Perhaps it is a difference of population. We are just so few by comparison."

She let out a gentle sigh. "If they are famed for their mushrooms, shouldn't we respect the ones who cultivate them?"

"We may never find out." He winked at her and heard approaching footsteps.

Havrshyk looked as worn as Leif and Fryn, despite his also being a Lich; his sword remained as anemic and pale as Fryn's knife. His tired eyes flickered over Leif and Fryn before shifting back toward his charge. He'd taken his role as Savis' protector very seriously since Ieffin had made his agreement with him. "Our mission is two-fold," he added, "first, we protect the Princess, and then we help her on her... quest."

Savis stepped around him and let out an amazed breath. She wore a borrowed set of garish clothing from Chall, a bright yellow skirt paired with a green blouse, and a pink neck scarf. One hand rested, as always, on her satchel—ensuring that the crown remained there. "I have a feeling this is going to be wonderful!" she declared, smiling warmly at them.

The Princess had recovered miraculously over the past two weeks from her lingering trauma involving her escape from Gaersheim, killing a fae, and losing her friends Trel and Yarrow. Even so, now, as at other times, her smile faded, and she looked down at the dark roots of the tree. "We can do this. No. I can do this."

"We will help," Fryn added, disentangling herself from Leif and taking Savis' hand.

Alyra strode toward the steps leading onto the dock branch with a small bag over her shoulder. Her crystal daggers were gone, and at the small of her back were six delicately formed wings that flickered and twitched, alive and restored. "I may tarry with you for a time, but I must find someone here, the true heir. Just as your people contend against a usurper, so do I… but I do so alone."

"Not necessarily," Havrshyk said, "if you continue with friends."

They followed her, and Leif noticed gratefully that one of the privateers carried his and Fryn's bags. Vinellin's letter promised them room and board in the short term, and hopefully that would be enough for them to get started on their next journey.

As he looked below one last time at the roots of the tree, shadow glowing with tiny lights, he thought of Grifton's final moments, falling through the air—wingless, and broken—only to sink into the unknown depths of the sea.

He shivered.

"May such a creature never come into being again," he muttered to himself, and followed the others.

Rosenkraun

Gaersheim

Archon's Estate

Hans sat behind his desk, where once the king had spilled a priceless two-hundred-year-old bottle of wine, and then complained that no one had thought to design a more stable bottle. He breathed in slowly, sorting through the nostalgia he had for a regime that had once been beautiful and proud, that had stood at the pinnacle of Fhoran civilization, and resisted the expansion of the Cherim into the Forest of Grass… and had decayed in two generations into a complacent, irrelevant nation, weak, and fat from idleness.

The desk, an antique dating back four hundred years, was recently refinished, and glowed with a slick black sheen. He only liked to have four objects on the desk at any given time: his pen, the latest report, a decanter of wine, and a glass that always seemed to have one sip left.

He scanned the notice again, frowning.

> *Per your last request, I followed the Hunter Grifton Francis to Norenan and beyond. As much as he was a threat to any around him, I was relieved you were correct.*

The president…no not anymore…The Archon crumpled the note, batted it off the desk, and smiled as it tumbled into the waste bin sitting just out of his view.

He poured himself a fresh glass of centenarian wine and allowed himself to enjoy a moment of celebration.

The other lands would see soon enough. Everyone prospers when there is no more competition.

"My Lord," his aide called from the hall, "the latest news-sheet has arrived. I think you'll want to read it."

Hans cleared his throat and set down his wineglass. The other paper was gone, so he could allow another object on the desk. "Bring it in."

Miln, a cunning and useful aide, stepped through the doorway with practiced grace. He did not wear any weapons with his green and white Commission uniform, unless you counted the pen in his jacket pocket. He slid the news-sheet across the desk so that it stopped exactly where the previous note had been.

One headline caught his eye.

"Cherim riders seen outside Haryn."

His jaw clenched. "Miln, bring me a fresh sheet of stationary. Oh, and burn this newssheet."

"Right away, sir," Miln said, whisking the news-sheet away. It puffed into ash and then smoke between his fingers, and a fresh empty sheet of paper appeared where the newssheet had been.

Hans started writing.

"Immortal Queen, Mother of All…" he scratched that out and threw the paper at Miln, "Get me another sheet!"

Miln slid a fresh sheet across the desk with one hand and caught the crumpled one and incinerated it at once.

No longer will this continent be named after you, Fhora, it will bear my name, my legacy, and you will be forgotten. A bitter fee who has only brought death and bitterness to our world. Sharpen your talons; I don't even care if you kill this messenger.

He gave the note to Miln.

Miln would see it sent.

Hans leaned back in his chair, shifted uncomfortably, and then stalked around his desk, pacing in circles… wine forgotten.

The door opened minutes later, and a youth with the pale skin and dark hair of northern Stanaedre entered. Ajak folded his hands and waited for Hans to notice him.

Hans poured a fresh glass of wine, and handed it to him, and frowned as the wingless youth took a long, careless sip.

"So, Fhora will come out of her forest at last? I'd prefer to address our rivals here first before we make any attempts to take on the Diad," Ajak said in a bored tone. He wore a simple black tunic trimmed in silver.

"I had not wanted to fight on two fronts," Hans replied, taking up his glass and drinking deeply.

"Froreholt is the lesser threat, and Waverly is yours. Surely you can defeat the Cherim singly if even the Rosenkrauns fought them at Haryn during the first Coup." Ajak set an empty glass on the desk and drummed his fingers on the wood.

"They had a much larger force then."

"Then your path is clear," Ajak replied, "do not forget why I brought you into my plans, Hans." He shook his head and looked toward the empty space at the center of the office. Then, with a snap of his fingers, a dark orb appeared in his hand and then twisted into a hole in the air. Light, birdsong, and the heady, humid scent of flowers wafted through the opening. Ajak spoke through the hole in a foreign tongue, and when a hand reached through with a small felt pouch, he accepted it. When the hand retreated, the hole closed, and Ajak eyed Hans, hefting the pouch. "Invest in more powerful, but stable servants this time. Use these shards if you must."

Hans, Archon of a new empire, bowed his head slightly as he accepted it. "Of course, Great One."

"Summon me when you have defeated the Cherim and Froreholt."

A larger window opened in the air behind the dark-clad, wingless figure, and he stepped from the office to a room of pure darkness and quiet. Then, the window closed, and Hans looked up with a sneer.

He would use anyone with the power and resources to help accomplish his goals. Even a deluded wingless cultist. He just needed to not fall completely under his power if he wanted to avoid the same fate as Waverly.

The End

THE JOURNEY WILL CONTINUE

For my readers, I beg a moment of their patience. Several iterations of this story have come and gone, and I am now working on the fourth book of this series, likely to be titled, "The Harvest Crown". The good news is that I will begin working on it at the same time as the first book of a new series in a new setting called "The Arcane Archaeologist". My goal is to publish that first book before Wingbreaker #4 and then alternate. Better news is that I have plans for more books in the Wingbreaker setting once this five-book series ends.

Some authors weathered Covid-19 by buckling down and writing five novels—looking at you, Brandon—while others have taken a pause from any creative works as they navigated working on the front lines, policing masking, and asking customers to leave when they become belligerent. Between those stressful times, getting married, having a high-risk pregnancy, and a son with Hydrocephalus and Chromosome deletion, it is a wonder to me that I somehow still stayed as motivated and focused on my art as I did. In fact, I realized one amazing fact. It is not intelligence I value most. The most important trait a person can have, or at least the traits I value most in a human, are kindness and creativity. Intelligence is arrogant and proud, kindness helps, and creativity frees. Do not worry if you are not the smartest in the room. Worry if you are the most critical and intolerant of others.

As conditions, and my responses to conditions, improve, I hope to be more prolific.

Thank you for waiting.

-Stephen Hagelin

About the Author

STEPHEN HAGELIN

Stephen is an author of epic fantasy books, including the Wingbreaker Saga and the upcoming Arcane Archaeologist series. Most recently he has published "The Lich's Blade," the third Wingbreaker novel. Between working full time, writing, and caring for his child with a chromosome deletion, he is not active on social media.

If you would like to follow his newsletter, please send an email to info@varida.com.

www.ingramcontent.com/pod-product-compliance
Lightning Source LLC
Chambersburg PA
CBHW051003180726

48291CB00006B/1954